RINGS OF SAND

Alan Murdoch is a one-time champion
decathlete, now a sports consultant, seconded
onto the Arab group to lure amateur athletes
into the Arab Olympic fold. It seems to him no
dishonourable task: world athletics has existed
on a bed of hypocrisy and double dealing
almost since the modern Olympics came into
being. But motives and principles become
more complex when Murdoch learns that the
Los Angeles Games is being used by the Mafia
for a multi-million drugs operation; and that
officials within the East European bloc have
strong political reasons for wanting a
'professional Games' to fail. And it is not long
before Murdoch's own life becomes an issue.
RINGS OF SAND reveals for the first time the
reality behind the façade of the modern
Olympic ideal, within the framework of a
thriller.

'The tremendous power of the book is in its
plausibility and acute observation ... A certain
winner'

Daily Mail

About the Author

Tom McNab was born in Glasgow in 1933 and obtained a Diploma for physical education at Jordanhill College of Education. The Scottish National Record Holder for the Triple Jump from 1958–66, he has enjoyed a very distinguished coaching career, serving as Olympic coach from 1972-76 (and attending the 1964 and 1968 Olympics as an observer). In 1966 he created the AAA Five Star Award Scheme, an incentive scheme which has reached seven million British school children.

He is the author of several books on athletics training, Chairman of the British Association of National Coaches, and was the script and technical advisor on the film *Chariots of Fire*. FLANAGAN'S RUN, his first foray into fiction, was an international bestseller and film rights have been bought.

Tom McNab was recently Head of Sport for TV-AM. He lives in St. Albans with his wife Pat and their three children.

Rings of Sand

Tom McNab

CORONET BOOKS
Hodder and Stoughton

For
Neil, Cathy, Sarah, Matthew and Kate

Copyright © 1984 by Tom McNab.

First published in 1984 by
Hodder & Stoughton Ltd.

Coronet edition 1985

British Library C.I.P.

McNab, Tom
Rings of sand.——(Coronet books)
I. Title
823'.914[F]   PR6063.C6

ISBN 0 340 37903 0

Printed and bound in Great Britain for
Hodder and Stoughton Paperbacks, a
division of Hodder and Stoughton Ltd.,
Mill Road, Dunton Green, Sevenoaks,
Kent (Editorial Office: 47 Bedford
Square, London, WC1 3DP) by
Cox & Wyman Ltd., Reading

**Also by the same author,
and available in Coronet Books:**

FLANAGAN'S RUN

I am grateful to *Track and Field News* for allowing me to use in amended form material from their magazine. I would also like to thank Heather Jeeves for her expert advice on the script.

Throughout the novel I have mentioned officials of the IOC, the IAAF and other governing bodies of sport. In each case the characters concerned are entirely fictitious. Sadly the problems that they face are still with us.

Tom McNab, St Albans 1984

Contents

1

Arrival in Tinsel Town

He could see only the tunnel – an alley filled with ten three-foot-six high hurdles. A warm trickle of sweat made its way down his temple, running into his left eye, blinding him. He blinked and turned, wiping the moisture away with the back of his hand.

He looked around him as he peeled off his tracksuit top, feeling it stick to his sweating arms, then dropped it into the metal basket behind his lane.

'Heat one, first round, men's 110 metre hurdles.'

The deep nasal voice of the American announcer resounded in the morning air of the Olympic Stadium. On his left, in the inside lane, stood the little Indian, Satajit Singh, a bearded sinewy man wearing a turban, prancing nervously on the spot. He had run 14.5 seconds back in India and would do well to survive this first round. Next to him stood the Pole, 'Jock' Joachimowski. He had run a windy 13.6 seconds in Warsaw and was a possible finalist. Then came the tiny Haitian, Thomas Colombo, who would feel happy simply to achieve three strides between hurdles all the way to the finish. For him, today would be his first and last experience of the Mexico Olympics.

'The first four finishers in each heat will go forward to the second round,' droned the American voice to the emptiness of the stadium. Murdoch slowly peeled off his tracksuit bottoms, as so often snagging his spikes on the bottom of the nylon suit as he did so.

To his right, the Russian, Andrei Korobkov, was flicking his bulky thighs as he tossed his own tracksuit bottoms into the

9

basket behind him. Murdoch had never beaten Korobkov, a regular 13.6-second runner. On the Russian's right, in the outside lanes, were the tanned, beanpole Frenchman, Michel Prost, and the third-string Italian, Marco Liani – head down, crossing himself, immersed in some remote Latin ritual.

'On your marks . . .' The starter's voice seemed to come from some far-off world. Murdoch turned to face his lane and licked dry lips with a thick, furry tongue. He peered down the corridor of hurdles as if there were only one to be cleared rather than ten, trying to remember what his coach, Hugh Grieve, had taught him. About the 'cocoon' – the cocoon of silence within which the athlete must live if he is to conquer, allowing nothing to enter to disturb his will or its sharp focus. Grieve, sitting up there in the stadium stands, hands clenched, eyes staring at the eight lanes of Tartan track – but fixed on one lane alone.

Then Murdoch's own ritual began. First the back foot placed squarely in its block. Then the front foot, 'screwed in'. Next, each hand placed behind the fresh-painted white line, in a tripod – delicately, as if each were made of fragile china. Now the light pressure on his fingers and front knee as he brought his weight forward.

He looked up.

'Set . . .'

Again the jagged trickle of sweat down his left temple, but this time he ignored it. He lifted his hips slowly, his weight feeling heavy on his hands, eyes looking down. Then nothing. His shoulders felt rigid and his fingers screamed for release.

The gun's report freed him, and the other seven hurdlers, and they sped from the starting line like water gushing from a breached dam. At once, Murdoch flowed into his whippy, high-cadence pattern: eight strides to the first barrier, then his right lead-leg spat out at the black and white hurdle rail. His head and shoulders penetrated the space above the hurdle and his lead-leg hit the ground early and active, his left leg following, loose and fluid.

Although he dared not look, he sensed that he was leading, for there were no menacing shoulders visible on either side. The second hurdle came as smoothly as the first, his leg action still fast and continuous. Three more strides, and the attack on the third barrier . . .

Still ahead, everything somehow slow and in control, nothing in vision but the sharp black and white of the next wooden slat. Four, five and six were taken with ease, gobbled up by legs that never lost their rhythm. Then, at hurdle seven, for no reason, ever so slightly high, with a minute loss of balance: it was enough to cause him to wobble and falter on landing. His flight path on hurdle eight was much too high, and suddenly he could sense shoulders on either side of him. He felt the muscles of his neck tighten. The ninth went down like matchwood and he staggered crazily out into Korobkov's lane, narrowly missing the white soles of the Russian's spiked shoes as he fell.

He kept rolling forward, ripping elbows and knees on the rough surface of the synthetic track. He felt his left leg connect with Korobkov's final hurdle, dragging it along with his heel. The skin of his left cheek parted as he slid on his face beyond the tenth hurdle and he was dimly aware of the athletes ahead dipping through the finishing line.

He lay flat on the track, the blood on his cheeks mingling with the salt sweat, unwilling to rise; but not because he was hurt.

Two white-coated figures were soon at his side, helping him to his feet, while another two ran up with a stretcher. He shook his head at them and looked into the stands. Grieve's face was not visible, only his bright red hair: his coach was leaning forward, his head in his hands. Murdoch tried to shout, but no sound came.

It never did.

Monday, 26 July 1982

Alan Murdoch woke, his face wet with tears. He had run that race so many times, but always it was the same. Grieve's red

11

hair, the silent tears, the awakening. No matter what he did, it was always there, the one race to which he continually returned, and always lost: Mexico City, 1968.

The Games had been like a hothouse – and what exotic blooms had flourished there. Tommy Smith, eating up the track in the 200 metres like some black giant in seven league boots. David Hemery, pouring over the 400 metre hurdles as if they had been spaced for his legs alone. Fosbury, arching over in a stadium which held its breath each time he began his magic circular run. The Russian, Yanis Lusis, like some god stepped down from Olympus, unleashing spears which hung suspended in flight as if gripped in space by his brother gods. And the American, Beamon! Running at the long jump take-off board as if pursued by devils, before launching himself into space and history.

Murdoch's right hand fumbled for the light on the table on his right and he pressed a button.

'My broker is E. F. Hutton and E. F. Hutton says – ' boomed a deep Californian voice at the foot of his bed. Murdoch jerked upright. At the end of his bed, at the centre of a semi-circular console, was a vast face in the middle of a colour television set.

'My broker is E. F. Hutton and E. F. Hutton says,' repeated the round, brown American face.

'Off!' growled Murdoch, pressing again on the console.

The picture changed and he immediately recognised Bugs Bunny being pursued by a pig with a hatchet. He pressed again, to see a sweating Alec Guinness constructing the bridge on the River Kwai.

Murdoch smiled, sat up on the pillows and pressed again. A lady from Sacramento had just won a thousand dollars' worth of groceries and was being urged to go for another two thousand.

Press. Johnny Weissmuller swinging through the air with Maureen O'Sullivan.

Press. 'On the Eastern Seaboard, today's weather looks fine and sunny . . .'

12

Press. 'Buy the beer with the built-in bite!' droned a bearded negro.

Press. 'My broker is E. F. Hutton and E. F. Hutton says . . .'

'Enough, E. F. Hutton,' said Murdoch, finding and pressing the off button. Almost as he did so, the telephone on his left buzzed. He picked it up.

'Prestige Studios Condo Catering at your service, Mr Murdoch,' said a voice. 'Mr Weir said that you had requested a nine thirty call. I hope that everything in your apartment is to your liking.'

'Beautiful,' Murdoch said slowly, his morning voice an octave lower than normal.

'You will find the television waveband, Band 20, contains a three-page breakfast menu,' the voice continued, mechanically.

Murdoch flicked on the television again and located Band 20, which contained a menu to dismay Falstaff.

'Got it,' he said. 'Nothing fancy. Toast, butter, marmalade, black coffee, no sugar.'

'You're certain, sir?' asked the voice anxiously. 'Page two has the Prestige Special . . .'

'No thanks,' Murdoch said quickly. 'Not the Prestige Special, thank you. Just the toast . . .'

'Butter, marmalade, black coffee, no sugar,' completed the voice.

'That's it.'

'It will be with you in five minutes, sir. Do you wish to be served in bed?'

'No,' said Murdoch abruptly. There had always seemed to him something decadent about breakfast in bed. 'I'll have it at the table. And please make that twenty minutes.'

'Thank you, sir.'

He threw aside the duvet top, stood up, stretched, and looked down at the vast circular blue bed. Jesus, if he'd made love on it it was big enough for a lap of honour, had he still the energy.

He wiped the sleep from his eyes and, standing naked on the

13

right side of the bed, stretched to his full height. Slowly he started to circle his arms, feeling a slight stab of pain in his right shoulder. Javelin, Papendaal 1969, he recalled with a grimace: his first year in decathlon.

He caught his reflection in the broad mirror on the dresser at the wall beyond the bed and checked himself out. At six feet and 185 pounds, he was still in good condition, only five pounds beyond his weight in the 1972 Munich Olympics decathlon, even if the balance between fat and muscle was no longer quite as favourable. Still . . .

Five trunk circles in each direction, then ten toe touches, hands flat on the floor, as he had every morning since 1960. He only just managed to place the flat of his hands on the ground as he pressed down over his right foot. The result of a hamstring pull; 400 metres, coming off the final curve, Athens 1971.

It was the ultimate paradox. The superfit athlete, possessing muscles able to exert enormous forces, served by a heart capable of pumping endless supplies of oxygen-rich blood, was as delicate as thistle-down. For the athlete, pushing remorselessly into the dim outer limits of his potential, also pushed himself ever closer to injury. All over Murdoch's body lay evidence of that fact, in tight knots of hard, fibrous tissue, the results of muscle pulls in competitions which he could now only dimly remember. And in the joints themselves lay practical evidence of torn ligaments which would never quite have the resilience of the past, and in tendons loaded with the debris of a dozen minor tears and years of inflammation. It was a price he had willingly paid and one of which he was daily reminded.

He leant forward and picked up from the dressing table the fat script of *The Nazi Games*.

It had always been a matter of wonder to Murdoch that he had ever written a novel in the first place. Yet when he had decided to write *The Nazi Games*, back in 1975, it had seemed the most natural thing in the world to do.

The 1936 Olympics had fascinated him from that first

moment down at Aldershot in the draughty cinema at the Army School of Physical Education back in 1964, when he had viewed a scratched and butchered version of *Olympische Spiele*, plundered by the army from German archives at the end of the war. Riefenstahl's masterpiece had been a revelation. Because of her, he would never view sport with the same eyes – nor consider himself as athlete in the same way. For Riefenstahl had seen the athlete as a god, transcending himself through the achievements of muscle and will.

Murdoch had been surprised that *The Nazi Games* had been accepted by the first publishers to whom he had submitted it. He had been even more surprised that, when the novel had been published, it had been a considerable success, and in late 1978 a film option had been taken up by Prestige Productions, headed by one of the world's leading producers, Andrew Weir.

His agent David Goldsmith had been blunt when Murdoch had asked what his likely future involvements in the making of *The Nazi Games* would be. 'Zero,' Goldsmith had replied tersely. 'When they take the book and you take the money then it's their property. They can do what they like with it – make it into a musical, if they want to.'

Goldsmith's words had tripped off a catch somewhere deep in Murdoch's mind. On impulse, he had spent several days in the library of the British Film Institute in Dean Street studying the structure of film scripts, before deciding to make his stab at writing the screenplay of his novel.

Even at the time Murdoch had realised the arrogance of his actions. On the other hand, he reasoned, it was no different from the moment when he had embarked upon his novel, for he had had no idea when he had first put pen to paper whether or not he could create a readable book. As Hugh Grieve had always said, the only certainty was that if you didn't enter the competition you had no chance of winning.

After reading a dozen scripts at the Institute, Murdoch had come to the conclusion that it was possible. He was fortunate that he had been nurtured on movies and thought in visual terms, and the novel of *The Nazi Games* as a consequence possessed several central set pieces which would transfer easily to the screen and form the spine of the screenplay.

It had taken him a month to complete the first draft which he had then submitted to Goldsmith. This time his agent had replied positively, but although he had acknowledged that Murdoch had a feel for the screen it was clear to him that the initial draft would last just short of four hours. Surgery was therefore required, and Murdoch and Goldsmith had spent many hours on their knees on the carpet of Murdoch's Hallam Street flat, sweating and cursing until *The Nazi Games* had been trimmed to a lean two hours and ten minutes of estimated screen time. Two drafts on, Goldsmith had submitted the final script to Weir.

A week later Andrew Weir had telexed to say that he was satisfied that Murdoch could write the final screenplay, and here he was now, in Prestige's vast luxury condominium. It had all happened too quickly – the movement from the world of muscle and stopwatch into sports consultancy, then into writing. Somewhere deep in Murdoch's thirty-eight-year-old body was a young man who still wanted simply to be an athlete even though that was no longer possible.

Breakfast would be arriving soon. He entered the bathroom. It was at least thirty feet long and twenty wide, its floor covered with non-slip, light-blue ceramic tiles, its walls with ones of dark blue.

In the far right of the room was a four-foot-deep wooden jacuzzi; on the left, a four-man log sauna. Murdoch smiled and walked over to the washbasin.

He rinsed his face with tepid water and checked the result. It would serve. The LA water was hard and good for shaving. He rinsed himself again, this time in cold water, groaning as he did so. He was not a morning man – Grieve had always said that Murdoch's heart did not start beating till noon. He hoped that Andrew Weir would not press him too hard and was glad that the meeting was not until four that afternoon.

He returned to the bedroom and donned his pants. Then he sat down and hooked his feet under the dresser and began his pyramid session. First, ten abdominals; next, ten press-ups. Then he performed nine abdominals, followed by nine press-ups. He continued without stopping down the pyramid: eight, seven, six, five, four, three, two, one – groaning as he squeezed out the final repetitions. At the end he lay flat on the floor like a stranded fish, gasping.

'Jacuzzi!' he said aloud.

Murdoch had luxuriated in the clear, swirling water, enjoying the play of the jets upon his body for fully ten minutes when the buzzer sounded at the apartment door. He hurriedly pulled himself out of the tub and reached for a massive white towel on the rail to his left. He draped it round his waist, re-entered his bedroom and opened the door, to face a black waiter on roller-skates.

'Breakfast, sir,' said the negro. 'At the window?'

Murdoch nodded, stuck for words.

The waiter glided across the thickly carpeted room and deposited the breakfast tray on the table beside the window. He turned.

'Mr Sylvester says he'd like to see you at one o'clock for lunch in his room, 11C, first floor, if that's all right by you, sir? Then he'll take you on to Mr Weir.'

Harvey Sylvester, who had dealt with Murdoch's needs since his arrival, had been a parody of the Hollywood 'gofer'. A soft little doughnut of a person, he was Andrew Weir's personal assistant, his task being to smooth the daily path of the great man. Concerned only to please, Harvey had already gone to immense pains to ensure Murdoch's comfort – after all, Murdoch had thought to himself, perhaps he was the Success of the Moment.

'Tell Mr Sylvester that will be fine by me,' he said.

'Thank you, sir.' The waiter nodded and was gone. Murdoch sat down and smiled. Waiters on roller-skates!

A thick wad of newspapers lay on his right, hot from the morning sun. He picked up the first, the *Hollywood Reporter*. '*Heaven's Gate* bombs', said the headline. Murdoch's brow wrinkled as he read the copy. Cimino, hero of *The Deerhunter*,

17

had apparently spent over forty million dollars on an unsaleable, unsalvageable western. A shiver ran down his spine. Perhaps that was what *The Nazi Games* was going to be: another bomb.

He sipped his drink thoughtfully. The Americans made good coffee at least, even if for some reason their 'cream' was never really cream. He looked around him once more at the vast apartment, then down at his watch: ten o'clock. Perhaps he could beam down enough of Alan Murdoch to deal with Andrew Weir in six hours' time. In the meantime, some word-editing on the screenplay.

He decided to run through the first Goebbels-Brundage sequence. It was essential that the clear purpose of the Nazis in planning the Berlin Olympics should be shown from the beginning, and that Brundage should be revealed as a willing dupe, easily capable of ignoring the true nature of the Nazi regime because of his naive belief in Olympism.

EXTERIOR: OLYMPIC STADIUM, BERLIN   MORNING

Below, massed barefoot female gymnasts dressed in simple white cotton dresses perform rhythmic exercises to the sound of Wagner's music. We move back to the central rostrum in the main stand, where Joseph Goebbels *and* Avery Brundage, *investigating official of the American Olympic Association, are sitting alone in an otherwise empty stadium.*

BRUNDAGE [surveying the display]: Remarkable, Herr Goebbels. The grace, the discipline.

GOEBBELS: You approve? Remember, Mr Brundage, this is merely a regional rehearsal for the Olympic opening ceremony with . . . [he consults his notes] only ten thousand gymnasts. We have nine other groups training in the various regions of the Reich, one hundred thousand in all. The cream of German womanhood.

Goebbels *picks up a telephone at his side and quietly speaks a few words into it. Below, in what seems like moments, the music stops and the arena empties, the gymnasts splitting into disciplined groups to exit through tunnels at the four corners of the stadium.*

GOEBBELS: And our facilities? Do you, in your professional opinion, consider that they are up to international standard? I can assure you that we have taken every possible advice.

BRUNDAGE: I have attended every Olympic Games since Stockholm back in 1912, Herr Goebbels. Without any doubt, the Berlin Olympics will have the best facilities of the modern era, bar none.

GOEBBELS: That is most gratifying, Mr Brundage. You competed with some distinction yourself, did you not? Fifth in the Olympic pentathlon?

BRUNDAGE [smiles]: That was way back in Stockholm in 1912, Herr Goebbels. Another time. Another world.

GOEBBELS: But you came ahead of your General Patton, did you not?

BRUNDAGE: No, I'm afraid not. George Patton competed in *modern* pentathlon. I was in the track and field event.

GOEBBELS: My error, Mr Brundage. [He picks up a clipboard, scrutinises it, and speaks as if by rote.] Modern pentathlon, created for the military in 1912 by General Balck. A simulation of combat conditions. [He looks up.] The Reich now have two good men in Gotthard Handrick and Hermann Lemp.

They step down the long stairway on to the track and walk along the home straight. Brundage *bends down to pick up some of the cinder surface, stands, then lets it slowly drift through his fingers.*

BRUNDAGE: A good track surface. Firm. Stays in the hand. It will be a fast track, no doubt about it.

GOEBBELS [smugly]: Built on strong foundations, like the Reich itself.

They walk slowly up the track and survey the surrounding stands.

GOEBBELS: The Fuehrer feels that there is one matter which I should bring to your attention, Mr Brundage.

BRUNDAGE: Yes?

GOEBBELS: The failure of your Olympic Committee to confirm the attendance of the United States team in Berlin.

BRUNDAGE: It is a complex matter, Herr Goebbels. I am afraid that my national association suffers from all the problems of being a democracy. That means that any rabble-rouser can put in his two cents and delay important decisions.

GOEBBELS: But what is the precise reason for the delay?

BRUNDAGE: Mainly Jewish pressure groups. Rabbi Wise, one of the country's leading Jews, has spoken out against the Berlin Games; so have many of our union leaders.

GOEBBELS: To what purpose?

BRUNDAGE: Wise says that Jews aren't getting a fair shake here in Germany and that the Olympic rules relating to race, creed and colour are being violated.

GOEBBELS [blandly]: The reason is simple, Mr Brundage. No Jewish sportsman is good enough. You must surely agree that it would be folly for Germany to risk success in the Games by artificially injecting a complement of Jews into our team, merely to placate international opinion. As a sportsman yourself, you will understand that.

BRUNDAGE: I surely do. You may know that the secretary of our Olympic Committee, Mr Frederick W. Rubien, has gone on record as saying that there are not a dozen Jews in the world of Olympic calibre.

GOEBBELS: That accords exactly with our own experience. It is nonsense to speak of prejudice if there are no Jews of appropriate ability. So all possibility of an American boycott is over?

BRUNDAGE: Not entirely, Herr Goebbels. There's still a lot of huffing and puffing and there's going to be some sort of mass meeting in Madison Square Garden in a month or so. But I've got a good hole card.

They turn and walk back up the home straight.

GOEBBELS: A hole card? I do not understand.

BRUNDAGE: An American gambling expression, Herr Goebbels. What you as a politician might call 'a reserve position'. I reckon that I have enough votes in my pocket to swing it when the time comes.

GOEBBELS: Good. You must realise that an Olympic Games without the United States would be unthinkable.

They walk back up to the main rostrum and sit down.

BRUNDAGE: No question of that, but I would be less than honest, Herr Goebbels, if I were to say that our troubles are over. There is even talk of the Russians organising their own Workers' Olympic Games.

GOEBBELS: The Russians! The Great Land of the future which has never been able to look the present in the face! I think, Mr Brundage, that we can safely ignore the Bolsheviks. The Olympic Committees of the world would undoubtedly see the Workers' Games for what they would be, a politically motivated charade. An empty mockery of sport.

BRUNDAGE [nodding]: Olympism is a holy crusade, Herr Goebbels, something that the world must respect and cherish. Its essence is tolerance and peaceful understanding. Politics has no place in its considerations.

GOEBBELS [smiling]: The Fuehrer himself could not have put it better. [He stands up and spreads his arms, looking down into the massive bowl of the stadium.] It is difficult, is it not, Mr Brundage, to imagine that, only a few months from now, this stadium will resound to the sound of one hundred thousand voices, as the world's greatest athletes march past the Fuehrer?

BRUNDAGE: Indeed, Herr Goebbels.

Brundage *looks down along the home straight and, as through a haze, we dimly see, as through his eyes, the marching American team and the sound of 'The Star-Spangled Banner'.*

Now we see Goebbels' *face and the same area through* his *eyes as the German team march crisply past dressed in white suits and white naval caps, to the growing sound of 'Deutschland Uber Alles'. We move from the athletes to the crowd and see only a forest of arms raised in the 'Heil' position.*

INTERIOR: HITLER'S OFFICE   DAY

Hitler *sits at his table, signing documents. He looks up as* Goebbels *enters, salutes and stands by a globe of the world, on* Hitler's *left.*

HITLER: You have met with Mr Brundage?

GOEBBELS: I have, my Fuehrer.

HITLER: And?

GOEBBELS [spins a globe of the world and his finger stops at the United States]: A simpleton, my Fuehrer. He is ours. [Turns.] The Americans will come to Berlin.

2

The Secrets of Astral Sex

Murdoch sat back in the soft dark shell of Prestige Productions'
Rolls Royce, dimly aware of the grey-uniformed chauffeur
separated from him by a glass partition, and of Harvey Sylvester
chattering away on his left.

Sylvester had spent the first part of their trip pouring out to
Murdoch the standard thumbnail biography of Andrew Weir.
Although he listened politely, Murdoch already knew it by
heart. First, Weir's leap from Madison Avenue in the late
1960s to the production of a series of immensely successful
low-budget horror 'quickies'. Weir had used hot-shot young
directors, miles of rejected footage from ancient movies and
equally superannuated actors such as George Sanders and
Lon Chaney Junior to make films whose power–weight ratio
had amazed the major studios.

His first big-budget production had been in 1969 – *The Black
Indian*, a western starring an unknown negro called Harry
Marsh, which had cleared over ten million dollars. Marsh had
gone on to become a world star and Weir to a succession of
films which had brought him six Oscars and had provided the
financial platform upon which his own company, Prestige
Productions, had been formed in 1974.

Weir had not been the old-style mogul-type Hollywood
producer. Rather, he had been deeply involved from the outset
of each venture, a Diaghilev who successfully brought together
highly specialised teams in photography, costume and production design. For each new project he had secured the best
screenwriters and directors, men who possessed the same

intense commitment as himself. Thus each Andrew Weir film had been suffused with his personal enthusiasm, and the ambience of a Weir film had been one in which actors had found themselves at ease – and so able to produce their best performances.

When, therefore, Prestige Productions had bought *The Nazi Games* Murdoch, an avid film buff, had known that his novel was in good hands.

He became aware of Harvey Sylvester's voice. 'Mr Weir broke the rule of a lifetime with you,' he said.

'I'm sorry, I'm not with you,' said Murdoch with a start.

'With *The Nazi Games*,' explained Sylvester. 'All his big movies up till now have come from bestsellers. But Weir always brings in screenwriters, big names like Nichols and Mann. No offence intended, but authors usually turn out lousy at writing screenplays. Won't butcher their own material.'

'I had that problem at first,' said Murdoch. 'The first draft was longer than *Gone With the Wind.*'

'It must have been tough,' said Sylvester, glancing anxiously out of the window as the Rolls glided to a halt at some traffic lights. He checked his watch, talking over his anxiety.

'By the way,' he said a few minutes later, sighing with relief as the studio at last came into view, 'you can meet some of the people you're going to work with tonight, at the party at Weir's house. If you check the file I gave you yesterday you'll see it's got all the details.'

Murdoch nodded, thinking of the minute-by-minute schedule that Sylvester had handed him on his arrival at Los Angeles airport.

Sylvester checked his watch as they came to the studio gates: it was 3.57 p.m.

The first thing that Murdoch noticed as Harvey Sylvester led him into Andrew Weir's sombre, oak-panelled room was a large black and white photograph of an athlete hanging up on the wall to Weir's left. Weir, a tall balding man in his early sixties, rose from behind his desk and walked towards Murdoch, arm extended in greeting. There was a simultaneous nod towards Sylvester, who immediately left, closing the door behind him.

'How are you, Alan?' said Weir, shaking his guest's hand. 'Good to see you.' His voice was dark and low. Noticing Murdoch's interest in the photograph he beckoned him towards it. A close inspection showed a black athlete on his marks with, a few metres behind, a racehorse ridden by an expectant jockey.

'The great Jesse Owens,' said Weir. 'Havana, 1937. He ran against a goddam racehorse. Did 9.4 seconds that day. The horse only shaded Jesse on the line.'

He put a hand on Murdoch's right shoulder and guided him towards a high-backed leather chair.

'Four gold medals in Berlin,' said Weir. 'Yet we couldn't offer him more than a lousy thirty bucks a week when he got back. And they called it the good old days.' He shook his head.

Murdoch ventured a glance round the rest of the room. It was much smaller than he had anticipated, its walls covered with photographs of past Prestige successes. On a shelf to Weir's left below the Owens photograph stood the four Oscars won by the company since its inception. Ten Oscars after only twelve years in the business, reflected Murdoch.

Weir's voice broke into his thoughts. 'Great you could come over, Alan. When I met you back in London it was all business, no chance to really talk.' He pressed a button on a console on his desk. 'Miss Spencer?' he said. He looked at Murdoch. 'Like something to drink?'

'Just a Perrier, thanks,' said Murdoch.

'Two Perriers, please, with ice.' Weir pressed the button, wrinkled his nose and leant back in his chair. 'I always think it best if two people are going to work together that they should know something about each other,' he said.

Murdoch nodded but remained silent. The openness and informality of Americans always made him feel uneasy.

'Me, I got to college in '38 on a track scholarship, believe it or not,' Weir was saying. 'I ran a college 9.8 a couple of times for a hundred yards. My old coach at Penn State always reckoned that to be worth 10 seconds dead with the wind behind me.'

Murdoch grinned. 'You were still a fair sprinter, Mr Weir.'

'Hey, no more of that "Mr Weir" stuff. This is the United States of America, not England. You Scotchmen are always so goddam formal.'

There was a knock at the door and Miss Spencer, a blonde in her early twenties, entered and placed iced drinks in front of each man.

Weir picked up his glass and grimaced. 'I've been drinking this stuff for six years. Doctor's orders. Hell, I'm so healthy if I sneezed I'd cure somebody.'

He sipped his drink and returned it to the table. 'Where was I? Yes . . . I pulled a hamstring in '39, left a hole in me so large you could lose your fist in it. So my coach pushed me up to half miles for my last year at college.'

'Did you give up after college?'

'After college it was Uncle Sam, a year in boot camp at Fort Wayne in charge of the athletics programme, then combat training and a couple of years in Europe against the Krauts. So my track career vanished somewhere in the Ardennes. By the time I got back in '45 it was time to earn myself a few bucks.'

Weir leant forward, both elbows on the table. 'You ever heard of Jolyo Joe, the Jellyo Man?'

Murdoch shook his head.

'Or Mr Moriarty, the Mop-Up Marvel?' Weir sipped from his glass, then laid it in front of him. 'Perhaps just as well,' he said, smiling. 'Well, Jolyo Joe and Mr Moriarty took me to the top in advertising in Madison Avenue, right through the '50s and '60s. It was a tough world. My theory is that the bottom is loaded with mediocrities. Only cream and bastards float to the top.'

He opened a brown cigar box on the table in front of him and withdrew a cigar, rolling it in both hands.

'I know you don't smoke, Alan. Hope you don't mind if I do. My only vice.'

Murdoch shook his head.

Weir wet the cigar with his lips, lit it and slowly inhaled.

'So in 1964 I put together all the money I had and came out west. I got myself some bushy-tailed young directors, a few million feet of stock footage and made myself . . .'

'*Men from Atlantis*,' said Murdoch promptly.

Weir smiled. 'We spent two weeks at the bottom of the Paramount pool making that one.' He sat back in his seat. 'So let's stretch you. What were my next two?'

'*Dementia*,' said Murdoch. 'Then *The Vampire Hunters*.'

'Go to the top of the class,' grinned Weir, obviously pleased. He stubbed out his cigar prematurely and stood up.

'Hindsight, Alan, is an exact science. Suddenly, all the big studios thought I was Wonder Man and I could have made a movie a month. But they all wanted me to make blockbusters, big versions of the horror movies I had made for peanuts.'

He moved away from his desk and pointed to a photograph on the wall on the left. It was of the black star, Harry Marsh.

'So I said, to hell with it, and ploughed my three million into this.'

'*The Black Indian*,' said Alan.

Weir laughed. 'Right again. Think of it! A western with an Indian in the lead – but not just an Indian but a goddam negro – apache crossbreed!'

He took the photograph from the wall and held it lovingly in both hands. 'It pulled in ten million bucks and two Oscars. And made Harry Marsh a star – the black James Bond.'

He replaced the photograph and turned to Murdoch. 'Let's look at *The Nazi Games*,' he said. 'A great book. No question of that. I'd already got two writers at work on a screenplay when your own script arrived on my desk. My first impulse was a "don't call us, we'll call you" letter. Then I decided I'd take a look for myself. The big plus was that you took out the carving knife – that's a bullet most authors won't bite. If you will forgive the mix of metaphors.'

Murdoch smiled.

'No,' said Weir. 'You cut *The Nazi Games* right down to the bone, even took out some of your best stuff. I'm with this guy of yours – what's your hero's name? Kane? – every frame of the way. And I'm with him because *you* believe in him.'

Weir bent down to pick up another cigar from the box on his table. He sucked on its tip for a few moments then lit the other end.

'But movies, Alan, are a team sport.' He puffed on his cigar and exhaled. 'A collaborative effort.'

He moved to the front of his desk and sat down on it, a tyre of flesh showing over the top of his trouser belt.

'I'm going to say something to you, Alan, which may seem a little hard.' He puffed slowly on his cigar. 'You need help, to knock *The Nazi Games* into final shape.'

Murdoch felt himself flush. Weir, sensing Murdoch's response, eased himself from where he was sitting at the front of his desk and walked round to take up a more formal position, seated at the chair behind it.

'Orson Welles calls it "the blind eye",' he continued. 'The point when the writer can't *see* the weak points any more. It must happen in track, when the coach can't see the athlete's faults, simply because he's been looking for too long.'

Murdoch nodded. Weir realised that the Scot had accepted the point, and relaxed.

'Not an overhaul, just some fine tuning?' said Murdoch.

'Exactly,' replied Weir. 'And you'll meet one of our best mechanics tonight at my party. Name of Ellis Payne.'

Murdoch walked up the grey marble steps from the black limousine, Harvey Sylvester once more at his side. Andrew Weir's house was early Errol Flynn, he decided – or rather, with its adobe-walled, hacienda-like aspect, middle Tyrone Power. Even from outside the solid oak door he could hear behind it the bubble of laughter, the buzz of talk, and somewhere in the background the remorseless sound of disco music throbbing in the humid night air.

The door was opened by a black butler dressed as a Tower of London Beefeater.

Harvey Sylvester grinned.

'My idea,' he said. 'Just a little touch of Ye Olde England. Thought it might make you feel a little more at home.'

Murdoch smiled politely and followed Harvey into the brightly lit entrance hall.

Facing him was a sweeping staircase of white marble, straight out of *Anna Karenina*. On his right lay the opening to the crowded lounge and he could glimpse, through the open French windows, the edge of a huge blue swimming pool. On the Astroturf lawn stood a vast marquee, within which guests danced and the disco band reverberated.

Weir, dressed in an immaculate white tuxedo, was walking towards them.

'Welcome, friends,' he said. He paused to sweep a glass from a tray on his right. 'Have some champagne. Californian style.'

Murdoch accepted the drink with reluctance. It was sharp and cold, but with a vile aftertaste.

'I want you to meet some people,' Weir continued, guiding Murdoch into the lounge.

Weir threaded his way through the crowds of guests, his hand on Murdoch's right elbow, with Harvey Sylvester following dutifully behind them. They made their way through the French windows out towards the edge of the swimming pool. A group of people were clustered round a burly black man with shoulders like a barn-door. The negro, who clearly dominated his audience, stopped in mid-flow as he saw Weir approach and gave a vast, white-toothed smile.

'Who you got there, Andrew?'

'Alan Murdoch, meet Bo Cannon, running back for the Los Angeles Rams,' said Weir. 'He ran two thousand yards with the ball last year. Round these parts they call him "Krazy-legs". Alan here ran track for Great Britain back in Munich in '72.'

'Nice to meet you,' said Cannon, engulfing Murdoch's palm in a massive hand. 'I used to run a little back at college.'

'When you was forty pounds lighter,' said a voice from the crowd.

29

Cannon grinned. 'You're damn right, Chester. But you can't bust your way through those goddam Dallas defences at less than two hundred pounds, can you, Honey?'

There were whoops from the assembled crowd and the feeling of strangeness which Murdoch had felt since arriving in Los Angeles again threatened to overcome him.

He stole a glance at Weir on his left, urbane and assured, then at Cannon. Murdoch knew that, for all Weir's hospitality and enthusiasm, he, Murdoch, was simply a transient figure and that Weir probably had half a dozen projects on the boil similar to his own. And the originator of each project would be treated by Weir in the same warm, solicitous manner, taken to the same extravagant parties and flattered by the same unctuous aides. For a moment he longed for something direct, something simple; the blank page, the stillness of a bar-bell.

Weir had been talking to Cannon. Now he turned back to Murdoch.

'I'll leave you two athletes together then,' he said, beginning to move off.

'I'se been telling these good folk here about getting dinged,' Cannon began.

'Dinged?'

'Getting dinged means getting hit in the head so hard you ain't got no memory. Okay, you can still walk around some. Hell, sometimes you can even keep on playing. But you don't feel no pain, you don't feel nothing. The only way coach and the other boys know you've been dinged is when they finally figure out you don't know the plays.'

'How many times you been badly hurt, Bo?' asked a grey-haired man in a Brooks Brothers three-piece.

'I been zipped ten times,' replied Cannon. 'I got legs on me like a road map. I do much more of this and I'll have to get me a recyclable body.'

'How long d'you reckon to keep going?' asked another man, dressed in a white corduroy safari suit and black polo-necked silk shirt.

'Till that unhappy day, sir, when my brain is writing cheques this ol' body can't cash,' replied Cannon, to whoops of laughter.

Murdoch smiled dutifully and drifted away to the right of the pool where a waiter had constructed on the centre of the bar a glittering fountain, pouring champagne from its peak. For a moment Murdoch watched the golden liquid bubble its way down to the base of the fountain.

He walked idly along the side of the pool. At the far end a bronzed, muscular young man was performing a double half-twisting somersault from the springboard, but no one else was watching.

Murdoch turned to his left and continued walking, to find himself on the edge of a group being harangued by a lean, cadaverous man with a moustache, dressed in evening clothes with a scarlet-lined cape.

'Dracula', as Murdoch immediately dubbed him, was, like Cannon, surrounded by a cluster of admiring men and women. He looked up and, spotting Murdoch, extended a lean hand.

'Pastor Leach of the Bella Vista Church of the Ministry of the Gospel of Light,' the caped figure intoned. 'Pleased to meet you.'

Murdoch introduced himself. 'Call me Murdoch,' he said.

'Perhaps you've heard of my little work,' said Leach. '*The Aesthetics of Bondage*?'

'Is it a novel?'

'Novel, but not *a* novel.' Leach smiled thinly. 'You see, Mr Murdoch, Bella Vista is dedicated to truth and light through chastisement. Angelica here' – he placed an arm on the shoulder of a tall brunette at his side – 'is our leading *dominatrix*.'

Enough was enough, Murdoch decided. Two could play at this game. 'Very interesting,' he said. 'But have you tried astral sex?'

'Astral sex?' said Leach, pursing his lips. The group was suddenly quiet.

'Something I've been developing in England,' said Murdoch. 'You people release yourselves through punishment; I avoid all physical hang-ups by homing in on the astral body.'

31

'How exactly does it work?' asked Leach thoughtfully.

'First, one has to have control of one's astral body. Total control. You can't fire a cannon from a canoe.' He did not notice that a blonde-haired young woman, dressed in a gleaming gold jumpsuit, had joined the back of the group.

'How long before this astral control develops?' asked Angelica, her brows set in concentration.

'There's no telling,' said Murdoch, warming to his subject. 'Top psychics are into it in a matter of weeks. For myself, it took three months before I could even get off the ceiling.'

'Doesn't it all depend on a sizeable population of similarly gifted psychics?' said a plump bearded man in a tartan kaftan, standing at the corner of the group.

'Not really,' answered Murdoch. 'A lot of people have the astral power – they're out of their bodies every night. They just haven't projected themselves sexually.'

'Like closet gays?'

'Something like that.'

'No moral problems, Mr Murdoch?' It was the young woman in the jumpsuit.

'That's the strength of astral sex,' said Murdoch. 'You wake up in the morning clean and refreshed. No guilt, no hang-ups.'

'What about the big O?' asked Angelica.

Murdoch paused to gather himself. 'It's got far beyond the big O,' he said at last. 'We're on an entirely different plane – the dimension of the spirit.'

'Have you written this up?' asked Leach.

'Not for publication, Pastor,' said Murdoch. 'But I do have an unpublished thesis on *The Sexual Power of Ectoplasm*.'

'That sounds one helluva work,' said Leach.

'Seminal,' said the young woman, pressing her way through the crowd. She reached Murdoch's elbow. 'I hope you don't mind if I take Mr Murdoch from you,' she said. 'We have a little business to do.'

'Not at all,' said Leach. 'Most enlightening.' He withdrew a black card from his pocket. 'My address, Mr Murdoch. You just keep in touch.'

'By ouija board,' whispered Murdoch under his breath as the girl drew him along the side of the pool. His legs felt weak.

'You really got beyond the big O?' said the young woman, smiling.

'I would if I knew what it was,' he replied.

He walked along behind the girl, intoxicated equally by the champagne and the heady pleasure of the verbal gymnastics in which he had engaged. The girl's proprietary attitude surprised him, but as he let her pass in front of him along the edge of the pool he took a more careful look: whoever she was he was not troubled to be in her company.

'Andrew tells me you're out here to work on a script,' the girl said, turning.

'*The Nazi Games*,' he said.

'I read the book.' She glanced to her left as a waiter came up to them with a trayful of drinks. 'I hear they got some smart-ass called Ellis Payne to work with you,' she added, taking a glass from the tray.

'Yes, that's what I'm told. You know him?'

'No,' she said. 'I don't. But I *am* her.'

For a moment Murdoch was nonplussed. Then he shook his head and laughed.

'Are you mad at me for fooling you?' asked the girl, looking up at him mock-anxiously. She extended a hand. 'I'm Ellis Payne,' she said. 'We're going to be working together on your screenplay for the next few months. We start in London next week. I've got a project for David Puttnam to finish, then you're my top priority. I'll give you a ring once I've got into town.'

'So what do you know about sport?' he responded cautiously.

Ellis stopped, a smile puckering the corners of her mouth. 'I've done a little in my time,' she said, draining the remnants of her glass. She put her hand on his shoulder. 'Come on,' she said. 'Scriptwriters aren't a bunch of vampires, you know. Anyway, I'd like you to meet some of our literary mafia. Then you can see what you're in for.'

They walked behind the diving board, with its lone, endlessly spinning occupant, towards a small group standing on the far side of the pool.

'Prestige Productions, meet Alan Murdoch,' said Ellis, smiling.

'Ah, *The Nazi Games*,' said a bronzed angular man, stepping forward to shake him by the hand. 'A fine novel. I'm Paul Slater.'

Slater introduced Murdoch to the other members of the group: Alvin Chambers, the writer of Weir's first big success, *The Black Indian*, a soft avuncular man, but younger than Murdoch had expected; the English writer Paul Bell; and Jack La Valle, who had written many of Weir's early low-budget movies. All appeared to have read *The Nazi Games* and each greeted Murdoch warmly. For the first time he felt as if he was among kindred spirits.

'The standard Johnny Carson question, Alan,' said Slater, after several minutes' conversation. 'How do you get sport on to the screen? Most sports films have been bombs up till now.'

'Until *Rocky* and *Chariots of Fire*,' interrupted Ellis.

Slater nodded. '*Rocky* isn't sport, it's Cinderella – with blood,' he said.

'Three times over, Rockies I, II and III,' said Murdoch. 'But then the essence of fairy stories is repetition.' He paused as someone handed him yet another glass of champagne. He shook his head and asked a nearby waiter for a Perrier. 'But the problem with most sports films is that they aren't really about sport. They always leave sport behind and get involved in side issues.'

Slater nodded grudgingly as Ellis Payne, standing near the back of the group, took up the baton. 'I'd like to ask you, Mr Murdoch,' she said, 'what in your opinion is the greatest athletic test?'

Murdoch turned to her. 'Decathlon,' he said. 'No question of it. The five S's: speed, strength, suppleness, stamina and spirit.'

'So you think that the decathlete is the greatest athlete in the world?'

'That was my event – ' began Murdoch.

'I see,' said Slater, smiling. 'Special pleading.'

'You could call it that.'

'What if I said that Ellis here could beat you any day?'

Murdoch flushed. 'At what?'

'Freestyle swimming,' replied Slater promptly. 'Two lengths.'

'I'd say put your money where your mouth is,' said Murdoch, grinning.

Slater raised his arm, beckoning Ellis to the front of the crowd.

'Young lady,' he said, 'you willing to take on Mr Murdoch?'

The girl smiled. 'Any time,' she said.

'Come on, Slater, give young Murdoch here a chance!' It was Andrew Weir, who had joined them. 'These boys are setting you up, Alan,' he rumbled. 'They've picked up a few bucks on Ellis before. She may look fragile, but she swam second-string in freestyle for UCLA back in '76. What was your best time, Ellis?'

'Fifty-seven flat,' said Ellis, blushing furiously.

'So you see, Alan, the boys have got themselves a little sting going here. You still game?'

Murdoch nodded.

'Right – we've got ourselves a deal,' said Weir, slapping him on the shoulder. 'Sylvester!' he shouted across the pool.

Harvey Sylvester was deep in conversation with a well-built blonde, but he immediately put down his drink and scurried towards them.

'Sylvester, fix up Ellis and Mr Murdoch here with some swimming gear. My people back in the house will tell you where it is.'

A sizeable group had already begun to gather round the pool as Ellis and Murdoch walked behind Sylvester towards the main building.

'Before I forget,' said Ellis, 'a couple of people will be here in about an hour's time. They want to meet you.'

'From the studio?'

'No,' said Ellis. 'These people have come a long way, from

New York. I thought I'd better mention it now, but I'll tell you more about them after the swim. Okay?'

Ten minutes later, both dressed in borrowed swimming gear, Ellis and Murdoch returned to the pool. The music had stopped, and so had nearly all the conversation. Two hundred guests were massed round the tiny twenty-five metre pool. What had started as a conversation piece seemed to have become the central point of the party.

The bulky Bo Cannon had taken upon himself the role of starter and stood, divested of his tuxedo, on the far side of the pool, a few metres from its edge. Like most athletes, Cannon took all competition seriously and his broad black face was now a mask of solemnity.

'You got two commands,' he said. 'Take your marks, then go. Got it?'

Ellis and Murdoch nodded. Murdoch glanced sideways at Ellis, but she seemed oblivious of him, her eyes staring ahead.

'Right then: take your marks,' shouted Cannon, lifting both hands for silence. The guests' light buzz of conversation faded dutifully.

For the first time since he had arrived at Weir's home Murdoch felt sharp and clear. His toes gripped the edge of the bath and he bent his knees, both arms forward, everything focused on the release which Cannon's next word would provide.

'Go!'

Murdoch's arms swung back in a reflex action, then powerfully forward to add to the strong horizontal drive of his legs. He hit the water over a metre ahead, striking out at once with a confident, rangy stroke.

He could sense that his start had put him into a solid lead, and started to cruise. Six years was a long time, even for a swimmer who had clocked 57 seconds for 100 metres, and anyway the short 50 metres was tailor-made for an athlete like Murdoch. But he could feel Ellis striking the water at a higher, faster cadence, shorter in range but more economical, while above him he could hear the growing shouts of the crowd. He sneaked a look to his left. Ellis was almost level, with only five metres to go to the turn. Murdoch stepped up his strike-rate, but still found Ellis gaining on him. They reached the end of the pool together.

Murdoch had always prided himself on the quality and strength of his tumble-turn. He half-twisted, touching perfectly with both feet, then drove off strongly, turning to his right to check on the girl. Ellis, turning neatly and swiftly, was ahead! Almost a metre up, she was keeping form superbly, and was making for home with crisp, remorseless strokes.

For the next thirty metres Murdoch drew upon a vocabulary of twenty years' track and field athletics, twenty years of holding form under stress – while cursing his earlier lack of drive. Stroke by stroke he clawed back at the girl's lead, feeling but ignoring the increasing heaviness in his arms and shoulders. To those above the pool now absorbed in the contest it seemed impossible that Murdoch could regain the lead: there simply wasn't enough time, not enough water remaining. But he powered on, as if he was going to drive straight through the end wall. When he touched, it was only six inches ahead of the girl's manicured fingers. Murdoch leant on the edge of the pool, gasping, his forehead on the back of his hands, his lungs stretched and screaming for air.

'Not bad for a track star,' said a gravelly voice above him, through the whoops and applause of the crowds. It was Weir again, who was kneeling between the two swimmers. 'You take good care of this boy, young lady. You hear me?' he said, patting Murdoch's wet shoulder. 'He's an athlete. He can dig deep.'

The girl had regained her breath and was looking at Murdoch. 'Whatever you say, Mr Weir,' she said, smiling.

Murdoch hauled himself out of the water and then helped Ellis to her feet. Together they walked through the crowds, towards the house.

As they dripped water through the lounge Murdoch, still breathing heavily from the effort of the swim, suddenly felt the incongruity of the situation. Ellis led him to the curving stairway and as she ascended the stairs he ventured a glance at her. Ellis's sleek, wet body still retained much of the tone of her swimming days, though she had mercifully lost the muscularity in the shoulders of that period.

'This meeting: how long do I have?' he asked.

Ellis looked down at her watch. 'About forty minutes.'

'And these people – who are they? How do they come to be here?'

Ellis paused. 'Let's just say I'm doing someone a favour. There'll be no problems if you see them in his library.'

'You're being very mysterious,' he said.

'Orders,' she smiled, putting a finger to her lips.

They sat without speaking in the stillness of Andrew Weir's study, only the sound of the china coffee cups upon their saucers breaking the silence between them.

'Tell me something,' Ellis said suddenly.

'Yes?'

'Back there, you asked them to call you Murdoch, not Alan. Why?'

Murdoch smiled. 'When I was a kid, there were two other Alans in my street. So the biggest one became Alan, the other was called Al.'

'And you became Murdoch?' She smiled, revealing tiny white teeth. 'It suits you.'

'I hope so – anyway, it's stuck.'

Ellis leaned forward. 'You like it here?'

Murdoch did not reply immediately but took a final gulp of coffee before replacing both cup and saucer on the glass-topped table at his side.

'Until about half an hour ago I wasn't too sure whether I was here or not,' he said.

'Then the swim,' she said.

'The race,' he corrected her.

'And that woke you up, brought you into reality?'

He sipped his coffee. 'It helped,' he said. 'One of the great clichés, Ellis, is that all over the world people are the same. Not

38

true. So you take a Scot six thousand miles and dump him in Los Angeles . . .'

'And it's strange.' She smiled a warm smile.

'Very strange.'

'Anyway, it's obvious you're not into astral sport yet,' she grinned.

'Who says? I've been in touch with Baron de Coubertin for the past couple of years. We're having the first Astral Olympics in '86.'

She laughed, white teeth showing behind full lips. 'It isn't that easy to con people in LA,' she said. 'But your astral sex really got to them.'

'Who says it was all con?' Murdoch said. 'I got the concept of astral sex years ago.'

'Don't tell me – you just haven't worked out the details yet.'

'Exactly. Just a few practical problems to iron out. After that it's all systems go.'

A telephone on a table at Ellis's right hand buzzed softly. She picked it up, listened for a moment, nodded and spoke.

'Please tell Mr Hall and Mr Stevens to come directly to the study.' She replaced the telephone. 'Well, they're here.'

A few moments later, as they heard a knock on the door, she stood up and extended her hand to him. 'We'll meet again in London. By the end of the year you're going to hate the sight of me, Mr Murdoch.'

She turned and he followed her to the door, which she opened to reveal two men, one tall, lean and tanned in a sober grey pin-stripe, the other a stocky moustached figure in a light cream summer suit.

'These are the two gentlemen who want to meet you,' she said. 'Mr David Hall' – he shook hands with the tall man – 'and Mr Leonard Stevens.'

The stocky man shook Murdoch's hand firmly. In his other hand he carried a black leather suitcase.

Ellis Payne stood with her back to the door and smiled. 'I'll leave you gentlemen to it,' she said. 'Goodnight.'

She closed the door behind her and the three men made

their way to where Ellis and Murdoch had been sitting. Hall and Stevens sat on the couch while Alan returned to his armchair.

'Sorry I can't offer you a drink,' he said.

'Not at all,' said Hall in a light Californian voice. 'We're pleased you could find the time to fit us in. You must have a tight schedule.'

'Miss Payne didn't really give me any idea of why you wanted to see me.'

'Then let me get straight to the point,' said Hall. 'We know, Mr Murdoch, from our sources in Hollywood, that you are here to finalise some work on your script for *The Nazi Games*. We also know that this work is in its final stages of drafting and that this might make you available for a project which we have in mind . . .' Hall paused.

'The budget is three billion dollars,' said Stevens.

Murdoch drew in his breath. 'To do what, may I ask?'

'To hold the 1984 Olympic Games. In Kudai.'

3

The Arab Olympics

Murdoch sat in the stillness of Andrew Weir's library, fighting to preserve some contact with reality. He took a deep breath.

'Let me see if I understand you, Mr Hall. You are proposing to hold the 1984 Olympic Games, already scheduled for Los Angeles, in . . .'

'Kudai,' said the man called Stevens, lifting his leather briefcase on to his knees, punching out a code on the computer on the handle and taking from it a thin blue file.

'One of the eight United Arab Emirates,' said Hall crisply, as if speaking from a prepared script.

'Established in December 1971,' chimed in Stevens, handing the file to Murdoch and tapping it confidently as he did so. 'It's all here,' he said. 'Ten pages.'

'Forgive me, gentlemen,' said Murdoch. 'I must confess that I didn't come to Mr Weir's party prepared to talk business. Even so, my immediate reaction is to say that your proposal is ridiculous. The next Olympic Games are already scheduled for Los Angeles, and that's where they'll be held, come hell or high water.'

'Then our plans may have to be a little more than either hell or high water,' said Stevens. 'But perhaps, Mr Murdoch, we have been a trifle precipitate. Let me explain who we are and how we come to be here.'

He paused to take off his glasses. He then took out his handkerchief and began to polish them meticulously. It was several seconds before he spoke again.

'My name is Leonard H. Stevens. Like my colleague, Mr Hall, I have never had connections with international sport.

Mr Hall is president and I am chairman of an international company called ITC – '

'The International Trading Corporation,' Hall broke in. 'We buy and sell mainly in the Middle East. ITC also has a building division, and we have constructed schools, hospitals and stadia both in the Middle East and throughout the world – '

It was Stevens who interrupted this time, as if on cue. 'It was just over a year ago, in March 1981, after a programme involving the building of hospitals and schools in Kudai, that we were permitted an audience with Prince Hassan, who had just succeeded his father. The Prince expressed an interest in building what he called a "stadium of the twenty-first century" including a totally automated track and field facility, capable of housing an Olympic Games.'

Hall took up the story. 'We went back to the States, did a little research and came back to him a month later with our own proposition – to hold a fully professional Olympic Games.'

'It was the Prince who set a date on it,' continued Stevens eagerly. 'The exact period of the 1984 Los Angeles Olympics. Prince Hassan was in his youth an athlete himself and has for years been disturbed by the corruption which has developed in the Olympic movement – '

'Drugs, shamateurism, politics, commercialism,' said Hall. 'But then you will know of these matters from your own experience.'

Murdoch nodded.

Hall placed both hands on the coffee table in front of him. 'In this document he proposes a streamlined Olympic Games, consisting of track and field, gymnastics and swimming – '

'A professional Games?' interrupted Murdoch.

'Exactly,' said Hall. 'The Arab Games will have first prizes of a million dollars per event.'

'A million,' said Murdoch. 'So the total funding for prize money is . . .'

'Eighty million dollars in the track and field programme alone,' said Hall. 'With proportional sums for the swimming and gymnastics programmes.'

'And the administration and officiating costs?'

'Budgeted at sixty million,' replied Stevens.

'And who's responsible for the funding? These are massive sums.'

Hall glanced sideways at his companion, who nodded assent. 'In 1974,' he explained, leaning forward so that his tanned face revealed the mottling of liver spots on brow and nose, 'using his own personal funds, Prince Hassan started to invest in the world commodity markets. By 1978 he had already established a financial platform for a major sports complex. It was in late 1981 that he brought in OPEC and a group of other like-minded young Arab princes to strengthen his financial base, and by the end of that year his Olympic consortium had produced a sum in excess of the finances required, capable of taking the programme beyond 1984.'

Stevens looked sideways at his partner. 'Rest assured, Mr Murdoch, the money is there.'

Murdoch stood up and walked away from the two men into the still shadows of the study. He turned to face them, his head down, as he tried to absorb what he had been told.

'Okay, gentlemen,' he said. 'What exactly do you want me to do?'

Stevens rose slowly, his stomach straining against the buttons of his suit. 'We have the facilities, we have the finance. We need someone to pull the whole thing together. A director.'

'But why me?'

'Our researches have been thorough,' said Stevens. 'Since 1977, you have, single-handed, created a successful sports agency which has raised money for sports ranging from bob-sleighing to volleyball.'

Hall took a red file from his briefcase and passed it to his companion.

'In 1979,' Stevens went on, opening and consulting the file, 'you created the Pepsi Superstar Sports Award for children. In 1980, you secured half a million dollars' sponsorship for the World's Masters Track and Field Championships. In 1981, the first adult fitness programmes for the World Health

43

Organisation, and quarter of a million dollars' sponsorship for the World Bobsleigh Championships.

'So that,' said Stevens, sitting down, 'is why we want you as our technical director.'

Murdoch too sat down, facing Hall and Stevens across the glass-topped table. 'What you're proposing,' he said, 'sets the world of amateur sport on a totally different course. Leaving aside the viability of the project, there is the question of the necessary infrastructure of supporting competition. Then there's the longer-term plans of the venture. Is it just a one-off Olympics? And what happens to the world's athletes if it is?'

Hall nodded to his partner. 'We realised, Mr Murdoch,' said Stevens, taking up his cue, 'that our proposals would raise many questions. For that reason we have prepared this document for your scrutiny.'

He withdrew a further folder from his briefcase, this time a yellow one, and slid it across the table.

'This paper,' he said, 'contains full details of our business credentials and a detailed profile of what we call "the Arab Olympics".'

'And what do you want me to do?'

'First, we'd like you to study the profile, give us your assessment of the project. Then we'd like to have your detailed recommendations and your decision on whether or not you would like to act as our technical director.'

'And how long would I have?'

'We understand that you are leaving Los Angeles for London in the next two days. If you could provide a verbal assessment by then we could discuss it on the plane to London. Kudai will provide the necessary transport. We will arrange with Mr Weir to cancel your homeward flight.'

'One other matter,' said Hall. 'Your scrutiny fee. Would twenty thousand dollars be acceptable?'

'I think it would,' said Murdoch, smiling.

'Please treat this file for what it is,' said Hall, getting to his feet. 'A time bomb, ticking away in Los Angeles, at the heart of the Olympic movement. Take it from me, Mr Murdoch, their days are numbered. This document represents the dawn of a new age in international sport.'

Stevens rose stiffly, his posture underlining a formality which he had preserved throughout the discussion, and extended to Murdoch a firm handshake. Hall did likewise, nodding to Murdoch as if they already shared in a secret and that the Scot's involvement was now inevitable.

The two visitors left the room, the sounds of the party outside intruding briefly as the library door was opened and closed. Murdoch was left in the quiet of Andrew Weir's library, the file inert on the coffee table. He looked at it ruminatively: in its ten pages might be the future of the Olympic movement. Or just the fantasy of an Arab prince.

In fifteen minutes Murdoch had said his goodbyes and was seated in the Prestige limousine, already deep in the Kudai proposals.

It was two in the morning and Murdoch was sitting upright in his bed in the Prestige condominium, the yellow file open on his knees. In the early moments of the dialogue with Stevens and Hall he would not have been surprised if the doors had burst open to reveal the crew of Candid Camera. Even the Royal Seal of Kudai, imprinted in red on the top right-hand corner of the first page of the document, could not remove the feeling of unreality which threatened to overcome him as he sat in pyjamas and dressing gown surveying the opening pages.

Leonard H. Stevens
Age 60, graduate Harvard Law School 1946. Practised law at Brubaker and Boyes, Chicago 1946–52. Legal consultant, Coca-Cola 1952–58. Chairman, Kia-Cola 1959–68. Chairman, International Trading Corporation 1968 to present. Board of Governors, Chicago University, 1970 to present.

David Hall
Age 52, graduate Cornell University 1953, with honours in Business Studies. Assistant Sales Director, Ford Motors 1953–58. Sales Director, Ford Motors 1959–65. Assistant

Campaign Director, Democratic presidential campaign (Lyndon B. Johnson) 1964. Director, Kia-Cola 1965–69. Managing Director, Kia-Cola 1969–72. President, International Trading Corporation 1973 to present.

Kudai
On 2 December 1971 the eight United Arab Emirates, comprising Abu Dhabi, Dubai, Sharja, Ras al-Khaima, Fujaira, Ajman, Umm al-Qaiwain and Kudai, were brought into being.

The UAE lie on the south-eastern corner of the Arabian Peninsula, with seven of the eight Emirates lying on the Arabian Gulf Coast and the eighth, Kudai, on the Gulf of Oman. With a population of 1,050,276 at the December 1980 census and an area of 50,000 square miles, it is small relative to the rest of the developing world, but the existence of considerable reserves of oil has given Kudai the capacity to embark upon numerous far-reaching development programmes. It has emerged with the Organisation of Petroleum Exporting Countries, OPEC, as a major provider of assistance to other developing nations.

Murdoch's eyes drifted idly down the page. Standard Saatchi and Saatchi stuff, the work of a bright-eyed young copywriter struggling along on ten grand a year. There were another six pages of the same.

His eye moved quickly through the PR material, only slowing when he came to the heading, 'The Arab Olympics'.

This section was leaner, more practical. It outlined the attempts of Kudai and the Emirates to reach the sports standards of the West, and of the difficulties in developing sport in a society with a small recreational base. Arab sports leaders had found that neither expensive facilities nor the employment of top Western coaches could produce quick results at international level. The nations of the West had a start of a hundred years and there was no way of closing the gap using 'crash' programmes.

Arab attempts to hold major international sports events had also been unsuccessful, foundering on the conservatism of the IOC, FIFA and IAAF, and the other international sports federations. The proposal in 1981 of Hall and Stevens to Prince Hassan of a professional Olympic Games could not therefore have come at a better time for Arab morale.

Saatchi and Saatchi had melted into the mist, thought Murdoch. The bland tone had gone. Now on to the meat of the proposal.

It is against this background that the following programme for the 1984 Arab Olympics is proposed.

1. *Date*
   28 July–12 August 1984.

2. *Venue*
   The de Coubertin Stadium, Kudai.

3. *Events*
   3.1 All men's and women's track and field events.
   3.2 All men's and women's gymnastic events.
   3.3 All men's and women's swimming and diving events.
   All events will be conducted by computerised methods of calibration, with trained Arab back-up in event of computer failure.

4. *Prizes*
   1 million dollars to each victor, running to 50,000 dollars for eighth place. A total of 2 million dollars per event.

5. *Management Structure*
   5.1 All logistics (stadium, housing of athletes, officials, spectators) is the responsibility of the International Trading Corporation.
   5.2 All training of officials is the responsibility of the executive director.
   5.3 All selection of competitors is the responsibility of the executive director.

Murdoch shook his head. The old sweet song. Throw a few million petrodollars at a problem and it would resolve itself. The failure of previous attempts to professionalise track and field athletics had foundered on under-capitalisation. The International Track Association, which had been launched in the United States in 1972, had twitched in its death-throes after the Montreal Olympics of 1976, simply because it could not attract investment. This failure derived from its inability to enlist any but a few dissatisfied American stars and a handful of faded veterans.

It was the classic chicken and egg situation. Because ITA could not attract sufficient stars it faded to a small circus of performers, with Olympians such as David Hemery often 'competing' in dismal two-man races. It soon degenerated into a tired band of gypsy athletes running in half-empty stadia, and the ITA had died in bankruptcy in late 1976.

Since that time there had been increasing discussion of 'open' athletics, with the IAAF, fearing some breakaway circuit organised by the agents of leading athletes as a showcase for their stars, desperately trying to find a formula which would gain both the approval of the East European nations and the developing nations. Meanwhile a handful of top athletes or their parents had begun to open Swiss bank accounts, and had delivered lofty perorations on amateurism and fair play at IOC congresses, whilst back home their medical advisors had continued to search for some miraculous and undetectable drug.

The jogging boom of the late '70s had added an extra dimension to the problem, for athletics ceased to be an elite sport and became a people's movement. By 1977 there were over thirty million joggers in the United States alone. They knew nothing and cared less for the American governing body, TAC (The Athletics Congress). Soon 'outlaw' races were developing, with massive fields, and in 1979 the Association of Road Runners of America, a body openly dedicated to professional road-racing, was formed.

TAC, fearful of what exposure to legal scrutiny might reveal of the true nature of amateur track and field, soon agreed that

ARRA athletes could place their winnings in trust funds to be administered by clubs to meet the athletes' training expenses. Meanwhile the IAAF and national federations wriggled desperately to retain both control of their athletes and the magic word 'amateur'.

Murdoch thought back to his meeting with Hall and Stevens. Since his retirement from sport he had tried to develop his ability to assess people, for the world of sports promotion teemed with shysters proposing half-baked schemes of minimum value to sport and maximum profit to themselves. Hall and Stevens, though manifestly knowing little of sport, struck him as men of weight and substance. Murdoch had early in his career identified in such men an element of repose and composure, a *gravitas* engendered by a mixture of past success and a healthy bank balance. Murdoch sensed that whatever the Kudai document lacked in detail Hall and Stevens had the clout to make a reality of their dreams.

He laid the yellow file on his lap. It was 3.00 a.m. and he was tired. He put the file on the bedside table and switched off the light.

As he closed his eyes, he saw only the image of a slim, firm woman in a one-piece blue swimsuit, walking towards him, smiling. Then the image changed and they were both in the pool, the water rippling over her sleek body, as she swam to his left, always only a tantalising metre away, out of reach.

Wednesday, 28 July 1982

Murdoch's passage through Los Angeles airport had never been smoother. A bland, efficient ITC aide had ushered him from the airport entrance to the runway in less than three minutes flat, a United States record, he observed, under his breath. The aide seemed quite unaware of her achievement.

He stood at the exit to Gate 14, looking for the executive plane which would take him home to London.

'Follow me, Mr Murdoch,' said the aide, and he took time to study the line of her slim legs as she led him out into the

49

whine of the runway. The girl walked purposefully towards a fat Boeing 737 and stopped at the foot of the steps leading to its entrance.

'Here we are, sir,' she said, smiling. 'Have a pleasant flight.'

For a moment Murdoch wondered if Hall and Stevens were really sitting up there in the fat belly of the plane or if it was all some monstrous hoax. He walked up the steps, to be met by an olive-skinned man wearing a light-blue uniform and peaked cap.

'My name is Captain Shuaibi, Mr Murdoch,' he said, saluting. 'It's my responsibility to ensure you have a safe and pleasant flight.'

He beckoned Murdoch further into the plane. Murdoch felt in his stomach the familiar knot of tension which always preceded any major moment in his life. It had all happened too quickly. His adaptation processes had just managed to handle Hollywood and now he had been placed at the centre of a revolution in world sport. The first compartment was a normal first-class area, with spiral steps leading upstairs to the bar, but Shuaibi led Murdoch through to the next section. The second was laid out like a boardroom, with thick brown pile carpet and a shining oval oak table, at which twenty places were set. But the compartment was empty except for Hall and Stevens, both of whom sat at the top of the table. As Murdoch approached them Hall rose, smiling, and put out his hand. Stevens was looking at his watch.

'Right on time.' He nodded to Shuaibi. 'We leave as soon as you get clearance, Captain.' He too now extended his hand, and soon the three men were sitting down at a block of seats to the left of the table and strapping themselves in.

'I believe you favour chilled Perrier, Mr Murdoch?' said Stevens. He pressed a buzzer at his side and the door behind him opened to reveal a waiter with a bottle and three glasses.

'I hope you had adequate time to digest our document,' said Hall, as the drinks were poured out.

'May I be frank?' said Murdoch abruptly, feeling the tension in him rise.

'We expect no less, Mr Murdoch,' said Hall, smiling easily, the whine of the plane's engines drowning his words as it prepared to take off. A moment later the 737 roared down the runway and Murdoch felt the familiar uncertainty in the pit of his stomach as it rose clear of the ground.

'There's not much to digest,' said Murdoch as the engine noise subsided. 'Part one covering Kudai – that's standard material.'

Stevens's and Hall's faces were expressionless.

'My first question is – and it's the first one that the world's press will put – exactly what financial security is there going to be, on a long-term basis?'

Hall looked at Stevens, who had unclipped his safety belt and was moving back to the boardroom table. Stevens nodded as Murdoch rose to join them.

'The consortium,' said Hall, picking his words with care, 'of whom the senior member is the head of the royal family of Kudai, absolutely guarantees the finances of the project. I can say no more than that.'

Murdoch nodded. 'The first section of Part two, dealing with the Arab world's attempt to catch up in international sport, has been written by someone with some knowledge of sport.'

He took a deep breath. 'It's the final part that presents the real problem. I always remember in the play *Cyrano de Bergerac* Cyrano suggesting a trip to the moon by standing on a metal plate and throwing a magnet into the air. The idea was to have the plate and passenger drawn to the magnet and make it to the moon in a series of throws.'

Stevens and Hall both laughed and Murdoch started to relax.

'I feel the same way about this proposal,' he went on. 'There's no detail, no understanding of the problems that would be encountered in getting the world's top performers to give up their amateur status and take part in such a venture.

'Let's first look at track and field. First, the Communist countries would put the blocks on their athletes coming.

'Second, top athletes do want to earn money, but above all they want to *compete*. So there would have to be a world support structure of at least twenty track and field meets, with good prize money in each. That would entail setting up a separate World Track Association to create rules and engage and train a body of officials.

'Third, two million dollars per event sounds great, but in my country most of it would vanish in income tax. There would have to be a basic sum, plus a guaranteed pension for life, with the balance held in trust, particularly if an athlete won more than one prize.

'Fourth, this computerised stadium. I read every track and field magazine in the world, but I've never heard a whisper of such a facility. It's like something out of *Brave New World*.'

Stevens looked sideways at Hall, and put up his hand, smiling. 'Could I stop you there, Mr Murdoch?' He placed two fingers to the side of his left temple and his thumb under his chin, and paused. 'When your appointment was first suggested our principal predicted your response. You have not therefore disappointed either him or us.'

'Our principal said that, no matter what money we offered, you would be extremely frank, even if it resulted in your losing your contract,' added Hall.

Stevens rose. 'I think it is time you met our principal.'

Hall also rose. 'Prince Hassan of Kudai,' he said.

Murdoch realised that someone else had entered the room, to his right. There, standing at the other end of the table, was a tall, bearded man clad in a white linen suit. Murdoch recognised him immediately. 'Woodie,' he shouted, walking towards him. 'Woodie!'

4

The Set-Up

Prince Hassan el Fahze of Kudai did not immediately smile in response, but surveyed Murdoch appraisingly. Then he stretched out both arms and broke into a broad grin.

'Murdoch!' he said, advancing down the cabin and putting both hands on Murdoch's shoulders before shaking him by the hand. They sat down together at the middle of the boardroom table, while Hall and Stevens remained in their seats, uncertain of the posture to adopt in view of the obvious intimacy between the two men.

'Mr Murdoch intended no disrespect, gentlemen,' said Hassan, only the slightest fleck of a foreign accent in his voice. 'From 1966 to 1970 I spent four years at Oxford University, then two more at the Royal Military Academy, Sandhurst. My special athletic talent lay in the 110 metres high hurdles. I gained the sobriquet "Woodie" because of my regrettable tendency to leave a row of broken wooden barriers behind me.'

'The Prince bought a fresh set of hurdles for the university just before he left,' explained Murdoch.

'It was only fitting,' smiled Hassan. 'After all, I had during my career destroyed barriers that had lasted a famous university for generations. Fortunately, by the time I left Sandhurst I had met your coach, Mr Grieve.'

'As I remember it, he got you down to 14 seconds flat.'

'Base metal into gold, the skills of the alchemist, that's what Mr Grieve used to say,' responded Hassan. 'He even awarded me a special honour – the OWC.'

53

Hall and Stevens looked perplexed.

'The Order of the Webbed Crutch,' Hassan and Murdoch said simultaneously, laughing.

'Those were good times,' Hassan continued. 'Moments when I was at my physical peak. Your Mr Grieve, I have much to thank him for, a wonderful leader of men. Am I wrong to say that he brought you into tobogganing after Munich?'

'Bobsleighing,' corrected Murdoch.

Hassan nodded.

'Grieve had learnt to drive a bobsleigh in the army and he reckoned that all he needed was athletic muscle to get the bob moving down the mountain. That was where I came in.'

Hassan smiled. 'Always the athlete,' he said. His face became serious again. 'And now we meet again, but this time for quite a different purpose.'

'Your Arab Olympics.'

'Yes. I must confess that I listened to your response upstairs. You did not sound . . . optimistic.'

Murdoch stole a sideways glance at the Prince's two cohorts. 'It isn't a question of optimism. First, it's a matter of defining objectives. If you hope to create a Games focusing on athletics, gymnastics and swimming featuring Western performers, then that *is* possible, but only if the proper structure is set up during the next eighteen months.'

'You discount any possible involvement by Eastern bloc nations, then?'

Murdoch shrugged. 'Poland is a possibility, but I doubt if the Russians would let them. The rest of the Eastern bloc is probably out, unless we can stimulate major defections.'

'What about the West?'

'If there's an adequate competitive support structure so that even the lesser performers make some sort of a living, then I think that Western athletes might buy it. But it's going to take some hard selling.'

'Athletes like Coe and Ovett, Thompson and Lewis?'

'Yes, if we offer them a secure, long-term deal. But not if

they think that the Arab Olympics is a one-off affair, like the International Track Association.'

Hassan nodded. 'And how do you see our structure developing?'

'First we have to set up our own organisation, with executive directors in each sport, each supported by a small staff. I would suggest an élite Olympics in each discipline, featuring no more than twenty competitors per event. I have some suggestions in gymnastics and swimming.'

'Yes?' asked Hassan, helping himself to a Coca-Cola.

'There I think we should have an over-eighteen qualification, so that we can distance ourselves from offering the fourteen-year-old Olga Korbuts and Sharron Davies's of the West million-dollar prizes. This would also have the advantage of providing a different type of gymnastics competition, taking it away from East European midgets and handing it back to properly proportioned young women.'

'All that you have said makes good sense,' said Hassan, nodding to Hall, who was making notes. 'But let us return to track and field, which I see as the key to the success of our venture. How do we set up a structure of meetings?'

Murdoch paused and bit on his lip. 'Two men are at the centre of world track and field athletics, the men who run the money meets. They're Claude "Bull" Buchinski in New York and Albert Quince in London. If we can bring their meetings into our orbit, in effect make these our Arab Olympic qualifying rounds, then we've cracked Western track and field athletics.'

Hassan looked sideways again at Hall and Stevens. The two names were obviously known to all three of them.

'You think it can be done?'

Murdoch nodded. 'But Quince and Buchinski are in the same position as the athletes. They'll want firm financial commitments to at least 1992, or they burn their boats behind them.'

'But surely the amateur authorities know quite well that these two men are already dispensing large sums to amateur athletes?' said Hassan.

'Yes, but they can handle that – it's a sort of black economy. Only the moment Quince and Buchinski become our men then they're outlaws as far as the IAAF and their own national bodies are concerned.'

Hassan's nose wrinkled. 'So what are the immediate priorities?'

'To set up a professional organisation, to commit meet organisers and a high fraction of Western athletes to our 1983 pre-Games programme.'

'In my country,' said Hassan, 'before embarking upon a project we divide the world into friends and enemies. Who are our enemies?'

Murdoch paused, just as the plane juddered its way through a pocket of turbulence. 'The International Olympic Committee; the international federations of athletics, swimming and gymnastics; and the organising committee of the Los Angeles Olympics itself. Then we have the national governing bodies in the three sports, plus the governments of the East European bloc who have pumped billions of dollars into sport. Not forgetting the national broadcasting associations, who've already bought the Los Angeles Olympics.'

Hassan nodded, his brow furrowing. 'I have always found that it is often individuals one is up against rather than organisations. An organisation is an abstraction and its control is usually left in the hands of a few. Who are these people?'

Murdoch pursed his lips. 'Maurice Delgado, the new head man at the IOC. He will have no desire to see the Olympics go down the drain in the first years of his reign. He's been a French Minister of State, so he's no fool. Then there's Harold Berne, the English chairman of the International Amateur Athletic Federation.'

'I know Mr Berne,' said the Prince. 'We met when I was in England. No friend of yours, as I recollect.'

Murdoch nodded. 'And of course there's Bruce Cohn, the chairman of the Los Angeles Organising Committee.'

'We know Cohn,' said Hall.

'All right,' said Hassan. 'And what can these people do?'

56

'In their place I would try to discredit your organisation – first by indicating that there was no money in the bank. So it's essential that your financial credibility is beyond reproach. Then they'll try to say that it's a fly-by-night set-up, that it will vanish after 1984. Another possibility is that they will try to discredit you man by man, to give the impression that you lack the individual ability to carry out the venture.'

'But Mr Murdoch,' interjected Stevens, 'our researches show that amateur officials have gone on record that they have no objection to professional sport so long as it is kept separate from the amateur section.'

Murdoch chuckled. 'That's true. They could afford to say that while the Olympics represented the peak of performance. Just as long as any alternative professional set-up was a minor circus, like the ITA. But the moment it becomes a successful big-money competition then their territory is threatened. Suddenly, being on the IOC or being the chairman of a national governing body will no longer be so important. Nor will Olympic medals have the same propaganda value for Communist nations, because now they'll be competing amongst themselves.'

Hassan smiled. 'We are a cat amongst pigeons. But who then are our friends?'

'You haven't any,' Murdoch replied. 'You'll have to earn them.'

Hassan tilted his head back against his seat and closed his eyes. A moment later he rose and paced slowly along the side of the conference table, his back to Murdoch. Only the thin whine of the plane's jets could be heard, and it was fully a minute before Hassan turned swiftly on his heel to face Murdoch.

'You are right,' he said. 'We cannot buy friends, only vassals.' He pressed thumb and index fingers to his lips. 'But one point you have not yet raised. It seems to me that the prize money which we offer will only increase the likelihood of athletes taking illegal drugs.'

'True,' replied Murdoch. 'If we can't crack the drug problem we're in trouble. As you probably know, there are two types of drugs. First, those relating to immediate performance – such as the amphetamines, easily detectable. These are still taken in countries like the USA where there are no drug-detection units, but they have been wiped out at Olympic level. The main problem is the anabolic steroids, which are essentially training drugs, undetectable if the athlete stops taking them about three weeks before competition.'

'How extensive are they?' asked Hassan.

'Almost total in power events and there is evidence that they have moved up into middle and long distances and walks. Some of the most recent suspensions occurred in women's middle distance.'

Hassan shook his head. 'Women,' he said. 'Girls. So sad.' He sat down at the table and pressed a buzzer on the table in front of him.

The door at the end of the cabin had opened and two waiters appeared carrying trays of canapés. They laid them on the centre of the boardroom table before making a discreet exit. Hassan lifted a tray and offered it to Murdoch, who accepted a quiche. He offered the tray to Stevens and Hall before taking his own and the conversation stopped for a moment as the four consumed their food.

'If we're going to have clean competition we'll have to be ruthless,' Murdoch resumed. 'There will have to be out-of-season testing on a quota basis. Luckily there are experts around, like Ernst Schmidt, a top East German doctor who defected at Lake Placid in 1980. He offered his evidence on drug-taking in East Germany to the Federations, but they didn't want to know.'

The waiters appeared again, this time bearing jugs of coffee. 'A choice, Murdoch,' said Hassan, his brown eyes twinkling. 'I seem to recollect you had no taste for Arab coffee. So I have provided both Arab and American.'

The coffee was served. Hall sipped his, then laid down his cup. 'You're saying that the federations ignored evidence which could have helped them eradicate drugs?'

58

'Precisely.'

'Our friend, Mr Berne – hasn't he been foremost in trying to wipe out steroids?' asked Hassan.

'Yes and no,' replied Murdoch. 'Berne saw early on that the anti-drug crusade would be a bandwagon he could ride for a lifetime. It was like being against evil. But he never formally proposed in Britain itself the single step that would have finished drugs in a single season.'

'And that was?'

'Compulsory random out-of-season testing,' said Murdoch. 'He knew that as a result British standards would drop like a lead balloon. He also saw that his dream of being Sir Harold would go straight down the drain.'

'Appalling,' said Hassan, pouring himself another cup.

'You've not yet mentioned the television networks,' said Stevens, reaching for a canapé. 'Surely they have a big stake in the success of the Los Angeles Olympics?'

'True,' responded Murdoch. 'ABC Television have paid the IOC 225 million dollars for the rights to the 1984 Games and they're selling them off now to national companies. An Arab Olympics bought up by NBC, or any other company, will be in direct competition with them.'

'So we have yet another enemy,' said Hassan, quietly.

'So far one hundred per cent enemies,' said Stevens.

'In my country,' said the Prince, 'we have the story of the old chieftain who was asked on his deathbed if he would forgive his enemies. He said that that would be impossible, since he had already killed them all.'

'Well, you haven't even faced yours yet,' said Murdoch.

Prince Hassan frowned. 'We have the facilities, as you'll see by the end of this month. And in the ITC we have a company capable of providing all that's necessary for the organisation of a major Games. What we need are the performers. Is it possible? Can you guarantee to bring the athletes of the West to Kudai?'

For some moments there was silence, broken only by the whine of the Boeing's engines as it cut west across the morning sky. Then Murdoch replied.

'The key lies with track and field athletics. First, I see Grieve as being vital, both to your development programmes and to credibility with the world's athletes. And the other keys are in New York and London. I've already named them for you: Claude Buchinski and Albert Quince.'

Thursday, 29 July 1982

Something had hit the street. Sergeant 'Bull' Buchinski could smell it, its odour as palpable to him as the stale smell of sweat which drenched every brown panel of the 82nd Precinct police gymnasium. Bull lay flat on his back on the padded bench, sweat dripping from his brow into his eyes, making them sting, and down into his grimacing mouth. Bull loved the taste of sweat. He relished the thick, hot, gorged feel of blood in his pectorals. Ten repetitions at 220 pounds had filled the wedges of pectoral muscle that formed his hairy chest, producing white stretch marks worthy of a pregnant woman. He sat up and wiped the sweat from his eyes.

'Okay, Sarge,' said Patrolman Maloney, behind him on the stands, wiping his nose with the back of his arm. But Bull had not really focused in as he leant backwards under the weight, narrowly missing it with the back of his grey, crew-cut head.

'Ready to take?' said Maloney.

Bull did not reply. His mind was elsewhere. *Something had hit the street*: Buchinski could taste it. There was money in the air, track and field money, but he did not know where.

'Ready to take?' growled Maloney, impatiently.

Bull raised his hands automatically round the warm metal of the bar.

'Yes,' he said.

Maloney stood above him and lifted the bar on to Bull's straightened arm, and for a moment Buchinski got a whiff of stale Scotch as he inhaled to fix his chest, to provide a solid platform up on which the weight would rest.

60

The first six repetitions came easily as he pushed the weight to arms' length, breathing out as he did so, each time returning the bar to lie across his nipples. But the seventh repetition was desperately slow and the bar suddenly felt heavy as he held it above him.

Maloney sensed Bull's weakness. 'Fix in, Sarge,' he growled. 'Fix in!'

Bull felt his triceps quiver and he slowly lowered the bar to chest-level.

'Hit!' shouted Maloney.

Bull pushed hard and just managed to squeeze the bar past the sticking point where the lower and upper arms were at right angles. The weight was now at arms' length and Bull felt himself start to shudder uncontrollably.

'Stay loose, Sarge,' hissed Maloney, his sweat dripping on to Bull's face.

Buchinski took the weight to his chest and this time hit it the moment it touched his skin. The weight stopped at the sticking point and Bull fought it, his breath escaping in a low moaning hiss. Slowly the weight inched up and Bull's hiss became a strangled squeal as it again reached arms' length.

'Last rep,' whispered Maloney. 'Eyeballs out!'

Bull fought to prevent the shuddering overcoming the whole of his upper body. *Focus in, Bull, focus in.*

He took the weight down to his chest, his mind now sharp, concentrating on lining it up with his nipples, for it was death to be out of line at this point, with muscles flushed with garbage.

'Shit!' shouted Bull, digging the weight from his chest, arching like a snake to give extra impetus to the bar. The black 110-pound discs slowly moved to arms' length and Maloney, poised above him, picked the weights from him and replaced them on the stands.

For a moment Bull lay still on the bench, lungs heaving. Then he lifted his trunk and leant forward, head in hands, the sweat streaming through his fingers.

'Must be getting old.'

'It ain't the years, Sarge, it's the mileage,' grinned Maloney. 'You know how it is with weights. Bio-rhythms. You tell *me* – you crapped twice in a row this week?'

'Ah, at my age once in a row is good enough,' groaned Bull, getting to his feet and reflexly rubbing the small of his back as he walked towards the exit.

'Think I'll have me a rub-down,' he said, picking up his sweat-top from a peg on the wall. He made his way through the dark clanking weights room, still rubbing the small of his back. It was like a nervous tic: there had been nothing wrong with his back, not since that Christmas morning twenty years ago when he had stretched a ligament bending down to check on the price of a pair of shoes at the Christmas sale at Macy's.

As he passed the mirror at the door he flexed the muscles in his chest and arms and checked himself out. Six feet, 200 pounds, only ten pounds up on the days, twenty years ago, when he had slung the shot out to over fifty-two feet at the old Travers Island track. Arms still seventeen and a half inches, chest forty-six, waist ten inches less. So some definition had gone, but what the hell did they expect at forty-nine? Arnold Schwarzenegger?

He entered the steamy shower room, peeled off his sweat-top, sweat-bottoms and jock-strap, sat on the wooden bench and unlaced his training shoes. Adidas had always done him right, always given him the best. And why the hell not? He had put plenty of track business their way.

He turned on the best showers in New York and smiled as the warm water gushed down. Bull Buchiński was proud of his name, the same as that of his hero Charles Bronson. He had seen *Deathwish* six times. Hell, if it had been up to him, had he been commissioner, he'd have let Bronson wipe out the whole motherfucking nest of muggers, spies, gays and liberals.

Bull had been the last of the breed of athletic New York cops which had begun with the Irish 'whales', Flanagan and McGrath, back in the last years of the nineteenth century. In those days no one could reach the top in the department without a shamrock in his jock-strap, and Bull's grandfather, Eugene, fresh from Poland in 1895, a natural strong-man, had joined the force, linked up with the 'whales' and immediately matched them in tossing the 56-pounder for height and the 35-pounder for distance.

Eugene Buchinski was a legend by the time Bull's father, Josef, had joined in 1925, and the Buchinskis had by then earned themselves the nickname of the 'Irish Polacks'. Josef had also been a 'natural', just missing the USA 1928 Olympic team for Amsterdam in the 16-pound hammer, and had been National Police Champion in the Olympic lifts eight times running.

The young 'Bull' Buchinski had also taken naturally to the heavy events, and in the early 1950s had put the 16-pound shot out to fifty-two feet and the discus to just short of a hundred and fifty. Like his father and grandfather before him, he loved exercise for its own sake and had continued to compete till into his early forties, well into the world of steroidal monsters.

Even before he had retired from active track and field Bull had officiated at Amateur Athletic Union meets all around the East Coast, mainly in his first love, the throws. In 1960, after fifteen years on the hoof on the East Side, he had been appointed police fitness officer, responsible for the physical condition of every cop from cadet to full sergeant, and this responsibility had limited his progress up the rungs of the Amateur Athletic Union hierarchy.

Bull had loved those first years in the job, when he had designed a rigorous and varied programme of jogging, circuit-training and weight-lifting to develop and maintain basic fitness levels. He had transformed most of the gloomy, old-fashioned gymnasia inherited from the Irish mafia of the nineteenth century into attractive modern palaces of fitness, and had established basic fitness norms for the whole force. Bull's 'Fit to Fight Crime' programmes had, by the end of the '60s – by every objective measure – brought the New York force to the highest levels of fitness of any police force in the world.

By then Bull had created a fitness programme that virtually ran itself. It was his view that men made themselves fit; all he had done was to enthuse them, provide the facilities and point them in the right direction.

It was in 1970 that an incident occurred that was to alter his life and to change the direction of world athletics. Bull had been officiating at the shot-put at the Garden Games in New York's Madison Square Garden when he had been summoned to the meet director's box. It was explained that Commissioner O'Rourke, who normally dealt with athletes' expenses, had been rushed to hospital with suspected appendicitis. Would Bull take his place?

It had seemed at first a simple task, merely to dole out expenses to one hundred and twenty athletes from all over the world. Bull had been under no illusions about what 'expenses' meant; even in his own day there had been plenty of loose money floating around, particularly on the indoor circuit. But what had amazed him was the depth and range of the deception. Athlete A, from just next door in Poughkeepsie, had somehow been on holiday in Mexico City and took 300 dollars on top of his 300 dollars 'sweetener'. Athlete B, who had already been paid travel expenses by the promoter of the Boston meet two nights before, charged the full air fare of 400 dollars from London, England. Many of the expense claim forms could well have been submitted to a publisher as works of fiction.

Bull had spent a hard, oath-filled night arguing and debating expenses with athletes from England to Australia and had ended up 500 dollars over budget, paying the excess from the evening's gate-receipts. A week later he had found no support when he had reported on the payments to the Garden Committee. No one on the committee wanted to know about illegal payments; that was something that happened in some dark underworld far away from the bright lights and the tuxedos of the Garden Classic.

After the committee meeting Bull had been sought out by

the meet director, Carl Merrill. Merrill had assured him that no blame attached to him. Indeed, the committee were delighted with the firm way he had handled what could have been an extremely delicate situation. There was another indoor meet in Richmond, Virginia, in two weeks' time. Would Bull handle the expenses there?

Thus Bull Buchinski's career as a 'fixer' began in Richmond, Virginia, in January 1971, just a year before his European counterpart, Albert Quince, the London bookseller, began in a similar manner. By the end of 1971 Bull had made links with every promoter on the Eastern Seaboard, indoor or outdoor, and by the Olympic year of 1972 had brought in the boys from the West Coast and the Mid West. Bull established the national rate for each man or woman, ensured no double claims for expenses and that no meet director was played off against another. He also made certain that the smaller meets did not lack for athletes by refusing to allow performers to compete in the big-money meets if they did not also support the smaller, less lucrative ones. And anyone who crossed Bull Buchinski could reckon on lean times – particularly by 1974 when Bull linked up with Albert Quince.

No two men could have been less alike: Buchinski, the raw, burly New York cop, and the lean, quiet Quince, expert in nineteenth-century athletics literature. By late 1973 Quince had linked up with the major West European money meets and had even 'bought' whole Cuban and Polish teams for 'hard' Western currency. The two men had met in the sticky heat of Hamilton, Bermuda, on 1 October 1974, and found that they had reached almost identical conclusions about the state of modern international athletics.

'A shit heap,' said Buchinski. 'Unsatisfactory,' had been Quince's milder response. In his measured way Quince had outlined the position. Illegal payments had, of course, been nothing new since the earlier days of the sport. In the late nineteenth century the promoters of English rural sports had found that 'stars' gave their meetings both status and income and paid them accordingly.

The re-creation of the Olympics in 1896 did nothing to improve matters. Indeed, by the 1908 London Olympics shamateurism was firmly established both in Europe and the United States. But no one was making much of a living out of the sport, and it was not until the rise of Paavo Nurmi, 'the Flying Finn', and the beefy extrovert American sprinter, Charley Paddock, in the '20s that any amateur was to make big money. Paddock had vanished into the world of Hollywood B-pictures in the late 1920s after a decade of shamateur life. Nurmi had lasted longer as an amateur – until 1932, when his status had been traded off at IAAF committee level by the Hungarian, Klics, in return for German support for his proposal for a 1934 European Championships. Nurmi had been banned for ever from amateur competition.

The big breakthrough had, however, come in 1935 when Hitler had decreed unlimited time off for German athletes training for the 1936 Berlin Olympics. This infringement of amateur ethics the IAAF had blithely ignored, and Nazi Germany had gone on to finish second to the USA in the track and field medals.

In 1948, at the first post-war Olympics, the nations of Eastern Europe, still shattered by war, had not taken part. 1952 saw the entry of the Russians, who finished second to the Americans in track and field and first on aggregate men and women's results. That year also marked a watershed in modern athletics, with Communist nations, using sport as an extension of political activity, pouring vast sums into facilities, coaching and sports science. To be an athlete in Eastern Europe was to occupy a privileged position: extra food, better accommodation, time off work, national recognition, foreign travel. In such nations as Russia there could be no such thing as a professional. In the eyes of the IAAF an amateur was whoever a national governing body decided was an amateur – and this suited the Eastern Europeans very well.

Bull Buchinski had listened patiently, over endless cups of tea in the strong Bermuda sun, as the earnest little Englishman had taken him through the history of the sport.

It was at 1960 that Quince's lecture became really interesting. That, said Albert Quince, removing his glasses to polish them, was the second breakpoint, the year in which the Olympics had first been extensively covered by television.

The 1960–70 period saw Western television mop up every track and field meet available and help bring into existence a multitude of new meets. Covering track events, like most sports coverage, was cheap when compared with a drama series or television movies; and there was a ready audience. Companies with products to sell also saw that the sponsorship of track meets was a cheap way of securing product exposure. But meets could only be successful when there were stars – and stars were scarce. The payment of large sums to top athletes had therefore become commonplace, and despite occasional press exposés of shamateurism (invariably by non-sports journalists) which were blandly ignored by amateur administrators, payments proliferated, with athletes doubling up expenses and faking travel claims as well as picking up appearance money.

The jogging boom of the early '70s had brought an added impetus to track and field, for thirty million Americans and perhaps another thirty million in the rest of the world were soon involved in running programmes. Established shoe companies such as Adidas and Puma had paid athletes since the 1950s and now thrusting new companies such as Nike, New Balance and Saucony competed with them. On the West Coast clubs like Pacific West and Los Angeles Runners had appointed professional managers to negotiate with promoters such as Quince, but in 1974, when Buchinski and Quince held their Bermuda summit, there were still many loose ends. West Coast Americans arriving in Europe stoned out of their minds, hotel thefts, sexual orgies, athletes failing to meet their commitments, the recurrent over-claiming of expenses – all were still rife.

'A shit heap,' repeated Bull.

'There *is* a need to rationalise, Claude.'

Bull had blenched when Albert had first used the name

Claude: only his mother was allowed to call him by that name. But he quickly realised that the little Englishman meant no harm. Hell, with a name like Albert, Quince had his own cross to bear.

'You're damn right,' he replied.

'First, I feel that we should have a division of territory. Might I therefore suggest that I take Europe and the Middle East and you the Americas, the Far East and Australasia?'

'Sounds fair to me,' said Bull, although he did not give a dime for the Far East and Australasia.

'I have the agreement of the major European promoters – Schumann in Germany, Liani in Italy, Paul in France, Haegg in Sweden – to speak for them. Britain I have completely under control.'

'I got the States in my pocket,' replied Bull.

'The first aim, therefore, will be to rationalise fixtures so that we minimise date clashes. Where there are inevitable clashes we must agree upon the division of athletes so that meets do not suffer unduly.'

'Right,' agreed Bull.

'Your federation, the AAU – how do you view them?'

'Cretins. Simpletons kissing other simpletons' backsides.'

'I see that we have the same problems,' said Quince, beckoning to a black waiter for more tea. 'But we cannot simply ignore the governing bodies. They do, after all, organise the sport. The important thing is to devise our programmes so that they cause minimum interference to the national and international competitive schedules. Otherwise we may face problems with getting IAAF clearance for our meets.'

'That ain't going to be easy.'

'The important things never are,' replied Quince. 'And now to discipline. If either of us blackballs an athlete – '

'Blackballs?'

'Suspends him from the money meets for any infringement, either personal or athletic. That ban must apply both ways. No matter who, no matter what his pulling power, he goes, both here and in Europe. That means all doors closed until he toes the line.'

Albert Quince sipped his tea and grimaced as Bull Buchinski nodded agreement. The Bermudans had taken to the vile practice of using tea bags. 'Any other points?'

'An ace in the hole,' said Bull. 'Against the federations, just in case the roof falls in on us.'

'You mean blackmail?'

'When you're with wolves you got to learn to howl like a wolf.'

Quince laid down his cup and reached for a buttered muffin. He took a bite and consumed it slowly.

'Bull, when drug-testing for anabolic steroids first started I secured the services of a brilliant young scientist by the name of Stephen Frost. As you know, our scientists cannot trace steroids much further back than a month from ingestion. I have no need to tell you that this is useless because the anabolic steroids are essentially training drugs. To detect them we therefore have to go at least nine months back. Stephen Frost, using a unique photographic method, has broken this problem and can detect steroids for nine months back.'

'But how does this help us?'

'Using a contact in the IAAF I have secured urine samples from the last Olympics and this year's European Games. These are clearly marked and Federation-stamped with unbroken seals and with them is a list of the athletes from whom they were taken. If the balloon goes up then the seals are broken and we test for steroids in the presence of medical witnesses. If the results aren't fifty per cent positive then my name isn't Albert Quince.'

'You got them by the balls.'

'Almost literally,' replied Quince. 'And what is your ace in the hole, Claude?'

'Thumbprints,' replied Bull, immediately.

'Thumbprints?'

'Every payment sheet at my meets is thumbed by the athlete. I got nearly a thousand illegal payment forms over the past four years. Borzov, Szewinska, Hammond, Major – I've got them all. There's no arguing your way out of it the way you can with a signature. It's foolproof.'

'So if we want to possess the hearts and minds of the IAAF we first take them by the balls and thumbs,' said a smiling Quince. 'Balls and thumbs.'

5

The Golf Ball in the Lettuce

Thursday, 29 July 1982

Agent Butch Pendleton entered his superior's office, pulling in his ample stomach as he approached Stafford's desk. He carried a single sheet of paper, to which was attached a glossy black and white photograph.

CIA section head Paul Stafford sat back in his leather chair, sipping his morning coffee. Mornings were not his time. He laid down the drink clumsily, spilling part of its contents into the saucer.

'What you got there, Butch?' he asked, scowling.

'Middle East, sir. Probably nothing, but you know how concerned the big man always is about the area.'

He laid the single sheet of paper and the attached photograph on the desk top in front of Stafford. The older man slowly scrutinised the photograph, detached the paperclip which held it to the sheet, turned the photograph upside down and shook his head.

'Those magnificent men with their flying machines. They can pick up a car number plate at twenty thousand feet. So what do you make of it? Where the hell is it from, anyway?'

Pendleton shrugged and walked timidly round the back of the desk to look over his superior's shoulder.

'It's from Kudai, sir. We only scan there occasionally. It's not much more than sand and oil, a couple of Hiltons and an airport.'

'Kudai? That's one of the Emirates, isn't it?'

'The richest, sir. Just been taken over by a young prince, name of Hassan. He's a soldier boy, trained in England.'

'Sandhurst?'

'Yes, sir; 1970–72. Very pro-English. Up till now they've kept their heads down, under his father. Developed their road, housing and education programmes, and left politics to their neighbours.'

Stafford shook his head and handed back the photograph over his shoulder to Pendleton, who returned to stand in front of his superior.

'It's a lousy picture,' said Stafford. 'I could take better with a box Brownie. You know what it looks like, Butch?' Pendleton shook his head. 'Looks to me like a golf ball in the middle of a mess of lettuce.'

'Agent Brix figures the lettuce might just be building equipment,' volunteered Pendleton anxiously.

'Then bully for Brix. And what does he make of the golf ball?'

Pendleton hesitated, his brow furrowed.

'Well?' said Stafford.

Pendleton paused. 'Brix thinks it looks like the Houston Astrodome, sir.'

Stafford groaned. 'Brix couldn't find his ass with both hands! Let me see that picture again.'

Pendleton obediently handed the photograph back to Stafford, who opened a drawer and withdrew a magnifying glass. He peered at the black and white print through the glass before putting both down and shaking his head.

'Tell the flying boys to make a mess of pictures from a lower altitude,' he said. 'And give them to Brix first. Tell him if he can pick out any bona fide tickets for the Astrodome to let out a holler right away. Then I can hightail it out to Kudai and see me a football game.'

He paused, then shouted after Pendleton. 'And get a couple for the big man – remember, he used to cover football for radio before he ever made the White House.'

*

72

At the time Berne had first contacted him IOC chairman Maurice Delgado had been concerned with a more important matter. Rumblings had reached him of a possible Russian withdrawal from the 1984 Olympic Games. Delgado knew that if the Russians went then they would take with them the whole Communist bloc. He had no intention of imitating the Emperor Theodosius who had achieved a dubious immortality by presiding over the demise of the ancient Games in 390 AD.

A week's prolonged telephoning to the Russian embassy in Paris had brought the response that any such decision was in the hands, not of the Russian government, but of its independent Olympic Committee, and that the Committee had expressed no intention of withdrawing. Delgado had breathed more easily, though he knew that the Russian Olympic Committee had about as much control over its decisions as the Dalai Lama.

Harold Berne's report had at first seemed the stuff of science fiction. A Shangri-la stadium in the middle of a desert, capable of holding one hundred thousand people, an unspecified track and field meeting in 1984 . . . Delgado knew only a little about the underworld of shamateur track and field athletics, but he took it on good faith that Quince and Buchinski were central to the world network of money meets. He had never heard of Grieve or Murdoch, but it still seemed clear to him that this group had been assembled for the purpose of some major undertaking. A call to the organiser of the Los Angeles Games, Bruce Cohn, had confirmed that rumours about a massive 1984 Arab money meet had been circulating for over a month in Los Angeles. The American had suggested a meeting in Paris or London to pool existing knowledge and to organise a plan of campaign.

Delgado had agreed, if only to see if fact could be separated from fiction, though he had no confidence in the outcome. Then a call from the authoritative French sports newspaper, *L'Equipe*, had brought matters to a head. They informed him that they had received inside information that a press conference was being called in October in London by a group called the World Professional Athletics Association, headed by one Alan Murdoch.

It was all beginning to fit together, and to Maurice Delgado none of it looked good.

A brown Daimler waited on the tarmac a hundred metres from the Boeing as Murdoch walked down the steps on to the runway at Heathrow. It flew the red and white flag of Kudai on its bonnet and at its side stood a sallow, mustachioed Arab in black uniform. He saluted as Murdoch approached.

'If you will give me ten minutes to have the luggage cleared at customs and installed, Mr Murdoch?' he said, with only a hint of an accent.

Murdoch nodded and was soon engulfed in the vast, dark softness of the Daimler. The flight from Los Angeles to London had given him time to collect and analyse the facts involved in staging an Arab Olympics.

He had committed himself to Hassan, Hall and Stevens before leaving the plane. Hassan's presence had sealed the project for him from the moment that he had entered the cabin. True, Murdoch's last memory of the Prince had been of a swarthy, spindly-legged hurdler chopping barriers like matchwood; but the man now wore power like a well-fitting glove. And behind Hassan lay the petrodollar strength of his consortium. There would be no financial problems, no living from hand to mouth as previous professional ventures had been forced to do.

Murdoch felt the adrenalin flow as he went back over all that had happened. Throughout his athletic life he had been an outsider, invariably at the mercy of people such as Harold Berne and his acolytes. Now, suddenly, he was at the crossroads of the sport, capable of directing it along a fresh path. He felt the blood throb and pulse in his temples as he scribbled on the clipboard on his knee while the Daimler cruised through the West End in the gathering darkness of the summer evening. The first calls would be crucial; from Buchinski and Quince, then to Grieve. Without them he would not be able to carry the project forward. His thoughts were interrupted by the subdued squeal of brakes as the car stopped at the traffic lights in Marylebone High Street. He was almost home.

It was 9.00 p.m. and his second-floor office in Hallam Street was dark as he inserted the key in the door. He could hear the raucous sounds of a party a couple of floors down. Checking on his desk for telephone messages, he saw that Quince had called from Helsinki. Mr Quince would call again in the morning. A Miss Ellis Payne was in London and would like to discuss the script of *The Nazi Games* with him. Could he call her?

A London telephone number followed: 499 0888. Murdoch wrinkled his nose. A West End prefix. He tried to think of the tanned, Californian Ellis ensconced only a mile from him in some luxury hotel, away from all the confidence and certainty of Los Angeles. Now she was in his territory.

There were four or five other calls, all routine.

A thick wad of mail lay bound on the table by the side of the telephone. He pulled out a copy of *Runners World*, locked the door behind him and walked slowly up the winding stairs, peeling off the brown wrappers of the magazine as he did so. He opened the double locks to his flat, put on the lights and closed the door behind him. His flat, his oasis. The living room had subdued lighting, but Murdoch could see the log-basket by the empty fireplace well enough to focus on it. Taking quick aim he threw the ball of brown wrapping paper at it, missed, and the paper bounced on to the sheepskin rug in front of the fireplace. Murdoch cursed softly to himself and walked over to the fireplace to retrieve his missile. Then he noticed that the empty log-basket seemed out of place. Instead of being snugly wedged, as it was usually, underneath the shelf of antique sports books, it had been moved slightly out. Some wood-waste from the base of the basket had spilled on to the rug, making a brown stain.

Murdoch bent down and dipped his fingers into the wood-waste. There was no doubt about it, the basket had been knocked over and replaced. He stood up and scrutinised the shelf of books, behind which stood his wall-safe.

They were all there: Shearman's *Athletics*, 1881 edition; Strutt's *Sports and Pastimes of the English People* (1801); and Thom's classic *Pedestrianism 1813*, the first modern work on track and field athletics. He had always, as a fetish, lined up the date '1813', which lay exactly in the centre of the book's leather spine, with the centre of the dial of the safe behind it. But now it was out of line, to the right of the dial.

He parted the books, revealing the complete dial, and slowly clicked it through its code – 8160, his best decathlon score. He opened the safe, inserted his hand and withdrew a sheaf of documents – mortgages, contracts, insurances. He again inserted his hand and withdrew a steel box. It contained over three hundred pounds in foreign currencies, which he had collected during his travels, and some jewellery. Again, all there. He shook his head and reached once more into the safe. Then as his fingers searched the back of the safe he made contact with a plump, soft package, only a few ounces in weight. He withdrew it carefully, flicked on a standard lamp at the side of the fireplace, and held it under the light. It was a sealed clear plastic sachet and contained what appeared to be sugar.

But Murdoch somehow sensed that this was not sugar. He ripped open the bag with his teeth and poured a few grains into the palm of his left hand, then warily dipped his tongue into it.

He grimaced. The powder was bitter – '*wersch*', his mother would have called it in Lallans. He replaced the remaining grains in the little bag which he put on the table in front of his couch. Murdoch sat down and drew both hands through his curly black hair. Somehow he sensed that a dark new element had entered his life, that forces were already gathering against him and the Arab Games, only a few hours from the handshake that had sealed his bargain with Hassan. There was only one man who could help in this. Birdie.

Commander Derek Sparrow took the glass of whisky which Murdoch offered him and raised it to his lips.

'Cheers,' he said.

Anyone seeing the lean mustachioed Sparrow on one of his regular training runs could well imagine that he was still as swift and aggressive as the 'Birdie' Sparrow who had run the mile with such distinction against Ibbotson and Bannister back in the early 1950s. The fifty-three-year-old policeman was now Britain's leading veteran runner in the 50–55 age band over 1500 metres and 5000 metres. He had, only a month before, taken early retirement and was now pounding out a hundred miles a week.

'Cheers,' replied Murdoch, sipping a glass of chilled Perrier.

Sparrow looked at his watch. 'Just gone half past ten,' he said. 'So it must have been something bloody important to have you call me out at this time of night.'

'Something or nothing,' said Murdoch, taking the little packet of powder from his pocket. 'Birdie, could you tell me exactly what this is?'

Sparrow took the sachet, sniffed it and sprinkled a little into the palm of his left hand. He dabbed at it with his tongue and grimaced just as his friend had done. His expression became serious.

'It's cocaine,' he said. 'No doubt about it. Now how the hell did you come by this?'

'I'm fresh back from Los Angeles tonight,' said Murdoch. 'I noticed a couple of books around the wall-safe were out of line, so I checked.'

'Anything missing?'

'Not that I've noticed, and I've looked pretty thoroughly. But I found this stuff stashed away at the back.'

Sparrow sniffed again at the grains in his hand.

'This is top quality stuff,' he said, pouring the cocaine back into its packet. 'The best. Uncut, no talcum or any other muck mixed in.' He looked up. 'I've got to say that this is serious. Athletes and coaches are horsing around with all manner of stuff these days: steroids, testosterone, marijuana, thyroxine. Man, if it were anybody but you – '

'But what's it all about?' Murdoch cut in.

'It looks as if you've been fitted up,' replied Sparrow, reaching for the decanter of whisky on the table in front of them. 'A set-up. I'll bet my month's salary we'll have an anonymous call tonight or tomorrow morning telling us to report to 51 Hallam Street if we want to get on to some cocaine. You could set your watch by it.'

He poured an ample measure of whisky into his glass. 'So who's got it in for you?' he asked. 'Berne?'

Murdoch shook his head. 'Those old battles were all over after Munich. I haven't crossed swords with that worthy for nearly ten years. Anyhow, that's not his style, is it? He kills you in committees, not like this. I'm out of his range now.'

'I'm not so sure,' said Sparrow. He leant forward and picked up the little bag of cocaine. 'Do you have any idea how much you could get for this stuff out in the street?' he asked. 'Cut it down a few times and you could make three, maybe four thousand pounds. No, whoever left this wanted you tabbed as a pusher, probably has some junkies set up to testify you supplied them. Whoever did this wanted to finish you off.'

Murdoch shook his head.

'You know what I do for a living, Birdie,' he said. 'I set up sports projects for companies, link up with sports associations to secure them sponsorship. And I write. It's not exactly the epicentre of the underworld.'

'And what about your trip to the States? What's that all about?'

'I've written a screenplay called *The Nazi Games*, from my novel. You think that I've got Martin Bormann after me?'

Sparrow shook his head, grinning. 'He'd be a bit long in the tooth by now,' he said. 'No, there's really nothing in your line of work that ties up with this kind of operation.'

Murdoch replenished his own glass. 'I haven't told you the complete story,' he said.

'Without that I'm no use to you,' said Sparrow. 'So let's hear it.'

'The object of the trip as far as I was concerned was to meet up with Andrew Weir, the head of the company who originally bought the book. Weir is probably one of the best producers in the world, right up there with people like Lucas or Coppola.'

Sparrow said nothing, just replaced his glass upon the table in front of him.

'At a party at Weir's house I was introduced to a couple of top American businessmen called Stevens and Hall. They were acting on behalf of the Government of Kudai.'

'Kudai? Isn't that one of the Emirates, out somewhere on the Gulf?'

Murdoch nodded. 'You remember Woodie?'

Sparrow shook his head, placing thumb and index finger to his lips. He snapped his fingers. 'Yes, I do,' he said. 'That Arab soldier who used to karate-chop hurdles before Grieve sorted him out.'

'Yes,' said Murdoch. 'He's the head of state there – you would hardly recognise him now. Well, he's working with a consortium of businessmen to create an Arab Olympics in Kudai, on the same dates as the Los Angeles Games.'

'Impossible,' said Sparrow, curtly. 'He'd never get the athletes.'

'Two million dollars' prize money per event?'

'I sit corrected,' said Sparrow, reaching for his glass. 'He'll get them all right.' He sipped his whisky. 'But surely not two million per event for the entire Olympics programme?'

'No,' said Murdoch. 'Only the men's and women's track and field, gymnastics and swimming. So it's a limited schedule.'

Sparrow shook his head. 'That's a far cry from getting Kelloggs to put up thirty grand for handball,' he said. 'But how many people knew about this deal?'

'Three, possibly four. An American script-consultant – a woman called Ellis Payne – introduced me to Hall and Stevens in the first place. Then there's Hassan himself. But there's no way any of them would want to leak the project at this stage.'

'No,' said Sparrow. 'Though we don't know about this woman Payne. But let's clear up one point first. What's going to be your exact role in this project?'

'Simply to get the world's best performers to Kudai in 1984

79

and to set up a support structure of competitions in 1983 leading up to the Games.'

Sparrow pulled with thumb and index finger on his upper lip.

'So let me see if I've got it right. Your Arab Games not only knock the stuffing out of the Los Angeles Olympics – your 1983 Million Dollar Meets will wipe out next year's Europa Cup and the first World Championships in Helsinki in August. The swimming and gymnastics are sideshows – it's the track and field programme that's the meat of the matter. By next summer you'll have to have in operation an alternative World Track and Field Association.'

'That's it,' said Murdoch. 'And not only at top level. We'll deal with ARRA.'

'The American Road Racing Association – the professional set-up?'

Murdoch nodded. 'We'll negotiate to absorb them within our Association and set up a capillary structure of people's road-races all over the world, running parallel to our élite track and field programme.'

'Whether or not you get the cream of the world's athletes to Kudai is very much dependent on your personal credibility. So you get pulled in to Marylebone police station on a drugs charge tomorrow, and it's Goodnight Vienna for you, and your professional Olympics.'

Murdoch sipped the last of his drink and leant forward, elbows on knees. 'So what's your advice?'

'There are two possibilities,' said Sparrow, stroking his spiky grey moustache with the tips of his fingers. 'But first I must be honest. Whatever happens I must report this, if only in case you're fitted up again. My people can either ignore it – or put your name on our observation list.'

'For God's sake, Birdie!' exploded Murdoch. 'Stop acting as if you're still a policeman. I'm not a criminal. After all, it was *me* who came to you with this bag of filth in the first place. You *know* me; you know I couldn't have anything to do with this. I don't even smoke, man!'

80

Sparrow shook his head. 'You always were a hot-head, Murdoch,' he said. 'Especially when you thought you were in the right. Which was most of the time.'

He sipped his drink. 'No,' he said. 'There's no question of any charge. The whole point of the exercise is to draw out the informers. We'd simply insert "A. Murdoch" on the sheet and set our drug squad to check if anyone reported a Murdoch who had been dishing out cocaine. Anyone who came up with evidence about you might bring us closer to whoever's behind it. It's a long shot, but it's possible.'

'And what if the press picked it up?'

Sparrow shrugged. 'We'd sit tight and deny point blank that the Murdoch in question was you. As I see it, it's your only hope to get closer to whoever's on your trail.'

'Then get my name put down on the sheet,' said Murdoch resignedly.

Sparrow smiled. 'I think you've done the right thing anyway,' he said. 'But let me give you some advice. You're in deep water now, as deep as any you've been in. This Arab Olympics deal isn't going to be any Sunday-school picnic.'

'I haven't agreed to take it on yet, not in writing,' replied Murdoch.

'You will,' said Sparrow. 'You've been itching to get your hands on the throats of Berne and all those other Olympic freeloaders for years. And here's your chance, handed to you on a silver platter. I'm going to enjoy watching you do it.'

After Sparrow had left, Murdoch sat in the semi-darkness of his room staring at the empty fireplace. In a matter of days he had moved from a cosy, uncomplicated world of sport through the unreality of Hollywood and on into the world of petrodollars. He had lived most of his life within his own head, but now for the first time he felt the limitations of his own powers of reasoning, and the strength of the forces massed against him.

Behind it all lay a growing doubt about Ellis Payne. When they had met in Los Angeles he had felt a strong frisson of recognition, as if he were renewing a previously established friendship. Since his last long relationship, which had ended three years back, Murdoch had failed to find that central essence of friendship without which a sexual relationship was meaningless to him. Somehow, though they had not even held hands, he had the sure feeling that with Ellis Payne something good would happen between them.

And yet, Hassan, Stevens and Hall apart, Ellis was the only one who, to his knowledge, could have known anything about the Kudai project. And the lethal little white bag of cocaine at the back of his safe could only be there because someone knew of his involvement with Kudai. Murdoch felt a deep lump of pain at the back of his throat as he checked his watch. Five minutes past midnight. He would call her in the morning.

Ellis Payne sat at the window of her room at the Inn on the Park, the weak morning sun casting its light upon the script which she cradled on her knee. She was working on the second major scene Murdoch had written, featuring the hero, Kane, the doctor athlete at the centre of *The Nazi Games*. Kane had already been introduced in the first fifteen minutes of the screenplay as an American postgraduate student studying at Oxford in 1935. He had just been asked by the CIA to travel into the Brazilian jungle to bring back the German Jewish doctor, Steiner, with his revolutionary discovery. It was essential that in the first part of the film Kane should not be some sort of Superman, emerging to pluck Steiner from the Brazilian jungle and return him to civilisation. Ellis had already severely edited an earlier sequence in which Kane and his CIA guides had confronted Nazi agents in Brazil, deleting from it the Bondery which might have made the Kane character less credible. She wondered what Murdoch's reaction to these changes might be.

The telephone rang at her right elbow. It was Murdoch.

'Your message,' he said, haltingly. There was a pause.

'How was your meeting back in LA?' she asked.

Again a pause.

'With Stevens and Hall?' she volunteered.

'Good,' he said. 'Very good.'

82

'They're both high-fliers. Ivy league.' She lifted the script on to her knee. 'So when can we meet? We've got a lot to do. I've just been working on the Steiner scene.' She waited for his reply, sighing. It was like pulling teeth.

'Stevens and Hall,' he said.

'Yes?'

'Did they say anything to you?'

'About what?'

There was another pause.

'Nothing. Forget it.'

Ellis Payne's brows furrowed. This was not the man she had met in Los Angeles, the inventor of astral sex.

'So when shall we meet?' She tried to milk the irritation from her voice.

'Make it eleven o'clock tomorrow. Here, at my office.' He gave her the address, and with a clipped 'Goodbye' hung up.

She put down the telephone, shaking her head.

Back in Hallam Street, Murdoch picked up the script of *The Nazi Games* and hurled it across the room.

Birdie Sparrow phoned Murdoch the next evening. Two junkies claiming to have been provided cocaine by a certain Alan Murdoch had been picked up in Trafalgar Square. Their description of Murdoch and his Hallam Street home had been meticulously accurate, too accurate for the interviewing officers, who had already been primed by Sparrow. The central flaw in their evidence was that neither had clearly identified Murdoch as a Scot, and soon their stories had started to disintegrate. A brief reminder of the stiff penalties for perjury had finally elicited from them the information that they had been provided with their stories by an unknown American who had communicated with them only by telephone. Two £200 bags of prime cocaine, stuffed into three letter-boxes in Holland Park, had been the payment, with a promise of more to come, and they had been advised to await police investigations before coming forward with their stories.

The next occurrence had been even more significant. That

same evening, whilst on his regular nocturnal run around Hyde Park, Hugh Grieve had been attacked by two men, both unknown to him. The victim's turn of speed had surprised the two assailants and Grieve had escaped with minor bruising.

On the morning following his call Birdie Sparrow leant back into the comfort of the armchair in Alan Murdoch's drawing room and sipped his coffee, looking across at Grieve and Murdoch.

'You know my first memory of you, Grieve?'

Hugh Grieve laid his own coffee cup on the table in front of him and looked sideways at Murdoch.

'Refresh my memory,' he answered.

'An elbow in the ribs,' said Sparrow. 'The Met police versus the army, May 1956, at the Old Imber Court track. They asked me to drop down to the half mile to take on the mad Scot Grieve.'

'I remember now,' said Grieve, grinning.

'I never had any sort of sprint finish so I decided to bomb it to the first bend to keep the pace fast all the way. You closed in on me from the outside and gave me a dig in the rib-cage that put me back about five yards.'

Sparrow groomed his moustache with thumb and index finger and leant forward. 'Still,' he said, 'that dig in the ribs did me a bit of good. It made me so bloody angry that I hung in and clocked one minute fifty-four, the fastest I ever ran.'

'And did you beat Grieve?' asked Murdoch.

'Are you joking?' said Sparrow. 'All I saw of him that day was his Scots backside. He ran just over one minute fifty-one. Still, that race taught me that middle distance running was a contact sport. The week after that I wiped out Derek Ibbotson over a mile.'

'More coffee?' asked Murdoch.

'Thanks,' replied Sparrow and paused as Murdoch replenished his cup. Then his face grew serious.

'Murdoch, you've come a long way since your years with Grieve here bashing your head against Berne and those other Establishment bruisers. But what you're into now is a totally different world. Your professional Olympics puts you head to head with the IOC, with national governments, and God knows who else. The cocaine plant and last night's little fracas at Hyde Park is just the beginning – a warning.'

'How do you mean?' said Murdoch.

'I think that you're both swimming against the stream again,' replied Sparrow. 'But this time it's a pretty strong stream.'

'A dead fish can float downstream. It takes a live one to float upstream,' responded Grieve.

'I think we know the score,' said Murdoch. 'The Arab Olympics menaces the whole rotten set-up.'

'All the knighthoods, the OBEs, the Légions d'Honneur, the whole freeloading Olympic carnival,' said Grieve.

'But have you thought of some of the people behind the carnival?' said Sparrow, pausing to sip his coffee. 'Some of the really nasty ones? We're talking about massive investments by governments, particularly in Eastern Europe. There's a lot of money involved. And a lot of pride.'

'When I first did that report for Prince Hassan I gave a detailed account of the sort of investment that had been put in by each nation, including the United States, for Los Angeles,' replied Murdoch defensively.

'And do you think those kind of people are simply going to watch their investment vanish into the desert sands of Kudai?' said Sparrow. 'No way, Murdoch. They'll fight like tigers. I think they've already started. And my first advice is to check on your lady friend.'

'Ellis Payne?'

'The very lady,' said Sparrow. 'I look at it this way. There's no way that Prince Hassan, Hall or Stevens would release information to anyone about the Kudai project. It isn't in their interests. But this girl, Payne, she must have had some inkling of what Hall and Stevens were going to ask you to do. Of course, it's possible that someone further down the line in the Kudai organisation has leaked it, but for the present the Payne woman is your only suspect. I'd keep a close eye on her.'

Murdoch stood up and let out a long sigh. This was information he had no wish to hear.

'And another question,' said Sparrow. 'How did anyone know that Grieve was likely to be involved? Did you tell the Kudai people?'

Murdoch shook his head. 'We did discuss Grieve but no firm decision was made,' he said.

'Then have you phoned him?'

Murdoch nodded. 'Twice.'

'From here?'

'Yes.'

Sparrow stood up and walked to the telephone. He unscrewed the voice-piece and scrutinised it for a moment before withdrawing from it a tiny black object, little bigger than a pea.

'You've been bugged,' he said. 'And by experts.'

Murdoch felt his heart sink. 'So what do you advise?'

'I know all you people think you can handle yourselves. But this is different. You don't even know who the enemy is, or when he's going to strike. For instance, these people who fitted you up with cocaine – who are they? What's their interest?'

'God knows,' said Murdoch dispiritedly.

'So what can we do?' said Grieve.

Sparrow paused. 'My first advice is to buy in some security,' he answered. 'Top men. To cover yourself, Murdoch – and Quince as well, because in London at least you three are the linchpins of the organisation. Without you – and Buchinski in New York – the Arab Olympics is like a chicken running about without its head.'

Murdoch put his hands to his lips. 'You're right, Birdie. But we need more than that. We need a fallback of some kind.'

'How do you mean?'

'I mean that Quince and Buchinski have got enough material on illegal payments and drugs to sink the whole lot of them if they try to lean on us.'

'That's a double-edged weapon,' observed Grieve.

'How come?'

'Shamateurism is one thing but once we start releasing lists of athletes who have taken drugs then we're going to be up to our ears in lawyers.'

'Another problem is that we may not be left with enough athletes to run the Arab Olympics,' said Murdoch.

'It's that bad?' said Sparrow.

'The fact is we're sitting on a vast pile of manure, Birdie. Who's clean at Olympic level?'

'We're going to be,' growled Grieve.

'I've been giving that a lot of thought,' said Murdoch. 'And I've come to the conclusion that we're going to have to declare some sort of amnesty on the anabolic steroids during the 1983 season.'

'Why?' asked Sparrow.

'Because if our medical experts can pick up the steroid imprint as far as a year back and we launch the Kudai project in October, then some of them will still produce positives next June and July.'

'Will this be an official amnesty, announced to the press?'

'I haven't made up my mind on that,' replied Murdoch. 'But it's something I have to consider. If the Kudai Games is going to be a new start, then I've got to give the athletes a chance to come clean.'

'If you're both out of the way no one's going to care who's clean and who isn't,' said Sparrow. 'But remember: you don't have to put your feet in the fire just to get them warm. Your ace in the hole can stay there. Just so long as the opposition knows you've got it.'

'And we thought we were only organising a sports meet,' sighed Grieve.

'Birdie's right,' said Murdoch. 'I knew it from the start, but I closed my eyes to it. Those bastards aren't going to let us derail their gravy train.'

He stood up and pointed his finger at the policeman. 'Birdie,' he said. 'You said we need security. I say we need you. So join us now, as Special Services Officer, Head of Security – call it what you bloody well like – and name your own terms.'

Sparrow lifted his coffee cup and slowly emptied it. He stood up.

He shook his head. 'I only retired a month ago and I'm piling in the miles like a youngster. When do I start?'

'Tomorrow,' said Murdoch. 'Check through the flat for any more of those bugs.'

Sparrow looked down at them both. 'I must be bloody mad, getting involved with you two. A junkie and a geriatric athlete.'

6

The Magic Stadium

Murdoch scribbled furiously, oblivious to the whine of the jets as they climbed above Heathrow on a British Airways Concorde to Kudai. Beside him Grieve sipped a glass of iced water.

Whatever Murdoch's worries over Ellis Payne, there was no doubting her industry. The three pages of notes on his revised script, written in her precise copperplate handwriting, represented at least two days' solid work. And it was work of high quality. Murdoch chuckled as he scanned the text. It was rather like having a coach again, constantly needling, coaxing, kicking him in the rump, pointing him towards his true potential.

Certainly, he could see no reason why with Payne's help the second draft of the script could not be finished by his trip to the European Games in Athens in early September, with a third and final draft completed by late October. His staffing budget for the Arab Olympics would ensure that there was plenty of time left for writing, and he had only one essential commitment, a trip to the World Bobsleigh Championships in St Moritz early in January.

He bit his lip as he studied the first pages of the scene on his lap. In it, Hitler and Dr Carl Diem, the architect of the 1936 Olympics, appeared for the first time, together with Goebbels. Ellis had already pointed out to him the lack of balancing humour in the screenplay. Perhaps this was the time to introduce it, in one of the few sequences in which Hitler and Goebbels appeared together. He reread the scene. Diem had just left the room, having proposed, to Hitler's delight, the first torch relay from Olympia to the Berlin Olympic stadium.

Murdoch smiled and started to write. The words came easily.

GOEBBELS: I fear only one problem, Fuehrer.
HITLER: What is that?
GOEBBELS: The lighting of the Olympic flame.
HITLER: But Krupps will surely take care of that?
GOEBBELS: That is not a problem. I have complete confidence in Krupps.
HITLER: Then where is the difficulty?
GOEBBELS: Vestal Virgins, Fuehrer. I seriously doubt if Greece now has a sufficiency, vestal or otherwise.
They laugh.

'You ready to talk yet?' said Grieve, unbuttoning his safety belt as the signal flashed above.

Murdoch loosened his tie and smiled.

'Sorry,' he said. 'That woman Payne gave me three full pages of notes in this scene alone. The besom wants me to change my hero into an American.'

Grieve drew his right hand through his shock of thinning, carrot-red hair. He was the epitome of the red-haired Glasgow Scot, always appearing to be on the edge of violence, his ruddy face ready to flush into flame and anger.

'Most men wouldn't be on the way to Wigan, let alone Kudai, on what you gave me over the phone,' he said.

'But you managed to read the Kudai proposals, and my notes?'

Grieve grunted. 'It's like James Bond in spikes,' he said. 'If Woodie wasn't into it with all those petrodollars I wouldn't give it ten minutes.'

Murdoch nodded. 'My sentiments too,' he said. 'But I've checked out Stevens and Hall with my business contacts here in London. They're both right out of the top drawer, no question of it.'

'And exactly why does Woodie want us out here?'

Murdoch put his script into his briefcase, locked it, and slid it below the seat in front of him.

'To show us his stadium and to get us to sign a contract to work for him.'

'What about Quince and Buchinski?'

'Bull will be in Kudai a couple of hours after us and Quince will be in an hour ahead of us from Nice.'

'Will they have sounded out the European and American money meet men by now?'

'The key men, yes,' replied Murdoch.

'What about the athletes and their agents? McCormack and their ilk?'

'That's our job,' replied Murdoch. 'Agents! Twenty-five per cent of an amateur should be one hundred per cent of nothing. Honestly, it's amazing how many athletes' wives, mothers and fathers have got agents these days. Like Seb Coe's dad. Not the athletes – their relatives!'

Grieve grinned. 'I remember the first time I got a pair of free shoes from Adidas.'

'I was thrilled,' said Murdoch.

'I'm not surprised,' said Grieve. 'You were painting three stripes on your bare feet when I met you.'

Murdoch laughed. 'It's a different world now, Hugh. A rotten world.'

'It was always rotten,' rumbled Grieve. 'Now it's just better paid.' He nodded to the stewardess poised above them. 'A Perrier for my friend,' he said. 'I'm beginning to think he's got shares in the company! Same for me too, I suppose.'

'Let's get back to Bull and Albert,' Murdoch mused. 'Will they have made up their minds about the Arab Olympics before they get to Kudai?'

'I don't think so,' said Grieve. 'Otherwise they wouldn't even bother to make the trip. My guess is that their meet promoters have given them a guarded yes – and what they want to see is the stadium. Plus the money on the table.'

'I'd have thought that fifty million dollars in escrow in the

Arab Bank, Park Lane, would have been just about enough to keep them sweet,' said Murdoch, accepting his Perrier from the stewardess with a grin. 'At least, that's what Hassan said when I phoned him yesterday.'

Murdoch sipped his Perrier, relishing the sharp impact of the liquid against the back of his throat.

'So what do you think?' asked Grieve.

'I think,' said Murdoch, 'that by tomorrow evening we will know whether the Arab Olympics is the *QE II* . . .' He paused to sip his drink. 'Or the *Titanic*.'

Murdoch, Grieve, Buchinski, Quince and Prince Hassan stood in the 'golf ball' which Agent Pendleton had described to his superior ten days before. A few moments earlier they had made their way through the 'lettuce', the broken remains of the construction site which was now being dismantled by teams of sunburnt, sweating Arab workers.

They now stood high in the stands, at the centre of the home straight. The red, synthetic track below them was, surprisingly, still lacking in conventional lane divisions. The track enclosed a grass infield, again pristine and unmarked by conventional throwing arcs. Indeed, to Murdoch the arena below looked like a scaled-down model of a stadium for giants rather than a practical sports arena.

Hassan broke the silence. 'Welcome to the de Coubertin Stadium,' he said, his pride evident in his tones. He beckoned them to follow him and the five men walked down the stadium steps to a small cordoned-off VIP area above the middle of the home straight, containing about twenty velvet-covered seats. At the centre of the area stood a small black console, rather like a miniature theatre organ, on a table. Hassan sat in front of the console, beckoning his four guests to sit down. He paused for a moment, then pressed a red button at the centre of the console, and looked above him at the curved translucent dome which encased the stadium.

'Now!' he said.

There was a slight whirring and the vast dome slowly started to open, allowing the harsh Kudai sun to engulf the grass surface of the stadium below. In a minute the opening was complete.

'The largest covered span in the world,' said Hassan proudly. 'Four times the size of any mechanically operated cover ever built.'

'What about the grass?' said Murdoch. 'How does it survive under cover?'

'A tough, hybrid grass, developed in Argentina,' explained Hassan. 'It is allowed several bursts of sun each day to promote growth. When the sun has gone the span can be left open.'

'The stadium capacity?' queried Grieve.

'Sixty thousand – all seated,' replied Hassan. 'Facilities for one thousand five hundred journalists, plus five hundred television and radio commentators.'

Murdoch pointed to the synthetic track. 'How many lanes?' he asked.

'Eight on the circular track, ten on the straight,' replied Hassan. 'Sprints can be run either way, though there is little wind to reckon with.'

They stepped down, then across the little wooden bridge that led on to the track.

Once there Quince bent down, digging his nails into the track's red-crumbed surface.

'What is it, sir? Tartan?'

Hassan smiled and shook his head. 'Obsolete,' he said. 'This is the Olympia surface, the world's first outdoor tuned track.'

'Tuned?' said Buchinski.

'A track geared to the natural contractile mechanisms of human muscle, giving back energy at exactly the correct time,' explained Murdoch. 'They've been working on it at Harvard and Cornell for years. Harvard thought they had it cracked back in 1980, but never really got it right.'

'Quite so, Alan,' said Hassan. 'But Cornell did, only last year. And now our experiments indicate the first electrically timed 9.8 seconds will be run here for 100 metres.'

'And what about Beamon's Mexico City jump of 8.90 metres?' asked Grieve.

'The best of the American jumpers such as Carl Lewis should go close to nine metres here, within accepted wind limits,' answered Hassan.

'But there are no long jump landing areas,' said Murdoch.

Prince Hassan nodded and beckoned the men to follow him back up the stadium steps to the console. They resumed their seats and Hassan quickly glanced along the length of the console unit. He nodded and pressed another button. At both ends of the synthetic areas between the track and the stands the track surface slid away, to be replaced by triple and long jump pits with take-off boards appearing at the appropriate distances from them.

'Hydraulically operated,' said Hassan, pressing another button.

Suddenly the track lanes appeared, but Murdoch and his companions could see that these were not the normal conventional painted markings. Hassan pressed again and the markings vanished; then reappeared.

'Lasers,' said Hassan. 'Any lane infringements will be immediately registered and keyed into the videotape of each race.'

'What about the vertical jumps?' asked Buchinski.

Hassan flicked a switch on the console, and at both ends of the ground high jump and pole vault landing areas rose from below the track surface, followed by vertical jumping stands.

'And crossbars?'

Hassan smiled and pointed to the jumping areas. Now, at about two metres in high jump and five metres in pole vault, solid beams of light appeared to join the two stands. As they did so digital scoreboard units rose, registering the heights of 2.05 and 5.10 metres.

Bull Buchinski looked around him in awe. 'Jesus,' he said. 'It's like *Star Trek*.' He looked up into the control area at the top of the stand. 'Who you got up there, sir? Mr Spock?'

Prince Hassan smiled. 'I'm afraid, gentlemen, that I have

been teasing you. The real wonder of this stadium is the structure of the area itself. What we have just seen, what we are now going to see, is simply the application of the best in modern technology to the problems of athletic competition. It is not essential to my Arab Olympics, simply a childish expression of my interest in modern science and its application to sport.'

He raised both hands. 'Let us now sit down for a moment,' he said, 'and view the first track and field meeting in history to be conducted entirely without officials.'

The five men climbed the steps behind them to the small VIP stand in the centre of the arena. Prince Hassan sat down in front of another console and once again pressed a button.

Immediately, from tunnels at either end of the stadium, Arab athletes ran out, taking up positions at the start of the 100 metres, at long jump, high jump and javelin.

'Their warm-up has already been completed in the adjoining underground area,' said Hassan. 'Competition can begin.' He pointed to the start of the 100 metres. 'Starting commands will come from a tape, with a standard thirty seconds between the first command to the order "set". Blocks are the standard pressure-sensitive type, gauged to detect any loss of contact inside one tenth of a second.'

Grieve and Murdoch nodded in understanding. No athlete was capable of breaking block-contact inside one tenth of a second unless he had anticipated the gun.

'Research shows that a maximum of two seconds should elapse between set and gun to ensure fair starts. Our computer is programmed for a variable set-gun time of 1.5 to 2.0 seconds,' continued Hassan.

The eight Kudai sprinters, responding to the commands of the tape and the bark of the pistol, were already surging down the track. As they finished their times flashed on to the giant scoreboard which dominated the track at the end of the finishing straight.

'11.16,' said Quince, flatly.

Prince Hassan shrugged. 'A little American Negro blood

would be welcome,' he said. 'No Kudai sprinter has yet broken 10.8 seconds using this equipment. But let us now look at the high jump.'

The holographic bar was at 1.90 metres and the first seven jumpers cleared easily. However, the eighth, though appearing to be clear, registered a foul on the scoreboard at the side of the landing area. Hassan pointed to the high jump.

'The holographic bar is force sensitive,' he said. 'A conventional crossbar would have been dislodged.'

'Says who?' growled Buchinski under his breath.

Over at the javelin, a burly young Kudai athlete launched the spear to well over seventy metres. The scoreboard showed 77.01.

'How does it register a flat or tail-first throw?' asked Murdoch.

'Only the point will trigger off the measuring mechanism,' explained Hassan.

The best of the long jumpers had cleared just over seven metres when the Prince turned to Murdoch and Grieve. 'You will notice that I retained the old-fashioned eight-inch take-off board,' he said, 'because of the leverage it gives the jumper, though the area beyond the board is pressure-sensitive. My biggest problem was the flattening of the sand after each jump. This was solved by having automatic rakes working immediately after the optical mechanism had measured each leap.'

He pressed a button on the console and a buzzing noise issued from the loudspeaker system. The athletes dutifully donned tracksuits and jogged from the stadium. Within moments all the apparatus had vanished, lane markings had been wiped clear, and the vast bowl was in darkness.

Hassan turned to face the group, arms folded on his chest. 'Well, gentlemen, you have seen the future. What do you think of it?'

There was silence. Then Murdoch spoke. 'It's magnificent, sir, but just a little . . .'

'Heartless?' Hassan smiled. 'Don't worry, Alan. I am not offended. First, let me say again that much of this technology is needless, done just as well by human hand. Much of it merely reflects my fascination with modern technology. But I ask you, gentlemen, think back: back to Munich when the German, Klaus Wolfermann, gained victory in the javelin by a mere two centimetres. Two centimetres, judged by an official finding by eye the mark of a javelin on grass and placing a peg in that mark.

'And think of Moscow, Mr Grieve. You remember the Australian, Campbell, in the triple jump, was fouled out by a Russian judge for trailing his rear foot on the ground during the step. Campbell was undoubtedly on the day the best triple jumper in Moscow. No subsequent study of videotape showed any sign of a foul. The Moscow Games had several such incidents.'

Murdoch and Grieve nodded and slowly the others followed suit.

'With two million dollars at stake for each event the aim of our Olympics must be complete fairness within the limits of existing technology,' said Hassan.

'But you do have some human back-up?' asked Murdoch.

Hassan nodded. 'You remember the American attempt to rescue the Iran embassy hostages?' he said. 'At the time I thought to myself, if the greatest nation in the world cannot ensure the working efficiency of a handful of helicopters what hope is there for any of us? Therefore, gentlemen, my aim is that our organisation will have a team of highly qualified officials, trained by us to take over in the event of any break-down.'

'Belts and braces,' said Buchinski.

'As you say, Mr Buchinski, belts and braces,' smiled Hassan. He placed both hands to his lips in a praying motion and bowed his head. Then he looked up. 'Gentlemen, you have seen the de Coubertin stadium. What do you think?'

Again Murdoch was the first to speak. 'Everything rests with Mr Buchinski and Mr Quince.'

There was silence. Then Quince spoke. 'I think that I can speak for Mr Buchinski,' he said in his thin, quiet voice.

Buchinski nodded. 'Before we came here we both thought this idea was a fantasy. But what we have seen here today, this stadium . . .' He spread his hands.

'They're ready,' said Bull. 'They're all ready.'

'Western Europe and the United States. We cannot speak for the East,' said Quince. 'All the meet organisers are with us – on one condition.'

'And that is?'

'Fifty million dollars in escrow in the Arab Bank, Park Lane, to finance the 1983 qualification meets,' said Buchinski.

'We'll call them the Million Dollar Meets,' said Quince.

Prince Hassan withdrew a slip of paper from his inside breast pocket and handed it to Murdoch. 'This is a draft for one hundred million dollars to an escrow account at the Arab Bank, London, on exactly the terms Mr Buchinski requests,' he said. He pressed a button on the console and the bright fairyland of the stadium slowly reappeared and the arena was filled with the boom of massed choirs.

'An Ode of Pindar,' he whispered, 'set to music by Vangelis.'

He slowly lowered the volume of the music and raised both hands.

'Well,' he said. 'Are you with me?'

There was no need for an answer.

Thursday, 12 August 1982

KGB General Boris Kutyenko looked at his diary with distaste. At 09.30, Igor Lysenko, director general of the KGB sports programme. Kutyenko scowled. He hated sport. In his early days as an agent morning callisthenics had been obligatory – an hour of sterile arm-swinging and toe-touching under the gaze of a crew-cut gorilla with muscles in places where the then slim Boris did not even possess the places. Thank God his swift rise in the service had depended on wit rather than muscle.

Three years before, his daily diet of camel-dung Russian cigarettes and an occasional golden American filter-tip had ended with a promotion which had given him access to the prized Berioska shops available only to the élite of the Party. It was there that Kutyenko and American cigarettes had formed a lasting bond – to the latter's profit and the degeneration of the former. Kutyenko had said for years that the Americans would dearly like to see him dead. However, his aides, daily penetrating the blue haze of cigarette smoke, listening to that inevitable wracking cough, were certain that cigarettes would be the death of him. What they did not know was that the assassin would be a certain Peter Stuyvesant.

Kutyenko gave a deep, rasping cough, just as his telephone rang. He picked up the receiver grudgingly.

'Yes?'

'Comrade Lysenko to see you, sir.'

'Give me ten minutes,' Kutyenko growled, replacing the telephone.

Lysenko. Master of Sport 1968, one of the Soviet Union's greatest all-round athletes. Although the director of KGB sport had no formal political clout he was someone to respect, and to watch. KGB athletes from the Dinamo Club had formed almost half the successful Moscow Olympics team, more than any other single club in the Union, and President Brezhnev himself had expressed his pleasure to Lysenko both by letter and in private audience.

Kutyenko lit another cigarette and drew long and hard, closing his wrinkled eyes. He hoped that Lysenko was not going to ask him again to infiltrate the East German Sports Institute at Leipzig in order to discover that secret cocktail of drugs which made women into men and men into monsters. No one, not even Andropov himself, had ever got beyond the first floor, so God knew what dreadful horrors lurked on the levels above. Better to ask him to breach Fort Knox and bring back the American gold reserves. The fact that the KGB had heavy representation on East German security forces carried no weight as far as Leipzig was concerned. Leipzig was Mecca, the Secret City.

Kutyenko had never borne any great belief in the value of sport as a political weapon, though he had never dared openly to express this view. Despite his hatred of exercise he saw some merit in national health and fitness programmes which might cut down on the number of vodka-sodden drunks littering the streets of Moscow. Or, even better, take a few inches from the lardy thighs and buttocks of Muscovite women. But he could see no great purpose in pumping billions of roubles into steroidal hulks scoring doubtful political points in the cities of the West. He had always taken the view that the thrower Tamara Press and her pentathlete sister Irina had put the international image of Soviet sport back at least ten years. He had met the Press sisters (or 'brothers', as they had sometimes been called) and found them to be the only women who had ever made him feel effeminate. But in his heart Boris Kutyenko suspected that there was a case to be made for Soviet involvement in world sport, and without his early experience of callisthenics he might indeed have taken a different view . . .

The door of his office opened and his secretary, Anna Touncheva, ushered in Igor Lysenko. Kutyenko rose to greet him, extending his hand.

'Comrade Lysenko,' he said. 'When was the last time we met?'

'At the Olympic Games, two years ago,' replied the angular Lysenko, his prematurely lined face impassive.

'I remember,' said Kutyenko. 'The day Dinamo took two gold medals in gymnastics.'

'Yes,' said Lysenko, sitting at a chair directly in front of the desk. 'Your memory serves you well.'

'So how can I help you?' asked Kutyenko, stubbing out his cigarette.

'It is not essentially an internal sporting matter,' said Lysenko.

'Not Leipzig again, I hope,' replied Kutyenko.

'No.' Lysenko's face was stern. 'I fear that door is closed for ever.' He paused. 'As you know, through a myriad of agencies from the trade unions to organisations like ourselves, our national funding amounts to close on one and a half billion roubles per year.'

'It surprises me that any accurate figure exists,' replied Kutyenko.

'It doesn't. The statistics are so vast, the organisation so complex, that all we can do is to hazard a guess, an informed estimate.' Lysenko paused again. 'I have quoted the approximate sum to emphasise the point that anything that menaces that investment must be damaging for the Soviet Union and for its political aims.'

'That goes without saying,' replied Kutyenko.

'Evidence has recently come to our attention that the Los Angeles Olympic Games face a dangerous, possibly even a lethal threat. It takes the form of an OPEC-backed alternative Olympics involving half a million rouble first prizes for each victor.'

'Surely that is to our advantage, Comrade Lysenko? The West will lose its athletes and we'll repeat our success in Moscow.'

'Not so,' replied Lysenko. 'In Moscow the defection of nations like Germany and the United States did marginally devalue many medals, but a loss of competitors on this scale would make the Los Angeles Olympics a mockery. The medals would simply not be worth winning.'

'But Comrade, surely a medal is a medal,' replied Kutyenko smoothly.

'Some more so than others,' responded Lysenko. 'It is my belief that the success of such a venture would be disastrous to Soviet sport and to our showcase, the Olympic Games.'

'Then not only Soviet sport,' said Kutyenko. 'Our East German colleagues would not exactly be dancing with joy.'

He lit a cigarette, mechanically proffering and withdrawing the packet to Lysenko, a non-smoker. He drew a deep, sweet breath of smoke, relaxing visibly as it slipped down his throat.

'Surely, Comrade Lysenko, the answer lies in diplomatic channels?'

'Comrade Kutyenko, what are our present relations with the OPEC nations?'

Kutyenko pondered. 'Not good,' he admitted. 'If they are

behind it there is not much we could do. My apologies. That is not a realistic option. So what service can I provide?'

'Our information is that a Western entrepreneur, a British decathlete, Alan Murdoch, against whom I competed in 1972, has been appointed to recruit athletes and meeting organisers and to set up the necessary infrastructure. The key to the success of the whole venture lies in his seduction of Western athletes.'

'With first prizes of half a million roubles your Mr Murdoch could empty the Soviet Union within a matter of days,' growled Kutyenko. 'So what do you want me to do?'

'Stop him,' replied Lysenko.

7

Tennis with Mr Ciano

Sunday, 5 September 1982

Murdoch closed his eyes and sat back in the sun. All he could hear was the steady, rhythmic 'clop' of tennis balls landing on racquets. For a moment he forgot that he was deep in autumnal England, in rural Hertfordshire.

He was sitting in a white wrought-iron chair at a circular table on the terrace above the sunlit lawns of Donne House, only half a mile from Shaw's Corner, near Wheathampstead.

Andrew Weir had decided to break clear of normal custom for the press preview of his three-hour science-fiction epic, *Galaxy*, and had taken the film away from the tiny preview theatre in West London and had renovated the ballroom at Donne House, creating a theatre more appropriate to what he felt was his film's immense scope. The morning showing had been a success, amply justifying the gamble, and had been followed by a sumptuous buffet lunch for the sixty-five-strong press corps, some of whom had travelled from as far as France, Italy and West Germany.

It did not surprise Murdoch that about twenty of the journalists had stayed beyond the preview and the lunch to enjoy Weir's hospitality and the company of his starlets, if not his public relations corps. For Andrew Weir had tried to bring Hollywood with him, or rather Hollywood's concept of an English garden party: cucumber sandwiches, white-coated butlers, cold, minty Pimms and suntanned girls with long, slender limbs beneath gossamer dresses. On the grass courts just below him, Ellis and the film's lead actor played doubles against two of Weir's Hollywood entourage, their grunting athleticism in contrast to the journalistic freeloading on the lawns above them.

As he watched, Murdoch felt that rare thrill on the hairs at the back of his neck as Ellis, the muscle in her bronzed legs flickering, leapt to make a high overhead smash. The girl could certainly play. Lethal at the net, she had been punching away volleys with accuracy and power. Ellis was clearly a natural athlete, rejoicing in challenge for its own sake, regardless of success or failure. Like him, she loved the game, the test of will and muscle, independent of result. Murdoch knew that in her he saw something of himself.

But how much of himself? Murdoch knew that the shadows were beginning to loom over his Kudai venture, and he hoped that Ellis was not a part of it. Before the day was over he would have to broach the drug question with her, with the possibility, indeed the likelihood, that their tenuous relationship would end there and then. That moment might also have grave implications for *The Nazi Games*, for if he failed to get the right answers then their professional relationship was over too. What a mess.

Below, the game was reaching its conclusion, with Ellis and her partner four-five and fifteen-forty down. Ellis reacted quickly to a powerful high-kicking service to her backhand. Somehow, at full stretch, she reached the ball, but was only able to lob it back high into the centre of the court. For a moment the ball seemed suspended in flight, with the server poised in a classic smash position, and Ellis and her partner scuttling back to the baseline. The smash bounced in the centre of the court, neatly bisecting the space between them and rising to an untouchable three metres. With a good-tempered 'damn you!' Ellis threw her racquet in the air and simultaneously ran forward to the net, right arm out-stretched.

Murdoch felt a lump in his throat as he watched the four players walk back up the slope towards him. He could put off the moment no longer; he would have to confront her. Ellis, after all, had introduced him to Hall and Stevens and had to know something of the Kudai project. It *had* to be her. But why?

'Not like you to be taking things easily.'

Andrew Weir's gravelly voice broke into his reverie. He was standing behind Murdoch with a squat mustachioed man dressed in immaculate tennis gear and carrying a £300 Prinz racquet.

'Meet Tony Ciano,' said Weir.

Murdoch stood and grasped the man's hand. The figure in front of him was about five foot eight inches in height and some 190 pounds, with that specific fatness Murdoch had once categorised as belonging to those who had taken up body-building working from the inside outwards. It was not a remark he felt it would be timely to repeat. He noted, however, that the American, clad in the most expensive Le Coq Sportif tennis gear, possessed a composure that outweighed the comic potential of his physique.

'Tony put five million bucks into *The Black Indian* a few years back,' said Weir. He turned as Ellis and her partner approached up the slope and beckoned them to join him.

Weir and Ciano sat round the table between Ellis and Murdoch. Ellis's partner excused himself and made his way back to a group of journalists drinking at a table just below them.

A waiter came up, carrying an empty tray.

'Four Pimms,' said Weir. He shook his head. 'Strangest goddam drink I ever did taste. Like a Dr Pepper with a kick.'

Ciano took off his glasses and polished them with a spotless white handkerchief which he withdrew from the pocket of his shorts. 'Andrew here tells me you got a hot script. *The Nazi Games.*'

Murdoch nodded.

'Tells me you got Ellis here to help you knock it into shape.' He replaced his spectacles. 'Then you got the best.'

Ellis smiled dutifully.

Ciano looked sideways at Weir. 'You found me a player yet, Andrew?'

Weir shook his head. 'I got these people here for the hype, Tony. They're not doers.'

'What about Murdoch here?' It was Ellis, her eyes twinkling.

Ciano looked at Murdoch. 'You game? Just one set?'

'I haven't played for years,' said Murdoch, shaking his head. 'Anyhow, I've no kit.'

'That can be arranged,' said Weir, grinning at Ellis conspiratorially. 'Easier than bathing trunks!' He beckoned to one of his staff standing a few metres away. 'Take Mr Murdoch here up to my room. Fix him up with some tennis equipment. Okay?' He glanced at Murdoch. 'Any preference for a racquet?' Without waiting for an answer he turned back again and said, 'Get him a heavy Head.'

He grinned at Murdoch. 'You're fixed,' he said. 'The Head is a beauty. Draws the ball on to the sweet spot like a thousand dollar hooker.'

'It looks as if you've got me hemmed in,' said Murdoch, rising. 'I just hope I can give you a game, Mr Ciano.'

Despite his shower Murdoch was still sweating slightly as he sank into a well-cushioned armchair in the air-conditioned living room of Donne House. On the couch in front of him sat Ciano, immaculate in a white linen suit which somehow managed to conceal his plumpness. He too was perspiring as he sipped a Pimms, his mouth almost engulfed by the forest of vegetation which the long glass contained.

Murdoch had been surprised when, walking up to the house, Ciano had asked if they could have a private talk together on what the American had described as 'a business matter', but he had agreed to meet him in the house after they had changed. Weir's social occasions, he reflected, were getting him into more 'business matters' than a day in the office.

'You dug deep out there,' said Ciano, parting the foliage on his Pimms to take a long draught. 'I thought I had you cold in that last set.'

Murdoch laid down his Pimms, withdrew a handkerchief from his top pocket and wiped his brow.

'I've got a system, Mr Ciano,' he said. 'I keep pushing my face forward until the other guy's knuckles break.'

Ciano's mouth made a moue.

'That's some system,' he said. 'It sure worked good today.' He paused, removed the vegetation from his drink and took another long gulp.

'I've been checking your Kudai operation,' Ciano said suddenly, his sharp brown eyes hardening.

Murdoch was surprised but tried not to show it. 'Then you've done well, Mr Ciano,' he said. 'Our official launch isn't for several weeks.'

'It's been all over LA for a month,' said Ciano. 'Not the detail, mind you: just the main Kudai deal. You can't keep an operation that size quiet for long.'

'Apparently not.'

'Things going well for you?' asked Ciano. 'In Kudai?'

Murdoch nodded. 'The track and field facilities are complete. Gymnastic and swimming stadia should be finished by the end of the year.'

'A million bucks a man,' said Ciano. 'Back in the Bronx, where I grew up, for five bucks the guys would take the hairs out of your ass and sell them for brushes.'

Murdoch smiled. 'I grew up in the same kind of place, Mr Ciano,' he said. 'Glasgow.'

'Glasgow, Scotland? I hear it's one helluva town.'

He removed the fruit from his Pimms, gulped rather than sipped the remainder, then sighed. 'That's better,' he said. 'You ever been to the Superbowl, Murdoch?'

Murdoch nodded.

'They pay those hulks forty g's a man for taking each other out. For a million dollars those boys would jump off a roof with a closed umbrella. So how you going to keep your Kudai Games clean?'

'You mean drugs?'

'That's exactly what I mean. Our footballers are full of the stuff. Some of my best clients.'

'We have the most advanced tests, Mr Ciano. No question of it.'

His companion pouted in reply. 'Every time you build a better mousetrap the mice get smarter too.'

'Mr Ciano, you didn't surely ask to talk to me to discuss the efficiency of my drug-testing procedures.'

Ciano's sharp, hawk-like eyes hardened. 'No,' he said. 'I didn't.' He leant forward, perspiration glistening on his round, tanned face. 'The Los Angeles Games are going to be a bonanza for California; four billion dollars coming in. Everything that gets built in Los Angeles – the harbour, the airport – I take a little piece of the action. Out in Vegas I own two clubs and a piece of another two. This time next year I'll own a couple of hotels in Los Angeles, just in time for the Olympics.'

He beckoned to a waiter passing the French windows leading out on to the lawn. 'Two more of these,' he said as the waiter entered, then went on: 'You don't have to be a Harvard professor to see that your little Arab venture is going to kick the Los Angeles Olympics right in the balls. And if the Olympics sneeze then I get a cold.'

Murdoch looked at Ciano closely. He had seen eyes like his before, only a few weeks back when he had met the board of the World Management Group, the agency which managed the majority of Western athletes. At its head had been the urbane Calvin Shaw, the 'Maestro of Muscle'. For Shaw, money had become an abstraction, a substitute for a sexual life which he had long since discarded in favour of the obligatory blonde on his arm. Ciano was like Shaw, for he had all the money a man could possibly use – thirty times over. Like Shaw, Ciano enjoyed men moving about the globe at his bidding, the flicker of fear in a subordinate's eyes, the personal infection he spread to others in his employ for whom money should have had some practical meaning. Ciano and Shaw came from the same distant eyrie, saw men and their problems from the same remote perspective. No life on earth meant anything to them except their own.

'I had a meeting like this a few weeks back,' said Murdoch. 'With someone you might know. A Mr Calvin Shaw.'

Ciano laid down his drink. 'Of World Management Group.'

'Yes.'

Ciano withdrew a white handkerchief from his jacket pocket and mopped his brow. 'Let me try to guess what he said to you, Mr Murdoch. He wanted you to lay off your Kudai enterprise until after the Los Angeles Olympics, so that he can keep picking up his twenty-five per cent from his athletes. But what he really wants you to do is to cut him in on your Kudai operation.'

'Exactly,' replied Murdoch. 'WMG told me they were planning to launch their own professional world road-racing circuit in 1985, completely independent of the national associations. They arrange the sponsor, the athletes, the television rights, the whole package. Take a cut every which way.'

'Shaw's a bright boy,' said Ciano quietly. 'He wanted to start his pro circuit last year, but I . . . persuaded him to delay his plans till after the Los Angeles Games.'

'And are you trying to do the same with me?'

The waiter had returned with their drinks, which he set down on the table in front of them. Ciano withdrew a slice of orange from his drink and sucked it.

'What's a year to you, Mr Murdoch? Start in 1985 and you'll have no problems with me.'

Murdoch felt a lump in his throat. 'And will I have problems in 1984?'

Ciano scowled. 'Almost certainly, I'd say. Indeed, I think I can guarantee it. You see, though I haven't yet met Mr Cohn or his Olympic Committee, we all want the same thing: the success of the Los Angeles Games. Hell, I've even had some of my boys helping out the LA police department when they were checking out terrorist organisations who might cause trouble in LA! As you can see I've got a lot riding on the Olympics.'

109

'So you want me to pack up my tents and go?' said Murdoch.

'Only until the LA Games are clear,' said Ciano, smiling reassuringly. 'Hell, it's not going to make much of a difference to your people. Wait till '85, and I might come in both ways.'

'How do you mean?'

'Cut you in for a little piece of the return in Los Angeles, then take a little slice of your Kudai project in '85.'

Murdoch shook his head. 'It's no go,' he said. 'It's not what I've been asked to do.'

Ciano's smile vanished. 'But it's what you may *have* to do, Mr Murdoch,' he said. 'You're in over your head.'

At the French windows behind Ciano Andrew Weir appeared, glass in hand, with Ellis Payne. Murdoch noted that Ellis shot a nervous glance towards the scowling Ciano and his heart sank.

'You boys getting to know each other?' said Weir, smiling. 'Good.'

Monday, 6 September 1982

The rumours reaching IAAF president Harold Berne about the Kudai Olympics could not have come at a worse time. The sale of television rights for the first IAAF World Track and Field Championships in Helsinki in August 1983 had not yet been concluded, and an alternative Kudai Games, backed by Buchinski and Quince and the world's leading money meet organisers, would put Berne in an impossible negotiating position.

To Berne the involvement of Grieve and Murdoch had been an added blow. Grieve and Berne's father, Benny Berne (né Bernstein), had been enemies since the early '50s when athletes such as the Londoner, Gordon Pirie, and the aggressive army 800 metres runner, Hugh Grieve, had put a cosy British athletics hierarchy under constant pressure in national press and television. Grieve, a remorseless radical, had roasted the hapless Benny on every occasion on which they had shared the same platform or microphone. And in 1952, in the national trials when the willowy, fragile Harold Berne had looked likely to scrape into the Olympic team in the quarter mile hurdles, the army, who had lost their best quarter mile hurdler through injury, had moved Grieve down a distance to take on the unfamiliar hurdles event. Grieve had gone on to wipe out Berne's chances – this a mere hour after the Scot had won the half mile title.

Grieve had retired in the late '50s, but even then Benny Berne had not been let off the hook. For the Scot had moved on into coaching and had produced a stream of tough, competitive athletes who had frequently bested Berne's Establishment protegés.

In the mid '60s Benny Berne, having achieved his much desired CBE, had eased himself out of his multitude of committees and slowly insinuated his son Harold into the administrative hierarchy. Harold had been made secretary designate of the British Association, taking over the reins from his father in 1967, the year before the Mexico Olympics.

The 1968–72 period had been one constant struggle between Grieve and the athletics Establishment to attain recognition for his squad of athletes and, in particular, for the budding decathlete, Alan Murdoch. As far as Berne was concerned the decathlon was an event for the mediocre, for those who could not excel in any event in particular, and the fact that Grieve was promoting and developing it simply confirmed him in his resistance. Grieve and Murdoch were starved by Berne and his associates of opportunities to compete abroad and, even when they used their own funds, either denied permission to compete in Europe or subjected to interminable prevarications.

But the Scots would not be denied, and in 1972, Murdoch, four years after his hurdles disaster in Mexico, was placed third in the world decathlon rankings and looked certain for a medal in Munich. Alas, in June of 1972 he had suffered a hamstring pull, missing the British Olympic trials. Berne pounced. The Olympics selection committee insisted that Murdoch attempt a trial decathlon at an inter-area meeting, a mere four weeks before the Munich Games. Grieve had pleaded in vain that his charge required a clear run-in to the Munich Games rather than a sapping test. To no avail. Murdoch had taken part in the trial and duly qualified: but at enormous physical cost. By Munich he had still not fully recovered and, though he finished a creditable fourth, he knew deep in his heart that Berne's 'trial' had put paid to any possible hope of Olympic victory.

The mid '70s had seen rapid changes in British athletics, changes which even Berne could not prevent. Television had brought sponsorship and with it large sums of money, and throughout athletics standards were rising at all levels. The professional attitudes of men like Grieve and Murdoch, so unacceptable only a few years before, now permeated the sport. Berne found that national team management was no longer the sinecure it had been, as athletes and coaches demanded the same high standards of accompanying officials as they were asking of themselves.

He had therefore moved upwards into a myriad of international committees, and in 1980 had become assistant secretary of the International Amateur Athletic Federation. The sudden death in 1981 of the Polish secretary Josef Jaskowski had thrust Berne into the plum position. The road was clear for Benny Berne's son, scourge of shamateurs and drug-takers, to become Sir Harold, all under the cloak of upper middle-class suavity and charm.

But now it appeared that his old enemies, Murdoch and Grieve, risen phoenix-like from the ashes, had again emerged to challenge him.

The temporary and artificial intimacy of Donne House had gone as Ellis Payne sat facing Murdoch across her room at the Inn on the Park in Park Lane. The coolness was almost palpable.

'This professor character that Kane has to get out across the Swiss frontier – ' she began.

'You mean Klaus Werther,' said Murdoch.

'That's the guy. Can we build him up?'

Murdoch sucked on the end of his pen. 'How do you mean?'

'I mean that he turns up' – she flipped through the script on her knee – 'on page 48 and has only about three pages before he competes in a track meet, then he hightails it across the Swiss border with Kane and – end of movie. Not much time to establish him, is there?'

'Do we really need to?'

'He *is* the pivot of the final part of the movie, so it's no bad thing if we get to like him a little. We've got to *want* him to get across the border with Kane.'

'Okay. What do you suggest?'

'Some earlier scenes,' she said, standing up, sleek and svelte in her brown velvet jogging suit. She placed her pencil across her lips as she turned to the open french window facing out on to a sunny Hyde Park. 'Establishing him as Mr Nice Guy. Doesn't have to be much. Just a chance to see him, place him in the audience's mind as someone good, someone worth taking risks for.'

'All right,' said Murdoch, leaning back in his chair, eyes closed. 'What about something earlier, with Goebbels, discussing Werther's comeback to track and field?'

Ellis turned to face him, the sun from the windows shining on her blonde hair. 'That might just do it, Mr Murdoch.'

He looked up. '*Mr* Murdoch. That sounds a wee bit formal.'

She sat down and placed her pad and pencil on the glass coffee table in front of her.

'Murdoch,' she said. 'I've always thought I could size people up. I thought I had you sized up back in LA.'

'As what?'

'A regular guy.'

'And how does that rate in your scheme of things?'

'A minus.'

'And when was the minus going to vanish?'

'Sometimes it never does. But I reckoned with you to give it a few weeks to eliminate the negative.'

'So?'

'Murdoch, can I level with you?'

'Level away.'

113

'When we first met back in LA I got good vibes. A couple of days back at Weir's place we had ourselves a great time even though we didn't get much chance to talk. Now I feel as if someone's opened the frigidaire.'

He did not answer immediately. Then slowly he told her of his conversation with Ciano and about the attempted cocaine fix. Ellis's face showed surprise, then concern. If she were acting, thought Murdoch, she was putting in an Academy Award performance.

'So how do you place me in all this?' she said.

'*You* linked me up with Hall and Stevens, *you* seem to know Tony Ciano well, *you* were one of the few people who could have tipped off the police about my flat. Two and two make four.'

'Sometimes only three and a half,' said Ellis sharply, tears coming to her eyes. 'So you think I helped set you up?'

'What the hell else *can* I think?' he shouted, standing up and throwing his script on to the coffee table in front of him.

She reached into her handbag at the side of her chair, withdrew a white handkerchief and dabbed her eyes. 'Okay, Sam Spade,' she said, sniffing. 'Let me make a stab at my own little scenario. Stevens and Hall met Andrew Weir a year ago last fall when he was looking for backers for *Galaxy*, and I arranged that they meet you back in LA. That much you already know. A couple of weeks ago my father phoned and suggested that you meet Tony Ciano when he was in London. But don't forget it wasn't me who introduced you to Ciano.'

'I don't understand,' he said.

'Neither do I,' replied Ellis. 'What exactly did Tony put to you?'

'He said that my project menaced the Los Angeles Olympics and that meant less money coming into California.'

'That's the key. Ciano is into every kind of racket in California and has a big stake in Vegas and Los Angeles. And they reckon the Olympics will bring over three billion dollars into the state.'

'Ciano reckons four billion,' he said. 'But where does your father come into all this?'

114

'My father, Robert Payne,' said Ellis, sighing, 'is a compulsive gambler and a born loser. At the last count he was into Ciano for a hundred g's. So it's my guess he's been feeding him everything I tell him about you. I swear to you I had nothing to do with what has happened.'

Ellis sensed Murdoch's uncertainty. 'Look, Murdoch,' she said, 'I've got no love for Ciano. He's made a fortune out of other people's pain. Cocaine, heroin, you name it. I just thought that if he met you it might take a little heat off my father. So let me put myself on the line.'

She paused, pushing away a strand of hair from her face.

'There's too much at stake in Los Angeles,' she went on. 'All the money that has been pumped in by the big companies like McDonalds and Coca-Cola, The Southlands Corporation. By opening day it'll be over five hundred million dollars. And a lot of the country's top executives – '

'Like Bruce Cohn,' interjected Murdoch.

'Like Cohn,' she agreed. 'Sure. They've put themselves and their reputations on the line for this Olympics. Cohn's become the Games' executive director working for peanuts and he's helped devise the first Olympics in modern times that's going to make a profit. But that'll only be the first step for Bruce Cohn, Murdoch. This guy sees himself as another Ronnie Reagan. First State Governor, then on to the White House. Sport, showbiz, politics, back where I come from it's all the same game. So he's got a lot riding on Los Angeles.'

Murdoch nodded. 'You aren't telling me anything I don't know,' he said, his face still dour.

Ellis shook her head. 'You're a hard man, Murdoch,' she said. 'You want to play it straight down the line, like when you were an athlete. But these people aren't going to play it that way.'

She laid down her script on the table in front of her. 'I read the papers,' she said. 'I can see what's being proposed at this week's conference in Athens – it's your friend Harold Berne. He's been a true-blue amateur since he first wet his diapers, but what's he doing now? He's standing on his head and

115

rustling up support so that athletes can get paid money into trust funds. Now you don't have to be Sherlock Holmes to see that he's got a whiff of your Kudai plans for 1983. That means your cover must have been blown weeks ago. Berne probably doesn't give a cent for the Olympics, but he wants to protect himself and his Federation. So what's coming up in 1983?'

'The first World Championships in Helsinki,' said Murdoch. He leant forward towards her. 'Ellis, don't get me wrong, I appreciate the lecture, but you still aren't telling me anything I don't know. Our 1983 Million Dollar Meet programme will finish the IAAF's first World Championships, probably destroy Berne's plans for the Federation's financial future.'

'Let me finish,' insisted Ellis, her face flushed and her eyes shining. 'Let's just look at Ciano for a moment. That cocaine set-up at your flat, that would never have stood up in court and Ciano and his London boys knew it. No, it was just a warning – Ciano telling you that you were in over your head, and back at Donne House he tried to spell it out to you again.'

Murdoch relaxed, though he did not know why. 'What do you think I should do?'

Ellis shrugged. 'If I were you I'd get out now. You don't need it, this Arab deal.' She too leant forward, lifting the script and tapping it with the knuckles of her left hand. 'You can write,' she said. 'You don't need to change the world of sport. Leave that to Cohn and Berne and their buddies.'

'So you want the same as Berne and Ciano?' he said, his voice dry. 'To get me to pull out?'

'No, I don't,' she replied. 'I just want you to see what you're up against, and to stop playing it like a boy scout.'

He sat back in his chair and sighed. 'You finished yet?' Despite what she had said he sensed that she was on his side.

'Not quite,' she smiled. 'I just want to say that if you want to come out of your corner punching against Ciano then I think I can help you.'

Her face became serious. 'Back in LA, a friend of mine, a reporter called Wayne Berbick, has been working on a story on Ciano for the past six months. He won't give me any details, but

116

he says it's a real ball-buster. What you need against Ciano is something you can use to stop him giving you any more trouble. So let me talk to Wayne, tell him about your situation, see if we can work out something to your mutual advantage. How does that grab you?'

'It grabs me,' he said, smiling. 'But the best man to deal with Berbick is a private investigator, and I think I know the man, too. An old friend, a cop – Birdie Sparrow.'

She raised an eyebrow. 'Birdie?' she said. 'Then he won't need a plane ticket.'

Murdoch smiled wryly. He picked up the telephone and dialled. 'Room service?' he said. 'This is 439. A bottle of champagne. Yes, immediately.' He replaced the receiver.

Ellis grinned. 'Champagne? At eleven o'clock in the morning?'

'Perrier wouldn't meet the mood of the moment,' he said.

'Which is?'

He sat down, lifted the script, then looked up at her. 'Relief.'

8

About-Turn for Berne

Wednesday, 8 September 1982

Sebastian Coe had made his move at exactly the right time. It was the European Games in Athens, the 800 metres final, and the English runner had cruised effortlessly into the lead, his unique sprint speed taking him easily clear of the pack as he cruised into the home straight. The time would not be fast, for it had been a tactical race, but Coe did not care; it would be his first major win at the distance.

Suddenly the chunky figure of the West German, Hans Peter Ferner, appeared on Coe's right shoulder. Surely, thought Murdoch, watching in the stands, Coe would simply slip into a higher gear. Up to his right in the commentary area the television commentators' voices were raised to a new pitch; but Coe, searching desperately for a speed which had deserted him like some fickle mistress, could not respond and the German surged on to win.

Heigh-ho, thought Murdoch; the only certainty in sport was that there were no certainties. Hugh Grieve came down the stadium steps towards him, side-stepping through the crowd and carrying two cans of Coca-Cola. 'Huh – Coe,' he said. 'Can't take the heat of the elbow brigade.'

He handed Murdoch one of the cans and both men peeled back the metal openers. Grieve gulped his drink down, coughing as he did so.

'Women, Murdoch, should be taken at room temperature. But not Coke. Only ice cold.'

They sat in the fading heat of the Athens afternoon, in shorts, road-shoes and T-shirts. For days they had lodged at the Athens Hilton, watching the good and the great of the International Amateur Athletic Federation flit through its grey marble halls. Murdoch had encountered Berne and his colleague Vera Goldberg at least a dozen times, but they had avoided his eyes, adopting a preoccupied stare into the middle-distance.

They all knew, there was no question of it. Quince and Buchinski, moving freely – as delegates – within the Federation conference, soon confirmed that the Kudai Games were a matter of common knowledge. Berne and his acolytes were also aware that Quince and Buchinski were themselves involved, though they could not prove it.

It was soon clear to Quince that a rearguard Federation action was being mounted. At surface level, the Federation, through its professional officers, pursued the formal IAAF conference programme to an exact and demanding timetable. But each night caucus meetings took place in Hilton bedrooms and at the Russian and East German embassies in smog-ridden central Athens. Berne and Goldberg, though never invited to these embassy caucuses, heavily influenced their discussions.

It was Berne's view that unless the Western athletes could be offered prize money then the defections to Kudai could prove mortal. True, throughout his life he had resisted the slide towards paid athletics, but he knew that if the West lost its stars the Federation would be dead. The lesser of two evils was to offer the athletes prize money at a limited number of meetings, as already proposed at the 1981 Rome conference.

The Communist bloc stood firm against giving money direct to the athletes – though they themselves had been doing just that for over thirty years. Berne therefore pressed them to his second option, which allowed athletes to accept cash for books, broadcasting and advertising, through their governing bodies, all earnings to be held in trust. He knew that the major sports agencies would be furious, for thus negotiations over fees would have to be conducted by the national governing bodies.

There would be no agents allowed to participate, and so no agent percentages from appearance money.

Berne's next step was to lobby for the votes of the developing nations, few of which, apart from Ethiopia and Kenya, would gain much advantage from the setting up of 'permit' meetings or athletes' trust funds. He gave convincing promises of additional aid for coaching and capital sums for development programmes, plus specific pledges to support particular Third World candidates in major IAAF committees.

By 12 September an exhausted Berne had secured the necessary votes for permit meetings, though the rigid stance of the Communist bloc was still a problem. His only remaining task was the designation of the limited number of permit meetings which would secure IAAF backing. He knew that Quince and Buchinski had probably contracted to Kudai most of those promoters to which the Federation were likely to grant official permit status. He also knew that there was no point in dealing directly with either Buchinski or Quince. He therefore set his officials to contact the major European and American meet organisers and convince them of the advantages of staying within the IAAF family. All evinced a reflex surprise when told about the coming Kudai Games – and promised undying allegiance to the IAAF cause. That worried Berne most of all.

Monday, 13 September 1982

It was only when he returned to his office that Murdoch realised the backlog of work which had piled up because of the Kudai project. He had anticipated the problem back in September and had advertised for two new account executives. One would handle the Pepsi Superstars Award Scheme, which Pepsi now wished to bring from the United States to Britain in 1983, and the other to handle Murdoch's new 'baby', his Superschool Competition, for which Murdoch already had three likely sponsors lined up.

Early in his career in sports consultancy Murdoch had realised that it was not enough to have a good and original sports sponsorship idea, to have it accurately costed or even to have television companies prepared to give it screen time. It was equally important to put the project with the right company, with no conflict between product and project. Thus, though Pepsi's involvement in youth and vitality in his superstar scheme was ideal, he had been less happy with Manulife's sponsorship of the World Bobsleigh Championships which would come up in January 1983 in St Moritz. However, the Manulife chairman had been a winter sports enthusiast and Manulife would make heavy use of the World Championships over its two-year sponsorship period as a means of entertaining both business associates and in incentive schemes for its top salesmen. Murdoch's aim in 1984 would be to press the company towards aims more directly in line with their business objectives such as the sponsorship of Veterans Athletics programmes. He had a soft spot for bobsleighing, having had a fleeting experience of the sport some years before, under Grieve's aegis. By the time of his trip to St Moritz for the 1983 World Championships, in early January, he would have another, more appropriate sponsor lined up.

By late afternoon he had made a substantial dent in the backlog, and had had time to reflect on the occurrences of the previous two months. His luck had been remarkable, and in a period of eight weeks almost every track and field meet director in Europe and the United States had been secured for Kudai. Not for the first time he felt glad of the counsel of Grieve, Buchinski and Quince. The meeting that morning at the Inn on the Park with fifty of the world's leading athletes had been a resounding success, and Grieve would have his first training courses for Arab coaches and officials by mid-November. The pieces were beginning to fit together, and all that remained was the formal press launch in a month's time.

The only surprise so far had been the amount of detail requested by Hall and Stevens in his reports to them. The two Americans had asked him for a day-to-day log on all developments, including minor meetings and telephone calls from journalists, sports administrators and government officials.

He reflected that this chore had been evenly balanced by the detailed reports on facility developments which he had received in turn from Hall and Stevens. His meeting with Mr Ciano was therefore duly logged and reported. He decided, however, not to report the result of the tennis game. Perhaps that might be too much, even for Hall and Stevens.

TRACK AND FIELD NEWS   OCTOBER 1982

TWENTY-THIRD IAAF CONGRESS — TRUST FUNDS APPROVED

Despite rumours of strong opposition the trust fund concept has breezed through. One can imagine the sighs of relief in Indianapolis, as the TAC had already collected a sizeable amount of prize money to set aside for road-racers, and if the IAAF had decided that the athletes couldn't have it . . .

Under the new concept athletes will be allowed to 'earn' money from competition. However, the money must be paid to the athlete's federation and put in a trust, from which the athlete can draw for basic training needs. Once the athlete draws some of the money for an unapproved reason he/she is open to suspension.

'Setting aside money for athletes is a violation of IAAF and Olympic rules,' argued Vladimir Efimyenko of the USSR. 'It is necessary to maintain the friendship between the sportsmen of different nations, but only by following the amateur ideal.' His request that the vote be set aside was rejected, however, and in the final analysis only the USSR and Rumania cast votes against the plan, which gained a 366–16 vote of confidence.

'Track and field doesn't just revolve around a few champions,' countered East Germany's Gerhard Schewinski. 'The athletes are like the cosmonauts who can't go into space without the help of many other workers. If money goes to the federation it must concern all the athletes, big and small.'

It would not be surprising to see many of the federations decide that a share of the loot is theirs. The British, for example, already take fifteen per cent of endorsement monies.

IAAF PERMIT MEETINGS

Going hand in hand with the trust fund concept is the new pro-gramme of IAAF permit meetings. These competitions, which will be controlled in number, will be allowed to pay 50,000 dollars in *per diem*, and will also be allowed to negotiate openly with a federation for an athlete's services.

For example, if Zurich wants to buy Sebastian Coe they strike a deal with the British federation. Their money (perhaps minus a percentage) is credited to Coe's trust.

While this is supposed to curtail under-the-table payments there will certainly be instances where athletes will choose to receive their money in the old fashion, be it for tax evasion purposes or whatever.

The list of official meets for 1983 will be set at the European Calendar Congress at Linz, Austria, in late October.

The concept of permit meetings passed by a 386–24 margin, Poland joining the Soviets and Rumanians in opposition. On both of the aforementioned votes the East Germans abstained because neither subject conformed to 'Olympic ideals'.

TESTOSTERONE BANNED

Now that a reliable testing method has been established the natural hormone testosterone has been added to the list of banned substances. Also proscribed is caffeine. Apparently urine samples from Moscow indicated very high levels of caffeine in many instances.

Dr Arne Ljungqvist of Sweden, head of the Medical committee, noted that random testing for drugs was still an impossibility. 'We simply do not have the laboratory facilities,' he explained, pointing out that there are still only six accredited laboratories in the world.

Wednesday, 6 October 1982

The world's press stood in total darkness in a bare, silent room. A few moments earlier they had poured into the London Hilton and had been shown to the small conference room on the first floor. But they had found it to be completely empty, its only distinctive feature being what appeared to be a number of cinema screens, about three metres high but covering the four walls. When they had all entered attendants had closed the doors and extinguished the lights.

Suddenly the screens became alive with film of runners, jumpers and throwers, to the boom of a stereophonic soundtrack by Vangelis, and for the next fifteen minutes the press were indulged in a display of the wonders of Prince Hassan's stadium and its attendant swimming and gymnastic facilities. It was a brilliant piece of salesmanship, and as the final images faded from the screen there was spontaneous applause from the hardened press corps.

The lights went on and uniformed attendants ushered the two hundred and ten journalists out of the conference room into an adjoining lecture theatre, where they took their positions in tiered seating. At each journalist's place was a fat folder of information and a video-cassette of the film they had just viewed.

At a long table at the base of the seating sat Murdoch and his staff, all dressed in austere blue blazers bearing the Arab Olympic emblem as designed by Prince Hassan.

Murdoch rose. 'Ladies and gentlemen,' he began. 'It is said that a picture is worth a thousand words. The film you have just seen is the most direct means we could devise to outline the nature of a unique sports venture, the Arab Olympics of 1984. The object of this conference is to allow you to put to me and my staff any questions relating to the project which may not have been met either by the film or the documentation. Anyhow, knowing something of your needs, I reckoned you'd want to speak to somebody rather than get your stories from a handout.'

From amid the second row of journalists Ralph Douglas of *Sports Illustrated* stood up. There was an atmosphere of hushed expectancy around him: his bushy shock of iron-grey hair and loud checkered sports jackets were known throughout international sport.

'Mr Murdoch,' he drawled. 'This is probably the most remarkable sports project which I and my colleagues have ever had placed before us. So I reckon the first question has got to be – is the money in the bank?'

'A few weeks ago,' said Murdoch, smiling, 'we had a meeting with some of the world's top athletes. Not surprisingly, that was one of their first questions.'

There was laughter.

He lifted two sheets of paper from a folder in front of him. 'These,' he said, 'are statements from the Arab Bank, Park Lane, and the Swissbank, Zurich. These show monies in escrow in my charge sufficient to take the programme to 1988. You have copies of these statements in your folders, on pages three and four.'

'Are you OPEC-based?' It was Emil Leclerc, the tiny representative of the authoritative French sports daily *L'Equipe*.

'Yes. As you may know, OPEC has massive sums lying in foreign banks, 70 billion dollars in the United States alone. OPEC monies, combined with the profits from share-dealings by Prince Hassan and his associates in the past six years, represent the financial base of the venture.'

'And where does the ITC come in?'

'The ITC is responsible for the building of facilities, accommodation – all the non-technical organisation of the Games. Mr Hall and Mr Stevens – both on my left here – are responsible for this part of the operation, and are my direct superiors. My job is to get competitors there and to organise the Games as a competition and as a spectacle.'

Klaus Stock, of the German magazine *Stern*, stood up.

'Mr Murdoch,' he said, 'I am not a sports reporter – I write what you might call the money articles – EEC, IMF, things like that. I have looked at your likely income and expenditure. There appears to me to be no way by which your Kudai Olympics can ever be in profit.' He sat down, his brow furrowed.

Murdoch nodded.

'That is correct,' he said. 'The Kudai Games is not a profit-making venture.'

'Can we call it a PR exercise?' shouted Sydney Bell of the *Daily Express*.

'You can call it an isometric exercise if you like, Sydney,' smiled Murdoch, and there was laughter.

William Carter, the plump, bespectacled representative of *The Times*, levered himself to his feet and raised his pencil in his right hand.

'All this is very well, Mr Murdoch,' he said. 'These wonderful prizes, these magnificent facilities. But where, I ask myself, does this leave the Los Angeles Olympics?'

Murdoch smiled and looked sideways at his colleagues. 'The proponents of the Olympic movement have always claimed that the Olympics are strictly for amateurs, for the cream of recreational sportsmen. We propose to deal with the professional cream, and to leave the Olympic movement with what they always said they wanted in the first place, the amateurs.'

Carter smiled. 'Fair enough, but not far enough. What about the Communist bloc? They certainly won't rush to your Arab Games. That means the remaining Western athletes will be second-raters and will simply be wiped out come Los Angeles.'

Murdoch's face was serious. 'A good point, Bill. But remember what happened when open tennis was first created. There the balance of power lay in the West; but in the end the best Communist nations put their players into open tennis: they had no choice. I agree that, in the short-term, they'll stay put, but when we succeed, as we will, I think that they'll have no alternative but to join us. The dollars will come in handy, too, to countries like Poland.'

Carter started to speak, but Murdoch raised his hand. 'If I could just finish,' he said. 'Athletics, swimming and tennis are individual sports and the Olympic movement has always claimed, despite all the flags and national anthems, that it was a competition between individuals. So if these individuals want to join WAPA and compete for money then surely that's a matter for them.'

Carter sat down, frowning.

Hugh Madden of the *Daily Mail* rose. 'WAPA? Could you explain?'

'The World Association of Professional Athletes,' said Murdoch. 'By the end of next year, 1983, when our competitive population is fully established, we will form WAPA. The sportsmen will elect male and female representatives to serve with me and my staff on the board of management.'

'Are you telling us that the competing athletes will have

a direct say in the running of your organisation?' pursued Madden.

'Yes. It's obvious to most of you that few governing bodies are truly democratic,' Murdoch explained. 'Because of our size and newness, we can have the type of simple, direct form of democracy that older associations have never been able to develop.'

There was a pause before a small, monkey-faced man stood up. 'Bons Maki, *Helsinki News*.' Maki had been one of the first runners to break two hours twenty minutes for the marathon back in the early 1950s. He spoke in measured, heavily accented tones. 'Mr Murdoch, the 1983 permit meetings created by the IAAF in Athens have enabled track and field athletes to put their earnings in trusts. Surely we have already accepted the fact that athletes can earn money from their skills?'

'Not really,' replied Murdoch. 'Even the creation of trusts doesn't overcome the basic question – which is why the best sportsmen shouldn't earn and pocket immediately what they can from their abilities.'

There was another murmur of agreement.

Roy Dellinger of *Time* magazine rose next. 'Mr Murdoch, with the massive financial inducements which you are offering, isn't there a strong likelihood of drug infringements?'

'Ladies and gentlemen,' said Murdoch. 'I refer you to sheet twelve of your brief.' There was a rustle of paper as the journalists sought the desired page. 'There you will see the West German, Dr Danike, has reported on the Moscow Olympics' urine samples. They show that forty out of the five hundred and sixty-four competitors he tested had taken testosterone, a natural male hormone. And sixteen of those forty were *women*!

'On the same page, there is a summary of a report in Finland, which found that thirty-six per cent of Finnish athletes and gymnasts had admitted to taking drugs. The project leader, Paul Voulle, was quoted as saying that he suspected that the percentage taking anabolic steroids was probably much higher.'

He turned to his left and pointed to the end of the table with his left hand.

'Dr Ernst Schmidt was until 1980 one of East Germany's leading experts in sports medicine. In January of that year he defected, and he is now in charge of our drug-prevention programme, on which we will spend three million dollars in our first year.'

Schmidt, a lean balding man with a hawk-like nose, rose and smiled, revealing flashing white teeth interspersed with gold.

'Dr Schmidt,' said Maki, his face stern, 'is it true that in your work in East Germany you gave anabolic steroids to women?'

'Yes,' said Schmidt. 'After the athletes' active athletic life had ended we provided a carefully monitored de-training programme to bring each woman competitor back to normal activity. There were, in our experience of ten years, no contra-indications.'

'What about testosterone?' pursued Maki.

Schmidt blushed. 'After the suspension of our best female shot-putter, Ilona Slupianek, for ingestion of anabolic steroids our sports administrators were censured by the party leader himself. Experiments with natural testosterone and other un-detectable or legal body-building drugs were therefore initiated. I disagreed with this policy which appeared to me to endanger health, but kept my own counsel. When in 1980 the first opportunity to defect occurred I took it.'

Ralph Douglas rose to his feet once more, his pencil pointed towards Schmidt. 'Is it true, Doctor, that you have devised tests which show if testosterone has been artificially injected and which can detect anabolic steroids well over six months after ingestion? Is it also true that the International Amateur Athletic Federation has ignored your conclusions?'

Schmidt looked uneasily at Murdoch, who nodded re-assuringly.

'To the first question the answer is "yes". To the second I can only say that the IAAF have been less than enthusiastic about pursuing my findings.'

'My question for Dr Schmidt is this,' said Mike Baum of

Newsweek. 'Could you say with certainty that any Olympic medallist in the 1980 Olympics had never taken illegal drugs?'

'Not with any degree of certainty,' said Schmidt. 'For any sport.'

There was a flurry of discussion and Murdoch had to shout to make himself heard.

Once the noise had subsided Felix Clark of the *Guardian* spoke from the back row. 'Are you dedicated to out-of-season testing, Dr Schmidt?'

'Yes,' replied Schmidt. 'There is no other sure answer to the anabolics.'

'And what about blood-doping?' persisted Clark.

Schmidt chose his words with care, his eyes half closed. 'That is a much more complex problem, the increase in haemoglobin in the athlete's blood caused by blood-doping. I have recently read the testimony of the Finnish runner, Mikko Ala Leppilampi, who claims that he was blood-doped before the Munich Olympics by a leading Finnish sports doctor. There is good evidence that this is common in Western nations, and it was certainly standard practice in East Germany before I left.'

'Have you any answer to this problem, Doctor?'

Schmidt nodded. 'Haematocrit levels must be tested close to the competitive period. This can be done by doctors in the athlete's own country. Then the athlete can be re-tested after competition. If there are any substantial changes then we can act.'

Murdoch stood up. 'I think, ladies and gentlemen, that we can close this area of questioning. I hope that it's clear that we are united on this front. We have the most advanced drug-detection system ever devised and all drug-suspensions will be for life. If we cannot control drugs then we shouldn't be in the business.'

There was prolonged applause.

Martha Smith of *Woman's Sport* magazine stood up, an attractive, dark-eyed brunette in her mid-twenties.

'Can you confirm, Mr Murdoch, that men's and women's prize monies for all sports will be identical?'

'Absolutely,' said Murdoch. There was an excited flutter of clapping from the half-dozen female journalists.

'Can you also explain why the gymnastics and swimming competitions are confined to women above the age of eighteen?'

'Yes,' said Murdoch. 'Though I would observe that this also applies to the male competitors in these particular sports. We felt that if we were offering big money prizes it was unfair to tempt adolescents. This ruling also encourages a type of gymnastics relating to mature women rather than to the Munchkins whom we have been viewing for the last ten years.'

There was again laughter and scattered applause.

Carter of *The Times* levered himself to his feet. 'You have been careful, Mr Murdoch, not directly to criticise the IAAF or the IOC. However, whatever weaknesses these institutions possess they do spring at their roots from recreational sport. And they do feed back into the developing nations at all levels, through their coaching courses and conferences. Does WAPA have any plans in this direction?'

Grieve stood up, his bright red hair and ruddy complexion in contrast to the blue of his blazer. 'That's one of my areas of specialisation,' he answered. 'On page fifteen you'll find our 1983–4 programme of coaching conferences and courses for officials in the developing nations.

'In addition, we offer the Superstar Decathlon awards for children and teenagers in the 9–18 age range. This is an all-round fitness award, providing incentives for kids of all levels of ability. A sample of the scoring tables is on page seventeen, and page eighteen has photographs of the badges and certificates.'

'Do these awards relate directly to the standards in the developing nations?'

'Aye. There are ten levels of award for each age group,' replied Grieve. 'You get the first level of the Superstar if you're warm and your heart is beating.'

There was laughter again. This was the Grieve they knew.

'The important thing with all kids, whether they're Chinese or Scots, is to recognise not their natural ability but their efforts. On page nineteen you'll see the special scheme for the disabled.'

Mike Baum of *Newsweek* was the next to speak. 'Mr Murdoch, the prizes being offered are vast, undoubtedly the greatest in the history of track and field athletics. Now: most Western nations have pretty strict tax systems. How do you propose to deal with this?'

Murdoch nodded. 'There are two options. The first is that we pay out any monies won over a period of years, thus diminishing the immediate tax burden. The second is to put substantial parts of the monies into pension policies. In any case, part of the service which we intend to provide will be advice on taxes, from top accountants.'

Baum nodded and made some notes on the pad before him. 'Another point, if I may. What relationship will WAPA have with athletes' agents, such as World Management Group under Calvin Shaw and IMG, Mark McCormack's organisation?'

'A friendly one, I hope,' replied Murdoch. 'You see, we do not pay appearance money. So if athletes want to slice off a percentage of their winnings for their agents then that's up to them.'

He looked around the room. The conference was beginning to lose pace, as the central questions and answers had been absorbed. He stood and raised his hands for silence.

'Ladies and gentlemen, I think that with the film, the dossier and your questions, which we have done our best to answer, you now have a comprehensive picture of our project. Next door in the reception area lunch awaits you. Also awaiting you – well, if I mention the names Lewis, Scott, Coghlan, Coe, Bank, Ashford, De Castella, you will have an idea of the calibre of athletes you will meet, plus someone who will be known only to track statisticians, a 14.1, 110 metres hurdles performer of 1971 . . .' He paused. 'Prince Hassan of Kudai.'

There was an immediate surge down towards the door. Murdoch looked to his side, to Grieve, Buchinski and Quince, and smiled.

Thursday, 7 October 1982

The golf ball trundled slowly across the deep pile of the carpet and landed neatly with a hollow 'clop' in the plastic coffee cup which lay on its side in the middle of the floor.

'So much for your golf ball,' said Stafford, bending to pick it up.

A few metres away, sitting in front of an ancient oak desk, Butch Pendleton raised a plump right hand. Stafford playfully tossed the ball underarm towards his junior officer, who adjusted nimbly to catch it before continuing to scrutinise the black and white photograph on his superior's desk.

'Have a heart, sir,' said Pendleton. 'From 40,000 feet it could have been a meringue. Our people in Kudai have checked it out. They say that it's the most advanced sports stadium of all time. Makes the Astrodome look like a high school ball park.' He paused. 'But then no law says you can't build yourself a sports stadium in the middle of a desert.'

'If it weren't for the Los Angeles Games the Company wouldn't give a damn,' said Stafford, shaking his head as his final ball stopped a foot short of the cup. He walked over to the desk and pressed a buzzer. 'Miss Clark,' he said. 'My Arab Olympics file – and two cups of coffee, milk and sugar.'

'Since we got on to this Kudai thing I've been checking back in our Olympics files,' said Pendleton. 'Before 1980, you couldn't have found enough paper on the Olympics in there to wipe your ass.'

'Then Afghanistan.'

'After that, there's everyone and his uncle in the files.'

'It was election year,' said Stafford.

'Then this guy, the President's special emissary, Cutler. Carter sent him everywhere to get the Europeans to pull out of Moscow.'

132

'Cutler, Nutler,' said Stafford. 'Nobody gave a damn about the Olympics till Afghanistan.'

'And nobody gave a damn about it since then till now.'

'Poland, El Salvador, the Falklands,' Stafford continued. 'Then Poland again. Next we'll be back with the Israelis. It never ends.' He straightened, waving his golf club for emphasis. 'But the difference is this time it's *our* Olympics. That's why when two hundred million-dollar golf balls start popping up in Kudai for a track meet on the same dates as the LA Games the Oval Office wants to know what the hell is happening.'

Stafford picked up the plastic cup, scrunched it into a ball and lobbed it into the wastepaper basket next to where Pendleton was sitting. He sat down in an armchair behind the desk and looked up as Miss Clark, a plump, thick-hipped woman in her mid-thirties, brought in two cups of steaming coffee. From under her arm she took a bulky file and placed it on the desk in front of Stafford, who immediately began to flick through it.

After a couple of minutes he sat back in his chair and sipped his coffee. No sugar. He grimaced and reached for a phial of Canderal in his drawer.

'This guy Murdoch. What do we have on him?' Pendleton asked.

Stafford leafed through the file and shook his head. 'Nothing much,' he said. 'Seems a pretty regular guy.'

'Who's he working with?'

'Prince Hassan of Kudai, aged thirty-seven, assisted by his brother Ryad. Ascended throne two years ago. Most liberal of Emirate rulers.'

Stafford went on leafing through the files. 'Now to the surprise packages,' he said. 'Messrs David Hall and Leonard Stevens. Blue-chip businessmen who have been in the Middle East since 1974. They got into Kudai in January 1978 with a big contract for schools and hospitals.'

'Haven't they been pushing for contracts in the Eastern bloc?' interrupted Pendleton.

Stafford inspected the file. 'Since 1976, mostly unsuccessfully.' he replied. 'But Stevens and Hall have worked for Hassan mainly on the hardware, the stadium and facilities. This guy Murdoch seems to be the technical linchpin.'

'Who else is in there?' asked Pendleton.

Stafford turned a page. 'Bruce Cohn – technical director of the LA operation. Ex-IBM whizz-kid, aims to make the LA operation the first modern Games to pay their way. Big Republican. On his way to the Senate if he can pull this off. I heard him speak once: good man.'

He reached forward, sipped his coffee and grimaced again. 'Harold Berne, president, International Amateur Athletic Federation. Son of Victor Bernstein, secretary of the British Athletic Federation. Took over from father in 1968. Chairman, British Olympic Committee 1974–9. Vice-chairman, Central Council of Physical Recreation 1978 to present. Turned a somersault just this September in Athens by supporting a proposal to give money to athletes.'

'What about the professional officers of the IOC and the IAAF?'

Stafford closed the file. 'The vanilla-flavoured men. Not fit to guard the fish in the aquarium. No, when the rubber hits the road it's the amateurs like Berne who run the set-up in sport, not the pros.'

He returned to the file on the desk and tapped it with his knuckles.

'One other thing. Last month the Brits let us have a KGB guy who had defected from the embassy at Istanbul. As I recollect, you were on vacation at the time. He didn't tell us much but he *did* mention that he had seen Murdoch's name on file.'

'So what's the bottom line?'

'That our man Murdoch is working for the KGB, either knowingly or unknowingly. How the KGB got to Hassan to set up this whole damn Arab Olympics, your guess is as good as mine.' Stafford stood up and shook his head. 'It doesn't add up,' he said. 'Who else has Murdoch got on his team?'

'Mostly sports people. A guy called Grieve, a bookseller

called Quince.' Pendleton lifted a sheet from the file and scrutinised it.

'Here's a beaut,' he said. 'Buchinski, Claude. A New York cop. Age, forty-nine. Heads fitness programme. Fixer for US track circuit.' He handed the sheet to Stafford.

'Buchinski?' said Stafford. 'His family's a legend in New York. When I was a kid my father never stopped bending my ear about the Buchinskis – the Irish Polacks, they used to call them. But he's way out to right field. There's no way he'd be linked up with Reds.' He scowled. 'What a mixture. In the white corner we have an Arab prince, a bookseller, a New York redneck, a couple of Ivy-league businessmen and an Olympic athlete. In the blue corner the next senator for California, the president of the International Olympic Committee and assorted Olympic deadwood, and the international track and field Establishment.'

'So what do we do?'

Stafford picked up a pencil from the desk in front of him and rotated it in a pencil-sharpener. He sucked on the blunt end meditatively.

'Okay,' he said. 'So this guy Murdoch is being trailed by the KGB. So Moscow is interested. That's no great surprise: so are we.'

He lay back in his chair and closed his eyes. 'Pendleton,' he said. 'When I get into something like this – something I don't know much about – I ask myself some simple questions.' He paused. 'Who wins? Who loses?'

He opened his eyes and leant forward, both elbows on the desk.

'Let's look at *us*. The Federal government, I mean, not our Olympic people. We spend seventy million dollars on security for the Games. If they're a success it's Cohn and his boys who get the glory, not the President. If they go down the tubes because of Murdoch, same thing. So we lose a few medals. Nobody cared much back in Moscow.'

'And the Russians?'

'How much d'you reckon the Russians, the East Germans,

the Cubans put into their Olympic teams, Pendleton? Put a figure on it.'

Pendleton shook his head. 'Impossible, sir. Nobody knows.'

'Our people say the East Germans put two per cent of gross national product into sport, the Russians a touch below that. For them the Olympics are the Fourth of July, Christmas, Mother's Day, all rolled into one. They're the ones who lose if Mr Murdoch has his way.'

Stafford stood up, lifted the file and hugged it to his chest. 'If the KGB *are* interested in Murdoch then they might snare things up, try to stop him. They win, we lose. So put a twenty-four-hour-a-day watch on our track star Mr Murdoch. And let's see which way he runs.'

9

Black Friday

For Los Angeles Olympic director of operations, Bruce Cohn, the previous day had been a nightmare. First, he had been kept an hour on the telephone by Hilda Stael, the secretary of the International Federation of Sport. She had called direct from Monte Carlo. Stael, who was embroiled in yet another of her endless translations of the works of Baron de Coubertin, had rambled on about the need for the Los Angeles Games to preserve 'the true and abiding spirit of Olympism'. Cohn had never understood exactly what 'Olympism' meant or how it differed in substance from simple, unalloyed sportsmanship. However, he had listened with courteous resignation, occasionally laying down the telephone to open a wad of letters.

About another learned treatise from a Professor Allen of Harvard Cohn was less sure. Allen believed that the Russians had devised some sort of ray which could, imposed upon an athlete from a distance, seriously diminish his performance. The Harvard professor announced that it had already been used in Moscow and had resulted in the inexplicable failure of such athletes as Sebastian Coe in the 800 metres and the Brazilian triple jumper de Oliveira. Several Western journalists, including the British *Sunday Telegraph*'s Peter Hildreth, had also suggested that the Russians had used such a device. Cohn had not read Allen's report, which spanned twenty-six closely typed pages, but had instead relied on a summary by one of UCLA's top sports scientists, Bill Wischnia. Christ, he thought,

137

it was all like something out of *Flash Gordon*. Who would deal with it? Delgado? Police Chief Brubaker? NASA? He memoed a polite reply to Professor Allen, indicating that the Los Angeles Committee would look into his study in great detail. Then he ordered his secretary to lose Allen's report somewhere in his already bulging 'Studies' cabinet.

Next in Cohn's in-tray was a learned paper from a Taiwanese professor of physiology declaring that Los Angeles smog might worsen times in the 10,000 metres by up to thirty seconds and might also cause irreparable lung damage, and result in crippling post-Olympic lawsuits. Enough was enough: the professor's paper was consigned to the trash bin.

Cohn sighed and looked out of his window on to the sunlit UCLA campus. It was 11.00 a.m. and most students were in class, though there were at least a dozen joggers in variously coloured sweat-suits making their way between the trees and along campus pathways. Cohn could always separate joggers from real track athletes. For one thing, their feet never seemed to leave the ground. Total contact running. No, it was all about rhythm. Runners had rhythm, joggers merely movement, a sort of healthy epilepsy.

He had never thought, when he had moved from IBM to become technical director of the Los Angeles Games, that it would be easy. Hell, even a millionaire like Jack Kelly, who had been up to his armpits in American Olympic geriatrics for nearly a decade, had got nowhere. Something happened, some strange transformation, when even eminently successful businessmen slipped into a shiny Olympic blazer. It was as if, in some strange way, they regressed to childhood.

The IOC: they were another breed entirely, and when he had got over the shock of his first meetings with the committee's octogenarians he had, in his methodical way, as a therapy, produced the 'Cohn classification'.

First, there were the Spiritualists who, wreathed in Baron de Coubertin's ectoplasm, had created a heady mixture called 'Olympism'. This was an odd mélange of *Tom Brown's School-days* and the Odes of Pindar strained through the fine mesh of a thousand idealistic academic minds since 1896. The Spiritualists rejoiced in holding endless congresses and seminars in luxurious hotels all over the world, congresses for which some sponsor or philanthropist would always pick up the tab.

The second group were the Ancients, the descendants of de Coubertin's first IOC. Although he had talked and written at great length about the democracy of sport de Coubertin had expressed his faith in the democratic process by appointing a collection of noblemen, clerics and princes to lead the Olympic movement into the twentieth century. This group had perpetuated itself ever since.

Then there were the Timeservers of the international federations. These were men and women like Berne who had come into sports administration after the Second World War, and had filled the vacuum at the top left by the war generation. They were often people who owned small businesses which allowed them freedom to act as unpaid, part-time administrators in their national associations.

The Timeservers had developed a taste for something with which they had never made contact in their undistinguished working lives: power. For they found that they could decide the fates of the finest physical specimens in the world. They held in their grasp the right to decide which athlete went to Baghdad or Albuquerque, which official to Moscow, Berlin or Adelaide – perquisites much desired both by athletes and by other ascending Timeservers.

Berne's swift volte-face at the IAAF Athens conference had at first surprised Cohn though a call to Berne had clarified the position. As a result, Cohn's estimate of Berne experienced a sea-change. Such a prompt and successful response to rumours of an Arab Olympics (which Cohn had discounted) deserved respect. The fact that Berne's main aim had been to protect the IAAF's 1983 European Cup and inaugural World Championships, rather than the Olympics, did not trouble Cohn. Neither did it concern him that the success of the 1983 **World Athletics Championships** would weaken the position of the Olympics movement as the acme of athletics perform-ance. That would be a problem for Seoul and the other in-heritors of the Olympic movement after 1984. Not for Bruce Cohn.

On his appointment in late 1979 Cohn had first met the formal leaders of world sport – the Spiritualists, the Ancients, and the Timeservers – but he had since become aware of one further tiny but important sub-group. This was the Chosen, a small knot of men who stood above the day-to-day affairs of sport and who could at a moment's notice return to a secure life outside. This group was typified by IOC chairman Maurice Delgado. Men like Delgado possessed a cool certainty of their moral strength; this, combined with the knowledge that they could simply turn their backs on world sport and return to pillared mansions, gave them a special authority.

The Cohn classification system helped him achieve some sense of reality in a confused world, but one which, like the world of the joggers outside, was at its core simply about human achievement. Cohn was in the business of helping the world's greatest athletes show their best paces before over two billion people. And that it was a business he had not the slightest doubt.

From the beginning the good citizens of Los Angeles, aware of the monstrous debts piled up by Mayor Drapeau ('we will just keep the tap running till the tub is full') in Montreal eight years before, had been cool about hosting the Olympics. Over sixty-five per cent had voted against the use of public funds for the Games, although a similar percentage had approved in principle of the Los Angeles Olympics. Early estimates had indicated that, without State or Federal help, the Games would result in a deficit of anything up to 336.5 million dollars. In 1978, Los Angeles Mayor Bradley therefore submitted proposals to the IOC for a 'spartan' Olympics, with total control of finance passing to the Los Angeles Organising Committee. This proved unacceptable, particularly as Bradley had added insult to injury by telling the aristocrats of the IOC that they could say goodbye to the free meals and hotel rooms that had cost the Montreal authorities over 23 million dollars.

Bradley and his Olympic liaison officer Anton Calleia and attorney John C. Andru soon found that they were fighting on two fronts, for on their flanks they were assailed by the US Olympic Committee and individual national sports federations, battling for the most expensive Olympic facilities they could secure.

The IOC, who had no immediate 1984 alternative to Los Angeles, had first tried to bluff their way out of it. Los Angeles would have to change the financial terms of its bid or withdraw. Indeed, it was darkly hinted, Montreal and Mexico City were again waiting eagerly in the wings.

By May 1978 Los Angeles's position looked bleak. Then, suddenly, the IOC caved in. At a meeting in Athens the 1984 Games were provisionally awarded to the city, with an IOC order that the award would be withdrawn unless Los Angeles signed an agreement 'to accept complete financial responsibility for the organisation of the Games' and IOC control over the money spent. Mayor Bradley agreed, on the condition that the city could secure some kind of insurance policy protecting it against financial loss.

Bradley was not surprised to find that no such insurance policy was obtainable. His next step was to press the IOC to negotiate with a private consortium of businessmen, thus taking the city officially out of the picture. On 15 June 1978 papers were filed incorporating a private, non-profit making Los Angeles Olympic Organising Committee. Bradley spent a month trying to get the IOC to bend its rules by allowing the consortium, rather than the city, to take on financial responsibility for the Games; but the IOC would not budge, and Bradley sadly recommended to his city council that it withdraw its bid. Then suddenly the IOC wilted once more, and within a month agreement was reached. One contract was signed between the city of Los Angeles and the IOC which freed the city from all financial responsibility for any deficits incurred. A second was signed between the US Olympic Committee and the Los

141

Angeles Olympic Committee dividing the responsibility between the USOC and the local group.

The next battle was between the consortium and the USOC, who reasoned that since they were assuming part of the risk they should have an even representation on the local committees. Faced with a fifty per cent loading of the Living Dead on their committees, the consortium dug in its heels and the struggle lingered on into early 1979. Then the IOC stepped in, warning that if no agreement were reached by 1 March they would reopen bidding on the Games. The two groups came to an agreement and beat the deadline by a single day.

The Olympic Games had been secured, but the troubles of Cohn and his newly appointed colleagues were just beginning. The Los Angeles Games were going to be a watershed in the Olympic movement in that they were going to be the first Spartan Olympics. For the first time in the modern era a Games was going to be in the black. This meant that, where possible, existing stadia, such as the Los Angeles Coliseum, were to be refurbished and used, and where new facilities had to be created they were to be constructed with only the basic technical amenities. Big business was ransacked for top executives willing to work for minimal salaries as commissioners of individual sports, under Peter Uberroth, and his technical director Bruce Cohn.

Cohn had started out with high hopes, but they were soon dashed. The original estimate for the refurbishment of the Coliseum had been a modest 4 million dollars; by 1980 it had risen to 60 million. Similarly, the initial security bill, using ten per cent of the Los Angeles police force, had come to less than 2 million dollars; by early 1981 this estimate had risen to 22 million dollars, was still rising, and would probably be over 70 million. The original estimate for a basic velodrome for the cycling events had been 500,000 dollars: this had now ballooned to 9 million. Estimates of 1 million for an archery range; 27 million for shooting and yachting facilities; 20 million for a new swimming stadium and 15.3 million for a rowing course had followed in swift succession.

There had been two immediate avenues of escape: big business and Congress. Unfortunately, though Congress would undoubtedly help out (had the USOC not loyally supported the President at the time of the Afghanistan crisis?) the machinery of government ground slow and would leave little time for actual construction of facilities. It was, therefore, to big business that Cohn and his colleagues turned for immediate short-term aid and Sam, the Animated Eagle, the Games' mascot, was asked to cast its shadow over America's largest corporations.

The Golden Eagle spread his wings and the Southland Corporation agreed to fund the velodrome; then McDonalds Hamburgers chipped in with the swimming pool at UCLA. After that Sam blew high and proud as Coca-Cola, the United California Bank, Anheuser-Busch and United Airlines became sponsors, and a 225 million dollar television contract was agreed with ABC Television. Soon sponsors were even found for Stael and Kramm's beloved artistic and cultural exhibitions. True, there were problems with the proposed minting of Olympic commemorative coins, but with the necessary lubrication the required bill would soon pass through Congress, thus releasing another 200 million dollars. Everything seemed at last to be going smoothly.

Then the previous morning had come the bombshell, the telex from Berne announcing the launch of the Arab Olympics in Kudai. At first the hastily convened Los Angeles Organising Committee, suspecting some gigantic hoax, had refused to believe it, and Cohn was instructed to check back with Reuters. The news agency responded by forwarding early that afternoon a verbatim account of the press conference of the day before.

The Reuters report had been rushed to the Committee's lawyers to check what restraints could be applied to the Kudai enterprise. The first telephone response by Alvin Klein, their legal advisor, had not been good. The athletes were free agents, though the moment they signed formal contracts with WAPA they automatically lost amateur status and forfeited any right to compete in Olympic athletics. Still, with the money on offer and the freedom to negotiate advertising contracts, most of the sportsmen would not be too troubled.

There was also the possibility, Klein pointed out, of having national associations put pressure on sports arena owners to deny WAPA use of facilities for the preliminary meets. However, most nations would consider such an act to be in restraint of trade and would be worried by the likelihood of hefty legal suits.

Another non-legal option, to avoid a direct clash of dates, was simply to switch the Olympics forward into August. But ABC Television would have none of it, since the schedules were fixed, immutable. And in any case, the ABC executives asked, what would be beamed to the American public in prime time other than an endless succession of Communist victories? If they had wanted to film a Spartakiade they wouldn't have put up 225 million dollars for it. Cohn had scribbled Klein's suggestion on a blank pad headed 'options' with a heavy heart.

Klein's final proposal was crisp and simplistic. 'Get Berne and his track boys to change the goddam amateur rules,' he said. 'Let 'em all take cash for the WAPA preliminary meets from 1983 to 1984 and keep their precious virginity. That gives you breathing space, time to make some sort of a deal with them before '84. If that fails, get Delgado to buy them off.'

Klein had done well from the top of his head in what had been a frantic afternoon, but Cohn dreaded facing the Committee later that day. For Bruce Cohn had ambitions far beyond the Olympics. Ronnie Reagan had made it from sportscasting to *King's Row*, then on to Governor of California and finally to the White House. Riding on a successful Olympics, Cohn knew that he might well take the Republican ticket for Governor. But on a Palookaville Games Bruce Cohn would not secure the nomination for town dog-catcher.

Cohn again looked out of his window at the joggers and wished he were out there with them in their simple world of sweating, shuffling effort. Then it came to him. He would sell off the Olympic torch relay across the States to the joggers at five thousand dollars a mile, perhaps more. He checked on his calculator; over fifteen million dollars. For a brief moment all thoughts of Murdoch, Berne, Delgado and Kudai vanished.

Monday, 1 November 1982

Kutyenko's meeting with Igor Lysenko had troubled him. True, there had always been a KGB influence in Russian national teams, usually in the form of 'masseurs' or 'coaches' who had no knowledge of either of those disciplines. But there the KGB had performed a different role, that of detecting or preventing defections and of protecting the team from the Western media.

This was not a simple sports problem. The Kudai Games had been sponsored by a nation in a sensitive area, one where recent Russian policy had been a dismal failure. Kutyenko had discussed Kudai with his department head Viktor Sherbakov, and had been surprised to find that Sherbakov already had a grasp of the problem, a sure indication that it had been discussed at a much higher level.

Sherbakov had brought new light to the issue. The Government still felt bruised, he said: hurt by the boycott by Western nations of the Moscow Olympics. The 1984 Los Angeles policy was going to be to let the Americans dangle until at least mid-1984. 'Twist in the wind' was how Sherbakov had put it.

Certainly, the Kudai Games would weaken Government Olympic policy for they would, in effect, be menacing an already crippled Games. And when Russia finally decided to compete after protracted wrangling about visas, security of the Russian team, cost of accommodation and the rest, they wanted to compete against a full-strength American team, not a handful of college boys left over after the stampede to Kudai. The Los

Angeles Olympic team were, as Sherbakov put it, 'part of the class struggle'.

So the Kudai Games had to be stopped, but quietly. Kutyenko's next meeting with Lysenko resulted in two parallel courses of action. The first, which he did not discuss with Lysenko, was to have a London attaché put Murdoch under regular surveillance, meanwhile compiling a detailed dossier on the Scot. Thus, if the time came to take more serious action, they would know Murdoch's strengths and weaknesses.

The second related to Lysenko himself. A deal must be tendered. Lysenko could himself offer it. After all, said Kutyenko, smiling, Igor and Murdoch had been 'brothers in sport'. Lysenko's face had not registered any feelings of brotherhood. Of course, Lysenko could not go into any such discussion empty-handed; there had to be something on offer. Igor Lysenko had felt relieved when he had heard the menu.

Claud Farrell Junior had been watching the Los Angeles Rams on Channel 4 when the call from Butch Pendleton in Washington had come. Growling, he had flicked on the video tape-recorder before levering himself to his feet.

He had listened for five minutes, nodding and grunting into the telephone. At six feet three inches and 230 pounds Claud Farrell was only twenty pounds lighter than when he had been 'cut' by the Rams at pre-season camp back in 1973. At the time it had been the worst moment of his life. Since then he had often reflected that work for the Company was considerably safer than facing the hulks of the NFL, which might otherwise have been his regular Sunday fate.

At least what Pendleton was proposing was about sport rather than trailing some Russki attaché or checking out the political background of some Greenham Common witch in order to 'leak' it to the British press.

Two days later the thin dossier on Murdoch had arrived. Farrell had reflected that the Scot had seemed to be his kind of guy. He had surveyed a photograph supplied of Murdoch

146

dressed in tracksuit with some interest. The Scot looked like a
quarterback, perhaps a running back. Certainly, Claud Farrell
might have to do a little blocking if the KGB were on Murdoch's
ass. He looked forward to the prospect.

Friday, 29 October 1982

Dr Caspar Goldstein opened the file on the bedroom table
and smiled. Even his secretary did not know his whereabouts.
He had hired a car in Los Angeles and driven here to the
Lucky Strike Motel in San Diego early that morning. Despite
himself, he felt like the head of some crime syndicate in an old
Hollywood B movie.

Claud Atkins was the first to speak, looking uneasily around
him at the other five athletes assembled in the motel bedroom.
Carl Luther, world leader in shot; Ben Gray, who had in 1981
run within a tenth of a second of Lee Evans's world 400 metre
best; Bill Ferris, closing fast on Daley Thompson's world
decathlon record; Sherry Clay, the fastest female sprinter
in the West; and Billy Salo, the best marathon runner of all
time.

'I think you have the picture, Doc,' Atkins said. 'From our
meeting at Santa Barbara two weeks back.'

'And what is the size of your little . . . consortium now – no
need to mention names?' said Goldstein, leafing through the
file on the table.

'We have five more, in men's and women's discus, men's
high hurdles, hammer and women's 800 metres.'

'And the total sum?'

'An immediate consultancy fee of fifty thousand dollars,
with a twenty-five per cent cut from everything we win in 1983
and 1984.'

'And how much could that be?'

'Impossible to say.' It was the massive Carl Luther, 260
pounds of muscle and bone, his bulk engulfing the light
wooden bedside chair on which he sat.

'If we all won in Kudai that would be a maximum of ten

147

million dollars, plus what we win in the lead-up meets,' said Atkins.

'And what would be my exact role?'

'To act as medical consultant to the consortium,' said Atkins.

'Why don't you cut the crap, Claud?' snorted Luther. 'The Doc's job is to get us the stuff.'

'The stuff?' said Goldstein.

'You've seen the reports, Doc. This guy Murdoch has the whole drug scene tied up tight. He says he can pick up steroids a year back! Take them away and that's two metres off my shot-put.'

'And three hundred points off an eight thousand seven hundred decathlon,' said Ferris, perched uneasily on the side of the room's single bed.

'The Doc knows the score,' said Atkins. 'I shot him the whole scene back in Santa Barbara. He wouldn't be here if he wasn't interested.'

Goldstein looked down at the file in front of him. 'Since speaking to Claud here I have been preparing a document which surveys the drugs scene, or at least as much as we know of it in the West. There's no doubt about it: the East Germans have the most advanced illegal drug programme in sport. Since the detection of Ilona Slupianek back in 1978 they have not been detected in a single drug infringement.'

'That don't mean they haven't been as high as kites,' growled Billy Salo.

'Indeed,' agreed Goldstein. 'The problem is that Mr Murdoch has the advantage of an East European sports medicine expert in Dr Schmidt. Now, if any athlete competing in the Kudai Games pursues the conventional drug options Schmidt will pick them up easily in his tests.'

Goldstein looked down at his file. 'As I see it there are two main areas. The first is in training and relates to anabolic steroids, which enable high training rates in every event, as well as helping produce muscle bulk in the throwers. My aim will be to find an alternative and legal drug producing the same results.'

'Testosterone?' asked Ben Gray.

'No,' said Goldstein, frowning. 'There are considerable contraindications, including cancer, with that. There's also some indication that the IOC will try to ban it by '84. My staff are at present working with two substances, one of which, a pollen derivative, looks like a strong possibility as an alternative to the anabolics.'

'So you think you can come up with something good?' said Luther.

'I'm quite certain, Mr Luther,' replied Goldstein.

There were sidelong glances and smiles. If a training drug could be secured then their main problem had been resolved.

Goldstein leafed through his file, then lifted it towards him. 'Now to short-range performance drugs,' he said, 'which even the IAAF have managed to control. Ladies and gentlemen, I think that it is in this area that I have recently made the biggest breakthrough: ATP.'

'ATP?' queried Atkins.

'Adenosine triphosphate,' said Goldstein. 'The very stuff of muscular contraction itself. My experiments indicate that an intra-muscular injection of ATP can produce an immediate two per cent improvement in contractile power.'

'And it's undetectable?' said Salo.

'Naturally,' said Goldstein, 'since it is already a natural part of the process of muscular contraction.'

He leafed through his file. 'Then there is the matter of vasodilators. This is of particular interest to the endurance events ensuring, as it does, greater blood supply to the working muscles. We have been experimenting with an as yet unnamed derivative of peyote, which has great possibilities. This is not yet on the IAAF list of proscribed drugs and is therefore unlikely to be on Mr Murdoch's lists.'

He thumbed further through his file until he came to the final pages. 'Finally,' he said, 'we have *el dopa*, much used as a pre-performance relaxant by dancers and musicians. Again, this is not yet on the IAAF list of banned drugs, though it is almost certainly already being used by the East Germans.'

'Sounds as if you've been burning the midnight oil, Doc,' said Atkins.

Goldstein placed the file in his briefcase which he locked securely. 'This survey,' he said, 'is the result of twenty years of research, most of it, admittedly, in areas quite unrelated to sport. When you first came to me it became clear that much of my work already had a direct application to your needs, though it had never been applied in any practical sense within sport.'

'So you're with us, Doc?' said Luther.

'Not yet,' said Goldstein, frowning. 'For what I have done so far the fee is five thousand dollars. If we don't reach an acceptable agreement on our future relationship then when I walk out of that door that's the end of it.'

'So just what are you trying to say?' said Atkins.

'Simply this. The service I would provide would probably not be technically illegal, since it would not involve attempting to help you to succeed fraudulently by using banned drugs. But any discovery of my activities would not be good for me – in the professional sense. I therefore require from you some insurance.'

'Insurance?' pursued Atkins.

'Either a bigger basic consultancy fee – say 250,000 dollars – or a bigger slice of your winnings.'

'How big?' asked Gray, suspiciously.

'Say forty per cent. For that sum you get a complete sports medicine service, treatment of injuries, nutritional advice, psychotherapy, the whole works. You keep all of your money on books, endorsements and the rest.'

'Thanks a million,' said Luther, morosely.

Goldstein stood up. 'Ladies and gentlemen,' he said. 'Don't be too greedy. For years you have been receiving coaching and medical advice for peanuts. And remember, when you pay peanuts you get monkeys. If you're going to be real pros then you've got to act like pros in buying in professional advice. Look at Navratilova or Borg. They pay big money to their coaches but they get the results.'

150

He laid down his briefcase. 'You can't lose. Look at it this way. Forty per cent of nothing is no good to me. Your little consortium of ten will have the best pharmaceutical advice that the world of Western medicine can offer. In my area, I'm a gold medallist. If it's to be a battle of doctors in Kudai, then I'm going to come out top.'

He turned, nodded to Atkins and closed the door behind him.

10

Sparrow Flies In

Monday, 1 November 1982

Murdoch disengaged his ear-mufflers and reeled in Ellis Payne's target. He and Ellis stood in the basement of the Regent Street Polytechnic, in the slim corridor of its pistol range. He ripped the target from its holder.

'Ninety-six,' he said, giving her the punctured card. 'Not bad for your third attempt.'

'But not good enough,' she said. 'You had a ninety-eight.'

Murdoch grinned. 'Beginner's luck.'

They walked over to the drinks machine which stood behind two chairs and a table at the back of the range.

'Coke?' he asked.

She nodded. He inserted the necessary coins and heard the thud as two cans were delivered. Murdoch opened them and handed Ellis hers. They sat down facing each other at the table.

Ellis sipped her drink. 'I've been checking the press. Your athletes are pouring in,' she said. 'Kudai is on its way.'

Murdoch nodded, reaching down on the floor for their tracksuit tops. 'We got great coverage. But the press were in a cleft stick,' he said. 'They've been pushing for open sport for years. Now it's come and they find that they're not quite certain.' He threw her track-top to her across the table.

'The devil they know,' smiled Ellis.

'Exactly,' said Murdoch. 'They may not have much love for Berne and his little mafia, but they've got used to them.'

152

'And now they've got you?'

Murdoch smiled. 'Yes, and it's as if somebody has redrawn the map of the world for them. At first they weren't sure it was all for real, but most of Fleet Street has been out to Kudai checking it out. So in a few weeks their whole world of sport has been rewritten.'

'They don't like change,' said Ellis. 'But then I suppose nobody does.'

'If they all liked change we wouldn't be down here,' he said. 'Playing toy soldiers. But Sparrow thought I should freshen up on my marksmanship. Just in case Mr Ciano starts to get serious.'

She looked at him apprehensively. 'Did you . . . ever see any action, when you were in the army?'

He shook his head. 'No,' he said. 'What you really mean, Ellis, is – did I ever shoot at anyone? The answer's the same. You often forget, when in the army, that you're there to kill people. Call it national defence, call it whatever you like, but that's what you're being trained for.'

'Do you think you could?' she asked.

'I saw a John Wayne western once,' he said. 'The Wayne character answered that question by saying, "You've got to be willing." I'm not sure. There's only one place to find out and there won't be much time to think about it if it does happen.'

She returned to sipping her drink. Murdoch felt that the silence was a platform for something she had to say, and waited.

'Murdoch,' she said. 'Can I ask you something?'

'Fire away.'

'Why are you in this Kudai business? You don't need the money, do you?'

'No, not really. I suppose because I've been asked to do it. And because I think it's got to be done.'

'But not necessarily by you,' she replied, her voice gaining strength. 'Hassan's petrodollars have a power all their own. And there's Grieve, Buchinski, Quince – they could carry it off without you.'

Murdoch pulled on his nose. 'The only way I can answer you, Ellis, is to say what sport means to me. Grieve used to call it the One Truth. The two of us used to pound up a sandhill down in Wales at Merthyr Mawr back in 1971. It was a killer – we called it the Big Dipper. He would end up flat on his face at the top of the hill, sweat drowning him, completely wiped out. He'd look up and say to me, "Murdoch, you can run this hill faster than me, but you sure as hell can't try any harder." Sport is about giving everything you've got, he'd say: will, muscle, soul. And more than that – commitment – effort – honesty.'

'Honesty. That's the key word as far as you're concerned, isn't it?'

'That's the only word,' he replied . 'Without honesty sport is a farce. Sport's something *we* made up. After all, we created the rules. It's a test of what we are and what we can make of ourselves through will and muscle. When we break the rules we destroy the essence of what we've created.'

'And you're going to be the Sir Galahad on the white horse who's going to clean it all up?' There was a fleck of sarcasm in her voice.

'No,' he replied. 'I'm just the one who's going to try.'

'I agree with everything you say. But can it work out there, in the real world? Think of those living steroids playing football in the Superbowl, those hulks they call women that put the shot and throw the discus for Russia. It's not sport, it's something else, don't ask me what. And at two million dollars an event some of those people will spike their own grandmothers.'

She stood up and moved to another machine at the side of the drinks dispenser. 'Potato chips?'

He shook his head. 'You think I'm too much of an idealist?'

She inserted some coins and withdrew a packet from the machine.

'It's not that, but it sure isn't a bunch of God-fearing athletes on one side and a bunch of dumb Olympic officials on the other.' She returned to her seat. 'Some of these precious athletes of yours have taken so many needles they can't find the freckles to put them in any more. And you're offering a million dollars a shot . . .'

'Look,' he said. 'I know just what you're thinking. God, I've spent nights tossing and turning thinking about it. But this can be the breakthrough, the chance for the athletes to be honest. Our drug-tests are foolproof, I really believe that. That means the athletes have no chance of faking. I'm *making* them honest, Ellis.'

She shook her head as she poured some crisps into her right hand. 'No, you can't *make* them honest. Those guys have been lying for too long. Now they've got doctors and agents to help them to lie and cheat, that's all.' She sighed and sat back in her chair. 'I just feel you don't *need* this Kudai business. You've got your agency, you've got the film. Isn't that enough? Hell, *nobody* wants you to do it – the East, the West, every national governing body –'

'You missed out the Vatican and the Ku Klux Klan,' he interrupted brusquely.

'If they had teams at Los Angeles they'd be against you too,' she said, smiling.

'Thanks for the vote of confidence.'

'It's nothing to do with confidence. You've cracked it already,' she said. 'You've already shown you can do it. You've got the meet promoters, you've got the athletes. If all you wanted to do was to beat those Olympic bozos then you'll have done it by the end of next summer. Their World Track Championships in Helsinki will be a shambles.'

'So what's your advice?'

'Get out while you're ahead. In the spring of '83. By that time we'll be into casting the film: we'll need your help for that, with your knowledge of track and field. There's a lot to be done.'

'No,' he said. 'I'm going to see it through.'

'Then it's because there's more to it than the Arab Olympics. This guy Berne, you got something against him? What did he ever do to you?'

'Berne?' he said. 'Nothing. Just that he killed me.'

Ellis's eyebrows rose in exaggerated surprise. 'Killed you?

Then who the hell am I speaking to? Not your astral body again?'

Murdoch's face relaxed. 'You clown,' he said. 'I was speaking metaphorically.'

'I thought you might be.'

They laughed, the sound filling the hollowness of the range.

Murdoch's face became serious again. 'It seems like ancient history now. Probably sounds trivial to you.'

'Try me,' she said, dipping into her bag of crisps. 'I've got the time.'

'It was back in 1972, when Grieve and I were getting ready for the Munich Olympics.'

'In decathlon?'

'Yes. Everything was going great. I'd broken eight thousand points twice and by the middle of June I was set for a medal. Then, a week later, I twanged a hamstring. Grieve and I thought that I had done more than enough to make the Olympic team without doing any more. All I needed was time for the leg to heal, then a little light training and on to Munich.'

Ellis's mouth puckered. 'Don't tell me,' she said. 'They wouldn't let you.'

'You mean Berne wouldn't let me,' growled Murdoch. 'He said that it was a committee decision.'

'So what happened?'

'A trial decathlon against a French B team only three weeks before the Games. It nearly finished me.'

'But you still made Munich.'

'Yes, I made it, but I had nothing left. No sharpness, no reserve. I should have been pushing for gold. Instead, I ended up struggling for bronze.'

'So Berne killed you.' She lobbed her empty can neatly into the litter bin, then placed both hands on the table, her face inches away from his.

'But this is 1982, Murdoch. Munich's a world away. It's over and done with. Getting back at Berne, lousing up his 1983 World Championships – that's no reason for ploughing on with Kudai.'

Murdoch held her gaze. 'Ellis,' he said. 'Do you really think that I would do that just to get even with someone? No, there's only one reason, and that's because it's worth doing, because it's a chance for a clean start.'

'And what about your Prince Hassan?' Ellis continued. 'Have you ever asked – what are he and his Arab buddies getting out of it?'

'That's a good point,' Murdoch said. 'I'd like to believe that Hassan has the same beliefs as I have.' He shrugged. 'Or perhaps it's just an Arab macho exercise, and that's the end of it. They show the world who they are. Good PR.'

'But not for you.'

'No, Ellis, not for me.'

Their discussion was interrupted by the buzz of the wall telephone to the left of the drinks dispenser. Murdoch picked it up. He listened for a moment before nodding into the telephone.

'Tell him to make it one o'clock.' He put down the telephone and turned to face Ellis. 'Well,' he said, 'it's lunch up at Camden Lock. With Birdie Sparrow.'

Birdie Sparrow looked out through the windows of Le Routier on to the oily winter waters of the canal, then glanced around him at the crowded restaurant. No question of it, his life had undergone a sea-change since he had linked up full-time with Murdoch and his strange entourage. Le Routier buzzed with the chatter of the bright New People, the executives of TV-am, Britain's first commercial breakfast television station soon to open in February 1983. On the other side of the muddy lock stood TV-am's bizarre studios, surrounded by a fretwork of scaffolding and alive with the buzz of drills. The atmosphere of the restaurant was heavy with the smell of impending success, the uneasy bonhomie of lunches paid for by other people.

At that moment Murdoch and Ellis entered the restaurant. As he watched them weave their way through the crowded room Sparrow reflected that it had not been so long ago that

Ellis had been a prime suspect in the cocaine affair. Still, Murdoch was the boss; he hoped that it had not been a case of heart over head.

Good posture, he thought, as Ellis approached him, smiling. Walks tall, like someone who knows what she's at, who she is. A formidable young lady.

He stood as they approached the table. Ellis was introduced to him and they shook hands.

'I've ordered the wine,' he said. 'Perrier '81.'

'A good year for water,' said Ellis.

'One of the best,' said Sparrow, pouring the icy drink into their glasses. 'To success,' he said, and the three of them touched glasses.

He picked up the menu, a handwritten affair covered in a plastic envelope.

'You'll have to help me here, Ellis,' said Sparrow. 'Deep fried camembert with gooseberry jam. Stuffed mushrooms . . . and that's just for starters.'

Ellis looked across at Murdoch. 'All depends on whether or not you want to eat like a bird, Mr Sparrow.'

'I'm on a seafood diet, Ellis,' he said. 'Every time I see food I eat it.'

Murdoch looked up from scrutinising his menu and gave a mock grin. As he faced Sparrow across the table it was clear to him that 'Birdie', just returned from Los Angeles, was revelling in his news. It was not long before the ex-policeman began to unveil the story of his visit.

'Your Mr Berbick, Ellis,' he said. 'He sees himself as another Bernstein – the writer, not the conductor,' he added, smiling. He looked up as a waiter hovered above him, having taken Ellis's and Murdoch's order.

'I think I'll live dangerously,' he said. 'The fried camembert and gooseberry jam to begin with.' He laid down his menu. 'Berbick thinks he's on to the biggest story since Watergate. He needed a lot of encouragement to tell me what I've brought back on Ciano.'

'How much encouragement?' queried Murdoch.

'You told me money was no problem,' grinned Sparrow. 'Five thousand dollars.'

'Petty cash,' said Murdoch. 'Now – what does it buy us?'

'Berbick had been looking into something quite different at the start,' Sparrow began. 'Complaints about malpractices in Los Angeles hospitals. Surgeons botching jobs, leaving apparatus inside their patients . . .'

'People coming in with one disease and leaving with another,' said Murdoch.

'Seems as if they could take their choice,' said Sparrow wryly. 'As with many such investigations, what started as a routine job suddenly changed its direction and took young Berbick into another world altogether.'

The turning point had been a meeting with Dr Paul Kahn, Sparrow said, a surgeon friend of Berbick's from college days. His purpose in seeing Kahn had been to establish the ground rules in his investigations, although his former friend had been strangely evasive about arranging a place to meet.

Eventually they settled on the bar at the Beverly Wilshire Hotel. When Berbick actually saw Kahn he had been shocked. The surgeon had been emaciated and incoherent, and had looked ten years older than his thirty-one years. Kahn had been a full fifty pounds lighter than when Berbick had first known him as a carefree sophomore with a passion for touch football. All that remained was a 120-pound shell. That evening Wayne Berbick had driven a drunken Kahn back to his 300,000-dollar home on Sunset and Vine.

What he had found there had shocked him to the core. For Kahn's palatial home was a shambles, and at its centre the once pretty Nancy Kahn was, like her husband, a shrivelled wreck. Nancy Kahn had explained that she and her husband had started on coke ('a little sniff on your hand') two years before at a hospital party. There they had merely been two of the five thousand neophytes in the United States who daily gained a cheap and pleasant introduction to the drug.

Berbick had made an impromptu meal for the Kahns while they had stumbled through their story.

The source of the Kahns' supply of cocaine had been a grateful patient, a Los Angeles businessman who had snapped an Achilles tendon during a ten-kilometre road-race. Kahn had taken easily to the stocky little man, no natural athlete, but who had, by sheer grit and determination, become competent in a wide range of sports. He had therefore made regular visits to his patient's palatial Beverly Hills home to advise him on a series of progressive post-operative exercises.

Kahn's diligence had been rewarded by his patient's complete recovery, and within months of the operation Tony Ciano was padding gently round a specially constructed two-hundred-metre-long path of brown peat which he had created in his grounds. Two months later Ciano again competed in a Riverside ten-kilometre race and ran a personal best of forty-two minutes thirty seconds. On the day following the race a set of golden coke spoons was delivered to the Kahns' home by a deferential, blond-haired young man – together with ten grams of cocaine.

Thereafter the path downhill had been slow but inexorable. By the end of 1980 the Kahns were up to five grams a week at 750 dollars a time, but still well within the range of Paul Kahn's 160,000 dollars a year salary. Then came 'free-basing', the ultimate high – and the most expensive, because of the amounts of cocaine used.

This involved the 'freezing' of the pure cocaine by dissolving it and adding sodium hydroxide and ether or baking soda. Half a gram of the precipitate was then filtered and dried. Next, the cocaine was 'smoked' from a small glass water-pipe which had been filled with rum or water, using a small butane torch. The vapour inhaled, said Nancy, gave a jolt far beyond orgasm.

The sole source of the Kahns' supply had been the ever-genial Tony Ciano, though they never dealt with him direct but rather with one of Ciano's acolytes, the blond laconic blue-eyed young man. At first there had been few problems, even on free-basing, but the Kahns sought coke of ever-higher quality at steadily increasing prices. The blue-eyed young man had been efficient and remorseless. By early 1982, their habit was costing them five thousand dollars a week. Ciano had melted into the background and the Kahns had burrowed deep into their savings. Then, in March 1982, Paul Kahn had only narrowly avoided a legal suit following his conduct of a simple hernia operation. The engulfing protective cloak of the St Thomas's Hospital administration had been thrown around him and he had been given a year's sabbatical, on condition that he and Nancy undertook a drug therapy programme.

Throughout the winter of 1982 they had attended Dr Segar's therapy clinics in downtown Los Angeles, had cried and crawled about the floor with the other ten addicts on the course, begging Segar for a sniff. But for them Segar's methods had not worked and by January they were again deep in the mire of cocaine addiction. By the end of February insurances, jewellery, furniture – everything saleable – had gone and they had re-mortgaged their home. And it was at that point that Wayne Berbick had come upon Kahn.

Berbick had at first been consumed with righteous indignation, that a man of Kahn's calibre could be brought to such a condition. For the journalist had never before come in contact with the effects of drugs upon someone of his own class and background. He reflected upon his personal experience of cocaine, the same first relaxed, social 'sniff', though for him there had been no follow-up, no addiction.

When his anger had subsided, his journalistic instincts had taken over. There was a big story here, if only he could stay cool, though his editor Lou Black was less than enthusiastic. He had seen too many bushy-tailed journalists vanish into the mire of drug investigations. He had therefore assigned another *Post* investigative reporter, Gus Morales, to the case, to work in tandem with Berbick. A fortnight later Morales had been found, badly beaten, in a Riverside parking lot. It was only then that the *Post* had put its full weight behind Berbick.

Tony Ciano, Berbick soon discovered, was not by any means the biggest wheel in the United States twenty-five billion dollar cocaine business, but he was certainly in the superleague class, slipping at least a ton of the forty-five tons a year which eluded local and federal investigators.

Berbick had pursued Ciano with fervour but with caution: with two billion dollars a year at stake Ciano was not going to be troubled about the death of an investigating reporter. Berbick's big breakthrough was the discovery of the sites of Ciano's bases in Bolivia and Peru, countries in which almost one fifth of their national product came from the sale of cocaine. The American had legitimate businesses in both countries, dealing in the sale of grain.

'Let's stop there for the moment,' said Murdoch. 'Okay, so Berbick is on Ciano's trail. But how does this help us, if he keeps it all to himself?'

Sparrow nodded, waving away cigarette smoke from a nearby table with a scowl. 'Fair point,' he said. 'But I hadn't finished. Berbick tells me that he thinks that Ciano's big drug push is going to be in '84 – Olympic year. Something really big, based on the Games.'

'But he didn't tell you what or how,' interjected Ellis, as the sweet trolley arrived. She surveyed the trolley. 'Let me guess what you'd like, Mr Sparrow,' she said, surveying him. 'You look like a Black Forest gâteau man to me.'

Sparrow raised both hands. 'ESP,' he said. 'Right first time.'

Murdoch exploded in mock-rage. 'Ellis, Birdie's just about to crack the Ciano problem and all you seem to care about is what he wants for pudding.'

'Dessert,' she corrected him.

'Pudding, dessert, who cares?'

Ellis and Sparrow exchanged glances across the table and burst into laughter.

'Two Black Forests,' said Ellis. 'What about you, Murdoch?'

Murdoch's face was resigned. 'All right. I'll have the same.'

Sparrow leant across the table, his voice lowered. 'Our Mr Berbick,' he said, 'isn't exactly Mother Theresa.'

'So?'

'So, put him on our payroll. We need someone good on our press team.'

162

Murdoch smiled as three great wedges of gâteau arrived. He shook his head and looked down at his plate. 'At least three hundred calories,' he groaned. 'How much to burn this off?'

Ellis and Sparrow's responses were simultaneous.

'Three miles,' said Sparrow.

'Two hours,' said Ellis.

Sparrow dug his spoon deep into his gâteau. 'I don't think we're talking about the same activity,' he said, smiling.

Claud Farrell had also tried the fried camembert with the gooseberry jam and had been surprised to find he had enjoyed it. At least, he reflected, Murdoch seemed to live in some style, a small recompense for his long hours of surveillance. He looked around the hot, crowded restaurant, beads of sweat beginning to form on the cheeks of his phlegmatic black face. The moustached man was still talking animatedly to Murdoch and his female friend. Farrell's eyes returned to the menu, and he frowned. What the hell was spotted dick?

11

Weighty Matters

Wednesday, 3 November 1982

Maurice Delgado was unhappy. His presence at the Heathrow Holiday Inn was at the request of Bruce Cohn, though Delgado would have preferred more time to consider the Kudai position. Cohn had been insistent, however, for in his view the future of the entire Olympic movement was now at stake.

This opinion was confirmed by a telephone call to Delgado from the director of the 1988 Olympics in Seoul, South Korea, and the IOC secretary had hurriedly convened a meeting of all interested parties. On his left were the officials of the International Gymnastics Federation, the German, Klaus Ritter, and the Canadian, Thelma Banks, and Harold Berne and Vera Goldberg representing track and field athletics. On his right sat Cohn, his aide Alvin Smith, Arthur Son, an official of the South Korean Olympic Committee, and Bill Dodge and Karen White of the International Swimming Federation.

'Ladies and gentlemen,' Delgado said. 'This is an ad hoc, unofficial meeting. It has no status relative to the IOC or, for that matter, relative to your individual governing bodies. I would therefore ask that what is discussed here be kept strictly confidential – '

'I think that you may be taking too much upon yourself, Mr Delgado,' blurted Smith, a young, tanned American official only ten years away from two gold medals in the 1972 Munich Olympic pool. 'My Association has been much disturbed by the announcement of the Arab Olympics. We came here in response to your call in the belief that this was some sort of formal gathering from which a serious statement of intent might be made. We didn't fly all the way from Illinois to come to some sort of Masonic meeting.'

Delgado flushed. He was not used to his authority being questioned. 'Perhaps,' he said, choosing his words with care, 'I did not express myself as well as I might have. It is only a matter of weeks since the announcement of the Kudai Games. During that time our investigators have been checking the credentials of Mr Murdoch and his associates, simply to verify their credibility. My information is that there is no doubt that the facilities, the finance and the necessary competitive infra-structure are there.

'As things stand, nothing prevents the holding of the Kudai Games – I will not dignify them with the name Olympics – from being held on the same dates as our own. Our meeting here, which relates only to the sports directly affected – athletics, gymnastics and swimming –'

'The core of the Olympics,' interjected Smith again.

'As you say, Mr Smith, the core of the Olympics,' continued Delgado, controlling his annoyance. 'This meeting can have no official status, since the sports represented are only a part of the Olympic programme, and since the structure of the IOC does not relate to representation from individual sports but rather to national Olympic Committees.'

'Can we cut through the crap, Maurice?' groaned Bruce Cohn, leaning forward on the brown oak table, head down. Delgado flushed.

Cohn lifted his head, his face lined with fatigue. 'We will have in 1984 the first Olympics in modern times which will make a profit. All our systems analyses show that when the Games are over Southern California will be left with some of the finest sports facilities in the world. Only unlike Munich, Montreal or Moscow *we'll* be in the black. Up till now nobody in your whole Olympic Committee ever gave a damn about who paid for the Olympics just so long as you all got your clambake once every four years. That's why the good citizens

165

of Montreal will be paying for their Olympics till somewhere into the twenty-first century.'

Delgado made to interrupt but Cohn continued, shaking his head. 'Hear me out. If this Olympics goes down the tubes then I think that you'll have trouble all the way from now on, for what's to prevent Murdoch and his merry men having another billion-dollar Games at the same time as the next Olympics? And the one after that?' He sat back in his chair with the air of a man exhausted by the incompetence of those surrounding him.

Delgado let out a long sigh, then spoke. 'Mr Cohn has summed up the position admirably, albeit in his own colourful way. In essence we have an alternative, fully professional Olympics in track and field athletics. The position in swimming and gymnastics is slightly different in that Mr Murdoch proposes to hold only events for senior swimmers and gymnasts. The swimming and gymnastic programmes are therefore probably not so seriously affected.'

'Agreed,' said Klaus Ritter in his clipped, precise accent. 'In this Mr Murdoch has anticipated changes which the IGF are already considering – that is, separate competitions for older lady gymnasts in the over-eighteen categories. However, men's gymnastics, which is essentially for mature men, *will* be affected. So I see the whole of Western men's gymnastics being devastated by the Kudai Games.'

Karen White raised her hand. 'Mr Delgado,' she said. 'The same applies in men's swimming which deals mainly with men of college age and above. I see our whole American collegiate programme being destroyed.'

Delgado's light-blue eyes settled on Harold Berne. 'Mr Berne, you have been silent up till now. What is your position in athletics?'

Harold Berne drew his hands through his shock of silvery hair. Like Delgado, he was unused to the rough and tumble of open discussion. 'A more comprehensive situation, Mr Chairman,' he said. 'If the competitive infrastructure outlined at last week's press conference really exists then the whole of

166

the Western 1983 men's track and field programme is going to be, for all practical purposes, a professional one.'

'Exactly.' It was Vera Goldberg, her lips thin and set. 'May I speak, Mr Chairman?'

Delgado nodded.

'Everyone is talking about the disadvantages of the Arab Games. What about the advantages? By taking away the professional element the Games will revert to their true nature as an amateur festival of sport.'

'Ma'am, you must be kidding!' It was Bruce Cohn. He reached below him for a thick wad of newspapers and dropped them with a flat thud on the boardroom table. 'Have any of you been reading the papers? Our athletes are going over to Murdoch in droves! They're queuing to get to Kudai and those million-dollar prizes. But what do you think will happen in Eastern Europe? They'll sit tight and keep pumping athletes into the army, the civil service and their physical education colleges. Have you any idea how much the East Germans *pay* their Olympic medallists, Miss Goldberg? What sort of world do you live in?'

Delgado raised his hands placatingly. 'Ladies and gentlemen,' he said. 'Let's try to keep the discussion at a civilised level. We have all read the newspapers and realise the crisis which we face. I would like to refer back to Mr Berne. Mr Berne, you must know Mr Murdoch and his colleagues better than any of us. What manner of men are they?'

'Troublemakers,' said Berne, sharply. 'Murdoch was prominent during his career in every group dedicated to questioning and changing the structure of British athletics. His then coach, Hugh Grieve, who has joined him in the present venture, in 1976 formed a coaches' association which became the breeding ground for every malcontent in the sport.'

Delgado placed his hands on the table in front of him, palms down. 'Ladies and gentlemen,' he said. 'It appears that the Olympic movement faces a formidable, well-financed and possibly unscrupulous adversary. The question is – what can we do?'

He pursed his lips. 'Our first option, as I see it, is simply to go ahead with our Olympic preparations in the hope that the 1983 Kudai season proves to be a damp squib. If, however, it is successful, then we undoubtedly face the prospect of a diminished 1984 Olympics.

'The second option is to bring into being swift changes in the amateur rules, so that between now and 1984 athletes, swimmers and gymnasts could profit directly from their skills. This might defuse the situation and mean that Mr Murdoch's programme would not be so tempting to amateur athletes.'

Delgado paused and looked around him. Cohn was first to speak. 'The first option is a do-nothing recipe for disaster,' he said. 'The second might just have a hope.'

Bill Dodge shook his head. 'No way,' he said. 'Track and field athletics with its new trusts and the like has very liberal rules. By our standards, the track and field athletes aren't amateurs. Swimming would never be willing to give way on amateurism in the same way, at least not by 1984.'

Klaus Ritter nodded. 'The position is exactly the same in gymnastics,' he said. 'They will never agree to go open. It is too early.'

Delgado beckoned to Berne and Vera Goldberg. 'And what is your position, Mr Berne?'

Berne fiddled nervously with his pencil. 'As you know, the Athens conference of the IAAF took a giant step in agreeing to trust funds for athletes. I was at first against such a change – I have always been a staunch amateur – but was convinced otherwise, and the conference took the same view. It is my opinion that a sudden step to open professionalism would be too much even for those who voted for the proposal, and would undoubtedly be resisted by the Eastern bloc. In any case, no full meeting of the IAAF is scheduled till our Helsinki World Championships next August. It would be impossible to make any major change in amateur rules till then, by which time the Kudai preliminary events would have occurred.'

'I can't believe what I'm hearing!' Cohn had risen to his feet. 'If we don't move our butts fast you people won't have anything *left* to organise. Your precious amateur status – whatever the hell that means – won't be worth a row of beans. So if gymnastics and swimming can't move their butts quick enough, who cares? Track and field is what the Los Angeles Games are all about. If they can change their rules, then we can salvage something.'

'That's true,' said Vera Goldberg. 'It is a matter of life and death.'

'It's more important than that,' said Cohn, without humour. 'With respect, ma'am –'

'There is a third option,' interjected Delgado, abruptly. There was silence. 'That is to make Mr Murdoch and his colleagues an offer, one which will keep them inside the world of amateur sport within which Murdoch has, after all, lived all his adult life. It has been my experience that many so-called "rebels" are simply little boys crying to be recognised, begging to be brought into the family circle. It is possible that Mr Murdoch may be one of these. If, therefore, we offer him both money and position within the Olympic framework perhaps that will be enough to draw him away from this Arab venture.'

'What can we possibly offer him?' Cohn's voice had dropped.

'Our public relations and advertising contracts come up after Los Angeles. In 1985 these contracts can be linked with the television negotiations for the 1988 Seoul Olympics. These contracts are both profitable and prestigious . . .'

'That is bribery,' said Thelma Banks.

'That is business,' said the little Korean, Son, speaking for the first time.

After the conclusion of the Heathrow conference an even less official meeting with Bruce Cohn revealed to Maurice Delgado that a certain Mr Ciano had been in touch with Cohn. Cohn's conversation with Delgado had been less than direct and Delgado had been relieved that it had been so. His life in the diplomatic corps had made him sensitive to nuances of speech and phrase and it was abundantly clear to him what the American was suggesting. In his discussion with Cohn, Delgado began to realise exactly what Ciano had proposed to the Los Angeles official. Ciano intended to stop the Kudai operation by the most brutal means, and wished to have the complicity of the Organising Committee. What troubled Maurice Delgado was that Cohn appeared to be seriously considering Ciano's proposition.

Maurice Delgado pulled rank on Cohn. He would have nothing to do with violence and if it did occur he would report the conversation with Cohn to the IOC. He therefore ordered Cohn to reject Ciano's overtures and to confirm with him that such a rejection had been made so that the IOC's books could be clear. In the meantime, they would negotiate with Murdoch.

Ciano pulled off his goggles.

'How'd I do?' he asked.

'Your best since July, Mr Ciano,' said the young man, as Ciano levered himself out of the pool and sat, lungs heaving, at the pool's edge, his stubby feet dangling in the steaming blue water. '71.6 seconds.'

Ciano smiled and nodded, then got to his feet as the young man handed him a monogrammed white towelling robe. Ciano pulled on the robe and pointed back at the pool.

'Eighty-one degrees, Blue,' he said. 'Yet I've never seen you in there, working out.'

The young man shook his head, no expression in his pale-blue eyes. He was dressed in dark-blue tennis shirt, light-blue slacks, and blue suede shoes.

'Not my style, Mr Ciano.'

His employer sat down at a circular white poolside table and slipped on a pair of cheap flip-flops. Blue handed him a towel and Ciano rubbed his face and thinning black hair vigorously.

'So this Murdoch guy, what do you reckon we do? Pay Mr Murdoch a visit?'

The young man's expression did not change. 'England, that's a whole new ball game, Mr Ciano. My father once told me never to forget one thing. You got to know the territory. You got to have people you can buy.'

170

'I see. You reckon we're too far away,' said Ciano. 'Six thousand miles.' He draped his towel around his neck. 'So?'

'So we hit someone closer,' said Blue.

Tuesday, 23 November 1982

The crack of the gun brought back a flood of memories. Murdoch stood with Grieve and Ellis by the indoor training strip at the Crystal Palace National Sports Centre: the longest piece of covered training track in southern England. Muddy rain dripped from the leaks in the ceiling above, making rust-red pools on the synthetic Tartan surface, as sprinters splattered past them.

Ellis wrinkled her nose as a drip from the ceiling landed on her wrist. 'Beats me how you ever produce athletes in facilities like this, coach,' she said. 'We had better back at college.'

Murdoch looked sideways at Ellis. In a matter of months the American girl had insinuated her way into the Kudai venture, into the British sports culture of which he had been a part for the past twenty years, into the warp and woof of his life. Ellis had become for him a point of reference for each new thought, someone who would cut through any weakness in his arguments. Because of her, *The Nazi Games* had become a sharper, tighter screenplay: because of her he had himself become stronger, more assured.

They were both standing in the alcove alongside the high jump landing area. He looked around him. It was like coming home. The cramped six-lane ninety metres of track had been the university within which his physical vocabulary had grown and flowered. Here he had run thousands of sprint and hurdle repetitions, building into his body that fine sensitivity of posture and muscle feel to which he would always subconsciously return in times of competitive stress.

There, on cold mornings, when warming up was like stirring treacle with a cold spoon, he and Grieve had silently jogged together. There they had sought that elusive, perfect technique

171

which was Grieve's in imagination but only Murdoch's in expression. There he and Grieve had sought that one miraculous moment when all the complex pieces of the moving jigsaw of skill fitted perfectly together across a hurdle or over a crossbar. Such moments of achievement were rare, when fitness and the neuro-muscular system reached a final agreement, when what had seemed unattainable suddenly became easy, and all that remained was the grooving that would permanently burn the new skill into him.

Murdoch's reverie was broken by a resounding clang as a 'flopper' on his left brought the steel crossbar to the ground in an unsuccessful jump. Murdoch grinned at the lanky beanpole of a jumper who had knocked down the bar and bent to pick it up. He replaced it carefully on the jump stands. The jumper nodded gratefully and jogged back to his starting point.

Murdoch looked again round the training area, and wondered what possible link there could be between this and the magic stadium three thousand miles away, with its million-dollar prizes.

Grieve nudged him. 'There she is,' he said.

Entering the area from a door immediately in front of them was a blonde girl in a yellow tracksuit. She waved to them, checked to the right to ensure that no sprinters were coming, then jogged across to hug Grieve.

'Katherine,' explained Grieve to Ellis as he disengaged himself. 'My daughter.'

Kathy Grieve was, like her father, a natural athlete. At first Grieve had coached her himself, never allowing her to specialise in her forte, middle distance running, but instead encouraging her to be an all-round performer. Kathy Grieve had responded well. At the age of sixteen she had won the English intermediate heptathlon championships before going on to specialise as an 800 metre runner.

It was at that point that Grieve, who had always resisted the desire to live through his daughter, had passed her on to a specialist middle distance coach, Tim Haller.

172

In her first two years she had gone from strength to strength. Then, at the start of 1981, a hamstring injury had taken her out of competition for the outdoor season. Haller had not panicked but had used the rest period to advantage, working on other areas of her body – the arms and shoulders, the abdominals, the back: the physical pillars of good running technique. Thus, Kathy Grieve had come back to track in the autumn of that year sharp and fast.

Haller had worked on two peaks of performance, known in the jargon of the sport as 'double periodisation'. The first was in the indoor competitive season, based on Britain's only indoor competitive facility of calibre, the primitive 200-metre track at Royal Air Force, Cosford. Kathy had dominated indoor competition in her first events and was, at two minutes and four seconds, not far from her best outdoor performance. In the spring of 1983 she planned to compete in the European Championships in Budapest and stood an excellent chance of becoming the second British woman to beat two minutes outdoors.

Murdoch watched her warm up. Kathy, he felt, though talented, had always lacked the one quality essential to an 800-metre runner: sheer sprint speed. Up till her injury in 1981 her best 400 metres had been only 54.9 seconds, and this had meant that when the first half of a race had been run inside 58 seconds she had been too close to her maximum speed. Similarly, when there had been a sudden injection of pace in the middle of a race, Kathy had always lacked the power to respond.

He watched her now as she moved into a series of silky repetition runs at eighty per cent effort, easily gliding past high jumpers and returning hurdlers, her golden hair streaming out behind her. Murdoch felt the familiar tingle in the skin at the back of his neck. Kathy Grieve had moved up a class. He could feel the power there, held in reserve, waiting to be unlocked.

Tim Haller entered the area from a door behind them. He was a squat, tubby man in his mid-fifties who looked incongruous in a tracksuit. His generally pallid face was distinguished by mottled red cheeks which sometimes had the appearance of rouge. Such looks were irrelevant. His record was impeccable, and since the early seventies he had produced a string of world-class middle distance runners. Haller lay on the obverse side of the coaching coin to Grieve. He was the gentle persuader, Grieve the ruthless martinet; both produced excellent results, only with different types of athlete.

Grieve introduced Haller to Ellis, and the coach shook hands with Murdoch.

'I don't suppose many of the officials have been speaking to you two,' he said.

'They never did,' said Grieve.

'Only the athletes count,' said Haller. 'After all, they *are* the bloody sport.'

Kathy Grieve jogged towards them, sweat beginning to bead on her lightly freckled brow. 'I'm ready,' she said.

Haller nodded to Grieve. 'One of your favourite sessions,' he said. 'Three by 200 metres, a shade away from flat out, with a thirty seconds' jog-rest between runs.'

Murdoch nodded. 'I remember. Rigor mortis sets in on the third 200 metres.'

'What did you run them in?' asked Kathy.

'The high twenty-twos,' interrupted Grieve. 'What will Kathy do?'

'The low to middle twenty-fives,' replied Haller. He turned to Murdoch. 'You like to tow her round?'

Grieve answered for him. 'Of course he will,' he said.

Murdoch shook his head. 'What are you trying to do to me, Grieve? Swimming, tennis, now running – everyone wants to test me to destruction. How come no one suggests Scrabble?'

'Twenty-fives,' said Grieve coaxingly. 'Come on. Twenty-bloody-fives. You could do that on one leg.'

Murdoch felt Ellis squeeze his hand. He looked down at her.

'This is a conspiracy!' he said, laughing.

*

He could not explain it, the feeling of unease. It came to him when Kathy Grieve had pulled off her tracksuit bottoms, revealing legs clad in black tights as protection against the cold breeze. Her thighs were thicker than he had remembered, the hard muscle flickering in relaxation before hardening to frozen isometric tension. When she removed her top, revealing her shoulders, Murdoch felt a sickness at the pit of his stomach. It was her deltoids, those converging fibres moving from the shoulders to their insertion in the upper arms. Kathy's had a clarity, a definition and a bulk which was unusual in a middle distance runner. Highly unusual.

'Ready?' said Haller.

They stood in the back straight of the outdoor track, the breeze fresh in their faces. Over in the far corner of the track, in the shadow of the main stand, stood Grieve and Ellis. Kathy took the inside lane as she and Murdoch jogged to the start. They passed Haller who dropped his hand to cue Grieve to start his stopwatch. Then they were off.

To Murdoch it felt surprisingly easy and the running flowed from him as he hung on Kathy's shoulder round the bend. In the straight the breeze pulled them in towards the finish, past Grieve and Ellis.

'24.8!' shouted Grieve to their backs as they jogged the diagonal across the wet infield grass back towards the start.

Murdoch was still breathing heavily as they came within twenty metres of the start, but Kathy, already recovering quickly, breathed lightly. Nevertheless, in the second run Murdoch, reaching back into his muscular memory for the relaxation and control which Grieve had taught him, managed to stay with the girl as they drove into the home straight for the second time, only feeling himself begin to tighten in the last fifty metres. When they hit the finish – to Grieve's shout of 'twenty-five seconds!' – he resisted the temptation to stop. Somehow, lungs heaving, he kept jogging across the pulpy field. Kathy looked over her shoulder at him, smiling. 'Last one,' she said. 'Flat out?'

'Yes,' gasped Murdoch, the breath coarse in his throat.

This time even the first fifty metres on the curve felt hard, but Kathy was remorseless, and it was all that Murdoch could do to stay with her. He pinned himself to her right shoulder, his breath now roaring through stretched lungs.

As they hit the straight he saw Ellis standing at the finish. Ellis and Grieve, the past and the present together. Murdoch started to sprint, creating a sudden gap between himself and the girl. But it couldn't last. Somehow Kathy was at his left shoulder and past him; with twenty metres to go she was two metres up. He did not hear Grieve's shout of 'twenty-four!' as he fell across the line.

Murdoch squatted, allowing the warm water of the shower to spatter on his head. He was still breathing heavily, the blood thudding in his temples. He would have vomited, but he did not have the strength. The years were pitiless, inexorable. Ten years before, the session with Kathy would have been little more than a warm-up, trotted out to help a club athlete in need of a partner before getting on to the real business of his training day. But now it gutted him, gorging his thighs with waste so that even standing up was difficult.

Murdoch let out a dry, acidic belch, and allowed some of the shower water trickle down his throat. The run had been good for him: a touch of reality.

He levered himself to his feet and made his way across the floor of the tiny dressing room allotted to coaches and officials, the water from his body dripping to the floor. He sat on a chair and reached for his towel as he heard a knock on the door. It was Ellis.

'You alive, Superstar?' she shouted. 'We got work to do. Then dinner. If you're too pooped then send your astral body.'

Murdoch summoned a smile. He had not squatted in the shower simply because of the weight in his legs; rather it was because of another weight, a suspicion that was now hardening into certainty.

HILLTOPICS

by Garry Hill, Managing Editor

Steroid testing will reach new levels this year with the institution of the IAAF's series of Permit Meets. Random dope-testing will become mandatory. I'm all for the elimination of harmful substances, but after years of being an interested follower of the subject I'm still not convinced that anabolic steroids are evil.

Are they 'ethically' wrong? I don't think so. From the first time somebody put nails on the bottom of shoes the 'natural' order of things was violated. The list of artificial aids is encyclopedic: sawdust, then foam to land on, synthetic all-weather surfaces, fibreglass poles, metal javelins, weight-training machines, electrical stimulation of muscles. The list goes on and on.

So does the list of things ingested by eager athletes. From electrolytic replacement concoctions to megadoses of vitamins. Looking at it from a biological standpoint I have to laugh when it comes to vitamins, which by definition are substances the human body is incapable of producing. Anabolic substances, on the other hand, are produced by all of us. And whether or not the steroids ingested by athletes are produced *in vivo* or *in vitro* they're still the same chemical. To me, it's simply another method of fooling your body into making some muscles it really didn't want in the first place.

We've all heard the horror stories about vicious side-effects of steroids, and about the shot-putter down in Texas (or wherever) who is on a dialysis machine, fighting for his life because he overdid it on 'roids. Well, I've been hearing the same story for almost twenty years now, and have yet to come across anyone with first-hand knowledge of any adverse incident of major proportions.

It's obvious that there are some possible deleterious side-effects from steroid usage, but from what I've seen they are strictly minor league compared with all the stress fractures I've seen from pounding the roads. How about chondromalacia and plantar fasciitis, those other runners' delights?

The other steroid bogeyman is efficiency. 'They don't work,' says most of the anti-steroid propaganda. 'I got unbelievable results,' say the advocates. Telling who is right is tough because of conflicting research. It's my feeling that steroids are not terribly damaging, while they can be very effective in increasing performance. Certainly, there's a bigger world out there than most surmise.

Wednesday, 8 December 1982

As Bull Buchinski inserted his key in the lock of the door of the 82nd Precinct gymnasium he reflected that it was indeed the end of an era. The gym had been the last of the sepulchral nineteenth-century sweat-barns which his father and his grandfather had so loved. The rigid black dumb-bells and bar-bells with which they had groaned and wrestled all those years back were still there, in honoured positions, still as difficult to lift as they had been almost a century before. But it would never be the same.

Bull closed the door quietly behind him, as he had done every Wednesday afternoon since 1951. Nautilus. He had kept the Nautilus machines out of the 82nd Precinct till the last possible moment, not because he lacked respect for these Rolls Royces of the strength world but rather because he felt that the old gym represented the past, his family's as well as those of New York's finest. But now they were in the main gymnasium, those Nautilus machines which represented the present like Space Invaders.

He walked slowly through the twilight gloom along the main lobby, his feet creaking on the thin, bowing floorboards, and flicked down a lightswitch on his right. Even with the lights on, the gym always had a dark, church-like quality, he reflected. Well, what had his father called it? The Temple of Muscle. Bull smiled and walked into the gym, flicking down a further lightswitch on his left.

There it was: the Nautilus. In two neat rows, black, padded, untouched. No question, it was great equipment, though it had none of the life of his Dad's old bar-bells, let alone an Olympic bar. He looked to the other half of the gymnasium where he had retained the best of the conventional weights. The best of both worlds, he thought.

He drifted over to the Nautilus area, took off his jacket and tie, and fixed himself below the squat-machine. After setting it at an appropriate load he fixed his shoulders below its firm black pads. Bull breathed in and drove upwards with both legs. The weight went up easily, albeit slowly, but the final part of the leg-straightening was tough, for that was the value of the Nautilus: it gave tension and resistance all the way, in contrast to conventional weights where resistance diminished sharply over the final part of each lift. By the time he had completed ten repetitions Bull was breathing heavily. He moved along the machines, occasionally pumping out a few repetitions on the more unusual pieces of apparatus. He nodded approvingly as he picked up his jacket and tie and made his way back towards the door. It was good stuff: strong, well-built, comprehensive in its muscular demands.

He walked over to the other half of the gymnasium which contained the old equipment. There it lay on the floor, that great beast, the Buchinski Bar-Bell, a massive solid bar, at each end a black sphere of 110 pounds, total weight 225 pounds. The Buchinski Bell, as the New York cops called it, was the standard by which any athlete had been measured on a two-handed strict military press. Only a handful of New York's best athletes had managed to lift it since Buchinski's grandfather had been given the bar-bell by the great strongman Eugene Sandow back in 1901. Their names were emblazoned in gold on a fading brown board above the main door to the gymnasium. He looked up at the board, dotted liberally with the Buchinski name over a period of almost a century, then round at the old gym.

On each side of the board hung brown fading Buchinski photographs which had been part of the gymnasium ever since Bull could remember. On the left, Grandad, with that funny old waxed moustache, wearing a one-piece leopard-skin suit and Roman sandals, poised under the Buchinski Bell in the classic one-arm-bent press position, a skill long-vanished. On the right of the board hung a photograph of his father, taken in 1933, during the USA Police Championships. Buchinski père was featured in the wide semi-split position of the old-style snatch, in perfect balance, a weight of 250 pounds fixed aloft above him.

Bull gulped, feeling an unexpected warmth and moisture in his eyes. The old place had absorbed the sweat of many good men, from the old Irish beer-bellies of eighty years ago to the present bronzed gods. It had been a good place, an honest place.

He placed his jacket and tie on a nearby bench and walked over to the Buchinski Bell. He placed his feet under its thick, rough black bar and lowered his hands to grip it, arms straight, back flat. He cleaned the bar easily, breathing in to take the weight on an inflated chest. He held the weight there for the regulation two seconds, then drove it overhead with both arms, breathing out as he did so. It was a beautiful lift, a lift from his youth. The bar went up smoothly, without stopping, and his arms straightened as the quiet hiss of his expiring breath ended. Bull smiled to himself and lowered the weight to his chest, then slowly to the floor. He had not strict-pressed the Bell for over two years. A pity the other boys had not been there to see it.

Bull felt good. He lifted the bell again and placed it on the squat-stands which stood above the low, flat bench used for his favourite exercise, the bench-press. He checked his watch: five o'clock. Time to pump out half a dozen repetitions before going home to put a call through to Murdoch, confirming the entries of more American athletes. He required replies from only three more college runners to complete his hand, before the American end of the Kudai project was complete.

He settled himself on his back on the bench underneath the bar-bell, placed both hands on the bar and levered it on to straight arms. He lowered it slowly to a high, air-filled chest, then pushed it up back to the straight-arm position. The first three repetitions were surprisingly easy. It was one of those days, he reflected, one of those 'hot' days when bar-bells felt light. The fourth repetition was strong but smooth, as Bull focused his attention on the bar above. He did not hear the light click as the gymnasium door opened behind him.

180

The fifth repetition was tough and sweat suddenly started to spurt from Bull's forehead. He pushed it to straight arms, breathing heavily. His eyes were glassy as he looked at the bar above him. Just one more, and it was going to be a grind.

He lowered the bar to his chest for the final time, then dug it viciously upwards, his breath exploding as he did so. The bar moved to within a few degrees of its final position, then stopped. Through the mist of his fatigue he saw two hands, fingers beringed, on the bar between his; above the hands a male face. He fought the weight of the bell as it dropped heavily back on to his chest.

The man moved round to face Bull, standing above him to the side of the bench. He was young, barely out of his teens, a slim, blond young man dressed in an immaculate black pin-stripe suit. Through his fatigue and the excruciating pain of the weight Bull knew that he would soon lose consciousness as the supply of oxygen to his brain rapidly diminished. He made one last effort, roaring as he did so. The young man above him did not move.

Bull arched his hips, giving the bar additional momentum, and slowly squeezed the weight towards the vertical. Then both brain and body surrendered, and he lost consciousness, his head lolling to his side, his arms limp, the weight again falling with a loud thud against his chest. He never heard the light, mocking applause beside him.

The young man reached into an inside pocket, withdrew a small hypodermic syringe and a phial of liquid. He inserted the needle into the phial and watched as it filled. He carefully squirted a small jet of liquid from the syringe into the air, scowling as some drops fell upon his suede shoes. Then he inserted the needle into a thick vein in Bull's thick, hairy right forearm, making sure that the syringe was completely empty before he withdrew it.

He placed the syringe back in its plastic cylinder and tucked the package into an inside pocket. Then with equal care the young man withdrew a handkerchief from his breast pocket and wiped the fluid from the toe of his suede shoe.

It had been an easy assignment, for Ciano's New York sources had been adamant on the inflexibility of Buchinski's Wednesday afternoon routine. Blue had simply followed their instructions. He checked his watch and placed his index finger on to the side of Bull's neck. There was no pulse; just another victim of the fitness revolution who had tried one lift too many.

He retraced his steps through the rows of equipment, stopping for a moment under the honours board and glancing at the framed Buchinski photographs. Then he flicked off the lights, plunging the gymnasium back into darkness, and made his way out into the street.

The outer door of the gymnasium clicked quietly behind him.

12

Eastern Approaches

Monday, 3 January 1983

Murdoch stood in Zurich station, gnawing at a tough, crusty *Schinkenbrötchen*, his breath creating a mist in the sub-zero temperature of the busy station. He checked his watch. The slow train to Chur would leave at 2.30 p.m., in an hour and a half; from there he would transfer trains and go on to the World Bobsleigh Championships at St Moritz, to his meeting with the Russian, Igor Lysenko. He shivered and closed the top button of his sheepskin coat.

Just two minutes passed before Murdoch again checked his watch. Joachimowski was late, but that was only to be expected. The crazy Pole had been the only man to have wangled himself practice jumps in the middle of an Olympic decathlon pole vault, and he had certainly been the only athlete to have been threatened with suspension for pushing in a decathlon 1500 metres.

Murdoch grinned as he sipped lukewarm coffee from a plastic cup. 'Jock' had been one of the few athletes who had lent colour and character to a sport in dire need of both. The Pole had even brought an occasional flicker of a smile to the faces of those hard-eyed automatons from East Germany. During the 1974 European Championships in Rome, he had clashed openly with the hurdler Schmidt, the political commissar of the Polish team. His later activities, following his retirement, had been even more outrageous: he had been with Walesa in Gdansk in 1980 and had been at the centre of the

Solidarity movement until martial law had been declared by General Jaruzelski in December 1981. Yet somehow, despite his wildness and his known Western sympathies, Joachimowski had survived within the Polish athletics hierarchy. Yet Murdoch had heard nothing of him since the spring of 1982 until his telephone had rung on Christmas Eve.

For some days he had wondered if there were any link between Joachimowski's call and the meeting in London which he had had a week before with the Russian attaché, Josef Klim.

Klim, a little football of a man bursting out of his double-breasted suit, had immediately disavowed any relationship with his famous hammer-throwing namesake Romuald Klim, Olympic victor in 1964. His reason for seeing Murdoch was, he admitted, connected with what he called 'light athletics'. It had been reported in Moscow, he said, his stubby fingers intertwining nervously, that Murdoch was embarking upon a major sports venture, involving an Arab nation.

Murdoch had been non-committal, but the Russian had continued, the words pouring forth from plump, wet lips. His old comrade Igor Lysenko would like to have the privilege of an informal meeting with Murdoch, at the Russian Federation's expense, of course, at St Moritz. At any time suiting his convenience in the week preceding the World Bobsleigh Championships. Murdoch had pressed Klim over the reason for such a meeting, but the little Russian would not expand further.

A week later the call from Joachimowski had come, suggesting in the Pole's words 'great happenings' if they were to talk privately. Murdoch, to kill two birds with one stone, had agreed to meet Joachimowski at Zurich station in the two hours between his arrival from the airport and his departure for St Moritz.

He looked yet again at his watch, then back up the station to either side of the central island containing shops and a cinema; at six foot six and 220 pounds Jock would still be easy to identify. Suddenly, there he was. Head and shoulders above the crowds, Joachimowski strode purposefully towards him with his strange, bouncy walk, clad in a grey double-breasted Bogart-type raincoat, snap-brim hat and sunglasses. Murdoch smiled. Though he had been born in Warsaw, Joachimowski's English was littered with the debris of a thousand American movies, from *Casablanca* onwards. The Pole also smiled broadly as he caught sight of his friend. He jogged the last few metres, arms out in front of him, and clasped Murdoch firmly with both hands.

'Great to see you,' he said in his pronounced Polish-American twang. He grabbed Murdoch's left bicep. 'You on steroids?' he grinned, pulling the Scotsman through the crowds, down towards the bar on the left-hand side of the aisle of shops.

'You know what they told me, those smart-ass doctors, when they wanted to put me on the anabolics back in '71?' He did not pause for an answer. 'They said to me, Joachimowski, take these and you'll be able to do it three or four times a night. Me, I said, no way – *I'm* not cutting down for *any* man!' He laughed, drawing Murdoch with him into the smoky crowded bar on the left of the central aisle of shops. They sat down and Joachimowski immediately removed a stub-filled ashtray to another table.

'Killers,' he said, grimacing, waving at the smoky air with both hands. 'How can they live their lives in . . . in such filth?' He beckoned a sweating barman towards them.

'Two Pils,' he said. 'You like Pils? Or is it still Perrier?'

'I'll try a Pils today.'

Joachimowski stood up, removed his raincoat and draped it over the chair behind him. Murdoch unbuttoned his own coat and did the same.

'The last time I saw you, you were flat on your back. After the Munich 1500 metres,' said Murdoch. 'Hard times for you?'

The Pole nodded. 'Living in a nutcracker, that's hard for any country.' He received both beers and passed one to Murdoch.

'*Nasdrovne*,' he said.

'Cheers,' said Murdoch.

'No matter what we do it's a goddam disaster,' Joachimowski went on. 'We do nothing and the people will not back Solidarity. We do too much and the Russian tanks cross the border to crush us. So we get Jaruzelski, who keeps out the Russians and crushes Solidarity. Then the Western bankers want to pull out the plug on us . . .' He shrugged. 'But we go on. Poland has always been a land of survivors.'

He laid down his beer. 'But you, Murdoch. I hear that you are sitting on a pot of gold.'

'How did you hear that?'

Joachimowski shrugged again. 'You cannot keep the lid down on such a project. The Russians knew of it in August, the East Germans only hours later. Then came your press conference in October. After all, it could mean the end of athletics as we know it. You of all people must understand that.'

'You know the details of the project?'

'I know that it will be held in the Emirates on the same dates as the Los Angeles Olympics, and that there will be massive prizes – some say two million dollars per event.'

'That's the long and short of it.'

'So you have the athletes and the meet directors? You have Quince and Buchinski's meetings?'

'Buchinski is dead,' said Murdoch flatly. 'A heart attack.'

Joachimowski shook his head. 'Yes, I know,' he said. 'Sad. A good man.' He looked up. 'And the East?'

Murdoch shook his head. 'Not worth the trouble,' he said. 'You know the problems there better than I do. The East Germans are all politically vetted and so to a lesser degree are athletes from the other Eastern bloc nations.'

Joachimowski laid down his beer. 'I think that you can reasonably forget about the East Germans, Murdoch.' He glanced around him then looked into his friend's eyes. 'But the East Germans, they're a particular case,' he said. 'So let me ask you this. How many Poles do you think are capable of qualifying for your Games and for your preliminary meets with a good chance of picking up some petrodollars?'

Murdoch paused. 'Ten for the Games themselves in track

and field,' he said. 'Ten others could pick up money in the preliminaries but probably wouldn't make it to the finals.'

'How much could they win?' pursued Joachimowski.

Murdoch shook his head. 'Impossible to say,' he said. 'At best, twelve million dollars. At worst, about three.'

'And our swimmers and gymnasts?'

Murdoch paused before replying.

'I'll tell you,' said Joachimowski. He withdrew a black notebook from his inside pocket and flicked through it before stopping at a page. 'Ten million at best, two at worst.'

'That's an optimistic figure.'

'So the total is twenty-two million dollars at best, five million at worst.'

'Something about that,' agreed Murdoch, sipping his beer.

Joachimowski leant on the table, his jaw jutting forward. 'Alan, have you any idea of what it is like now in Poland? The very basics – bread, meat, butter, the things that fill Western trashcans – we stand in queues a kilometre long for these things.'

He looked over his shoulder. 'Two more Pils, please,' he said, pulling on the apron of the waiter behind him.

Leaning closer to Murdoch he said, '*Twenty-two million dollars*. Dollars are blood to Poland. Blood! What would you say if I could deliver the cream of our athletes to you?'

'How?'

Joachimowski again looked around him. 'Our teams will defect,' he explained. 'En masse. At your Pepsi Cola Multi Games in London next month, in February. The only time the three sports will be together in the West at the same time.'

Murdoch leaned back in his chair. 'Let me get this clear, Jock,' he said. 'You're telling me Solidarity will organise the defection of Poland's best performers?'

'Yes.'

'Jesus Christ! And what then? What will become of these defectors?'

'They will be taken care of by Solidarity sympathisers in London until your competitive season begins.'

'But what about their relatives?'

'They will do well,' said Joachimowski. 'We will get money back to them – extra food, summer holidays at centres in Hungary and Yugoslavia. They will not be persecuted. When the time is ripe those who wish to come out of Poland to join the athletes will be allowed to slip quietly across the border without any hassle.'

'You seem to have it all worked out.'

Joachimowski nodded, his lean, tanned face creasing into a frown. 'Murdoch, do you have any idea how much Poland owes? Seventeen billion dollars to Western banks, eleven billion to Western governments. Goddammit, we can't even service the interest on the loans! So now we sell our sportsmen.'

'Won't the Russians suspect?'

Joachimowski shrugged once more. 'Perhaps, but so what? They don't want to take over our economy; they're in enough trouble themselves. The Soviet State is not an intelligent creature, Alan. It is a brainless reptile with a limited set of responses.'

'And what do you want me to do?'

'For the moment, nothing. Closer to the time I suggest that you arrange training facilities for the athletes, swimmers and gymnasts, and include them within any international training clinics you have planned. For the rest, our people in England will take good care of them.'

'Let me sleep on it,' said Murdoch. 'I'll let you know within the week.'

'What's there to think about?' pursued Joachimowski impatiently. 'You *must* want these people.'

'Of course I do,' said Murdoch, placatingly. 'But this thing is bigger than sport. There's the question of political asylum, for one thing. If the Thatcher Government doesn't give it, then your people are in deep trouble.'

'But your Iron Lady will be able to give the Russians a bloody nose for Afghanistan. Okay, so it's a couple of years late . . .' Joachimowski took another tiny notebook out of his pocket and placed it on the table. 'Anyhow, Poland is just for openers,' he said. 'This notebook contains the names of fifty-one performers of high calibre from the USSR, Czechoslovakia, Rumania and Bulgaria, all of whom would be willing to defect at the same time. Alan, you can split the whole of the East wide open. What do you say?'

Murdoch looked out of the train window on to the white, pine-speckled mountains. He had long ago given up trying to find a comfortable posture on the stiff green seats of the train to Chur. The last time he had come to St Moritz had been eight years ago, when Grieve had formed a bobsleigh team to take on the 'Hooray Henrys' of the Bobsleigh Association.

Grieve had put Murdoch on the brakes, a Welsh sixteen-metre shot-putter at number three, an Irish javelin thrower at number two, and had driven the bob himself. Only Grieve himself had ever ridden before, but to the Scot the winning equation was both simple and clear. One tenth of a second gained at the start equalled three tenths of a second at the finish. Thus, if he and the 600 pounds of athletic muscle-power behind him could push the four hundred-pound bob down the first fifty metres three tenths of a second faster than any other team then that would give him almost a second in hand to make up for any errors in his driving. That, at least, was the theory. In practice, their first trial starts were slower than expected, caution blurring the pushing power that Murdoch and his two colleagues undoubtedly possessed. After three practice starts that were no faster than any of the other British teams, Grieve had gathered the three athletes round him in the bob hut bar.

'Have a look over there,' he had said, pointing to a group of British officers sipping Glühwein over in a corner. 'Those physical illiterates are laughing their bloody heads off. We're clocking 5.90 starts, exactly the same as them. They've got the jump on me in driving experience, so they end up with 72 seconds and I get 73. Next time, no excuses. Okay?'

Their next start time had been 5.5 seconds, only a tenth short of the course record for that season. Grieve and his crew had gone on to win the national four-man title and to represent Britain in the World Championships in Cortina. To Grieve it seemed unremarkable: winning on snow was just an extension of winning on the track.

Murdoch watched the miles slip past as a blue dusk gathered over the Swiss countryside. He glanced again at his watch: it was getting to be a fetish. Still, only ten minutes to arrival. Things had been so simple then, so carefree, trekking across Europe in army Land-Rovers, borrowing starting-shoes from friendly Swiss bobbers. Now, as in track and field athletics, success in bobsleighing no longer lay with husky Swiss farmers but with steroidal monsters from East Germany. The disease had followed everywhere, even into innocent sports like bobsleighing. The decline seemed inexorable once a certain level of personal and political commitment had been reached. He settled back in his seat.

He had always thought of sport as the Great Purity. The challenge of stopwatch and tape, the stillness of a cold, dead stainless steel Olympic bar which either rose smoothly to its ultimate destination or simply lay there inert. The inner demands of lungs ripped as if by thorns during a lonely training run where no one would know if you stopped for a breather – no one except the most important person. Sport was a fantasy but one bounded by the most rigid of rules, a series of tests that man had devised for himself and freely entered. And inside that fantasy lay the training process which contained its own particular and personal rules.

Murdoch had never really competed with anyone. All that he had done was to use competition as territory for a series of personal journeys towards personal goals. Just as in training he had always signed unwritten contracts with himself, so for him competition had always been a struggle against the man he had been yesterday.

He checked his watch. The train would be in Chur in ten minutes. First Ciano, then Joachimowski had brought the Arab Olympics further away from his first simple conception. It was not going to be a matter of 'take the money and run'. He knew too that his meeting with Lysenko would take him even further away, into a world where he did not want to be.

Igor Lysenko sat on the wooden bench across the table from Murdoch, his severe crew-cut and his ascetic face looking out of place in the après ski bustle of the Hotel Steffani dining room. Murdoch had always thought that Lysenko had looked like the knight from Bergman's film *The Seventh Seal*. Now, ten years after his bronze in the Munich decathlon, long vertical lines had set in the Russian's face, a legacy of years with Dinamo Sports Club.

'Ten years,' said Lysenko, lifting a glass of foaming Tuborg.

'To three minutes fifty-nine point six,' replied Murdoch, lifting his own glass of Perrier. 'To Igor Lysenko, the only man to break four minutes for the 1500 metres in Olympic decathlon.'

'It was necessary,' replied Lysenko, sipping his beer. 'I was lying eighth after nine events. An Olympic medal of any colour meant a position in Dinamo for me. No medal and I would have been teaching physical training to fourteen-year-olds in Smolensk.'

He wiped a fringe of foam from his upper lip. 'It was only pain,' he said. 'But the last three lap-times are burned in my memory.'

'Mine too,' said Murdoch. 'Sixty-six; sixty-five; sixty.'

Lysenko's face crinkled into a smile. 'Those were two good days,' he said simply. 'Though I will never forget the day we were to begin.'

'The Israeli deaths,' said Murdoch.

'Yes,' said Lysenko. 'Even on the victory rostrum I wept. Here we were, having run our hearts out for two days, mere hours after the butchery of all those brave men. Somehow it did not make sense.'

The Russian's eyes fluttered as if he were wiping the memory of death from his consciousness. 'Lunch,' he said, picking up the menu. 'You have been here before. What is best?'

'They do a great hamburger,' said Murdoch. 'Prime beef.'

'Then hamburger it shall be. For you?'

Murdoch nodded and watched as Lysenko ordered. On the track Igor Lysenko had possessed almost the same physical balance in his 190 pounds of muscle, tendon and ligaments as Murdoch himself. Off it, Murdoch reflected, the Russian lived in a world as far from his as that of the nomads of the Kalahari.

Lysenko drained his glass and looked over his left shoulder for a waiter, nodding to indicate two more of the same.

'How much has my colleague Mr Klim told you?'

'Nothing,' said Murdoch. 'But I thought it worth the earlier trip to St Moritz. My company acts as consultant to the sponsors of the British team competing here: two birds with one stone.'

'Or three.'

Murdoch's pulse quickened. Did he know of Joachimowski? 'Three?'

'I believe your old regiment has a team here, competing for Great Britain.'

'Of course. Old comrades.' Murdoch sighed.

'We too have been old comrades, Murdoch, albeit as rivals. I always feel that there is a special bond between decathletes, possibly because they live together over such long periods.'

Not with you, you old bastard, Murdoch thought. He said, 'Possibly too because we lack competence in so many events. A brotherhood of insecurity.'

A smile flitted across Lysenko's face. 'A brotherhood of insecurity,' he said. 'Yes.' He shook his head. 'I often think that my failures are more a part of my memory than my successes. Is it the same with you?'

For a moment Murdoch's mind leapt back to Mexico, and the pang of pain was almost physical. He looked at Lysenko and smiled. 'My coach called decathlon a series of disasters waiting to happen,' he said. 'The bad times, the javelins that won't land point first, poles that come back and hit the crossbar after you are well clear . . .'

Lysenko nodded. 'I seem to remember we both had many such moments of failure.'

192

He turned as he felt the presence of a white-coated waiter on his left shoulder and paused as their drinks were put down before them. Then he leant forward, both elbows on the rough wooden table, his beer enclosed between his arms.

'Murdoch,' he said, 'we have both come a long way since Munich, you in your world and I in mine. But this adventure which you plan in the Emirates . . .' He sipped his beer.

'Adventure?'

'It is science fiction. How long can it possibly last?'

'You haven't yet seen our protocol, Igor. You might think differently if you had. The money is guaranteed, the facilities built, the event organisers already appointed.'

Lysenko's mouth tightened. 'And the athletes?'

'That's confidential information, you must realise that.'

'Then you are committed?'

'Completely.'

'And what of the American meets? I have been told that Mr Buchinski is dead.'

'I didn't think you would have heard,' replied Murdoch.

'Our intelligence on such matters is excellent,' said Lysenko, his voice strengthening. 'We have been informed that the official cause of death was a heart attack.'

Murdoch nodded. 'Yes. Lifting weights on his own. I suppose it could have happened to him at any time.'

Lysenko lowered his voice and looked around the crowded restaurant, then back at Murdoch. 'Alan, do not ask me how I know. But your Mr Buchinski did not die from natural causes.'

Murdoch looked at Lysenko's eyes. The Russian was telling the truth, he felt sure, and for some reason was taking a chance in telling him. He opened his mouth to speak but Lysenko anticipated his question.

'Do not ask me any more. I have said too much already.'

Lysenko frowned as two plates of hamburger and chips were placed in front of them. 'Do you know who sent me here?' He did not wait for a reply. 'The Supreme Council of Soviet Sport. The Supreme Council itself. And I was sent because I had known you as a competitor, to speak to you as a friend in the name of sport.'

Murdoch slowly sliced into his hamburger, speared a piece on his fork and put it in his mouth. He chewed slowly, then swallowed.

'As I understand it, Igor, the Soviet Union has always resisted all changes to the amateur laws within the IAAF and other Olympic-related governing bodies. It has always been to your advantage to do so because your internal interpretation of the word "amateur" has been so flexible: your teams have always had more than their fair share of soldiers and eternal students. All that is being planned now is the ultimate option that already exists in tennis, soccer and boxing. Our Arab Olympics merely brings track and field athletics, swimming and gymnastics into line with other sports.'

'But you must see that it is not as simple as that,' persisted Lysenko, his lunch untouched. 'You will destroy the Olympic movement, the International Amateur Athletic Federation, all for –'

'Come off it, Igor. Your people have been flouting the rules for years.' Murdoch cut strongly into his food and chewed vigorously. 'Anyway,' he said, 'surely you didn't come all this way just to discuss the ethics of amateurism with me. So why the trip?'

Lysenko sipped his beer. 'I came here to try to stop you,' he said.

'Surely you didn't think I was going to give up, just because we sweated out for a couple of days together in Munich ten years ago?'

'No,' said Lysenko slowly.

'So your people gave you something to bargain with?'

'Yes.'

'And that is?'

'We know of your work in sports consultancy. We understand that you have been linked with Spartan, the sports shoe company, who have been trying to set up a factory in Russia and market their products there for some years. That contract and planning permission can be Spartan's.'

'And?'

'We are putting up for tender the on-ground advertising on all our leading soccer and athletic grounds. It can be arranged that the contract can be yours.'

'And what do you reckon these two deals are worth?'

Lysenko flushed. 'We are not experts in capitalist finance, but we consider the two to be worth about 200,000 dollars a year.'

Murdoch pursed his lips. 'And what about the rest of you?'

'What do you mean?'

'I mean that you didn't make this trip just for the Russians – you came here on behalf of the whole Eastern bloc.'

'Not the Germans,' said Lysenko.

'Okay, so leave them out. Have you other sports trade concessions in countries like Poland, Czechoslovakia and Hungary?'

Lysenko hesitated. 'There have been indications that some other Warsaw Pact nations might contribute . . .'

'I'll bet they will,' said Murdoch. 'Television rights?'

'That could be part of the agreement,' said Lysenko.

'Access to Eastern bloc athletes for major Western meets which I designate?'

'Yes,' said Lysenko.

Murdoch sat still for a moment and considered. Igor Lysenko was handing him most of Eastern Europe on a plate. 'And how would this be formalised, made watertight? What would prevent your people pulling out after the first year?'

'Binding contracts,' replied Lysenko, cutting into his hamburger and taking his first mouthful. He appeared to be relieved that he had now unburdened himself of the details of his offer.

'And all I have to do is to abandon the Arab Olympics?'

'As late as possible, say in June, when it would be difficult for anyone else to re-create it. You and your advisors are the heart of the concept. If you give up it is dead.'

'And what about the East Germans? Where do they stand?'

Lysenko broke his bread and scraped butter thinly along its

195

soft brown surface. He inclined his head and sniffed. 'The Germans have always gone their own way,' he said. 'They would not enter into negotiations, though I am certain that they will be delighted if we can reach some sort of agreement here in St Moritz.'

'Have you any formal documents of proposal with you?'

'No. But they could be here by tomorrow from our embassy.'

'Then I would like to have them.'

'And your answer?'

'Before the end of the week. Before the last practice run in the championships.'

'So the Russians are worried,' said Grieve, hopping from foot to foot. It was nine thirty in the morning and he and Murdoch stood on the snow-covered lake on the outskirts of St Moritz, dressed in bulbous padded ski-suits, woollen berets and fur-lined boots. Frost glistened in Grieve's greying red hair and his nose glowed like a plum. Behind them the coach's ten-man British bobsleigh team brushed the snow from the surface of the lake and furrowed starting grooves in the ice with hot wires under the supervision of Staff Sergeant 'Buster' Lloyd.

Murdoch thumped gloved hands together, feeling the hairs in his nose freeze as he breathed in the cold air. His face felt as if it had been dipped in snow.

'Lysenko's offered us everything but Stalin's jock-strap,' he said. 'Let's run.'

The two men jogged slowly up the path surrounding the lake, their feet crunching on the frosted snow, their breath spuming in front of them.

'There must have been a lot of heart-searching in Russia before they came up with this deal,' growled Grieve, stepping round an elderly matron on the narrow snow-path. 'But it's interesting to know that even the great dictatorship of the proletariat is willing to get into bed with us capitalists.' He frowned. 'Some of my mates back on the Clyde would puke if they knew this.'

'It's just that they don't want our Arab Olympics,' said Murdoch, beginning to breathe more heavily as the heat built up inside his ski-suit.

'I get nervous when people try to do us favours,' said Grieve, running with low, economical strides, his feet crunching rhythmically on the frozen path. They turned left, parallel to the home straight soon to be used for St Moritz's unique horse-racing on ice. 'How much is all of this worth?'

'Impossible to say until I've costed it,' replied Murdoch. 'Certainly not less than a quarter of a million a year. But the real value is that it gives me an inside straight to Eastern Europe. I've been trying for the past five years for that.'

Grieve looked sideways at Murdoch. 'You could make a lot of money.'

'We could eat it with a knife and fork,' Murdoch replied. He was aware of a stillness – that the older man was waiting for a response.

'And all without hassle?' prompted Grieve.

'That's right. No hassle.'

'You've got some doubts about our Arab deal?' said Grieve, his breath spuming around him.

'Not about Hassan, or Stevens or Hall,' replied Murdoch. 'Nor the development programme that you've got your teeth into.'

For a moment he said nothing more, as he sought words which would accurately convey his misgivings.

'It's the breaking away from everything we've spent our lives in,' he said. 'We know that a lot of it stinks – '

'But it's been our sty,' said Grieve.

'Yes, that – and the feeling that we've got into forbidden territory.'

'You mean Ciano?'

'And now Joachimowski and Lysenko,' said Murdoch. 'It's a new can of worms.'

'Or hornet's nest,' said Grieve.

The two men matched each other stride for stride along the long path, covering a further two hundred metres before

Murdoch spoke again. He felt, in the running, the re-establishing of an old link, that physical thread which had bound them during the years when Grieve had coached him. If the master–pupil relationship was in many ways reversed he still felt that Grieve was standing somewhere in his moral centre, testing him.

They continued to run, their breathing now synchronised. At last Grieve broke the silence.

'When do you have to give Lysenko an answer?'

'Before the end of the week, before the last practice run.'

Grieve eased off and stopped. He pointed ahead to a bench by the side of the path, its outline only dimly visible beneath a fluffy mound of snow.

'We've worked out that it's four hundred metres back round to where the bobbers are setting up the start.' His finger traced a curve running from right to left round the frozen lake, then he looked down at his digital watch and pressed it to its stopwatch function. 'My best is seventy seconds flat in boots and ski-suit. You game?'

Murdoch nodded, smiling, already feeling a surge of adrenalin. First Kathy, then her father . . .

The two men crouched, hands on knees.

'Five, four, three, two, one,' hissed Grieve. 'Go!'

They surged off, their feet slipping and skidding as they accelerated on the uneven surface. It was impossible to run with any fluidity or rhythm, and after fifty metres Murdoch settled into a fast, choppy, chugging action. After only a hundred metres he began to breathe heavily, the icy air freezing on the back of his throat. Just a few feet to his left Grieve plugged on remorselessly, his breath billowing in clouds around him. In these early moments Murdoch realised that he had been set up, that Grieve must have run endlessly round the rutted path with his bob squad.

His face cracked into a grin. It was like old times. Single arm push-ups, three standing hops, one finger dead-lifts: Grieve could always produce some esoteric physical challenge in which only he could succeed. The man would never change. Further, unlike Murdoch, Grieve had never stopped competitive running and was still, at fifty-two, capable of achieving inside two minutes for 800 metres. In contrast, Murdoch, though fit, was running on a memory dim from years away from competition.

Involuntarily he began to sense the type of surface which would give him grip, picking it out with quick changes of cadence, though he received little 'feel' through the rigid, grooved soles of his boots as they crunched into the broken ice and snow.

They completed two hundred metres, curving left back to the bob start, each in turn narrowly missing a bewildered schoolboy cyclist. Murdoch could feel the heat building up on his thermals beneath his ski-suit, the sweat drying on his frozen face.

With one hundred and fifty metres to go his eyes focused on the bobbers to his left. They had left their practice, seeing that Murdoch and Grieve were no longer jogging and sensing that something was up. The two men were still neck and neck, just a few feet apart. Then without warning Murdoch felt soft: his knees started to bow, his lungs feeling as if they were being rubbed with iced sandpaper. For the first time he could see Grieve's back and tried to focus in on it, to create an umbilical cord on which he could pull.

One hundred metres to go. Suddenly Grieve was five metres up. Ahead of them the bob squad were screaming encouragement. Murdoch could feel his lungs roaring with pain and his legs felt as if they had been filled with water, but he tried to maintain his rhythm, to preserve the inner stillness essential if he were ever to regain those lost, elusive metres.

Slowly he began to pull Grieve in, his breath ripping through him like a saw. One metre gained, then two . . . But Murdoch was spent. He kept drilling on, legs bowing, his feet landing flat on the frozen surface, until he staggered through the finish two metres down, tumbling on into a soft, powdery snowdrift alongside Grieve.

Staff Sergeant 'Buster' Lloyd stood above the two men,

hands on hips. 'Mad buggers,' he said. 'What do you think this is? The Olympics?'

Murdoch sat up, his hands sinking deep into the powdery snow, lungs heaving. He nodded towards Grieve.

'Every day's the bloody Olympics to him.'

The slim brown envelope, its corners sealed with red wax, had been delivered to Murdoch's room at the Steffani, and lay on his bedside table. Murdoch did not open it. There was no point in delaying a decision until Saturday, for he now knew what he had to do. He telephoned Lysenko's room and was pleased to find that the Russian coach was there. They arranged to meet in five minutes in the lobby below.

For a moment, as he stood on the stairs above the lobby, Murdoch felt sorry for the ascetic Russian, standing surrounded by the lunchtime ski crowd. Lysenko had come a long way to achieve nothing, and his masters would surely show him little pity on his return.

He walked towards Lysenko, withdrew the envelope from his inside pocket, and handed it back to the Russian. Lysenko noted immediately that it had not been opened and frowned.

'Then it is no,' he said. 'I'm sorry.' Carefully he slipped the package into an inside pocket. 'Sorry for all of us,' he added, looking into Murdoch's eyes. 'The matter is now out of my hands,' he said. 'Those who follow me will not be athletes.'

The Russian pursed his lips and gave a slight shake of his head. Then he turned smartly on his heel and made his way through the crowded lobby, through the swing doors of the Steffani, out into the bitter cold of the streets of St Moritz.

13

Danger Run

It was midday and the World Bobsleigh Championships two-man practice runs had just been completed. Murdoch stood at the top of the run on the verandah of the Sachs restaurant and looked down from the starting-box into 'Wall', the tight left-hand turn one hundred metres from the start. St Moritz was unique: a man-made course constructed from snow and ice first scooped then hammered and caressed into fifteen hundred metres of challenging bob run. And all shaped from the contours of a lush summer meadow only a few hundred metres from the centre of St Moritz itself.

If snow conditions were favourable then course-creator Franz Knabel had the run ready by mid-December, possibly even a week earlier. In bad years nothing was possible till early January, and the Swiss and European bobsleigh calendar would then be thrown into temporary confusion.

Each turn had its own name, some like 'Wall' or 'Telephone' descriptive of the immediate geography, geography with which no bobber wished to make contact. Others, like the 'Gunter Sachs', named after the millionaire who had built the bob hut with its bar and 'Dracula' restaurant, or the 'Nash and Dixon', named after the British 1964 Olympic gold medallists, honoured those who had served the sport.

Murdoch went through the course in his mind. First, the left-hander at Wall, the shallow, wriggling Snake, then the tight right-hander at Sunny. The shallow Nash and Dixon corner, then the tricky Horseshoe left-hander, followed by Telephone, Shamrock and Devil's Dyke. By this time a 400-pound racing bob would be rocketing along at seventy miles an hour. Then Tree and the desperately tight turn at Bridge. From then on there was a little dent of a curve at Leap and the soft, shallow left-hander at Bariloche, finishing with a sharp right-angled left-hander at Gunter Sachs, and finally Martineau and a ride up to the soft snow of the finish. The St Moritz run was not the fastest in the world – that distinction belonged to the artificial run at Lake Placid – but its natural quality made it a classic driver's course, tricky and unpredictable. It could never be taken for granted, even by the experienced Swiss drivers like Eric Scharer or Hans Hildebrand, who knew every groove and bubble on its icy surface.

Murdoch had spent the morning watching the final two-man practices. The first of the four practice runs, held the previous day, had been performed with brakes applied before the most difficult curves to enable drivers to have time to pick out a good line on each curve. Many drivers, impatient to get a full speed run, had done without brakes the second time round; but less experienced crews, such as the Japanese, the British and the Russians, had touched the brakes a couple of times. Few national teams, however, used brakes on the last two practices, and Grieve had instructed the four British teams to 'make it real' in the final two runs, as only three teams per nation were permitted to compete in the championships proper. Grieve had posted observers at each curve and video cameras at Horseshoe and Bridge – crucial corners – choosing his three teams at the end of the fourth run. All that remained was a day of rest from training and the final tuning of the sleds before the first round of competition began.

He turned to see Grieve approach him, carrying two steaming glasses of red Glühwein. He took a glass with his fingertips and sipped it tentatively.

'They always get the cinnamon right here,' he said, grinning.

Grieve nodded. 'I've got us a run in half an hour, if you fancy it,' he said. 'In an old tub of a feuerabend. We'll take it down slow, in eighty-five or eighty-six seconds. You game?'

Murdoch nodded. 'No big push at the start?'

'Act your age,' growled Grieve, mock-stern. 'You can just jump in and we'll trundle down easy. But if you're looking for a wee thrill Eric Scharer says he'll let us go down in a couple of hours in something a bit faster, an old Swiss racing bob.'

'Where's the gear?'

Grieve drew him downstairs along to the tiny, fetid bob hut beneath the main restaurant. On wooden pegs on the walls hung half a dozen British helmets. Grieve took one down.

'Try this,' he said. 'It's Buster Lloyd's. He's more or less your size.'

He bent down into an Adidas bag and picked up a pair of gloves and protective sponge elbow pads.

'No need for spikes for the first run,' he said, throwing the gloves and pads at Murdoch. 'But I'll get you a pair of size ten racing shoes for the run this afternoon with the Swiss bob.'

He bent down again and withdrew his own helmet, pads, gloves and spikes, then sat down on the bench and took out his boots.

'I took this up too bloody late,' he said, easing on his spikes. 'Thirty-five.' He pulled on his elbow pads. 'Perception. You've got to *feel* the bloody ice under your arse and see the corners early. By the time I'd begun to get some idea of it my legs and reflexes had gone.'

He donned his helmet, then looked at Murdoch keenly before adjusting the younger man's chin strap.

'Okay,' he said. 'Let's go.'

Grieve and Murdoch were the first of the 'tourist' bobbers, scheduled to start at one o'clock. They were driving in a sluggish, ponderous feuerabend, a machine used by instructors at St Moritz to take tourists down the famous course in a leisurely ninety seconds – twenty seconds and twenty-five miles an hour slower than the world championship bobbers would achieve. Murdoch adjusted his goggles and took up his position at the back of the bob, fixing his hands on the starting handles in front of him.

The buzzer sounded and the red light ahead turned to

green, signalling that all was clear. On his left, Grieve stood with both hands on the stubby horizontal starting handle. A light push was enough to set the bob moving gently, and after a couple of trotting strides Grieve jumped into the front seat of the bob, snapped down his starting handle and engaged the steering ropes which controlled the two front runners. Murdoch too now jumped in, settled in his seat, and gripped the bars on each side of him to fix his position.

They took the first turn, the left-hander at Wall, with ease, hardly moving, then picked up speed into the gentle curves of Snake. Murdoch could hear nothing but the grind and growl of the runners on the uneven ice as they picked up speed into the wide, sweeping, 180-degree right-hander at Sunny. Grieve was able to take the curve and its exit low and controlled. Nash, and the transit into Dixon, came up with a rush and Grieve was only just able to hold a straight path into Horseshoe. Even before Grieve had shouted 'brake' Murdoch had reflexly touched lightly on the brakes for thirty yards and their teeth bit ice, slowing them into the mean, difficult left-hander. Grieve took a low line on the curve and shot out of the exit perfectly balanced, to pick up the short straight into Telephone, in control.

A second touch on the brakes brought them into the right-hander at Shamrock in good order and the bob, flowing easily, was now up to close to fifty miles an hour. A further pull on the brakes before Tree and another before the tight curve at Bridge took them roaring round the twenty-foot-high ice wall, and Murdoch felt the centrifugal force press him down into his seat as he tried to fix his gaze on Grieve's helmet, to maintain the line and necessary balance of the bob. Through Leap, over a blind brow into Sachs, and they were almost there, ripping down towards the finish on the steepest part of the course. He kept off the brakes at the final curve at Martineau and let Grieve have his head. They crossed the finishing line to plough into the soft snow of the rising straight. Murdoch pulled back hard on both brakes, feeling their teeth grip the ice below the fluffy snow.

The two men got out as the Swiss labourers pulled the

feuerabend to the bob truck for its return to the start. Murdoch looked up at the digital clock: 80.5 seconds. He grabbed Grieve's hand.

'You cunning old sod,' he said.

Grieve grinned, his ruddy face glowing. 'A piece of pie,' he said. 'Just you wait till we go down in the Swiss bob.'

It was a quarter to three. Murdoch and Grieve watched from the verandah of the Sachs restaurant as plump, middle-aged Swiss drivers took tourists down the bob run in sturdy, ancient feuerabends. In half an hour they would go down in a fast Swiss bob, loaned to them by the great Swiss bobber Eric Scharer, a friend of Grieve and Murdoch's from their bobbing days of the '70s. From the Cresta Run, two hundred metres away on the other side of the road running through St Moritz, floated the plummy voice of the commentator and club secretary, Eric Everton-Jones.

'Would the lady who has placed her Pekinese at Junction kindly remove it? Thank you very much . . . Next on the run is Sir Ronald Digby, Royal Fusiliers.'

Grieve shook his head. 'Sir Ronald Digby,' he said. 'And they talk about the changing anatomy of Britain.'

'Eton,' said Murdoch.

'Eton, Caius College, Cambridge, then on to the Cabinet, and his feet won't even touch the ground on the way.' He pulled a tube of Smarties out of his top pocket and beckoned. Murdoch put out his gloved hand.

'Do you think we can pull it off?' Grieve said, pouring out the sweets.

Murdoch slipped a handful of Smarties into his mouth and crunched happily. 'You mean our Arab Olympics?'

Grieve nodded.

'Why do you ask?'

'The athletes. Some of them have been living too long in brown paper envelopes. No moral sense. With two million dollars per event some of them will be so high their feet won't touch the track.'

Murdoch's face became serious. 'You said it once, Hugh. Sport without ethics isn't sport. We've got the best brains in sports medicine working in our team. We've got out-of-season testing. We'll wipe drugs off the face of the earth.'

'I hope you're right,' said Grieve, as another bob trundled down the run below them. 'I was talking to a couple of weight-lifters a few weeks back. They were telling me that some lifters are injecting themselves with other people's urine just to beat the drug-tests. Straight into the bladder. When I heard that I wanted to puke.'

Murdoch felt a bitterness in his mouth. 'That's why we've got to beat the drugs.'

Grieve's eyes became distant. 'Do you know how many international athletes I've coached?' he said. 'Thirty.' He reached down into his hip pocket, withdrew a crumpled hand-kerchief and blew his nose vigorously. 'I never even get a Christmas card from most of them.'

He replaced his handkerchief and zipped his pocket. 'The mistake I always made was that because *I* put all I had into coaching athletes I thought that I had some sort of real relationship with them. But they always let me down. Every bloody time.'

He put his hands on Murdoch's shoulder and smiled. 'Except you,' he said.

'Herr Grieve.'

Grieve turned in response. Behind them stood the figure of Hans Muller, the Swiss official in charge of the afternoon's runs.

'Fifteen minutes to your run.'

Grieve nodded and he and Murdoch crunched back through the ice towards the bob hut.

'We'll hack it,' said Murdoch. 'Kudai.'

'Just wanted to hear you say it,' Grieve replied.

3.00 p.m. Murdoch, clad in a pair of borrowed brush starting spikes, settled both feet into the raised wooden start block behind the bob and with gloved hands pushed the Swiss podar lightly up and down in the starting grooves. It felt heavy. On his left, the British bob team had left the restaurant above the run to watch their two compatriots, and stood silently at the ice wall, just in front of them.

Murdoch pulled down his ski glasses and made his ritual twitching movements on the two start grips, simulating the first outward throw of the hands. This would change in a stride to a bent-arms, thumbs-in pushing position so that the maximum forward impulse could be given to the bob, transmitted efficiently from both legs through the hands as he ran, his back horizontal. After that it was push, push, push for thirteen strides down the sloping ice before he would leap into the bob behind Grieve. He hoped that the old reflexes would take over, for it was eight years since he had first thundered down the first fifty metres at St Moritz behind his coach. Then he felt the cold fear in the pit of his stomach and was glad: it was fear that was his friend in such situations, fear that brought into play the essential reflexes that meant the fine difference between success and failure.

He snatched a glance at the clock to the right of the start which recorded the time of the first fifty metres. Back in 1974 he and Grieve had made a swift 5.52. But the years had taken the sap out of the legs of both men, and anything near six seconds over that initial fifty metres would be excellent now. He made a final ritual adjustment to his goggles before nodding as Grieve looked back at him for assurance that he was ready. The coach turned, screwed his spikes into the hard ice, and took a low start position.

'Ready?' Grieve roared.

'Ready.'

The two men gently started to rock the bob back and forward on the starting grooves.

'One . . .' shouted Murdoch, sliding the bob lightly forward.

'Two . . .' He could feel the tension building up in him like a coiled spring.

'Three!' With stabbing, thrusting strides he launched himself out from the wooden start block with both legs, feeling the bob's 400-pound weight as he overcame its inertia. Simultaneously Grieve drove out from his more conventional starting position into a strong running action, and the two men hurled the podar down the icy slope, their spikes biting into its rutted surface.

In nine strides Grieve was in, under the cowling, his hands on the steering handles. Three strides later Murdoch had leapt in too. Grieve had snapped down his starting handle, which would otherwise have fouled the wall on the first curve. The start had been fast and controlled, and the two men were now pressed in tight within the narrow shell of the bob as it gathered speed. Behind them the clock showed 5.98 seconds.

This time the first curve, the left-hander at Wall, came up quickly but they took it with ease and rattled through Snake into Sunny.

'Brake!' roared Grieve.

Murdoch pulled back on the brakes. Nothing happened. As they swept into the left-hander Grieve obviously realised that the brakes had not bitten, but he did not look round, instead concentrating on handling the curve at the unexpectedly high speed.

He took the next corner – Sunny – well, on four runners, deliberately understeering, and they came off down into the shallow Nash and Dixon with only two hundred metres to go into the tight left-hander at Horseshoe.

'Brake!' roared Grieve again.

Murdoch pulled back hard and felt the brakes sunder and go limp. They had snapped.

They roared round Horseshoe, with massive pressure pushing them into the bottom of the bob. Grieve kept his nerve, avoiding the tendency to tug too hard, too early, on the steering ropes. The pull off the curve had to be high and late. Grieve steered it well, but the 400-pound bob was now going at almost twice their expected speed, bringing curves in at a rush, and stretching the veteran's reflexes to their limits.

Coming out of the exit of Horseshoe into Telephone they

touched the top of the wall on the right runner, and as a result the right-hander at Telephone was taken badly, with the sled bumping both sides of the ice wall. Murdoch felt as if he had been hit with hammers as both shoulders in turn smashed against the ice.

They bounced through Shamrock and Devil's Dyke, with the bob shearing ice as it scraped and roared through Tree towards the tight right-hander at Bridge. He could feel his stomach muscles tightening, not far from spasm, as he fought both to fix his body in line behind Grieve's and to make the minute adjustments that might keep the sled on four runners.

But Grieve was rushing towards Bridge in a bob that was sliding across the bubbly ice at speeds far beyond his reflexes. His brain held him from the temptation to oversteer, but the Scot simply did not possess a sufficient reservoir of skill or experience from which to draw. The bob hurtled low into the right-hander across its line of curve and climbed to the top of the turn. For a moment, Murdoch glimpsed the blue sky and the valley below. Then he saw no more.

He was in the magic stadium but he could see only the legs of runners, the muscles of their thighs as they flickered in flight, bulged and set in relief on landing, before extending for the next giant stride. It seemed as if he would never rise above their legs, yet suddenly he was no longer in the race at all but in the midst of the crowd.

Or rather, he was deep in the roar of the crowd as it raged and urged the runners round the track. But, on inspection, it revealed itself as an audience of men in the white jackets of surgeons, their mouths closed and silent, their eyes hidden behind dark sunglasses. Behind them, at the back of the stands, teleprinters clacked automatically, shuttling back and forward, spewing out an endless flow of paper which piled up in front of them before cascading down on to the tiers below. Behind the teleprinters journalists gossiped, oblivious to the race on the track or the endless, senseless chatter of their machines.

Then came the boom of a victory anthem signifying the start of a medal ceremony. The blonde girl on the top step of the victory rostrum bent forward to receive her medal, but as she lifted her head he could see that her skin was stubbled with facial hair. She smiled a toothless, sexless smile, and lifted her massive arms to receive the applause of the crowd.

On the track the race continued, only now Murdoch could see the torsos of the eight runners – sickly, white and shrivelled, while the athletes' eyes had the dark, haunted look of men long imprisoned. Yet above them the vast television screens at either end of the ground showed a quite different picture of the runners – handsome, bronzed athletes in the peak of condition.

The roar of the crowd increased as the finalists swung into the finishing straight. Once more Murdoch could see the flash of spikes as the runners surged towards the line, but now also their hollow, desperate faces contorted as they elbowed and clawed their way towards the finish.

All eight hit the line together, to fall sprawling on the ground. Blood began oozing from their cuts and bruises – only it fizzed and bubbled as if it had a life of its own, one man's blood mingling with another's as they lay spread-eagled on the rapidly reddening track.

Within seconds the bodies were empty, like the Witch in *The Wizard of Oz* when Dorothy had doused her in water. Attendants arrived and heaped the limp carcasses in piles at the back of jeeps, whilst others began to hose the track down with water.

Next came the rain – only it was not rain but millions of fluttering dollar bills, cascading from the roof of the stadium. They landed on the track, absorbing the blood of the runners as it mingled with the water with which the attendants had hosed the surface.

Then, above him, the roof of the stadium slowly opened, revealing an inky, starless sky. When he looked down again at the stadium it was empty. A breeze whirling the notes round and round the track. He bent down and picked up one of the blood-sodden dollar notes and examined it. The face on the note was not that of George Washington: it was his.

He raised his eyes again to the sky and found he was looking up into the clear blue eyes of Ellis Payne. He tried to rise but she pressed him gently back on to the bed. Beside her he could make out a severe grey-haired man in a black pin-striped suit. The man smiled.

'My name is Dr Rosenthal,' he said. He lifted a clipboard and surveyed it. 'The last time you were here, Mr Murdoch, was back in February 1974. Shoulder bruising when you hit the wall at Sachs.'

For the first time Murdoch realised where he was: the Krankenhaus, the refuge for all the strained ligaments and torn cartilages of the holiday skiers of St Moritz.

Rosenthal was still consulting his clipboard. 'Concussion. Badly bruised ribs and gluteals. Minor facial cuts, requiring only six stitches. You have been very fortunate, Mr Murdoch. Few men come off Bridge at a hundred kilometres an hour without at least two fractures.'

'What about Hugh?'

Rosenthal's face became more serious. 'Mr Grieve was not able to get clear of the sled.' He again consulted his clipboard. 'Concussion, severe. Cracked right clavicle, three broken ribs. Considerable facial bruising.' His own lined face creased into a smile. 'But your Mr Grieve does not appear to be made like ordinary mortals. Twenty minutes ago he was awake and demanding copies of *L'Equipe* and the *Guardian*. Already he is asking the nurses for pulley-weights in order that he may rehabilitate himself.'

'He's going to be fine, Murdoch,' said Ellis, her lips puckering in concern.

Dr Rosenthal whispered a few words in Ellis's ear and moved silently from the room. As soon as the door closed behind him Ellis slid a chair to the side of Murdoch's bed and sat down.

211

'They checked the brakes,' she said. 'Sawn through. Sabotaged.'

Murdoch groaned. 'I checked them before the start. I should have found it then.'

'Herr Muller said it would have been impossible for your check to have detected the damage. They were three-quarters sawn through. It took your first braking to finish them off.'

Murdoch slowly eased himself up and Ellis placed pillows behind him. The effort brought beads of sweat to his forehead.

'Jesus Christ,' he said. 'We could both be dead.'

He reached for a glass of water from the bedside table and slowly sipped it. 'But how do you come to be here?'

'It came through yesterday on the evening news,' she replied. 'I was in Zurich by midnight and caught the morning train to St Moritz.'

He looked over to the table by the window. It was engulfed in baskets of flowers. She caught his glance.

'All the world championship teams have sent something,' she said. 'Murdoch,' she said. 'You're crazy. These people are out to get you. They've nearly killed Grieve. You've got Ciano on your tail . . .'

'And there's something else,' he said. 'Buchinski. It looks as if his death wasn't an accident.'

Ellis's lips quivered and she exhaled slowly. She made to speak, but Murdoch interrupted her.

'Not the Russians. Because Lysenko told me, don't ask me how he knew. Perhaps the Russians had put a tab on Buchinski and someone else got to Bull while they were watching him. I don't know.' He sighed, wincing as he felt the bruising in his ribs.

'What about this bobsled accident?'

Murdoch shrugged. 'Not Ciano this time. Probably the Russians. After all, it's not exactly a top security area up there in the bob hut. A few minutes' work with a hacksaw could have done it. But I don't think they meant to kill us.'

'Thanks for nothing,' she said. 'So where are we now in the Kudai stakes?'

'Your Americans are all still behind us, to a man. Bull's death hit them hard, but in some strange way it stiffened their resolve, made the Kudai Games a sort of memorial to Bull. It's odd how people's minds work.' He coughed, feeling another sharp pain in his ribs.

'Not just their minds,' said Ellis, smiling. Then she placed her hands on his stubbled cheeks and kissed him.

The softness of her mouth surprised him. Ellis's lips parted and her tongue darted delicately to touch the inside of his lips. There was nothing lewd in its movement, only a blend of affection and passion, which in its suddenness made him, at that moment, incapable of response.

'You surprise me,' he said. 'Taking advantage of a man in bed.'

She smiled. 'Can you think of a better place?'

14

Kathy

Maurice Delgado awoke to the bleeping of his wrist-watch. Eight o'clock; he was to meet Murdoch at eleven. He lay back, stretching.

The Kudai Games had come as a surprise to him, although he had of course heard rumours about them weeks before the Athens Games. But his diplomatic antennae had been pointing in a different direction, towards a reciprocal Eastern bloc Olympic boycott and the still-dangerous issue of British rugby and cricket teams touring South Africa. Delgado knew that these were issues which would haunt the Los Angeles Olympics to within days of their official opening.

He was also aware that his own position owed little to merit and more to an IOC commitment to the Good and the Great which stretched back into the nineteenth century, to de Coubertin himself – that great democrat who had created in the IOC the most undemocratic organisation imaginable. Yet somehow it had all worked, this self-perpetuating jumble of millionaires, generals, archdukes and princes, in a way which no democratically elected body could ever have done.

Maurice Delgado knew that he lay in a direct line with Lord Burghley, Avery Brundage, Lord Killanin and the other blue-bloods and millionaires in whom sport had placed its trust since the 1896 Olympics. He would truly have preferred it otherwise, that some world democracy of sport had freely elected him, like an American President. But this was the way of the world, or at least the world of the IOC.

214

Delgado had liked Lord Burghley. The Englishman's charm and dignity had been no surface veneer; rather, it had been the product of centuries of breeding, and Burghley's central unstated assumption of moral superiority had held sway over even European Communists, let alone capitalists like Avery Brundage.

Brundage, Delgado had both despised and admired. For the arch-vulgarian of Munich, this humbug of infinite sexuality, had been the saviour of the Olympic movement. Paradoxically, it was probably only a barbarian like Brundage who could have protected the Games from the encroachment of commerce and politics in the period from 1950 to 1976. Delgado knew in his heart that neither he nor Killanin could have done it, for both knew too well the central inconsistencies of the purist amateur position. Their sophistication, their intellect, would have left them defenceless in the post-war battle for the preservation of the movement. No, it was Brundage who had saved the Olympics, and they should all be thankful.

For Delgado, his Olympic appointment had come like a rope to a drowning man. His political life had been all but finished, as the France he knew and loved had moved inexorably to the Left. Long before 1976, when his children had left home, his marriage to the estimable Marie Saint-Saers had been over. They had not married for love, so he had not lived through the slow wearing away of passion. Yet even in early middle-age Delgado had been aware that he still needed affection, and when he had met the young Madame Louise D'Asterac in 1973 he had known that she was the woman with whom he wished to share the rest of his life.

Marie had known of Louise D'Asterac from the beginning, but it had not troubled her. Instead it took a weight of guilt and responsibility from her shoulders, for although she had never loved Delgado nor indeed any man she had sensed her husband's unhappiness. The appearance of Madame D'Asterac had come as a relief.

Louise appeared to ask nothing of him. Indeed, she seemed to come from some older, selfless tradition of feminine commitment. Her pleasure came from involvement in his thinking and his doing. But though she had no creative intellectual abilities of her own, Louise possessed that most valuable of qualities, the capacity to cut through cant. Thus her slim, manicured fingers handled each Olympic document in the same way as they expertly fondled Maurice Delgado's lean, Riviera-bronzed body. So after his first meeting with Cohn and the representatives of the governing bodies, it had been to Louise D'Asterac that he had turned. Her response had been immediate: 'Murdoch wants money or respectability, perhaps both. Money you have in the Olympic commercial contracts, though not till after Los Angeles. Or perhaps a direct bribe.'

'And respectability?'

'Your Mr Murdoch has, according to your researchers, always been a classic outsider. So go to your precious Committee, go to Berne. Ask them to make the second IAAF World Championships and World Cup available to Kudai, in return for the delaying of their 1984 Games. And your IOC contribution is Kudai as the site of the 1992 Olympics.'

'But you know I have no control over the IAAF, Louise.'

'Their 1983 Helsinki World Track and Field Championships is dead if Kudai hold their Million Dollar Meets in 1983,' she had replied sharply. 'So Berne will *have* to bring something to the negotiating table. And it has to be a major Games, Maurice.'

Of course she had been right, although it had taken two months of negotiating and bullying before Delgado had the central bargaining counters he required.

His watch bleeped again and he turned on to his side and pressed the stop button: 8.15 a.m. As he did so he felt Louise's fingers slide across his left hip and gently but purposefully fumble for him. No matter how often it happened it always came to him as a sweet shock. He gave a reflex sigh and gratefully allowed her to have her way.

Murdoch had surprised Maurice Delgado. The IOC president had expected to meet a Mark McCormack-type executive,

Savile Row-suited and Gucci-shod, remote from the day-to-day world of sport. Instead, he found someone to whom he could relate far more directly than men like Berne or Cohn.

The Scot had been completely frank, and his revelations on his meetings with Ciano and Lysenko and his St Moritz accident had shocked Delgado. Yet, on reflection, he knew that Murdoch's experiences had probably been inevitable. His own negotiations with the Los Angeles Olympic Committee and his more recent dealings on the North American television rights for the 1988 Winter Olympics were proof, if any were needed, that the Olympics, whatever their ideals, were now essentially about money and politics. The 1988 Winter Olympics would realise 300 million dollars in North American TV rights alone and the 1992 Summer Games well over twice that sum. Bruce Cohn had reckoned that the Los Angeles Olympics would bring 4 billion dollars in trade into California.

The reserve between the two men had broken down quickly as a result of Murdoch's openness. As their discussion had progressed, Delgado had realised that Louise D'Asterac's proposals might prove to be irrelevant. For, in principle, what Murdoch was proposing in Kudai was what Maurice Delgado himself desired. Delgado saw in Murdoch, not someone awash in petrodollars and dedicated to the overthrow of his Olympic movement, but rather a man with a single, almost Messianic aim: open, honest sport. And that troubled him, made him for a moment wish that he was dealing with a naked commercial entrepreneur.

Delgado decided to avoid making any offer to Murdoch of the IAAF contracts which Harold Berne had brought to him; those were clearly bribes, more directly concerned with saving Berne's 'baby', the Championships in Helsinki, than preserving the Games at Los Angeles. Instead, Delgado suggested delaying the Kudai Games till 1992, when the Emirate could be offered the entire Olympic programme; postponement rather than cancellation.

He could feel that his offer had made an impact upon the

Scot and had pressed forward with a supplementary offer. If Murdoch would make his revolutionary drug-testing procedures available to the Los Angeles Olympic Committee then they would be applied at the Los Angeles Games.

Delgado knew that he had gone beyond his own remit in making such an offer, for the actual consequences might be appalling and the damage to the Olympic movement beyond repair. On reflection, perhaps Murdoch had infected him with his own simple – possibly simplistic – view of sport as a form of ultimate truth.

He saw too that this final offer had come as a surprise to Murdoch, and had pressed home his advantage. The Kudai track and field programme would not start until the summer, with the swimming and gymnastics in the autumn. All three groups would not therefore have crossed the Rubicon until that time and Delgado proposed to leave his offer open till the end of May.

The meeting had ended amicably but Delgado had not been optimistic. The Kudai venture had possibly gone too far, and Murdoch and his colleagues were now in too deep. These reflections were strengthened by a telephone discussion later that day with Harold Berne. Delgado had been guarded in his discussion with Berne. Nevertheless, he had decided to test his British colleague. If a deal with Kudai were possible, would the IAAF agree to Murdoch's drug-testing procedures being used in Helsinki? The silence on the end of the line had been almost palpable. When the conversation had resumed Berne had said that he would have to go back to his committee for a ruling. It was at that moment that Delgado knew that he could not rely on Berne or the IAAF, and that no drug 'positives' would be discovered at the inaugural World Championships. He had put down the telephone slowly.

Saturday, 29 January 1983

It was the first time that Murdoch had seen Grieve close to tears. His old coach had arrived at Hallam Street unprompted and he had sensed that there was something wrong the moment he had opened the door.

'A dram,' said Grieve, walking past him into the living room. 'A double.' Grieve normally drank nothing stronger than lager.

Murdoch had asked no questions but had poured out a large Glenfiddich as his friend sat in the centre of the sofa, head down. Grieve suddenly looked his age, a grey fifty-five, the bruising from his St Moritz crash still visible on his cheeks. Murdoch handed him the glass, which he emptied in two gulps before laying it on the table in front of him. Murdoch recharged it and waited for Grieve to speak.

'Kathy,' he said at last. 'They've got a positive.'

For a moment Murdoch could not take the information in.

'From that big indoor meet in Paris a fortnight ago,' explained Grieve. 'Her, a Rumanian and a German. The samples have gone to Duisburg for final scrutiny.'

'Hold on. Let me get this clear,' said Murdoch. 'You're saying that they've picked up Kathy for drugs? Who told you this?'

'Berne,' said Grieve, as Murdoch replenished his glass. 'He called me this afternoon at home. Said it went beyond his remit, but thought that as her father . . .' Grieve made an uncomfortable choking noise. 'Of course he admitted that the first sample wasn't conclusive.'

'I see. But he just thought you'd like to know,' said Murdoch. 'As an old friend.' He poured himself out a whisky and sipped it slowly. 'Have you spoken to Kathy yet?'

'Yes,' said Grieve, thickly. 'On the phone.'

'And?'

'Stromba,' said Grieve. 'Five milligrams a day. It all started when she got that big muscle pull back in '81.'

'Speeded up the muscle repair?'

'Aye. Her coach Haller advised her, then kept her on them into '82. Of course she found that she recovered her training volume quickly. Then she found that she could get in two sessions a day without fatigue.'

'Did she take medical advice?'

'Some Harley Street quack called Leadbetter. She's been tested before and both times Haller had pissed in the bottle for her and given his *own* sample. You know what testing's like in Britain.'

'Yes,' said Murdoch. 'Sure I know.'

'They've got her, Murdoch,' said Grieve. 'No doubt about it.'

'Wait a minute,' said Murdoch. 'This doesn't add up. Kathy must have known she'd be likely to be tested in a major meet like the Paris one. Wasn't she checked out by Leadbetter before she left?'

Grieve nodded.

'Leadbetter had her flushed out to clear her of the drug, and then checked her. Her London tests said she was clean. Otherwise she wouldn't have gone to Paris in the first place.'

'She'd have gone sick, or pulled a muscle?'

'Yes. That's the usual form.'

Murdoch stood and placed both hands to his lips. 'Let's look at two possible scenarios,' he said. 'The first is that they *do* have a positive sample, that Leadbetter boobed. The only reason Berne phoned is that he wanted to use Kathy's exposure as a lever on us to pull back on our 1983 Kudai programme. Blackmail again.'

'Or to discredit us in the press,' said Grieve.

'Yes,' said Murdoch. 'And don't let's forget that *Daily Express* picture a few months ago of Kathy and me training together at Crystal Palace. It'll be all over the front pages. I can see it now. "Arab Olympics leaders in steroid scandal."'

Murdoch sat down facing Grieve. 'But let's just look at the second scenario,' he said. 'Let's say Kathy *was* clean in Paris. That means Berne is bluffing. After all, we've no means of knowing whether he has a positive sample or not.'

'And Berne doesn't know for certain that Kathy has been on the anabolics.'

'No,' said Murdoch. 'He didn't even specify anabolics, did he?'

Grieve shook his head. 'From what Berne said, it could have been anything, amphetamines . . .'

'Okay,' said Murdoch, leaning forward. 'Berne knew that there was a good chance, probably around eighty per cent, that most of his international athletes have been on some drug or other at some time. He also knows that the athletes have no means of knowing the sensitivity of any new testing procedures. So let's just say our Mr Berne takes a gamble – and it's not a long shot by any means – on Kathy being on something.'

'It's possible,' said Grieve. 'So what do we do?'

'Did Berne say that he would call you back?'

'Tomorrow,' said Grieve.

'Then tape his call,' said Murdoch. 'Get him to repeat his statement about Kathy being a positive. And get him to talk as much as possible.'

'What are we going to do?'

'Nothing,' said Murdoch. 'We'll sit tight and gamble that Berne's bluffing. If he isn't bluffing then he'll come back to us with some sort of deal. If he is, we have his tape – and that's the last we'll hear of Mr Berne.'

Berne's call to Grieve on the following day was duly taped. Investigations by Quince during the next day showed that there had been no drug-testing in Paris; the French had too many skeletons in their own cupboard for that. On Monday, 31 January Berne's secretary phoned, requesting a meeting with Murdoch. It was refused.

On 3 February Kathy Grieve, after a stormy afternoon with her father, ended her coaching relationship with Haller and gave her father a firm promise that drugs would play no further part in her athletics career. On the same day Berne's recorded discussion with Grieve was placed in a safety deposit box in Barclays Bank, Tottenham Court Road.

If Delgado's meeting with Alan Murdoch had been a surprise to him, then it had been equally surprising to Murdoch himself. The Scot had expected a combative encounter, albeit at low key, ending in a bribe, disguised in one form or another. Now, as he sat in his flat in Hallam Street, awaiting Ellis Payne's arrival for their first script conference since St Moritz, he reflected that Delgado had not been what he expected at all. True, the IOC president had an urbanity which Murdoch tended instinctively to distrust, but as the meeting had progressed so he had been drawn to Delgado.

Murdoch knew that his attitude to men of Delgado's background was an unthinking response, born of a working-class background. He could no more help having it than he could avoid being six feet tall, but he was glad that such knee-jerk reflexes could be overridden by the reality of Delgado himself.

In other circumstances the Frenchman's offer, resulting in a saving of hundreds of millions of dollars for Kudai, would have been an excellent one. But Murdoch's brief from Prince Hassan had been clear. It was to produce the first open, professional games, conducted with the utmost probity. He had, however, felt duty-bound to relay Delgado's offer by telex direct to the Prince. Hassan's negative reply had come within the hour.

Murdoch flicked through *The Nazi Games*. Even in the over-simplified world of his script, the 'Goodies' and the 'Baddies' were not always clearly etched. Was, for instance, Brundage 'bad' or merely dim? Similarly, Delgado was certainly a moral man, albeit one in charge of a corrupt enterprise. Brundage's support for American participation in the Berlin Olympics had been a major factor in the Games' success, which, in turn, had strengthened the prestige of the Nazi regime. Kane's scene with Rabbi Wise had been intended to show the complexity of a situation in which Kane would face the choice between withdrawing from the Olympics in protest against persecution of Jewish athletes or performing a patriotic duty.

He checked his watch. Ellis, invariably punctual, would be with him in a matter of moments. They had not met since after the St Moritz crash, as Ellis had been forced to return to Los Angeles to tie up some loose ends on her Puttnam project. He felt that in a single moment in St Moritz they had cut through weeks of preliminaries, but he could not be sure.

It was strange. He wondered what she saw when she looked at him. The gap between friendship and something more could be millimetres, or it could be a chasm. Perhaps he would find out tonight.

He heard the buzz of the bell at the front door. It was Ellis. She stood, her face wet with rain.

'You're edible, Ellis,' he said, involuntarily. The words sounded ridiculous. For a moment Ellis was taken aback. She handed Murdoch her dripping umbrella and entered the flat.

'So you've woken up at last, Murdoch,' she said, over her shoulder. She took off her wet raincoat and handed it to him, then removed her neck-scarf and placed it on top of the coat. She sat on the couch as Murdoch moved off to hang up her clothes. When he came back Ellis was deep in the film script, flicking through the pages in search of a particular scene. She looked up at him.

'This sequence with Kane and the girl athlete . . .'

'At the *thé-dansant* at the Uberstrasse?'

'Yes.'

'What about it?'

She picked up a bundle of pages and surveyed them.

'It's no good. It's got about as much sex as a Tarzan movie.'

Murdoch reddened and, although he tried to control it, his voice became harder. 'And what exactly would you suggest?'

'Contact, physical contact. After all, these are fit, vibrant young athletes, at the peak of their powers.'

Murdoch did not reply, but waited for Ellis to continue.

'You know, even back in 1936 there was *some* physical contact between the sexes. People haven't changed *that* much. You've got Kane treating the girl like a piece of bone china.'

'So?'

'So we've got to have a scene where they get to grips with each other.'

'It isn't a wrestling movie.'

Ellis grimaced. 'You know what I mean.'

'Perhaps Kane isn't that kind of man.'

'You mean he's gay? You're telling me we got a gay athlete for our hero?'

Murdoch relaxed and grinned.

'You know what I mean, Ellis. Kane, he's an athlete, and it is 1936. They had a lot of hang-ups back in those days. He's dedicated. Committed.'

'He's still a man.'

Murdoch took the script from her and scrutinised it. 'Okay,' he said. 'So you've convinced me. I'll try to write it – in the interests of art. But where can we place what you so delicately call a "contact" scene? Not in the Olympic Village.'

'No,' she replied.

'And there's no way he could get her away somewhere for the night. Not with Avery Brundage around. They'd both get taken off the Olympic team.'

Ellis sucked on her pencil for a moment. 'That's true. What about starting something in training?'

'In training?'

'Let's say we make the girl a hurdler. So's Kane. So they're doing hurdle drills together. You know, little practice exercises. Kane's helping her out.'

'How do you mean?'

'I've seen the track and field athletes work out at UCLA. Putting their lead legs over the hurdle. Then the rear leg.' She got to her feet. 'Stand up, Murdoch. I'll show you.'

He stood up obediently.

Ellis moved into the middle of the room, beckoning him to join her. 'Just imagine,' she said, 'a hurdle right here.'

Murdoch nodded. She leant forward and placed both hands on his shoulders. Murdoch smelt the delicate fragrance of her cologne.

'Now, I've seen them do it down at the track. They circle their rear legs round the hurdle, like this.'

Murdoch nodded.

'Well, support my rear leg, dummy.'

He placed his right hand uncertainly on her knee, feeling the warmth of her flesh through her jeans.

'They circle it, then they pull it through into running action.'

She pulled through her knee and as she did so her lips brushed his lightly, as if by accident.

'So let's choreograph this. First we can get them going through a range of exercises, each drill building up to this final one. Kane gets his hand on her thigh . . .'

Murdoch placed his hand on the inside of her thigh.

'Further up, closer to my crotch.'

Murdoch felt himself flush and harden.

'Now the pull-through of the lead leg.'

She pulled through her thigh and Murdoch's hand involuntarily moved between her legs. Ellis groaned. Her voice dropped.

'And the oh, so-gentle brush of the lips. No kiss, mind you, they're in strict training. Just like you said.'

Ellis pushed herself away from him. She was breathing heavily.

'Got it?' she said. 'Then we cut in to an idyllic woodland scene with them in tracksuits in a big necking session.'

'You've sold me,' he said. 'But shouldn't we choreograph that too?'

She stood close to him, her breasts lightly brushing his chest, lips parted, her face set in a quizzical smile.

'Only if you really think we should, Mr Murdoch. In the interests of art.'

15

A Visit to Leningrad

Tuesday, 22 February 1983

Murdoch always took particular care over his laces. There was nothing worse than starting a run flat out and then to find your rhythm destroyed by a flapping lace. He double-knotted them now, zeroed his digital stopwatch and rehearsed the run in his mind. The usual ritual: warm up with a slow jog along Hallam Street, into Portland Place, then across Euston Road to the edge of Regent's Park. His first contract with himself began there, a contract to run strongly and evenly to the start of the canal towpath. He would work hard up the long straight along the side of the park towards Camden Town, then sharp left for two hundred metres and then left again on to the steep narrow lane that led down to the Grand Union Canal towpath. On a good day he would make it in six minutes five seconds; when he was 'hot', inside six minutes.

Then came the Big Contract, a hard run for one mile along the towpath; his best had been five minutes twenty-eight seconds – on a still day in May. Then the turn-round at the bridge, and the attempt to match his time on the way back. There, his best had been a lung-bursting five minutes twenty-six seconds. Finally, a rubber-legged struggle up the short path back on to the pavement and a slow recovery jog back home to Hallam Street.

Those were the ground-rules, the unwritten contracts which Murdoch regularly made with himself. There was no dishonour in failing to achieve the time requirements of the contract; only if he failed to try would there be dishonour. Every day Murdoch made such inner contracts, and each time attempted to meet their demands, ones of commitment and effort before all else.

He looked out on to the street. It was a cool, breezy February afternoon, and he had given Sparrow's man the day off from his security duties. He stood up as the buzzer at the door of his flat sounded.

It was Ellis, bearing a massive Harrods carrier. She wryly looked him up and down. 'You want some company on the road, Murdoch, or is it banjo strings today?'

'Banjo strings,' he said. 'Full stretch.'

'Then you're on your own,' she replied. 'I'll have a drink ready when you get back.'

He attempted a brief kiss on the lips, but she pulled him in, open-mouthed.

'Easy,' he said. 'I thought we'd finished on the sex scenes.'

'Only in the script,' she said to his back as he made his way down the hall.

Murdoch jogged along Hallam Street, side-stepping the pedestrians out walking in the fading, late-afternoon light. He passed an obese, puffing, fellow jogger shuffling towards Broadcasting House and raised his right hand in salute. The jogger grinned in recognition of their shared pain. Nowadays you were never alone on the roads.

As he ran, Murdoch's mind was free to drift back over the events of the past month. The defection of the East Europeans had brought Kudai back under the spotlight of the world's press, away from the sports pages into the editorial columns. The numbers involved had surprised him, and had put the Thatcher government in a dilemma. A hastily convened Cabinet meeting had resulted in asylum being granted to all the defectors, and with that decision Communist sport was dealt the biggest blow in its history. The immediate reaction of the Communist press had been one of outrage, with talk of boycotting the Los Angeles Olympics again surfacing. He wondered what their next move would be. Fortunately, the logistics of caring for the defectors had been taken up by

British Solidarity, with some help from the Kudai coffers. It had all been surprisingly painless, and even now Grieve was busy planning how he would use the best of the Communist sportsmen in his clinics in the Emirates.

As he ran, Murdoch also wondered what would have happened to Lysenko. Would his head roll? He felt some sympathy for the ex-decathlete, out of his depth in the politics of the Kudai situation.

He had reached the traffic lights at Regent's Park. Glancing to both sides, he crossed the street and ran on through the Park gates. Murdoch checked his watch, pressed, and heard the confirming beep as the stopwatch mechanism was activated. Immediately he started off on the first contract.

Even at this higher speed his running action felt artificial and alien, for he had been a sprinter–hurdler, his musculature ideally suited to the explosion of sprint-starts but useless for the oxygen transport involved in running distances of half a mile and above.

Thus he ran with frugal, heel-first strides, his breath coming easily after the inevitable early breathlessness of the first half mile from Hallam Street. It was flowing, going well, and by the left turn at the traffic lights, just before Camden Town, he was only a little over five and a half minutes, close on his record schedule. He nevertheless held himself back, gathering himself for the hardest part, the two endless straights down by the canal.

As he turned on to the towpath he checked his watch. Five minutes fifty-eight, only a few seconds outside his best. He zeroed the watch again and controlled his strides down the steep incline leading to the towpath. Murdoch reached the base of the hill and pressed the stud on his stopwatch.

He felt crisp. His eyes were fixed to the middle distance and in his concentration he missed the greetings of fellow-runners coming towards him on the narrow path. On his left stretched the dark, oily canal, and above the canal he could see the twinkling lights of a junior school. Murdoch ran fluently, his feet somehow missing the grooves and ruts in the towpath's

228

asphalt surface. He hardly noticed the shadows and silence as he passed under the canal bridges. Soon he saw the mile point, an empty wooden towpath bench.

He looked at his watch. Five minutes twenty seconds, eight seconds inside his best, and it had been surprisingly easy. He turned for the return journey, breathing lightly. Perhaps it was one of those days when mind and body would reach agreement. But even in the first hundred metres he knew that it was going to be hard. To begin with, he found that he was now running into a head wind, and he had to struggle to achieve his previous rhythm.

After only a quarter of a mile Murdoch was breathing heavily and felt the stretch on his diaphragm and the respiratory muscles of his chest, the legacy of his St Moritz injuries. He was balancing on that narrow knife-edge between discomfort and pain. Any slower and his chance of a record would be gone; any faster and the fine balance between input and output would slip away.

He could hear clearly his own breath, feel it rip through lungs and chest, apparently incapable of giving him the oxygen he required. But he could also see the finish now – a bench occupied by two groping, middle-aged lovers – just below the path leading up to the main road.

Murdoch's legs had almost gone. He lurched past the bench, stopped the watch and stood, hands on knees, sobbing, a few feet beyond the two lovers, oblivious to them. He checked his watch: five minutes twenty-one seconds. The contract had been met, the record secured.

He trotted, head down and heavy-legged, up the steep path to the main road and turned right, his feet hardly leaving the ground. In the gloom he did not see the black Rolls Royce parked forty yards ahead of him.

Murdoch now shambled rather than ran, his bent-kneed action a parody of the purposeful stride with which he had attacked the towpath run. Every breath seemed to come from lungs hedged with thorns, but he was beyond caring. He had cracked it, and was content.

He was only a few feet from the Rolls when both its doors opened simultaneously. Murdoch cursed and moved out to his right. As he did so, he was held firmly by both shoulders from behind. He turned, his fatigue momentarily forgotten, but smelt only sickly sweetness as a white handkerchief was thrust over his nose and mouth. His legs buckled and it was only the strength of the other man in front of him that prevented him from falling to the pavement. He was unaware of the two men half-pushing, half-carrying him to the car, or of being thrown in a heap on to the leather seats within.

Only a hundred metres away a tracksuited Claud Farrell cursed and sprinted as the Rolls eased out into the road, soon to be swept up in the Regent's Park traffic.

Farrell weaved and dodged through passers-by, praying that the car would be caught by the first set of lights, now only a hundred metres away. But the black Rolls sailed serenely through on green and Farrell, struggling for speed, zig-zagged through a crowd of students at the crossroads. The Rolls was still only about two hundred metres away, its progress slowed by the density of the traffic. It had signalled to go left, towards central London, but for the first time was forced to wait as a line of cars swept past it in the opposite direction.

Farrell gathered himself for a final burst. He had to salvage at least something before it was too late. Grunting as he ran, he side-stepped an elderly woman and a young courting couple and, ignoring the growing pain in his throat and chest, kept on running. He was only fifty metres from the car as it at last found space in the traffic. As it turned, he caught sight of the licence plates: MFU 109T. He stopped running and leaned, sobbing, on the park railings on his left. He had almost blown it. But not quite.

Murdoch was in a tunnel, facing himself. But he faced an unlined, younger self, a trickle of sweat pursuing its jagged path down his tense, young face. The man before him made a reflex pre-race gulp and he followed suit, without knowing why.

Behind him came a steady purr in the darkness, and he realised that he was facing on film the man of his nightmares, the Murdoch of Mexico City. He felt an itch on the tip of his nose and made to lift a hand to scratch it. But the hand would not rise from his side. He looked down to see that he was firmly bound to a wooden chair four metres away from the screen, where the Mexico debacle flowed inexorably on.

Inevitably all went smoothly at first: one-two-three, one-two-three, his legs windmilling on and over each obstacle, the running between the barriers fluid and balanced, sweet product of hundreds of hours with Grieve. Then that minor, crucial loss of balance at the seventh. It was a flaw so subtle that only he and Grieve in that whole vast stadium would have detected it.

His neck tightened as he saw himself struggle to regain control at the eighth hurdle. But his clearance was too high, always would be, and he smashed through the ninth and fell, ploughing through the fresh surface of the Tartan track, underneath the tenth hurdle. He clenched his fists as he again felt his skin rip and shear on the rough Tartan. The film froze on him flat on the track, his anguished face looking up towards the stands where Grieve sat, head bowed in private pain. The screen went blank, but the room stayed dark.

'Mexico City, 1968,' intoned a voice from somewhere behind him. 'Failure.'

Despite the coldness of the room Murdoch was drenched in sweat. He shut his eyes and tried to take in the situation. First, a physical inventory. He could feel the ridges of his jock-strap on the seat of the stiff wooden chair to which he was pinioned so it seemed that he was still dressed in his full running gear. He tried to move his ankles, but they were also bound tight, although he could feel the hard ridge of his Adidas road shoes on the floor, and by pushing down on his toes he could raise the chair slightly.

As the projector began again, its purr filling the silent room, he tried to cry out, but a plaster strip across his mouth reduced the attempt to a muted grunt. Forced to continue looking at the screen, he saw a javelin hanging for an instant as if suspended in flight before plummeting to stab turf. But the athlete, smiling as the distance of 62.84 metres appeared on the primitive manual scoreboard, was not Murdoch but Igor Lysenko, crew-cropped and bronzed, an almost frivolous figure as he skipped back to retrieve his tracksuit. Murdoch tried to establish the venue, as the camera showed some general shots of an almost empty stadium.

The camera closed in on a hand brushing earth from the tip of a 60-metre Berg javelin, and moved back to show the figure of Murdoch, but a heavier, more muscular version than the hurdler of Mexico City. Suddenly he could identify the moment, and felt the sweat spurt from his forehead as he struggled impotently against his bonds. Papendaal 1969, the ninth event of the decathlon. He had led Lysenko narrowly after the eighth event, the pole vault, but had thrown only a miserable 55.02 metres in the javelin after two rounds. Lysenko's third and final throw had gone out to a fine 62.84 metres, putting him back into the overall lead with his strong event, the 1500 metres, still to come. Now came Murdoch's own third and final attempt to catch up with the Russian.

It was a long throw, with a powerful, direct pull through the shaft of the javelin. The spear flew into the light breeze, rifling flat and steady, certain to land at well over 65 metres. But as it dropped it was caught by a sudden gust of wind, its point rose and it hit the ground ominously flat. Murdoch could almost hear the clang of its landing, though the film was silent.

The camera focused on a flag: a red flag. Murdoch felt sweat and tears flow down his face.

'Papendaal, 1969,' intoned the deeply accented voice. 'Failure.' The screen again went blank, then the projector recommenced its steady, insistent whirr.

It was a pole vault, in double slow motion. Murdoch experienced the familiar gunpowder taste of his teeth grinding together, could feel the ropes cutting into his wrists and ankles. This time he knew exactly where he was: Leningrad 1971, Great Britain versus Russia and West Germany. He had entered the competition at a modest 3.40 metres, simply to get some points on his card, and had cleared easily. Wishing to conserve energy he had left his next vault till 4.00 metres, a height he would normally clear with ease. But at 3.80 metres there had been a sudden downpour of rain, leaving the runway slippery and dangerous.

The film followed his third and final vault, from take-off to landing. It had been an all-out effort but he had managed to summon the correct level of control and coordination at take-off to ensure a balanced drive, his horizontal speed transferred directly into the flexible pole. It was a strong, easy clearance, his hips well clear of the bar, and the cameraman had done well to capture the smile on his face as he flopped backwards into the engulfing softness of the blue-foam landing area.

But the pole had not responded to his backward push. Instead it had drifted into the bar and he had watched as it dropped slowly down on to his chest. The film froze on his despairing face.

'Leningrad, 1971. Failure,' intoned the voice again. The screen went blank.

Murdoch sagged in his chair, and shut his eyes. He felt a lump in his solar plexus, just as he had when he had first been told of Buchinski's death. The voice appeared to be only a couple of metres behind him. It was deep and assured, undoubtedly foreign, but he could not identify it or move to see behind him. Surprisingly, it sounded almost sympathetic, parental.

He opened his eyes again and stared at the screen. Now they were in Munich at the Olympics in a sequence he had seen a dozen times. It was the final event, the 1500 metres, and the camera followed Lysenko and Murdoch through the final three laps. By the end of the third lap the Russian was over sixty metres ahead, with Murdoch struggling to find room in the following pack.

But the sound of the bell for the final lap seemed to galvanise the Scot. He got on to his toes, his knees lifted and he set off in strong pursuit. Even in the silence of the room Murdoch imagined that he could feel the roaring of his lungs, hear the shouts of the crowd give him a strength to which he had no physiological right.

Lysenko had been only fifteen metres ahead when he hit the tape, with Murdoch staggering behind him. The film stopped on Murdoch, sprawled on his back.

'Munich, 1972,' said the voice behind him. 'Failure.'

This time the room stayed in darkness. There were footsteps, and a range of unidentifiable sounds. A few moments later there was a click, and the room was bathed in light. Murdoch looked around him to see that he was in a stone cell, with cracked, yellow plaster walls. On the wall where the films had been, just to their left, were pasted some tattered posters. He was close enough to see that they were for long-past sporting events. He could also see that they were in an unfamiliar script. He screwed up his eyes to identify it: Russian. The poster on the left featured soccer, a 1980 cup match between Zenit Leningrad and Dynamo Moscow, the middle one some sort of local Spartakiade in 1979, and the one on the right a 1980 swimming tournament.

Murdoch could again hear in his mind the roar of a crowd, which stopped abruptly. Or was it just his mind? How much was he imagining things, how much – ? About a quarter of an hour later there was a further roar, unmistakable, then silence. Suddenly, above him, there was the tramp of feet and he could see the shadows of spectators passing the grille high on the cell wall to his left. He made to shout, but could not. Then he looked again at the wall and realised where he must be. The Leningrad stadium!

Then the room was once more plunged in darkness, and again the film was repeated. He estimated that it lasted five minutes, and that he saw it a dozen times, often without any break, before the light was switched on. Murdoch began to feel weak. This was just the beginning of the process, the slow erosion of the spirit. But the bastards had it wrong. The first three sequences on hurdles, javelin and vault were failures, true enough. But not the 1500 metres. There he had given everything, then found more. It was a run of which he would always be proud. Whatever they knew about psychology, his Russian gaolers knew sod-all about track and field athletics. Not every loss was a defeat – and that they would never understand.

Murdoch shut his eyes. Somehow, the pain in his solar plexus had gone, just as the sick feeling before competition had always vanished. For Murdoch was intent on focusing in upon his situation, his intelligence cutting through his fear.

Why had they not killed him? That would surely have been their simplest course of action, the one, after all, they had presumably adopted at St Moritz. It could only be because this was only the first part of a programme to weaken him psychologically, in order that he not only withdrew from the Kudai project but totally renounced it, making it impossible for it to be revived under alternative leadership.

Was that why they had brought him so far, to deprive him of hope, to put him into a situation where there was no possible means of escape?

The projector had stopped, but there was no further noise. Presumably the first break in the films had been to set the machine on some form of automatic control. Murdoch opened his eyes but his mind continued to race. But why had his captors remained anonymous? After all, there was no way by which he could identify KGB agents working on their home patch. And why Leningrad stadium? Probably, he reasoned, because it was the only one in Russia in which he had ever competed.

If they had made their first mistake with the Munich 1500 metres, he was certain that the programme would not simply consist of endless re-runs of his past athletic failures. There would be more to come. But why Leningrad stadium? Just a further move to disorientate him? But how had they managed it all?

He tried to cast his mind back to Leningrad stadium. He had last been there in 1977, for a decathlon match against Russia and West Germany . . .

His thoughts suddenly jumped, as again above him he heard

the roar of the crowd. There was no logic in the jump. It was simply the realisation that he did not feel hungry. He had begun his run at five o'clock, finished it about five thirty. His last meal, a light lunch, had been at one thirty. There was no way he could be in Leningrad any earlier than midnight. And yet he did not feel hungry at all.

Leningrad. Even by plane it would have taken over four hours to get him there. Under the plaster he drew his tongue along his lower lip, then along his upper. Both smooth. Of course they might have shaved him, but it was unlikely. Could they have fed him whilst he was unconscious?

There was one other test. He drew his tongue along his front teeth. Smooth. He was not far from home, for they would certainly not have troubled to brush his teeth. To be sure he checked the back of his teeth. Again, still smooth. He must be no more than a couple of hours from Hallam Street – and a long way from Leningrad.

He began to scrutinise the room carefully, rotating his chair as he did so by pushing it slowly round with his feet, the sweat pouring in streams down his face. Behind him the projector had been left on a small wooden table, already spooled up for the next session. Otherwise the room was completely empty, with no clue as to where he was, or who else had been there.

And yet there was something in the damp, musty smell which was familiar. He kept the chair rotating slowly, re-examining every detail of the little low-ceilinged room, dreading the sound of a returning captor. They could not be long in arriving, for their methods were dependent on constant pressure, lack of rest. But they also relied heavily on despair, that loss of hope created by entombment in some foreign place far from the security and succour of familiar things. But if he was not in Leningrad, but rather somewhere not far from home, where was he? All that he sought was a clue, a hint that he might be correct.

On his fourth rotation he found it, nestling in the right-hand corner of the room, a metre to the left of the grilled frosted glass window. It was only a few centimetres of sticky red and black paper, probably jammed into the corner by a negligent cleaner. Murdoch edged the chair towards the corner, fearing that the grating of its legs might arouse his captors. He managed to get within a foot of where the paper was lying, close enough to examine it carefully.

There was no question of it. It was part of the wrapping of a Mars bar, the beginning of the red 'M' clearly visible. He was still in England. The realisation gave him new strength and he strained against his bonds. But the cords which bound him hand and foot, though thin, had been well tied and he succeeded only in rubbing his ankles and wrists until they were bleeding raw.

He checked his bindings. There were three, one each at his wrists and ankles and another, looser binding fixing his trunk to the chair.

Murdoch ground and twisted his way back to the centre of the room, then towards the projector which stood on a low table by the far wall. He paused, lungs heaving from the exertion, and looked at the machine in front of him.

For a moment he was at a loss. As he examined the projector he cast his mind back to when he had first operated Grieve's tired old Specto-Analyser. On it they had endlessly dissected film of Murdoch's athletic techniques. He could also recall clearly the number of times he had cut his hands on the edges of sharp film-spools. Perhaps now that experience might work to his advantage.

He edged his way to the front of the machine where the lower reel projected, turned round and bent forward in an attempt to make contact between its bottom edge and his wrist bindings. But, however he manoeuvred, the bindings were at least six inches below the reel.

He sat back, sweat and blood from his wrists dripping on to the stone floor. There was one other possibility, but it was a long shot. He dare not try to push the projector over on to the floor, for that might alert his captors. If, however, he could tip himself on to his back and lift the ropes round his ankles to the reel's cutting edge then he might at least release his legs.

Murdoch slowly turned so that the chair faced the projector. This first part of the exercise would hurt, but less than falling directly backwards which would risk crushing his hands. He braced himself, then tilted the chair to the left until he fell. He grunted as his left shoulder crunched on to its hard stone surface, then lay gasping for a moment in a miasma of pain.

The next effort would be against gravity, and with all the leverage to his disadvantage. He placed his left elbow firmly on the floor then, with all his weight to his left, started to rock the chair, gradually gaining momentum. Fortunately the chair legs were short, enabling him to develop a limited rhythm. Finally, levering with his left elbow, he lurched his body to the right.

It took four attempts before he managed to lie, gasping, on his back below the spool arm of the projector. Next he lifted his ankles to the spool, maximising the limited slack of the ropes around his chest.

Luckily he had judged the distance between him and the spool almost exactly right, and it took only a moment before he was able to manoeuvre the spool's cutting edge next to the ropes between his legs. Murdoch made half a dozen small twitching movements with his legs and the rope began to fray. But the leverage was now against him, the rope was strong, and it was not long before his abdominals began to go into spasm. He dropped back, the ropes still a tantalising foot away from the sharp rim of the aluminium spool.

Murdoch lay gasping on the stone floor, his body drenched in sweat, his ears straining for any sound of his captors' return. He had not much left in him. Once more he raised his leg ropes to the spool and this time managed four cuts before falling back exhausted. He looked at his legs: the binding ropes were over halfway gone. One more big effort could do it.

This time Murdoch's abdominals immediately locked into deep cramp, but somehow he managed to make six cutting movements before the ropes sundered and he fell backwards on to the floor.

He lay, recovering, for two minutes or more, then dropped again on to his left side, his cheek and knee on the floor. Then, rotating the chair anti-clockwise, he turned on to his back and shuffled along the floor towards the wall below the grilled window. He placed the legs of the chair against the base of the wall, flexing his legs and fixing the soles of his feet against the horizontal spar at the bottom of the chair.

With a sudden jerk he pushed with all his remaining strength. To his delight, he came immediately clear of the chair. He levered himself to his feet and limped to the projector, the blood rushing painfully into his stiff legs. There was no time to rest properly. He stood with his back to the spool arm and started to saw. It was only a matter of seconds before he had cut through the third binding. He was free. He ripped away the plaster from his mouth and massaged his jaw.

Not bothering with the chair, he moved quickly to the wall, tore down the Spartakiade poster and, folding it clumsily, stuffed it inside his tracksuit. As he did so there was a sound down the corridor outside, about twenty yards away. He looked around the room for a weapon. There was nothing. He tore the two metres of flex from the projector and pulled the projector plug from its socket. Then he moved quickly to the right of the door and flicked off the light.

The squat figure who entered met only darkness. First the darkness of the room, then that of Murdoch's grasp, as the flex around his throat quickly tightened and he lost consciousness. Murdoch lowered him to the ground, then delved into the little man's right inside pocket, which was empty. His gun, a squat little automatic, turned out to be in a holster just below his heart. Murdoch flicked the light back on and located the safety catch. He pushed it to 'off' and slowly opened the door.

He stepped out to find himself in a dank, curved corridor, about fifteen metres wide. Directly in front of him stood high iron gates and on both sides of the gates, set into the wall, a series of little windows, resembling those at railway ticket offices. Murdoch looked above them and heard the coo and flutter of pigeons. He knew where he was: in the White City Stadium, London. He had last been there only eight months before, filming a commercial. The old slum of a stadium, built

239

back in 1908, had once been the home of British athletics and was now used mainly for greyhound racing.

To his left was the main exit and he made his first steps towards it, thankful that he was still wearing his road-running shoes. He checked his left wrist for his watch, but it had gone. He started to jog, painfully at first, as the blood moved back into his limbs, but gradually more easily.

He could hear only his breathing and the sound of his feet landing on the concrete floor. There was always a strange, specific deadness about an empty stadium, particularly one that had been charged with activity less than two hours before. Each time he came to an exit gate he checked it, in case by chance it had not been locked. After unsuccessfully checking on four of the gates he decided that it might be worth trying to clamber over the next one.

He slipped the automatic into a tracksuit pocket, first turning on the safety catch, then jumped to place both feet on a horizontal steel strut about a metre up the three-metre-high gate, his hands on a similar strut just a metre above it. The rattling noise was appalling, and the gate continued to shake and rattle as Murdoch placed both hands on the spiky top of the gate and attempted to pull himself up. But the sharp steel of the triangular spikes bit into his fingers, ripping them, and he dropped back down, retaining his hold on the lower horizontal bar, gasping and licking the blood from his hands.

Suddenly there was a crack and the wall to the left above him splintered to the shock of a pistol shot, spattering him with soft blue plaster. Murdoch jumped to the ground and saw in the gloom to his left about thirty metres away a large man in a dark blue raincoat and black Homburg. He took out his gun and scampered off, following the clockwise route he had previously taken. The second shot was a vast boom behind him, filling the emptiness of the stadium corridor.

The adrenalin lent power to his stiffened limbs and Murdoch ploughed through drifts of betting slips along the dark, concrete corridor that surrounded the greyhound track and terracings. He came to the next exit gate, one of a series spaced fifty metres apart circling the outer perimeter. Bolted. He shook it impotently, then ran on, fumbling as he did with the butt of the automatic.

The second gate was the same. Murdoch stopped, lungs heaving, hearing behind him the scampering of feet – one person? two? – how many he could not be sure. If there were two of them then it would be a simple matter to close in on him from either side of the 800-metre interior tunnel around the track in which he was now trapped. With the exit gates too high to be cleared his only hope was to get into an area which he knew intimately, the infield of the stadium or the terracing.

He sprinted along the inner curve of the tunnel, his breath spuming in the frosty air, his sweat cooling quickly on his skin. The first inner gate leading to the terracing at the end of the home straight was locked. Perhaps they all were? Cursing, he ran to the second on the curve, opposite the area where the long jump pit had been sited. It was open.

He bounded up the steps leading to the terracing, then ran down the terracing itself, miraculously managing to keep his feet. The moon, appearing suddenly behind the skirts of a cloud, revealed the shadowy stadium and reminded him that there was a small one-metre-high mesh fence to be cleared at the perimeter of the track. He scrambled over the fence on to the mushy grass greyhound track, his feet crunching on the red cinder of its curve. To his relief, the moon was soon once more covered in cloud, leaving the stadium in darkness.

He was now on the curve of the athletics track, mossy and overgrown, soft after a thaw, and he slithered over its slimy surface, knees bent, aware that another shaft of moonlight might reveal his position. He tripped over the inner curve of the track, tearing the skin of his wrist on the wooden board which framed the long jump pit, and rolled into the pit.

It had been twelve years since the White City had housed a major athletics meeting and the sand level was low, a foot below ground level. Murdoch was therefore for all practical purposes invisible from the terracing where he was now being hunted. He rolled over on to his back, wiping the automatic clean of sand with the bottom of his tracksuit, disengaged the clip and laid the empty gun on the grass to his left. He pushed on the top of the clip: the spring was stuck. He quickly prised the first bullet out with his finger-nails, then the other four, laying them behind him with the automatic on his left, then gently pushed on the spring-mechanism of the clip, a horizontal strip of metal linked on its back with a series of simple springs. He worked his index finger along the spring, lightly pressing each section. Suddenly the spring relaxed. Murdoch slid each of the cartridges back into place, licking each one as he did so to lubricate them, an old army dodge, then eased the clip back into the butt. He turned on to his face, his chin in the sand, his eyes scanning the stadium section by section. First, behind him at the area on the curve which he had entered: nothing. Then up the home straight where back in 1963 he had seen Ron Jones lead the mighty American Olympic champion Bob Hayes in the final leg of the sprint relay: nothing.

The box at the entry to the greyhound track. Perhaps only a cloud crossing its glass panes but also possibly a movement. He strained to follow the shadow. Yes, it was moving, across the track and on to the infield, into the grassy centre of the ground. Murdoch screwed round in the sand, spitting grit from his mouth as he did so. He released the safety catch and cocked the gun, never letting the moving shadow escape from his gaze. Now it was over thirty metres away and coming towards him, but still much too far for the toy pistol Murdoch was carrying.

Then the stadium was ablaze, as the full floodlights engulfed the ground with light. If he had been seen, there was no evidence in the other man's movements. Like his colleague, he was clad in a blue raincoat. That meant that the big man had put on the lights and was still around: so there had to be at least three of them.

The man, stocky and bearded, stood erect and walked with purpose directly towards the long jump pit. It was obvious from the man's manner that Murdoch had not been seen, but every metre that shortened the distance between them diminished

Murdoch's chances. It was time to act. He jumped to his feet, adopted the two-handed stance he had been taught, feet spread, and fired.

It was not a perfect shot but it was enough. The bullet hit the man on the right thigh. He screamed and fell writhing to the ground, clutching the wounded leg.

Murdoch immediately ran back the way he had come, scaling the low perimeter fence. He had placed his foot on the first step of the terracing when he became aware of someone above him. At the top of the terracing stood the tall man in the Homburg, his face shadowed in the gloom of the upper stand, his automatic held in front of him with both hands. There was no way Murdoch could react in time.

The shot was immediate, echoing in the empty stand.

The tall man fell to his knees, and as his face came into the light Murdoch saw that it bore an expression of surprise. For a moment the man stayed kneeling, as if about to pray. Only his hands did not rise in prayer. Instead he fell face forward, hands at his side, his gun clattering noisily down the terracing.

Above him, at the top of the terracing, Murdoch could now make out another figure, a burly black man in a tracksuit. He seemed to be grinning, despite the gun in his right hand.

Murdoch hesitated, then slowly walked up the terracing towards him.

'My name's Farrell,' the black man said, 'Claud C. Farrell. CIA.' The negro extended his hand. 'Nice to meet you, Mr Murdoch.'

Farrell looked with mock distaste at Murdoch's bloodied hands and filthy tracksuit.

'You got yourself quite a little life, Mr Murdoch,' he said. 'Let's get you back home to Hallam Street. I imagine your Miss Payne's going to be a mite concerned.' He looked down at the man below. 'Don't you trouble yourself about him,' he said. 'Or the other two out there. Tomorrow morning no one will know they've ever been here.'

Farrell descended the stadium steps, withdrew a small torch from an inside pocket and leant over the fallen man, shining the torch in his face. He then placed his index finger on the man's neck and stood up, nodding.

'Pulse strong,' he said. 'He'll live.'

'You *did* say CIA,' said Murdoch, as they walked up the terracing towards the exit. He had begun to shake and he was suddenly aware of the depth of his fatigue.

'Yes,' said Farrell. 'Just here to see fair play.'

16

The Trojan Horse

Friday, 25 February 1983

Claud C. Farrell Junior stood before Paul Stafford's desk, shifting his weight nervously from foot to foot as his superior leafed through his report.

Stafford looked up irritably. 'Sit down, man, for Christ's sake. You're making me nervous.'

The massive negro did as he was bid, engulfing his chair.

'Farrell,' Stafford said. 'When you came into the Company and someone told me you had been an all-American running back I thought, Shit. What is this place coming to?' He tapped the file. 'But this is good.'

Farrell's broad features relaxed visibly.

'Two, possibly three Russian agents taken out, and no mention of them in the British press. Why do you think that was?'

'I reckon they cleaned up at the White City when their men didn't come back to the embassy. It's only a few blocks away.'

'And what were they up to?'

'It's all in the report, sir.'

Stafford grunted. 'And what do you suppose they hope to gain?'

'This guy Murdoch's the key to the whole operation. If he gave up the Kudai Games then they'd fold. The Russkies were using standard deprivation techniques, trying to make Murdoch think he was in Leningrad, trying to get inside his head.'

'But he held out?'

'Yes, sir. Murdoch tagged on to what was happening, got clear and took two of them out. He could well have taken the other if I hadn't gotten to him first.'

'You've spoken to Murdoch?'

'We had a couple of beers.'

'And?'

'If he's a KGB man then I'm Elizabeth Taylor.'

'Why didn't they just rub him out?'

Farrell considered the question. 'If he'd been killed then there was always the chance that the rest of his organisation would have toughed it out. If, on the other hand, the Russkies got him to pull out of the Games then the likelihood was that his people would have come out with him.'

Stafford nodded. 'Farrell,' he said, 'this Olympic business is a bucket of shit. Problem is, for once the KGB and the Company want the same thing – we want this guy Murdoch to pull out. There's no way the Oval Office wants a bargain-basement Games. Los Angeles has to be the best ever, bar none.'

Farrell's face was sombre. 'You're saying, sir, that I should have left Murdoch back there with the KGB?'

Stafford nodded again. 'It might have been better,' he said. 'But let's look at it another way. The Russkies are making noises already about pulling out of Los Angeles, and they probably plan to keep us on the edge all the way into 1984. If they're worried about Murdoch it means that they plan to compete in LA for sure. That tells us something we didn't know.'

'That they'll come to LA?'

Stafford placed his pencil ruminatively against his lips. 'They'll be there,' he said, 'with a regiment of KGB agents. And I've been checking around. The International Olympic people have made Murdoch an offer to pull out – he's got till April to make up his mind.'

'So we sit tight?' said Farrell.

'Yes,' said Stafford. 'At least, till April.'

Sparrow's trip to Los Angeles to meet the young journalist Wayne Berbick had proved fruitful. Berbick had at first been

246

reluctant to volunteer information on his Ciano investigations, but Sparrow's offer to provide him, in return, with the exclusive story of the Kudai Olympics had proved irresistible to the young American. So had a salary of 4000 dollars a month.

The salary paid to Wayne Berbick soon brought other dividends. The young journalist had, in his capacity of press officer, dealt superbly with the defection of the Eastern bloc athletes, the major issue with which Murdoch and his organisation had been faced since their October launch.

Nor did Berbick's work for Kudai interrupt his investigations on Tony Ciano, though he had joined forces with Sparrow to ensure that their enquiries would be pursued with professional rigour.

Berbick had, in any case, reached a dead end in his investigations. True, he had discovered that Ciano planned something big for the Los Angeles Olympics but he had no idea of its nature. It was at this point that Sparrow's expertise proved invaluable.

A scrutiny of Ciano's business interests revealed a recent and rather unusual addition. In March 1982 a company called Spartan Sports had been created, its purpose the production of track and field equipment. Further investigations showed that no Spartan equipment had yet been sold, and that the company factories were in Thailand, Bolivia and Peru.

It had not taken long for Sparrow to realise the nature of Ciano's plans. The Los Angeles Olympics, a festival dedicated to youth and fitness, were to be used to bring in a massive cache of cocaine and heroin.

It would come as no surprise to the American Olympic authorities or the FBI that the Eastern bloc teams had been swollen with extra doctors, physiotherapists, masseurs and technicians, though sorting out the genuine officials from KGB agents would be difficult. What would be surprising was the size of the teams from Thailand, Burma, Columbia, Peru and Bolivia, nations with no great sporting heritage.

For what Ciano planned to do was to use the clothes and equipment of the teams from these nations to bring into Los

Angeles the biggest single cache of drugs in history. Vaulting poles, javelins, discoi, training bags, tracksuits, road shoes, medicine balls – all would have a rich filling of prime cocaine.

Ciano had rightly reasoned that scrutiny of Olympic teams would be cursory and had already set up 'factories' in all five nations to produce the necessary sports equipment. He had also suborned local officials to ensure teams of a sufficient size and extent to justify the amount of equipment he planned to bring to Los Angeles. Thus Bolivia would bring a pole vaulter who had cleared a metre less than the Olympic qualifying height, Thailand a javelin thrower whose best throw was over twenty metres short of his nearest Olympic opponent's. Fortunately for Ciano, Olympic rules allowed one person per nation in each event, regardless of standard.

By the beginning of February, Sparrow had located Ciano's 'factories' in both Bolivia and Peru: the time had come to hand the information on to the FBI. It was on 14 February that Ciano had made his first mistake, when on a 'trial' run he had used a Peruvian pole vaulter, Manuel Perez, arriving in Los Angeles to train at UCLA, to bring in two poles each containing four pounds of cocaine. Customs officials had allowed the poles through and the FBI had followed the unfortunate athlete to Ciano's home.

For Ciano there was no way out; the FBI videotape of the stocky little Italian receiving the poles from Perez was on national networks by nightfall of the fourteenth. Tony Ciano was taken into custody that evening.

Tuesday, 1 March 1983

He knew that it was going to be a formal meeting when Hassan addressed him as 'Murdoch'. The Prince had always used the more intimate 'Alan', one of the few people in the world, apart from Murdoch's parents, to use that form of address.

Hassan had from the outset kept to his original word. He had left Murdoch and his colleagues to get on with the business of creating WAPA and the network of supporting competitions.

The Arab development programme for coaches and officials in swimming, athletics and gymnastics was, despite Grieve's incapacity, already under way. There had been little need for formal meetings, and regular progress reports to Hassan, as well as to Stevens and Hall, had been all that had been required. The sudden request for him to visit Kudai had therefore come as a surprise.

The Kudai Hilton was like every other Hilton Murdoch had ever been in, only twice as large and three times as sumptuous, its marble halls and lush velvet tapestries like something out of *A Thousand and One Nights*. It was a cool, still limbo-land, remote from the boiling world outside. As he had pressed the button for the elevator which was to take him to Hassan's suite he had felt a pang of uncertainty. Could he really bring the greatest sportsmen in the world to this hothouse?

As he entered Hassan's suite he realised it was the first time that he had seen the Prince in full Arab dress. Clad in simple white robes and burnous, Hassan looked what he undoubtedly was, a man from an inscrutable culture as foreign as that of an eskimo. Murdoch could no longer picture him as he had been years before, the swarthy barrier-breaking high-hurdler or, even more recently, the suave and Westernised businessman.

'You seem to have been through the wars,' Hassan said, as Murdoch sank into an armchair on the other side of a round mahogany coffee table. 'How is Grieve?'

'You remember what he always used to say – sport is what happens between injuries. He's getting stronger all the time. He's knocking out two hundred press-ups a day and ten miles a week on his jogging machine. He'll be back at full strength in a couple of weeks.'

'Good.' Hassan reached forward, withdrew a slim cigar from a box on the coffee table and lit it from a silver lighter nearby. 'You have not been entirely frank with me, Murdoch.'

Murdoch flushed. 'In what way?'

'The St Moritz affair, of course, I knew of – after all, it was international news. But the earlier matter in London – the

249

'drugs – I knew nothing of that. Neither did I know of this most recent and more serious matter at the White City.'

For a moment Murdoch did not know how to address Hassan, whether to respond naturally or in a more formal manner. His tongue moved faster than his thoughts.

'You said back in Los Angeles that I was to have a free run, that I was only to get in touch with you if I needed help. I took that to mean what it said.'

'You think being kidnapped, almost losing your life in St Moritz – that does not constitute requiring help?'

'With respect, there was nothing that you could have done in either of those circumstances. They were matters which I had to sort out for myself.'

Hassan nodded. 'And how exactly do you propose to sort out the repercussions?'

'First there's the London drug business, then the assault and kidnapping. I've been into the cocaine plant with my security man, Sparrow, and with Ellis Payne, and we think that it's the work of an American gentleman called Ciano.'

'Ciano? A Los Angeles businessman?'

'You know of him?'

Hassan nodded. 'He applied to open a casino here two years ago. And what was Mr Ciano's reason for setting you up?'

'Drugs,' said Murdoch flatly. 'He planned to bring close on ten million dollars' worth of cocaine into Los Angeles, hidden in the equipment of Olympic teams.'

'Is there anything I can do?' asked Hassan, concerned.

Murdoch shook his head. 'It's already been done.' He went on to explain the investigations of Berbick and Sparrow and the results.

Hassan nodded and drew lightly on his cigar. 'You have done well. But Mr Ciano will try again, I feel sure of that. What of St Moritz?'

'The Russians,' replied Murdoch.

'Can you be absolutely certain?'

'I think so.' Murdoch told Hassan of his meeting with Lysenko and of the Russian's cryptic reference to Buchinski's

250

death. 'Anything that hits the Los Angeles Olympics also devalues Olympic medals for the Communist bloc,' he added.

Hassan pursed his lips. 'Buchinski was a great loss. I met him only once, when he came here in August, but I know from your reports the contribution he had made.' He paused. 'Could it be the Russians who were behind his death?'

Murdoch shook his head. 'Lysenko would never have volunteered the information he did if the Russians had been responsible. No, it's on Ciano's patch. I've no evidence that it's him, but if it was murder he's the more likely bet.'

'And you think it was the Russians in St Moritz?'

'Yes,' replied Murdoch. 'I'm also certain they were responsible for the White City affair, no question of that. They want to rub the Americans' noses in the dirt in Los Angeles. They're pooling resources for the first time with the East Germans and dividing up the Olympic cake so that neither ventures into the other's territory. The East are going to be out in force in Los Angeles but with our Arab Olympics the medals won't be worth a docken.'

'A docken?'

'A Scottish phrase. Worthless.'

Hassan smiled, then his face became serious again. 'My younger brother Ryad has a passion for foreign affairs,' he said. 'His sources say that the Russians will cause trouble all the way to Los Angeles, as revenge for the Moscow boycott. Ryad thinks, for instance, that they will plant well-known KGB agents in their team and force the Americans into banning them. Thus an international incident will be created, and the Russians will threaten to withdraw. If we devalue the Olympics then that type of strategy is no longer available to them.'

For a moment Hassan closed his eyes. 'It was predictable. I should have anticipated the Communist response,' he said, laying down his cup. 'Though Mr Ciano's interest does come as something of a surprise. So, first, what do you plan to do about the Russians?'

'Blackmail,' said Murdoch. 'We have official urine samples from both the 1976 and 1980 Games which will show that

Russians and East Germans took both anabolics and testosterone. We will bring to the fore all of the East German sports defectors since 1976, including our own Dr Schmidt, to flood the airwaves with material on East European cheating. Quite simply, I'll inform them that if there is any further interference with me or my staff we will release these materials. Similarly, we have Buchinski's expense accounts and videotapes on thirty-seven East European athletes, showing that they took appearance money whilst on the US indoor circuit in the 1972–80 period. Again, we will release this evidence both to the media and the international federations.'

'You were going to do all this without consulting me?'

'Your brief was to get the athletes to the Games. I'm doing that.'

Hassan drew again on his cigar, the smoke forming a light wreath round his bearded face.

'When I first conceived the Arab Olympics,' he said, 'I had two objectives, one noble and pure, the other possibly less so. Self-delusion is a snare which I have always tried to avoid, so I will outline my position to you. Like you, I have always seen sport as the ultimate truth. Man against himself, with Allah the final judge. The Olympics, the whole infrastructure of world amateur sport, offended against this, being simply a battle of drugs and chauvinism. My Games, though offering massive money prizes, also offered the chance of removing steroids and the rest – and of diluting the nationalism.'

His mouth twisted slightly. 'That was the noble part of the enterprise. Now to the less noble element. You may remember that back in 1971 Kudai applied for membership of the IOC. It was refused, on a technicality. You may also recall that I was at the time running regular 14's . . .' He raised both hands deprecatingly. 'I know that Grieve will say these times were only achieved in Kudai with my father timing me, but I was at my peak. I would never run better. So I did not participate in the Munich Olympics. A year later my father became ill and I had to take over his responsibilities. My athletics career was, for all practical purposes, over.

252

'The failure to reach a possible destiny is a form of death,' he went on. 'In sport there is no going back, no way by which the muscles of a middle-aged man can regain the spring of youth. So my Arab Olympics are a kind of revenge – I admit it.'

'My use of the word "blackmail" doesn't disturb you?'

'I would be troubled if you did not suggest something of the kind. When one is with wolves one has to learn to howl like a wolf. So what is your first priority?'

Murdoch sat back in his chair. 'To let the East know what I have got on them – photocopies of all depositions. I will give them a simple warning: if I or any of my staff are harmed or troubled in any way then the material goes off to the media.'

'That will be enough?'

Murdoch shrugged. 'Impossible to say. The evidence I have exposes the last decade of East European sport as a total sham. I'll have everything lined up – doctors, universities, handwriting experts – to validate the materials which I'll bring to light. It will put a bomb under the whole of Eastern bloc sport. If that doesn't hit them, nothing will.'

Hassan smiled. 'You have them, as our friend Buchinski might have said, between a rock and a hard place.'

'You agree with what I'm doing?'

'Murdoch, these people have already shown you no mercy. None should be shown to them.'

Hassan placed his fingers in a triangle to his lips. 'But before we go on to discuss Mr Ciano let us move to an equally serious matter. From the beginning I have given you a free hand. This meeting has been occasioned only because of the serious and dangerous problems which you have recently encountered. It is my view that you are going to need more rather than less help in the weeks to come. The problem is that I am not going to be available for consultation.'

He leant forward and poured himself a cup of coffee.

'Just over a month from now I will be in Mount Helen Hospital, Los Angeles.'

He smiled.

'I have discovered that my propensity for smashing hurdles

was caused, if only in part, by bad eyesight. In recent years I have had recurrent eye problems. A month ago I had a brain-scan.'

He paused, his breathing heavy.

'It turned out to be more serious than I had expected. A brain tumour. My physician has advised me that an immediate operation is imperative. Thus I will next month enter Mount Helen for an operation, one which will put me out of commission for several weeks. I am arranging through Ryad that you will have complete executive control over the Games' preparations, though naturally I will expect you to keep Mr Stevens and Mr Hall fully informed.'

Hassan paused. He noted the reaction on Murdoch's face and smiled. 'Don't worry, Alan. The operation, though complex, has an eighty per cent chance of success. By April I will again be in action, by which time your teams will have completed their final site inspection here and all will be ready for the 1983 season.'

'When will that be?'

'Mr Hall has arranged, on 26 March, a flight from Gatwick for your staff.'

'Will everything be completed by then?' Murdoch asked doubtfully.

Hassan nodded. 'When you came here last time the swimming and gymnastic facilities were unfinished. Mr Stevens and Mr Hall have promised that by 8 March all competitive facilities will be completed and from that date until the 1984 Games we will be testing them, using local competitors and officials.'

He picked up his cup and sipped from it ruminatively.

'And I have a plan – perhaps a more subtle plan than you have so far envisaged – for the men of the Eastern bloc.' He smiled. 'We will make them an offer.'

'An offer?'

'Yes,' said Hassan. 'An offer they must refuse.'

THE DAILY MAIL   4 March 1983

Arab Olympics boss Alan Murdoch last night lit the fuse which may blow up the cosy world of Olympic sport. In a statement from Los

254

Angeles Murdoch offered to abandon his controversial Arab Games if the amateur authorities would submit their athletes to the scrutiny of his medical experts.

'Let my staff make random tests of the world's top athletes *now*, during the training period. If we pick up less than thirty per cent positives on steroids or testosterone then we will abandon our project. Either way, amateur sport wins. If we pick up less than thirty per cent then the Arab Olympics vanishes; if we pick up more then we stay in business. Whatever percentage the results will be forwarded to the amateur authorities to help them in their crusade against drugs.'

IOC chairman Maurice Delgado was not available for comment at his Lausanne office. Harold Berne, IAAF official and a leader in the anti-drug drive, said that the proposal would be considered by his committee when it met in three weeks' time. Murdoch has given the world's sports federations a month in which to respond. It may well turn out to be the longest month in the history of sport.

NEW YORK TIMES   Wednesday, 23 March 1983

PRINCIPLES AND PETRODOLLARS

It looks as if Mr Alan Murdoch and his Arab Olympians have called the bluff of the world's sports federations. It is now almost a month since Mr Murdoch made his offer of free drug-tests to the federations, with its attendant offer to abandon his 1984 Kudai Olympics if he failed to secure more than thirty per cent positives.

The world's sports organisations, despite the exhortations of the IOC's Maurice Delgado, have treated the Kudai offer as a Trojan horse, one which they have resolutely refused to allow to enter their gates. An infinity of reasons have been offered, ranging from questioning the validity of the tests themselves to the practicality of random tests in totalitarian states. So it appears that, though, like St Augustine, the world's sports leaders wish to be chaste, it cannot be just yet. Mr Murdoch has, in his little exercise, told us more about world sport than many of us would like to know. Petrodollars and principles are, for once, linked. We wish Mr Murdoch well.

Thursday, 24 March 1983

Hassan had been right, thought Murdoch, as he laid the *New York Times* on top of a fat pile of newspapers on the coffee table

255

in Ellis's Los Angeles flat. It had been so simple; the cheapest piece of public relations in history.

The world's press had had a field day, or rather a field month, roasting Berne, Hilda Stael and the other flustered leaders of world sport as they wriggled and writhed in their attempts to evade acceptance of Murdoch's offer. He had, only a week before, given the knife a further twist by offering to halve his required percentage of positives to a mere fifteen per cent. It had, of course, made no difference.

But, Murdoch reflected, as Ellis entered from the kitchen bearing a steaming mug of coffee, the joke was now over. The media – and with them a large section of the world's population – now saw exactly where the federations stood on drug enforcement. There was no need for him to twist the knife further.

Similarly, his letter to the Russian attaché Josef Klim, with its threat to release information on the 1976 and 1980 Olympic drug-tests, appeared to have had the desired effect. He had retained contact with Claud Farrell on an informal basis, and the burly American had confirmed that KGB activities appeared to have ended. All seemed at last set fair for the million-dollar track meets of the summer of 1983 and the swimming and gymnastics programmes of the autumn.

17

Showdown

Friday, 25 March 1983

It was always unsettling to Murdoch to see someone he had previously associated with health and fitness laid up in bed. Thus it was now with Prince Hassan.

In the sterile luxury of Mount Helen Hospital Hassan, in sickness, looked like what he would soon be: a middle-aged Arab.

'No grapes?' Hassan said as Murdoch approached.

Murdoch shook his head, instead placing two magazines on the table beside the bed.

'*Track and Field News* and *Sports Illustrated*. We keep getting good write-ups in both. The athletes are now committing themselves to us publicly in droves. The American women are one hundred per cent behind us, and the road-racers were signed up last Friday.'

'So we are nearly there?'

'Yes,' said Murdoch. 'Grieve and the rest of my staff fly out to Kudai to inspect facilities tomorrow. I go out in a couple of days. It's all coming together.'

'In that case it is time that I apologised to you for a certain duplicity,' said Hassan. 'Sincerely.' He beckoned to his visitor to sit beside his bed. 'It will not have escaped your notice that OPEC has been in some disarray these past few months.'

Murdoch nodded and sat down. Hassan reached over to a table on his left and poured himself a glass of water. He sipped it slowly, then replaced the glass.

'A dreadful mess. Even Yamani himself could not handle it. What you may not have learned, though, is that our whole Arab Olympics enterprise was for some time in danger. Several contributors wished to pull out of the Games. It was only by doubling my own personal contribution that it was possible to stop the rot.'

'How did you manage to keep it quiet?'

'With great difficulty,' smiled Hassan. 'I knew that the slightest hint of doubt would give strength to our enemies and cause withdrawals of competitors. I therefore bound my colleagues to strictest secrecy. Not even Hall or Stevens knew. Now our funds are assured, the stadium complete, and we are ready a year ahead of time.'

Behind them the door opened and the face of a pert blonde nurse appeared, young and mock-stern. She put up three fingers and Hassan nodded, smiling.

'They have been strict with me here. No telephone calls for the past two days, not even from my brother Ryad.

'I am going to be even less use to you than I thought,' he went on. 'It looks as if I will be out of commission for at least a month, possibly longer. During that period I wish you and your colleagues to take complete control of the Olympic project, in collaboration with Ryad. Mr Hall and Mr Stevens's work is all but finished, but I would like you to keep them informed on all major developments.'

Hassan then opened a drawer in a bedside locker on his right and withdrew a square piece of plastic, similar to a credit card. He handed it to Murdoch.

'This is the key,' he said, pointing to a squat steel safe set on a table in the right-hand corner of the room. 'Open it.'

Murdoch walked over and slid the card into a slit at the top of the safe. The door snapped open, revealing a single shelf on which rested a blue file and a bulky sealed package.

'The file contains an up-to-date account of the whole project, much of which is already in your own files,' Hassan explained. 'The brown package contains other relevant papers, in particular my written authority to you to take over all matters concerning the Kudai Games. In effect, it means that whatever action you take between now and the end of April requires no counter-signatures from myself or any of my officials to make it legal and binding.'

Murdoch withdrew the documents and stood by Hassan's bed. The Arab's face wrinkled into a smile and for a moment he again looked young.

'You're in charge now, Alan,' he said.

Behind Murdoch the door opened and the face of the blonde nurse appeared. Her expression was now an imperative.

Saturday, 26 March 1983

He would never know why he had opened the sealed envelope; possibly it had been the news of Hassan's successful operation. Whatever the reason, he had done so, and things would never be the same again.

The envelope had been specifically addressed to Hassan, and marked with the royal seal of Kudai. It had nestled amongst a sheaf of official papers relating to the Kudai Games, some of which required his signature, others merely information reports on the Arab Sports Development Programme and on the condition of the swimming and gymnastic facilities.

Murdoch had left the envelope for a day, preoccupied with final revisions to *The Nazi Games* at Ellis's Los Angeles flat. The script had now been sent to Andrew Weir and Murdoch was experiencing the same knot in his solar plexus that he always had when his work was under scrutiny.

Then had come news of Ciano's indictment. Plea-bargaining had brought the sentence down to five years and there would be several more months of appeals which would keep Ciano steadily ploughing a daily furrow in his swimming pool for some time yet, but for all practical purposes the Ciano threat was over.

But now he was in deeper trouble than he could possibly have imagined. For even to a non-expert the evidence provided by the unexpected 'report' was brutally clear. He reached to his bedside table for his translucent pen, took off its top and began to mark the relevant sections in yellow.

The document was less of a report than a series of notes prepared by Henry Martin, an ITC engineer who had worked for the past five years on various Kudai projects. Martin had written what had amounted to a secret dossier on the projects and, fearful of going through formal Kudai Government channels, had slipped his sealed report into a batch of Government papers destined for Hassan.

According to Martin, the students' quarters at Kudai's national computer school had been the first to show serious defects – initially, a fire caused by a faulty wiring system, then deep cracks in the bedroom walls on the first and second floors of the tower blocks. The college of physical education had been next, with the warping of the floor of the gymnastics hall, followed by leaks in its translucent roof.

But it had been the collapse of the second floor of the Orthopaedic Hospital only a day after Hassan had entered Mount Helen which had resulted in the preparation of the hasty report which Murdoch now scrutinised. There had been no deaths, but two student nurses had been badly injured and the entire hospital evacuated.

There had undoubtedly been corruption on a massive scale. This related essentially to the quality of materials used in the five-year three-billion dollar schools, colleges and hospitals building programme which Hassan had initiated in 1979. The materials used in construction had not been those specified in the tenders, but false bills of lading had been provided to cover the fraud. Now the flaws were beginning to show, and the engineer's report showed conclusively that there had been a calculated and massive misappropriation of funds to the tune of close on 30 million dollars over the first three-year period. And behind it all lay the two men for whom he had so far had total trust.

Murdoch sat upright in bed rereading the report as Ellis wandered in from the bathroom, towelling her hair. She stood by the end of his bed, sensing his mood.

'Trouble?'

Murdoch nodded.

'The worst kind,' he said. 'Just have a look at these.'

She took the report and sat on a sun-lounger by the window, as the morning Californian sun streamed into the room.

Murdoch rose and went to the bathroom. He was shaving his upper lip when Ellis's voice reached him through the open door.

'This stinks,' she said. 'But why has it taken so long for anybody to notice?'

Murdoch leant forward and lapped cold water on to his face.

'Stevens and Hall,' he said, reaching for a towel. 'The building programme was their direct responsibility. They must have had some idea that there might be an investigation. Perhaps they managed to slow it up until Hassan got into hospital. Certainly they wouldn't have expected me to get a hold of it.'

'D'you think it means the stadium is in the same shape, same defects?'

Murdoch shook his head. 'Not necessarily, though my guess is that it is. They obviously gambled on the cheaper materials, hoping that any defects wouldn't show up for years.'

'Or perhaps the company that supplied them went even lower on material specifications and skimmed off a little more,' she said.

Murdoch poured some after-shave on to both hands, winced as its sharpness hit the skin, and surveyed her from the entrance of the bathroom.

'It's possible,' he said, re-entering the room as he tied his towelling bathrobe at the waist. He sat down opposite her at the table.

'But how could it have got past Hassan?' she asked.

Murdoch shrugged. 'There was no way he could have kept in contact with all the building programme, and anyhow these flaws have only come up in the past few weeks. He's been more worried about the operation than the on-site building.'

'So what can you do?'

'In the short-term, nothing – at least till Hassan is back in action, and that won't be for several days. The building programme is none of my business, but Hall and Stevens are. They brought me into this, they built the stadium, and they've been kept in touch every step of the way with the Olympic project.'

'And what clout have they got while Hassan's in hospital?' asked Ellis.

'I have to report back to them, that's all,' he replied, biting his lower lip.

'What about your site inspection tomorrow?' Ellis rose and walked back towards the bathroom.

'I have an architect on the team, on a consultancy basis. He'll pick up any structural flaws – I can call him now with some of the technical data from this report, so that he can look out for similar problems.' He shook his head. 'What I don't know is whether or not Stevens or Hall have seen this report.'

Ellis glanced back at Murdoch through the open bathroom door.

'They must know that inspections have been made,' she said.

Murdoch stared out of the french windows down into the yacht basin below, his mind racing. The decisions that he made now would be the most important of his life.

'Let's look at what you would call a scenario,' he said. 'Hassan has always taken a personal interest in all his public building projects. No one else has had any involvement – he always dealt direct with Hall and Stevens. So let's say we're the only ones who know about this.'

'Then we're in trouble,' she said, through toothpaste foam.

'You mean *I'm* in trouble.'

'I mean what I said the first time.'

He walked over to her, drew her to him and kissed her.

'Look,' he said. 'You came into this to knock *The Nazi Games* into shape, not to get stuck into my problems.'

'But then came those Kama sutra hurdle exercises.'

'An optional extra.'

'But I'm in whether you like it or not. I know all those kooks, Sparrow and Grieve and the others. I'm on the team – even if I'm not on the payroll yet.'

'So what do I do?'

She gently disengaged herself and walked back into the bedroom.

'We've got to think on our feet and we've got to be right first time. Let's look at the worst scenario. News of the report gets out to the international press. There'll be a massive scandal. Kudai's credibility as the base for the Arab Olympics goes down the tubes. Athletes will leave in droves. By the time Hassan gets out of hospital his Arab Olympics won't be worth a row of beans.'

Murdoch nodded and followed Ellis through.

'And what's the best scenario?'

She looked sideways at him. 'That you can keep it all under wraps. That the stadium is in good shape – or can be repaired. That Hall and Stevens can slip quietly from the scene, with no fuss.'

'Too much to hope for,' he said, shaking his head. 'You got any other scenarios in that head of yours? Something that'll take this lump from my throat?'

'Yes,' she said. 'But you'll have to work fast. Save what you can.'

'A salvage job?'

'Yes,' she said, nodding. 'Delgado's put a lot on the table for you: the 1992 Olympics, and the possibility of other World Championships in Kudai in the next few years. What was the deadline for reply?'

'Three days from now. The end of March.'

'Then the third scenario,' she said, 'goes something like this. You get signed and sealed contracts for the 1992 Olympics and the meets he's offered you, and you, on your part, agree to pull out of the 1984 Kudai Olympics.'

Murdoch let out a deep sigh. 'Then it's all over,' he said. 'Hassan's dream.'

'He made a mistake,' she said. 'He trusted the wrong men. Anyhow, he'll get his Olympics, just eight years late. It's better than nothing. But you'll have to work fast.'

Murdoch sat on the edge of the bed and pulled on his trousers.

'One thing doesn't fit,' he said. 'There has been no cancellation of our inspection flight to Kudai. And there's no way Hall and Stevens will want my people out in Kudai poking around.'

Ellis moved across the room and sat at the window. She looked down into the harbour for a moment then turned to Murdoch.

'That worries me – that bothers me more than anything. When do they leave?'

Murdoch checked his watch.

'We're eight hours behind,' he said. 'It's ten o'clock. They were due to depart at five in the evening from Gatwick. They've gone by now.'

'Jesus,' said Ellis, her voice rising. 'Get on to Gatwick now.'

The fog which had delayed all Gatwick flights throughout that day had just cleared and the Kudai Airways jet which had been delayed for an hour was ready for boarding when Murdoch's call to Sparrow had reached him in the airport lounge. Sparrow's response had been immediate and within half an hour Gatwick's runways had been cleared and incoming flights 'stacked' or redirected. The Kudai executive jet was gingerly trundled off the runway on to a stretch of concrete in the corner of the airport and ringed by security staff, standing at a respectful distance. The inspection took place at eight o'clock that night under a battery of floodlights. Two well-hidden delayed-action explosives were discovered, the first in the baggage compartment, the second in the rear toilet. They had been timed to detonate over the sea, so that there would be little likelihood of adequate investigation. Thus, in a single action, the entire senior staff of the Arab Olympics would have been killed.

Sunday, 27 March 1983

Maurice Delgado had been surprised by the abruptness of Murdoch's call.

True, he and Murdoch had agreed to have a final discussion at some point before the April deadline, but Delgado, aware of the near-total support of Western sportsmen to the Kudai cause, had already resigned himself to a devalued Olympics, as had Bruce Cohn. The Los Angeles director had, however, been surprised at the continuing support for the Games from major American companies, a sure sign that somehow, somewhere, a deal with Kudai might be under way. Unfortunately Delgado could offer Cohn no support for such a hypothesis, for as the days had slipped by no further contact had been made by Murdoch.

Not, that is, until this Sunday, when a call from Murdoch to IOC headquarters in Lausanne had been redirected to him at the Westbury Hotel in New York, and a meeting had been immediately arranged for breakfast the following day.

Murdoch's requirements had been simple. In return for the cancellation (press-releases would call it 'a postponement') of the 1984 Kudai Olympics Murdoch required IOC guarantees of the 1992 Olympics, and in the 1984–1992 period the world championships of athletics, gymnastics and swimming to be held at least once in Kudai.

This had presented no great problem to Delgado – most of what Murdoch was asking for had already been on offer at their previous meeting – and it had only taken a couple of hours' telephone calls to the officers of the relevant federations to ensure their compliance.

Murdoch's final request was probably the most difficult for Delgado to implement. It was that the Kudai drug-testing procedures be adopted by the IOC for Los Angeles. Delgado hedged, pointing out that the tests would have to be accepted by his medical commission. But Murdoch was adamant – for this much he owed to Hassan – and the Frenchman had finally agreed.

Delgado had telephoned Louise D'Asterac in Paris, and jubilantly announced his good news. Her response had been immediate and damning. Murdoch had won, though she did not know how. Listening to her, somehow, deep in his heart, Maurice Delgado sensed that she was right.

Yet he had asked no questions of Murdoch, and had spent the next two days further sealing up the deals with the IAAF, IGF and FINA. There were no problems, for each organisation was at one stroke both exorcising the spectre of the Arab Olympics and setting themselves up with a financially viable world championships; but it had all happened too easily and for Delgado the feeling remained that somehow he had been duped. What did it matter? By the end of the week he would be hailed as the saviour of the Olympic movement, and in 1984 the first profit-making Olympics of the modern era would at last definitely be held. All had therefore been for the best; if not in the best of all possible worlds.

Monday, 28 March 1983

Blue – or, as he had been christened, Ernest Sefton – had always been flattered when people had told him that he appeared to glide rather than walk. It fitted exactly his image of himself, an image nurtured by a thousand movies and videos.

Tony Ciano's fall had affected him little, for the Ciano empire had a momentum that went beyond any temporary indisposition of its leader. Thus Blue still had tasks to fulfil, and as he left a message for Murdoch with the clerk at the Beverly Wilshire Hotel he reflected that an enterprise which had begun so efficiently with Buchinski back in December was now drawing to a close.

Blue sat in his red Volkswagen 'beetle', reached into the glove compartment and withdrew a small plastic bag. He carefully broke it open before sprinkling a 'line' of the fine white powder on to the back of his hand. Then he sniffed it up in a single inhalation and started the car. He smiled. The contract on Murdoch would be a pleasure.

The call to meet Weir and Ellis had not been a surprise, for the studio head had already two days before put to Murdoch six pages of detailed notes on his revised script.

However, Weir's request to Murdoch that they should meet

266

in Calico Ghost Town, south-east of Las Vegas, where he was producing his latest film, *Comstock*, had been particularly inconvenient. True, nothing could be done about Hall and Stevens until Hassan was fit enough to make decisions, and that would be at least two days hence; but for the first time since Murdoch had arrived in Los Angeles his work on *The Nazi Games* seemed an ill-timed and frustrating commitment.

As he drove through the Mojave Murdoch felt alone. He had entered the negotiations with Delgado impulsively, instinctively, without reference even to Grieve or to Quince. His gut had told him that the Arab Olympics would collapse like a pack of cards if any hint of the Kudai corruption got into the press, and so he had had to act quickly, or his bargaining position could well have been eroded completely.

The agreement to hold the 1992 Olympics in Kudai and the attendant world championship contracts were now snug in his briefcase on the car seat behind him. There would now be no Arab Olympics in 1984, but part of Hassan's dream had been salvaged, and that might be enough.

Driving through Victorville towards Barstow Murdoch realised just how tired he was. He had taken too much upon himself, in essence the purification of a large section of world sport. He checked the signpost on his right. Thirty miles to Barstow, with Calico a few miles to the east beyond that. No, let Berne and the others sort it out. He would provide them with all the necessary medical research, *gratis*. It might mean the banning of a whole generation of the world's top athletes but that was their problem. More than likely, they would simply ignore the Kudai tests, finding in them some minute procedural error which would spare them the inevitable embarrassment that drug-testing in the Los Angeles Games would bring.

Despite his tiredness he also felt light, as if a weight had been lifted from him. It was over, the dream – or rather the nightmare – of trying to organise a totally honest and open professional Games. For nothing could make international sport clean again, not him, not Hassan, not Schmidt and all his wonderful tests. He had been foolish to imagine they ever could.

Yet there was a lot to be thankful for. He and Grieve and a handful of men had shown that they could develop in less than a year an infrastructure capable of supporting a major international sports festival. Throughout that year they had been tried, and not found wanting.

And there was Ellis. In her he had found both lover and friend. He had lived too long inside his own private world, with his solitary dreams. Now there was someone with whom they could be shared.

He looked to the roadsign. Ten miles to go.

Calico Ghost Town was an ideal location for Weir's latest film. In fact, *Comstock* concerned the Comstock Lode, a discovery of gold near Virginia City in 1859 by the liar and claim-jumper, Henry T. P. Comstock, while Calico had been the home of a silver mine; but in the movie world that was a minor detail. Calico's perfectly preserved main street with its bars, shops, hotels and livery stables enshrined the world's concept of the western boom-town.

Every day, throughout spring and summer, tourists streamed down its one main street. Calico's peak period had been from 1880 to 1900, when the hills above it had been raped of their rich veins of silver. By 1900 the silver-vein had been played out and the population, which had swollen to over three thousand at its peak, had shrivelled to a tenth of that number. Attention had then shifted to a less profitable mineral, borax, and this had sustained the survivors of the silver-boom into the late '20s, by which time the borax too had been exhausted.

A handful of dogged prospectors had lingered on, literally scraping a bare living from the brown, pock-marked mountain above the town, but by the late '40s only a trio of haggard eccentrics remained.

Then came the revival. Calico Ghost Town became part of the Old West, a national tourist attraction. Its main street was rebuilt and repaired, car-parks and camping sites were created below the town, and franchises sold for the main shops. The

Maggie Mine, the Mystery Shack, the Last Chance Saloon and the Calico-Odessa railroad lived again.

For Prestige Productions, the period immediately before the spring rush of tourists had been ideal for filming. Weir had been able to negotiate a week's shooting in mild, warm spring weather and the filming had gone well, the empty hills reverberating to the noise of daily gunfire.

Murdoch came off the road and drove towards the car-park which lay on a tarmac terrace just below the town. He was surprised to find none of the camera trucks, caravans and catering vans that he had expected. The car-park was almost empty, with only one silver Volvo estate and a Volkswagen 'beetle' parked immediately below the winding wooden steps leading to the town.

He trotted up the steps and stood by the town's well, its wooden bucket creaking quietly on its axis, and looked up the main street. Deserted.

Murdoch had seen Calico a hundred times, although he had never before set foot on its dusty Main Street. It was *Shane*, *High Noon*, every western he had ever watched. He was surprised that a fluff of tumbleweed did not bobble down the street towards him in the light breeze.

On his left stood the Last Chance Saloon, with its toffee-glass windows. Immediately beyond it was the Calico Theatre, and beyond that the photographer's shop where tourists could dress up in cowboy gear and buy sepia tints of the results. On his right was the Silver Queen shopping area, Lane's Store, a livery stable, the sheriff's office and the undertaker's. Above it all, on the mountain at the end of Main Street, were the words 'Calico', irregularly etched in chalk.

There was no sign of Weir, and Murdoch noted that the main street bore on its dusty surface no evidence of recent activity. Rather it looked as if it had been carefully rolled and brushed, ready for filming or for another rush of sightseers. As he walked up the street the sun hid behind a cloud, casting a shadow over the brown hill above him, itself dented like a piece of gruyère cheese with the endeavours of men long dead.

To his surprise, beneath the tourist gloss Calico had a gritty reality that he had not expected. Somehow the town, now a century distant from its halcyon days and tarted up for jaded twentieth-century tourists, still bore the marks of the toil of those who had travelled there in hope over a century before.

For a moment, lost in reverie, Murdoch forgot why he was there. Then came the sound of a voice, behind him to his left.

'Mr Murdoch?'

It was not the voice of Andrew Weir. He looked behind him. On the verandah of the Last Chance stood Leonard Stevens and beside him David Hall. For a moment he was taken aback. Then he walked on to the boardwalk, up the steps towards them. They all solemnly shook hands, as if the meeting was wholly expected and agreed upon. Murdoch did not speak.

'I think we might go inside, Leonard,' said Hall. 'The sun is just beginning to go. Getting a mite chilly.'

Stevens nodded and the three men pushed through the swing doors into the saloon. Murdoch saw in front of him an exact replica of a western bar, or rather a replica of its Hollywood mutation. Above them hung a heavy crystal chandelier, while behind the polished oak bar stood the inevitable mirror, always certain to be smashed in the equally inevitable bar-room brawl.

Stevens went to a refrigerator behind the bar and withdrew two cans. He handed one to Murdoch and one to Hall, then returned to the refrigerator to take out a bottle of brandy.

'Both David and I apologise about this necessary . . . deception,' he said, beckoning Murdoch to drink his beer. 'Only we feared that if approached in the normal way you might have felt constrained about joining us.' He sat down at a table and poured himself a large measure. When he had finished he beckoned Hall and Murdoch to join him. 'As it is, you must be wondering why we are here, so let me start at the beginning.

'When, in 1980, we initiated the concept of the Arab Olympics we had already spent several fruitless years trying to break into trade with the Communist bloc.'

'Seven,' said Hall, sipping his beer.

270

'The 1980 Games was a revelation to us,' Stevens continued, 'in that we realised for the first time exactly how much money and prestige was involved in the Olympic movement. We realised that any opposition, any alternative to the Olympics, menaced millions of dollars of investment – and, more important, it threatened a massive political commitment.'

Hall took up the story, speaking in his light, Southern accent. 'We reckoned that the Arab Olympics, or rather the threat of an Arab Olympics, could be a mighty useful lever for getting us where we wanted to be. And where we wanted to be was east of the Iron Curtain.'

'Trade concessions,' said Stevens. 'We knew it would take a while, and a whole lot of planning, but we got them – on condition that we pulled out of the Kudai Olympics.'

Murdoch felt his heart sink. And yet he knew that he had sensed something wrong from a long way back, and that all Hall and Stevens were doing now was to confirm his own doubts, give strength and substance to something he had already felt in his bones – an unease about the whole venture.

'So there was never any intention of having an Olympics in Kudai?' he said dully.

'Never, on our part,' said Hall, smiling. 'From the start we were only shooting for the Communist bloc. That's where the big money's going to be for people like us, smuggling in high technology goods. As for Prince Hassan – well, he's a mite like you, Mr Murdoch. A dreamer. He wanted to break all those IOC bigwigs, wanted to prove that he could hold a clean Olympics, all that stuff. No, it was the threat that was worth a fortune.'

'But the threat had to be real,' said Stevens. 'And that was where you and your people came in. If the Commies didn't think that we could swing the athletes of the West then there was no threat; we were just a paper tiger. But when you got those defections back in February and when you called the IOC's bluff over drugs then they were ready to make a deal.'

'They could see the whole damn card-castle going down the tubes,' said Hall, grinning widely at Murdoch. 'They had played all their cards, and you had trumped them. That was when they came to us and made their offer – what we'd been waiting for all along. The only danger was that someone might kill you off before we had set up our deals.'

'We first thought that we would buy you and your people off,' Stevens explained. 'But we soon came to realise that it was going to be too big a job, what with Grieve and Quince and Buchinski. Too many of the kind of person it would have taken a long time to persuade.'

'What about Buchinski?' said Murdoch harshly. 'Were you responsible for that?'

'Nothing to do with us,' said Hall. 'That was Mr Ciano, before we came to terms with him. And before the FBI started to take an interest in his activities.'

'Mr Ciano – well, that was a bonus we hadn't planned for,' said Stevens. 'We first met him in October, had several fruitful meetings, then again last month. He said he was going through a little temporary trouble, but that he would be clear of it by the Los Angeles Olympics. Mr Ciano cut us in on a little piece of his pie if we pulled out of Kudai. You see, your regular reports were like gold to us – they put us in touch with everyone who wanted the Kudai Olympics to fold – everyone who was willing to pay big to get us to fix it. When you reported back to us about your meeting Ciano early in September, at Weir's preview, we were on to him right away.'

'So you arranged the Gatwick trip?'

'Yes,' said Hall. 'I'm afraid we did. You see, what we did not expect – indeed, *couldn't* have anticipated – were the structural defects showing in our Kudai enterprises at such an early stage. True, we had shaved a little here and there, but we had no idea of the short time scale involved. We thought we were clear till 1986 at least. Arab workmanship – and probably some more shaving by our suppliers – that brought it back to 1983.'

'Thus,' said Stevens, 'when our man in Kudai told us that a sealed report from that guy Martin had been sent to Hassan and that your security people had checked the Gatwick flight,

272

we assumed that you had laid hands on the Kudai report and had somehow put two and two together.'

'I hadn't,' said Murdoch. 'Not till now.'

Hall, noting that Murdoch had finished his can of beer, walked back behind the bar, withdrew another can from the refrigerator and returned with it to the table.

Stevens had both his hands to his lips, as if considering some unspoken proposal. He lowered them briefly and said, 'So let us summarise the present position. The engineer Martin who spoke to Prince Ryad has been bought off. There are no copies of his report still in existence.'

'Except mine,' said Murdoch.

'Yes. Except yours.'

'The trade agreements with the Eastern bloc are ready to be signed,' Hall continued. 'All that is required now is the receipt of the report and the withdrawal of your organisation from the enterprise, at a time of our choosing. In return, we will make you and your colleagues a generous settlement.'

'Wait a minute,' said Murdoch. 'Only last week you tried to kill my entire staff. Now you want to forget it all and buy them off.'

Stevens winced. 'It was a mistake,' he said, looking sideways at Hall. 'I said so from the beginning. It was always my view that we should simply reach an accommodation. Blood is always an expense.'

'But that's water under the bridge,' said Hall, again intervening. 'We want you with us now. There's more than enough for all of us, with Mr Ciano's contribution.'

Murdoch did not reply.

'Let's lay it on the line,' said Stevens. 'Since January, we have been contacted by several major American companies who have an interest in the Los Angeles Olympics as sponsors. They've agreed to make their own subventions if we pull out.'

'It's much bigger than we ever expected,' interjected Hall again. 'It's the Businessman's Olympics.'

Murdoch did not reply at once. 'The problem, gentlemen,'

he said at last, 'is that you no longer have anything left to sell.'

He paused again, enjoying the moment.

'Yesterday, in New York, I signed binding agreements with Maurice Delgado to cancel the 1984 Kudai Games.'

Stevens's jaw dropped. 'And what did he give you in return?'

'I'm not at liberty to say,' said Murdoch. 'But by this evening the world's press – and that includes *Pravda* – will have the story. And that means that unless you've got your deals with the Communist bloc already signed – and you've just told me that you haven't – then you no longer have anything to offer them.'

Murdoch looked at the two men before him, weighing the effect of his words. He was gambling. No press-release about his arrangement with Delgado would be made until the following day, while the Kudai-IOC agreements were in his briefcase. And his briefcase was in his car.

Hall's face became serious and he looked across the table at Stevens. 'We must assume that your negotiations with Mr Delgado have been secret and that the agreements have not yet been finalised and signed.'

Murdoch did not reply.

'We must also assume that, since Prince Hassan has only just been operated on and has not yet seen a copy of Martin's report, he knows nothing of your negotiations. In short, you are out on a limb, Mr Murdoch.'

'How do you know that Grieve and all the members of my organisation haven't already been told?'

'Unlikely,' said Hall.

Stevens nodded. 'Too delicate a matter to spread around. Swift and secret is always best under such circumstances, and I am sure that you have been both. No, I too am quite certain that you are on your own.'

'So where do we stand?' said Murdoch, an animal suddenly sensitive to the area immediately surrounding him.

'That depends entirely on you, Mr Murdoch,' said Hall, taking another pull of beer. 'You see, you have throughout acted entirely consistently and honestly and if you hit below the belt, as you did in offering the federations your drug-tests, it was all within a strictly moral context. What Mr Stevens and I have to ask ourselves is whether or not you are likely to break what seems to us an outmoded moral code.'

'Try me,' said Murdoch.

'As I have said, blood is always an expense,' said Hall. 'I think that we can agree to settle on you a million dollars for a four-week delay of your press-release concerning your withdrawal from the Kudai Olympics and the receipt of the original Kudai report. This will give us time to conclude our agreements with the East, and will serve both our purposes.'

'Plus prominent media statements by you on the non-viability of the enterprise when the time comes,' added Stevens. 'In order to deter Hassan from restarting the whole affair.'

Stevens paused. 'All that we are asking for is a little time – and your silence,' he said. 'If the media ever get to know that the whole Kudai venture was from the beginning a – '

'A fix,' said Murdoch grimly.

'If you like, a fix. Then not only would our personal reputations be at stake but also possibly our lives.'

'It's been rather a lot to absorb,' said Murdoch. 'In one afternoon.'

'I'm afraid your decision will have to be made here,' said Stevens.

Murdoch felt a familiar lump at the bottom of his stomach. 'What are my options?'

Stevens paused, looking sideways at his colleague. 'We are all gentlemen,' he said. 'If you want to think about it why don't you have a stroll outside? Get a little air into your lungs?'

Murdoch recalled that there had been two cars in the car-park beside his own. There was someone else in town.

'That might be a good idea,' he said, his eyes fixed firmly on the two businessmen.

'Take as long as you like,' said Stevens, and smiled.

Murdoch stood up, turned and made his way out of the saloon. His breathing had quickened, and he felt his pulse throb like a drumroll in his right temple. He pushed through the swing doors.

Part of Murdoch's attraction for Ellis Payne had always been the fact that she had never been certain what he would say or do. Murdoch came from a culture quite unknown to her, and that element of surprise had been unnerving, and exciting. Even his first sexual advance had had a freshness and an innocence which still made her flush involuntarily whenever she teased it back into her waking thoughts.

She knew that these were cloudy times for Murdoch, and had therefore concluded her business in San Francisco peremptorily and had caught the first plane back to Los Angeles, bent on a surprise visit to his room at the Beverly Wilshire. She had lain back in her seat, eyes closed, and luxuriated in sexual fantasy, feeling her face warm and redden as she anticipated their meeting. She wondered if the other passengers had noticed.

It came, therefore, as a disappointment to arrive at Murdoch's hotel to find that he had gone out.

As she was leaving, she had asked the hall porter about Murdoch's departure-time, and he had mentioned that Mr Murdoch had asked for directions to Calico. Ellis knew that Andrew Weir was shooting *Comstock* at the old ghost town. However, a call to Weir's office revealed that shooting had ended the previous Friday. Ellis returned thoughtfully to her flat, and was soon setting out east on the road to Calico, breaking speed limits every mile of the way.

Blue had left his rifle back in the car, and had opted instead for a hand gun, a Buntline Special, which had been part of his collection for four years now but which he had never yet used in his professional life. Horses for courses, Blue had thought, when he had been asked to take on the Calico assignment. The old Buntline Special: a replica perhaps, but in perfect working order and just as capable of dealing out death as it had been in the days of Wyatt Earp. As a finishing touch Blue had slipped on his new three-hundred-dollar boots, and had gunned his Volkswagen Beetle east for the showdown in Calico.

Once there, he had conferred briefly with David Hall before positioning himself in the shadows of the boardwalk, outside the undertakers, on the other side of the street from the Last Chance Saloon, and about fifty yards further down. He had been told that if Hall and Stevens came out of the Last Chance first, then the contract was off, though he did not know why. If, on the other hand, Murdoch hit the swing doors first, then he was his.

He watched Murdoch as he sat on the boardwalk only sixty yards away. No need to rush things, he thought. Let the old Buntline have a moving target.

Once outside, Murdoch decided not to walk, but made his way across the street and sat on the boardwalk, elbows on knees, both thumbs firmly placed under his top teeth. He had to think, and think quickly.

He knew that he had blundered: he had told them more than he should. If only, in his anger, he hadn't told them of his deal with Delgado then he would have given himself some room for negotiation. Across the road Hall and Stevens were undoubtedly working out their options, probably telephoning Reuters to check if a Kudai or IOC statement were in the pipeline and, if so, if it could be stopped. If they found out that he was lying and that there was no press-release then his position was bleak. Their own position was precarious too, but it could be salvaged, though how they would deal with Hassan on his recovery was not clear. Or how they would deal with him.

Murdoch's mind raced. The problem was that he knew too much. Indeed, he was now the only person, outside of Hall and Stevens themselves, who knew everything.

He stood and started to walk slowly up the right-hand side of Main Street, towards the glowering mountain. Above him a light breeze blew brown dust from the mountain down into the street, forcing grit into his eyes and making him cough.

The first shot was from behind him and to his right, hitting the soft wooden beams of the nearby store and showering him with splinters. He felt warm salt blood on his lips, coming from a fretwork of little cuts on his brow and cheeks. There was little to be gained from hugging the line of buildings – he was still an open target – so he ran out into the middle of the main street where there was more space and sprinted up its light gradient towards the base of the mountain.

The second and third shots hit the ground in front of him, peppering him with dust and stones. He was only twenty metres from the base of the mountain – and the protection of its shadows – when a sharp pebble bounced up and opened a small cut on his temple, causing blood to flow freely down his left cheek.

The fourth shot took the lobe of his right ear. He fell, rolling and cursing, the pain forgotten as he got quickly back to his feet and once again began to sprint. Gasping, he zig-zagged towards the shelter of the brush at the bottom of the mountain, somehow keeping his balance through the broken rocks.

Behind him, Blue ran, cursing, up the centre of Main Street. Murdoch was now over two hundred yards away, scrambling up through the rock and scrub. Blue reached the base of the mountain, breathing hard and peered up into its gloom. He had lost him.

Murdoch moved out to the right, continuing upwards, following the smooth surface of the path parallel to the railway track, all that was now left of the old Tecumseh mining line. He could feel the blood from his ear begin to drench his collar and tie, and to clot on his chest.

The next shot was well behind him. He smiled through a grimace. The gunman was having difficulty picking him up in the gathering dusk. He began to hit the steeper gradients and felt the air begin to rasp in his throat as he tried to preserve his speed.

At the base of the mountain Blue reloaded the Buntline and frowned. If he had taken the rifle it would all have been over by now, with twenty thousand dollars snug and warm in his hip pocket. The Buntline's recoil had been heavier than he had remembered, nothing like the customary soft hit on his right shoulder of his rifle, and he had been close only once.

Above him he could hear Murdoch scrambling up the steep rocky surface. Blue completed his reloading and pushed the cylinder back into line with the gun barrel. He looked up at the mountain. Time was on his side. He would wait, then circle up the rail track and try to get behind his man. It might take him a little longer, but for Murdoch there was no way out.

Above him the sun was dying fast and the mountain assumed a slumbering, crumbling brown. Murdoch cut to his left, off the path, and scrambled almost vertically up the uneven gradient towards an overhang twenty feet from the foot. He pulled himself up with both arms, levering himself on his elbows and slithered into the hollow beneath the overhang.

Safe, for the moment at least. He lay in the welcoming shadow of the rock, flat on his face, attempting to muffle the sound of his own breathing, his blood staining the earth and pebbles around him.

Murdoch looked below. The town was in twilight now, and there was only one light – in the Last Chance Saloon. Hall and Stevens were probably still sitting there, sipping their drinks, waiting for their man to return to report a job well done.

At least he was above his anonymous enemy. But that enemy had a gun, and was probably a professional. His only friend was the gathering darkness. He fumbled in his jacket pocket and withdrew a handkerchief, rolled it into a ball and placed it against his left temple. The cut was about an inch long, but was superficial and was already beginning to coagulate. The blood from his earlobe dripped steadily down his cheek and neck, but he could live with that too.

Murdoch again looked down into Calico. No sign of movement. His only hope was to get to the car-park just below the town – though even then he had no idea whether or not this was being covered by another gunman. There was certainly no point in staying overnight on the mountain, for even if he didn't freeze he would be picked off with ease in the morning light.

He looked to his left, to the railway line about a hundred yards away. It moved east another five hundred yards into scrubland, then reached a dead end. No good. But two hundred yards below that the track had a fork, only dimly visible in the gloaming, and just above the fork were three mining trucks about five yards apart. The right-hand fork led down to the top of Main Street, to a tourist ticket office; but the left fork wound behind the town to the bottom of Main Street, only a couple of hundred yards above the car-park.

His breathing had recovered and he turned over on to his back, grit and blood matting his face and hair. It had to be the lowest truck. If he could get it moving the truck would trundle down on its own momentum. There was no knowing whether or not the junction points were set for the left, towards the car-park, or right, back into Calico.

If the latter, he would have to jump clear and take his chance – and hope that its noise on hitting the station buffers would create a diversion.

If it went left, he could try to control it with the brakes to the bottom of the track, then jump off and run from the bottom of Main Street down into the car-park, probably across a line of fire.

He turned on to his stomach and peered through the gloom. The bottom waggon was about two hundred yards away, below him diagonally to his left. It was too dark to see the exact nature of the ground, but it was certain to be rocky and uneven. He breathed in deeply, then began to crawl off the ledge, on knees and elbows, down the mountain.

He stifled a groan as a rock bit into his side and he lay for a moment, his face against the earth, gasping. Then he pursued his painful way through the scrub towards the railway line below.

A shot rang out, hitting rock about a hundred yards above him. The gunman was gambling, hoping that the noise would force him out of cover. He lay still, his head pushed into the rock face, then looked up: the nearest mining truck was just a

280

hundred and fifty metres away, its form dimly outlined in the blue-grey light.

Despite the cold, the sweat beaded on Murdoch's brow, mixing with the dirt and blood. The incline suddenly steepened and he slid down, head first, into a clump of saguaro bushes. He stifled the temptation to shout, but lay in the centre of the bush, gripping it on both sides, before sliding the rest of the way down, rolling sideways to the path alongside the railway track. He lay on his back and looked above him. Already the night sky was speckled with stars.

The truck was now only twenty metres away. He turned on to his face and crawled the final few yards, then sideways on to the line, feeling the rusty ridges of the rails with his hands before lifting himself on to his feet.

The top of the truck was just above head height. Murdoch placed his right foot on the ledge above the wheels and his hands on the rim of the truck and levered himself up and into it.

Again a shot rang out, hitting rock fifty metres or so up the mountain. Still guessing, but closer. Murdoch groped along the rough metal base of the truck, feeling for the brake. He finally discovered it at the far end.

It was right-angled, with the horizontal handle made of steel – obviously a primitive screw-mechanism. Murdoch knelt above it and pushed clockwise on the handle. It would not budge. He tried again, but still there was no movement.

The handle, he reckoned, was at a position about twenty minutes to the hour. He jammed his back against the front wall of the truck to give himself a firm base for a pull, then man-oeuvred his left foot till it was at the base of the brake. Thus fixed, he pulled with both hands, at the same time pushing hard on his right leg. The pressure brought a stream of blood spurting through the wound on his temple into his left eye and down into his mouth.

Somehow the blood gave him strength. He stifled a grunt as he again pulled on the rusty brake. It was like the last lift in a long weight-training session, the final nightmare moment when the weight will not even clear the ground.

Suddenly the brake gave, squealing as he pulled through the winter rust. Murdoch stopped and listened. There were voices in the darkness somewhere down below to his right at the top of Main Street, at the base of the mountain. He pushed the brake back to the left, engaging it again, kneeled on the bottom of the truck and peered above its lip. Down on the right fork, at the tourist station at the base of the mountain, he could see a torch. It moved upwards, making its own path of light towards him. Someone was coming up the track from the top of Main Street.

Murdoch dropped down and braced himself behind the brake. Then he pulled again, viciously, pushing backwards against the truck wall. All at once the brake gave completely and the truck trundled forward in a slow, miserly movement down the mountain and into the darkness, its rusty axles squealing after a winter of inactivity.

As the truck gathered speed he once more looked above the lip. Still the torch travelled inexorably up the track to his right: it was now about two hundred metres away. He could only be about a hundred metres from the fork, the point at which he was going to have to make his decision.

Below him, at the base of the track at the top of Main Street, Blue had heard the noise but could not, in the darkness, see the truck, and he started to make his way slowly up the rough path beside the railroad track, his stiff new boots allowing him only slow progress. After tripping up several times on rocks and bushes he decided to walk up the centre of the track, where the regularity of the sleepers provided firmer footing. Unfortunately, his car torch provided merely a pencil of light, sufficient for only a yard or so ahead. Blue heard the rattle of the truck, but the noise appeared to be moving away from him as the truck negotiated a shallow anti-clockwise curve.

Murdoch could feel himself gaining speed on the steep incline. He peered ahead, no longer caring about the torch. Then suddenly he felt the vehicle lurch as it hit the points. He was there.

It went right, towards the station. Murdoch ignored the taste of fear in his mouth as he jumped into the void, leaving the truck to career down towards the town.

Blue, standing on the line, was smashed backwards by the two-ton truck, his shout echoing above the silent town.

Murdoch landed luckily, on the flat path beside the line, giving reflexly as his feet hit the ground. He rolled down the embankment, hearing the chink of his car-keys as they were flung clear of his jacket pocket.

He lay for a moment in the darkness, cursing, ignoring his ripped knees and elbows. The keys could not be far, and he couldn't go on without them. Murdoch took off his jacket and placed it on the ground: the garment would at least provide him with a central point of reference in the darkness. He inched forward exactly three body-lengths and scoured with his hands the ground a metre clockwise and marked it with a small rock. Nothing.

He crawled back to his jacket, then made his way another three body-lengths to his left in a clockwise direction, and again searched on either side of him. Again, nothing.

He made his way back to his jacket, got up on to his knees and looked up the track. The torch had vanished. He crouched lower and moved out another twenty degrees anti-clockwise. On his first sweep he made contact with the plastic disc to which the keys were attached. He was back in business.

He stuffed the keys deep into his trouser pocket and replaced his tattered jacket. Then he jogged the final two hundred metres down the path towards Calico.

He was now at the base of Main Street, just behind the blacksmith's smithy, standing in the shadow of its side wall. Ahead of him lay the breadth of Main Street, the lights of its empty shops illuminating the darkness. Below it were the steps to the car-park. Murdoch remembered the voices at the base of the mountain: there could be another gunman. And what had happened to the first?

That twenty metres could be killing ground. His only advantage was surprise, the surprise of speed. Murdoch made his decision and sprinted across the bright, dusty street, every stride expecting the roar of gunfire. But no gun sounded. In seconds he had scampered down the steps into the car-park. He crouched along the side of his Renault, fumbled for his keys, then inserted the door key into the lock.

For a moment he was blind.

'Trust is important, Mr Murdoch,' intoned the voice of Stevens. The businessman stood above him, a powerful torch in his right hand.

'And integrity,' said Hall, who held in his hand a small automatic pistol. Murdoch rose. As he did so Stevens stepped forward, extricated the keys from the Renault and pocketed them. The two men led him back up the steps to the base of Main Street. There, by the town well, was a short history of the town on a mock-ancient poster.

Hall and Stevens sat on the wall of the well. Hall kept his automatic pointed at Murdoch. Both men were dressed immaculately in well-cut gaberdine raincoats, neither giving any indication of the drama of the evening through which they had passed. Murdoch stood before them, bloody, sweating and dishevelled.

'We have come a long way, Mr Murdoch,' said Stevens, 'since that first night in Los Angeles. Back there we thought it would be neat and simple. We never thought that our little venture would arouse so much interest.'

Hall interrupted. 'But we have both come to the regretful conclusion that it will not be possible to come to any agreement with you.'

Murdoch had always speculated on how he would feel when death was only moments away. Now he knew. First sick and weak, then increasingly strong, knowing that nothing worse could happen.

He looked at the two men sitting only a couple of yards away from him, and strained to hear a hint of the gunman who had pursued him up the mountain. Murdoch looked again at Hall. The man was no gunman, but marksmanship was not required at this range, only will. And there would be only one chance to find out if Hall had that will.

'You look like shit, Murdoch.' It was a female voice, though where it came from in the darkness it was impossible to tell.

Both Hall and Stevens spun round and peered into the gloom, but they could see nothing.

'Put down the gun, Mr Hall – on top of the well.' It was Ellis.

Hall fired blindly three times into the darkness beyond the well. There was only silence.

'It's all over, Hall. Put it down,' came Ellis's voice again. Hall looked desperately at his colleague, then pumped three more shots at shoulder-height into the void.

'You've had your six,' said Ellis, stepping from the darkness only a few yards beyond the well. Murdoch searched for some sign of a weapon in her hand, but there was none. As she ran, wobbling, towards him there was the faint whine of a police siren from the road below.

Ellis almost fell upon him, her breath coming in deep sobs. He pulled her up to him, kissing her wet, tear-stained cheek.

He looked at Hall and Stevens. Both men seemed somehow to have grown smaller. Only a few hours before they had held in their grasp the future of the entire Olympic movement, and with it the certainty of their own prosperity. Now they had nothing.

Hall made to speak as the police siren reached a wailing crescendo in the car-park below, but the words would not come.

Murdoch looked down at Ellis, his voice hoarse. 'Game's over,' he said. 'Time we went home.'

Epilogue

In September 1984 the 1992 Olympics were awarded to Prince Hassan el Fahze of Kudai, and in 1985 the second world athletics championships were held there. At these championships world records were broken for the 100 metres (9.91 seconds), 1500 metres (3 minutes 30.1 seconds) and long jump (9.05 metres).

In November 1986 Kudai hosted the world gymnastics championships, and in the same year Prince Hassan became the first Arab member of the IOC. January 1987 saw the first world swimming championships in Kudai, at which nine world records were broken.

The Nazi Games was released in America in May 1985 to unanimous critical and popular praise. Collaborators Alan and Ellis Murdoch secured an Oscar nomination for best screenplay.

TOM McNAB

FLANAGAN'S RUN

The greatest running race in history – it was the glorious, crazy idea of promoter Charles C. Flanagan: 3000 miles from Los Angeles to New York, 50 miles a day, every day, with prize money for the winners – should any survive – of $300,000.

In the heart of the Great Depression, an unforgettable cast of characters flocked to the start: heroic Mike Morgan, beautiful Kate Sheridan, desperate Hugh McPhail from Glasgow, the veteran Doc Cole and Lord Thurleigh running for a bet. Each day the brutal odyssey of endurance took its toll but still a gallant band edged mile by mile towards the well-nigh impossible.

Tom McNab, a British Olympic coach and technical adviser to the award-winning film *Chariots of Fire*, has written a wonderful and heartwarming novel, brimming with thrills and joy, friendship and love.

ALSO AVAILABLE FROM CORONET BOOKS